"*Laws of Depravity* by Eriq La Salle should be on a fast track to Best Seller status. It is the story of good vs. evil where it's not always clear who are the good, and who are the evil. *Laws of Depravity* may be the most engrossing book you read this year, bar none."

—Lee Ashford, *Reader's Favorites*

"Eriq La Salle, in *Laws of Depravity*, has written an utterly compelling and riveting thriller with echoes of the dark master, Thomas Harris. Here, La Salle also adds a surprising twist by weaving in a spiritual component that raises the narrative to lofty and thought-provoking levels. It's a wonderful accomplishment."

—Leonard Chang, author of *Over the Shoulder* and *Crossings*

"Actor and director Eriq La Salle's intense debut is a modern day parable cleverly masquerading as a crime novel. A muscular, gritty and spiritual thriller."

—John Shors, bestselling author of *Beneath a Marble Sky, Beside a Burning Sea, Dragon House, The Wishing Trees*, and *Cross Currents*

"*Laws of Depravity* will take you on a heart-pounding ride of vengeance, murder and atonement, never letting you rest until you've reached the final page. Eriq La Salle deftly draws unforgettable characters who tangle with good and evil and seek spiritual understanding and forgiveness for some of the most dastardly deeds human beings are capable of committing. Drawing on his talent as an acclaimed actor and director, Mr. La Salle digs deep into his characters' psyches, delivering a group of bruised and tarnished individuals you won't soon forget."

—Neal Baer, coauthor of *Kill Switch* and former executive producer of *Law and Order SVU*

"The surprises keep coming in La Salle's twisting debut thriller, in which good and evil aren't always black and white. In addition to the absorbing, fast-paced plot that will keep readers guessing until the end, each wonderfully sculpted character has a distinct, lifelike personality. The plot offers catalysts for change while raising spiritual questions and blurring the line between good and evil, which propels the story upward from being merely a solid, entertaining thriller to being a gripping must read that could have readers pondering right and wrong long after they've finished."

—*Kirkus Reviews*, Starred Review for *Laws of Depravity*

"A serial killer known as the Martyr Maker is on his final round of murdering 12 clergymen once every 10 years. Two New York City detectives and the FBI are on his trail, but maybe the dead clergy aren't as innocent as they appear. A gritty crime thriller, spiritual quest, and love story all woven into one compelling tale."

—*Publishers Weekly*

"Fast-paced… Characters are richly textured [and] none is without faults. Sets the hook for the captivating series."

—*Kirkus Reviews*

ALSO BY ERIQ LA SALLE

Laws of Depravity

Laws of Wrath

LAWS
OF
ANNIHILATION

ERIQ LA SALLE

Lavette
Books

PRESS

Published by Poisoned Pen Press, an imprint of Sourcebooks
P.O. Box 4410, Naperville, Illinois 60567-4410
(630) 961-3900
sourcebooks.com

Published in association with Lavette Books
5318 Weslayan St. Ste. 154
Houston, TX 77005
Lavettebooks.com

Cataloging-in-Publication Data is on file with the Library of Congress.

Printed and bound in the United States of America.
VP 10 9 8 7 6 5 4 3 2 1

PART I

1

I n Hell.

It was the only way to describe the hottest summer on record. Even under the daily clamor of city life, if one listened intently it was still possible to hear the faint echo of the Devil's joyful laughter. He was the only one who could have taken any pleasure in the torturous heat, the ungodly stench, and, of course, the gorge of hatred.

It felt like the cruelest summer ever. New York was taking gut punches from a punishing heat wave that showed no signs of easing. The Big Apple was in dire need of relief. It was thirsting for summer rains, cool merciful drops that fell from somewhere at least in the proximity of Heaven. Of all of the East Coast cities that were being strangled by the heat, New York was choking the most.

FBI Special Agent Janet Maclin drove down to the Big Apple

from Washington, DC, where it was also hot, yet much more tolerable. She suffered through the slow roast of being in Manhattan because her trip was mandatory. Of her numerous visits to the city, it was the first time she had come to New York and hated it. What she hated most was her reason for having to come.

From the time she was a child, Agent Maclin had had grand dreams of becoming the first female director of the FBI. She'd entered the Bureau knowing that as a woman she would have to run faster and jump higher than her male counterparts just to be considered *half* equal. Fueled by her dream, she outran and outjumped the best of them. Though sexism had hindered her at numerous turns, it was good old-fashioned bureaucracy that left her dream all but wilting on the vine. It didn't matter that seventeen years into her career she had acquired quite the reputation, as not just a rising star but a bona fide standout. She had certainly accomplished more than all of her peers and most of her superiors. Bringing down two major serial killers within a month of each other was just one of the many achievements on the impressive résumé she had built on the journey toward her lifelong dream. Ultimately, none of it really mattered because, even though she had entered the Bureau as a young attorney, she had blossomed into a talented field agent and not a bureaucrat or politician, which, throughout the history of the FBI, had been the traditional path to directorship.

It was public knowledge that the long-standing, current director of the Bureau was being vetted as the heavily favored vice-presidential replacement after the current VP had suffered irreversible brain damage from a severe stroke just five months into the current administration's incumbency. Now that the director was more than likely leaving, all types of rumors were spreading. There was speculation, thin and unsubstantiated, that he was aggressively looking for a woman to succeed him. Although she knew, both logistically and realistically, she didn't stand a chance, the spark, however faint, still reignited the flames of her most desired dream. Under normal circumstances, she wasn't the type to allow herself to get caught up in things she considered highly improbable. But for once, she embraced the distraction of hope—because, unfortunately, the current circumstances of her life were unfolding as anything but normal.

She'd started the day with a stomach full of butterflies. By the time the receptionist ushered her into the penthouse office on Park Avenue, they had mutated into angry dragons that were currently wreaking havoc on her intestinal fortitude. She wore her favorite navy-blue pantsuit with a crisp white collarless top beneath. She wasn't much on jewelry. She wore no earrings, bracelets, or rings— just a simple, rose-gold Lady Bulova and a silver *hamsa* necklace barely peeking over the second button of her blouse.

The tiny hand-shaped amulet had several names and meanings. In the Jewish faith, it was referred to as the Hand of God, but Agent Maclin didn't wear it for any religious reasons because she was definitely not the religious type. She had worn the necklace for the last thirty-four years because it was all that she had left of her mother, who had passed away when Maclin was seven years old. Born into a proud Protestant family, her mother converted to Judaism just before marriage to hopefully establish spiritual consistency for her impending family. The irony was that although Maclin's father was raised in a Conservative Jewish family, by the time she was born he had at best grown indifferent to the faith.

Maclin wasn't a woman who was easily intimidated. Yet, the large office made her feel like a truculent child waiting to be reprimanded by the principal. She stuck her hands in her pants pockets in an attempt to stop them from trembling. She wasn't the most patient of women. Agent Maclin was a verb, a ball of kinetic energy who found her greatest peace when she was *doing*. The helpless waiting was nerve-racking. The quiet office didn't help in any way; the silence was burdensome. She looked through the twelve-foot-tall windows facing 49th Street and could see down the corridor of high-rises all the way to the West Side.

The inside of the building was unfazed by the scorching heat wave that was punishing everything outside. The office felt like the coolest place in New York, both thermally as well as esthetically. She tried to distract herself by taking in all that she could of the space that was unabashedly vying for a shot on the cover of *Architectural Digest*. Everything about it screamed of money. The address, the bone suede walls with coffered ceilings, customized fixtures, and intricate appointments throughout. The room even *smelled* rich; the scent of some high-end fragrance floated in the air like a perfect reminder of a tropical island. There was an original Picasso as well as one of Degas's famous paintings of a ballerina.

It was not surprising to her that the man she came to see had an "ego wall." It was the one wall solely dedicated to the long list of his accomplishments over an extremely successful career.

There were multiple degrees from Harvard and Princeton along with his photo on the cover of *Time* magazine, not to mention the framed pictures of him with three different presidents. There were tchotchkes and even artifacts in display cases from various parts of the world, no doubt collected during his extensive travels. Despite how much she had read up on him, he still held the upper hand because he knew more *consequential* things about her.

Agent Maclin analyzed the office in the same way she ran a crime scene. She gathered facts based on meticulous observation. Even though she had already read as much information as she could, she still gathered clues about the man who knew more about her future than she did. Maclin hated more than anything that she no longer controlled her fate. After being seated for two minutes, she concluded that the leather Barcelona chair she sat in was intentionally only mildly comfortable. As beautiful as the office was, it was never designed for meetings lasting longer than necessary. It was fine by her because she certainly didn't want to be there any longer than she needed to be.

She stared at a Swarovski crystal clock on the desk, irritated that she had now waited six long minutes past the designated time of the meeting. Just as her hands stopped trembling, one of the double doors to the office opened. The man breezed in and greeted her with an apology that she felt was filled more with etiquette than sincerity.

"My apologies. My staff meeting ran longer than normal," he offered.

Maclin hated the man the second she met him. She thought

he looked too slick with his gelled hair, artificial tan, and two-thousand-dollar loafers.

She was a bit surprised that he was younger looking than his online photos and even the magazine covers. He looked too young, she felt, to have acquired all the expertise he was renowned for.

"It's quite all right. I was just admiring the view," she lied. She reminded herself to smile because her natural disposition was sometimes a bit off-putting to people. Today, more than any other, she needed not to put anyone off and certainly not the man she came to visit. Maclin wasn't an unfriendly woman by any means; but unfortunately, she had the kind of pensive face that more often than not seemed frozen in a permafrown. Her lifelong habit of pursing her lips made her seem as though she was just two ticks away from a full-on scowl. Whenever she was contemplative— which was most of the time—the corners of her mouth turned downward like a grumpy fish. Her malady only added to the pile of misogyny that she waded through on a semiregular basis at the Bureau. *"You know, Janet, maybe if you smiled a lot more, you'd go a lot further."* She'd once overheard two of her male colleagues laughing about how she had a terminal case of Resting Bitch Face.

Maclin extended her hand and smiled hard, as though it were the most natural thing in the world for her. She smiled like a woman who was certainly worthy of her host's empathy. He had small, manicured hands that looked better than hers ever had. There was a softness to them. His handshake had the tentativeness of a man afraid that a firm greeting might somehow jeopardize his liveli-hood. He was the type of man that Maclin usually easily dismissed;

she had very little tolerance for men with tepid introductions. Yet, she was in no position to rebuff him, because regardless of the unimpressive measure of his hands, they still held all the power.

However, the minute they shook she knew that things weren't going to go her way and all the smiles in the world wouldn't change that. Now she had to wade through indeterminate minutes of polite chatter before he confirmed what she already knew.

The man's name was Dr. Winston Quinlan III, and he was widely regarded as one of the top five oncologists in the country. Maclin had traveled from DC to New York to see him so that he could offer his professional opinion about how much time she had before she died.

"…and, unfortunately, after looking at your CT scan we weren't able to find anything that contradicted your previous two doctors' prognoses. Stage IV metastatic ovarian cancer is certainly a huge challenge on its own, but now that it's spread to your pancreas and other parts of your body, I'm afraid we're terribly limited in what we can hope for. I do have to say that in some cases—although it is rare—we've seen people beat the odds and live another three to five years."

Maclin stayed standing and looked at him directly. "The thing about working in law enforcement is that I've given enough bad news over the years to have learned how to take it. There's no need for you to feel that you have to give me some false sense of hope. I just need the facts so I know what to expect and when to expect it."

"Well then, I would have to start by saying, frankly, I'm surprised that you're currently functioning as well as you are. In the next month, two max, things are going to get pretty bad and then only worse from there."

"Would chemo and radiation help any?" she asked.

"In your case, I'm afraid not. Your cancer is much too aggressive."

"At the risk of sounding clichéd, how long before I, uhh… you know?"

"I think we're looking at three months. Four, tops. I'm sorry I can't give you better news."

Agent Maclin looked over the doctor's shoulder and stared at the painting of the ballerina, and for the next minute was able to shut out everything else. Dr. Quinlan continued speaking, but his voice became nothing more than a steady whirr of garbled apologies. Maclin looked so hard at the painting that she thought she saw it come alive. She found escape in seeing the ballerina move. She saw grace and perfection. She could even smell the hard work and hear the applause of the faceless audience. She felt the warm footlights that lit up the stage. The more Maclin looked at the painting, the more she thought about how much it was filled with life and possibilities that were no longer available to her.

2

They were identical twins, Israel and David Abramovitz. To look at one was to see the other. They moved alike, they sounded alike, they were in every perceptible way each other's mirror. The brothers were two Reform rabbis, thirty-six years old, deeply rooted in their faith. Their father and both grandfathers before them were rabbis. They came from a long line of sacrifice and philanthropy. Their grandfather on their mother's side marched and bled with Martin Luther King, Jr.; he'd even shared a cell with Ralph Abernathy in Mississippi the summer that Bull Connor declared open season on the Northern agitators.

The twins had coal-black hair and soft blue eyes. They were five feet eleven and built like they knew their way around the gym. They resembled soap opera actors more than they did men of God; they contradicted the stereotypical image of Jewish holy men. They were by all accounts good men, both virtuous and humble. Like their father and grandfathers, they held on to the inherited belief that there was more light in man than darkness. They were hip, handsome, and highly respected. The mayor personally called them to help quell tensions that had been steadily escalating between the Hasidic community in Bensonhurst and Borough Park and outraged members of New York City's African American community.

The trouble had begun three weeks earlier when a group of angry Hasids chased a black teenager named Devon Timmons to his death after he sprayed graffiti on the side of a synagogue. When no one was indicted for the boy's death, the steady unrest left Borough Park feeling a lot like Ferguson, Missouri. "Black lives matter. Black lives matter," echoed in pockets of New York day and night. There were protests and even small riots, from Do or Die Bed Stuy all the way up to Money Makin' Manhattan and the Boogie Down Bronx. The Abramovitz brothers went to some of the black churches and spoke directly to the congregants, pleading for peace. Even though most of the violence and riots had slowed, parts of New York still walked the thinnest of tightropes.

The Sinai temple on East 73rd Street was unusually crowded. Throughout the two-hour-long evening Shabbat service, Israel and David took turns addressing their members and invited guests. The brothers played off of each other very well. Although they treated the recited scripture with the utmost reverence, they each took their turn injecting a respectable amount of humor while addressing the crowd. A half dozen African American preachers and community leaders sat in the sanctuary amongst regular members who quietly translated both the spoken or written Hebrew pronunciations. The sanctuary smelled of aged paper. The scent was emitted from the siddurim—old prayer books—which rested in holders on the backs of pews. David took the lead as the service was nearing its end.

"'For his anger endureth but a moment; in his favor is life; weeping may endure for a night, but joy cometh in the morning.' As we conclude tonight's service we would like to leave you all with something that the Torah teaches us."

The brothers then recited in unison, "Grant us peace, Your most precious gift, O Eternal Source of peace.

"And give us the will to proclaim its message to all the peoples of the earth.

"Bless our country as a safeguard of peace, its advocate amongst the nations.

"May contentment reign within our borders, health and happiness within our homes.

"Strengthen the bonds of friendship and fellowship

"Among all the inhabitants of our world.

"Plant virtue in every soul,

"And may the love of Your name hallow every home and every heart.

"Shabbat Shalom."

After the service, along with their wives, Israel and David hosted Oneg Shabbat dinner in the open courtyard behind the temple. Platters of food were placed down the middle of the long table, which seated twenty. Before they ate, three prayers were offered.

The first was the blessing of Shabbat led by the women as two candles were lit. The Abramovitz brothers then offered a blessing over the wine. The guests were then asked to place their hands over their eyes as the third and final prayer was offered over bread covered in white linen. After the prayers, everyone feasted on salmon, brisket, green beans and carrots, warm challah, and kugel. There was kosher red wine served, lots of wine.

"The kiddush cup represents unity under God," Israel said as he sipped from a silver cup and passed it to his brother. David sipped then addressed all those assembled. "If I am not for myself, who is for me? If I am only for myself, what am I? If not now, when?"

The brothers then told stories of when their grandfather marched with King. Although the two groups came together because of the racial conflict that had New Yorkers unusually tense, the brothers and their guests spoke more about their similarities than their differences. Before the night ended, they sang songs together. Two Yiddish songs were taught, and the night ended with everyone joining hands and singing "I've Been up the Rough Side of the Mountain."

An hour after everyone had left, David and Israel stayed behind to put the finishing touches on a speech that they were to give at a rally the next day at the Harlem State Office Building. They both loved the quietness of the temple when they were the only ones there.

"It's almost eleven thirty. We can tweak it in the morning if we need to," David said.

"I just want to come up with a better ending while I'm think-ing about it," Israel responded.

"The ending is fine—just leave it. Let's go home. I'll make sure everything is locked up."

Being the more pedantic of the two, Israel ignored his brother and continued working on his laptop as David exited the office. Israel was so caught up in his work that he didn't notice that David had been gone for twenty minutes. Once he stopped typing on his laptop, he became quickly aware of how intensely quiet it was. Only after he heard a strange noise coming from another room did he look at the clock and realize the passage of time.

"David?"

When his brother didn't answer, he called out again, a little louder.

"David?"

He waited for a response that never came.

"I just finished with the speech. Stop clowning around."

The only thing that came back to him was the hollow echo of his own voice.

"All right, moron, you made your point. I'm coming now."

As Israel turned off his laptop and stood to leave, the lights went out. Since their office had no windows, everything imme-diately turned black. He reached for the beaded chain of his desk lamp, but when he tugged it nothing happened.

Israel feared darkness even more than he feared God. When he was nine and playing a game of hide-and-go-seek with his brother, he had accidentally locked himself in an abandoned refrigerator for the worst four minutes of his life.

David knew better than anyone Israel's paralyzing fear of the dark. The more Israel pulled on the lamp's chain with growing desperation, the more he felt like a scared nine-year-old again. The black office felt tight, like a slightly larger version of the refrigerator in his childhood. Try as he might, he couldn't slow his overactive mind. He could only think of the horrible possibilities lying in wait to take advantage of his temporary blindness. The darkness was unending, a frightening ellipsis. His lips and mouth were dry from the heavy breathing he wasn't aware that he was doing.

The temple had two generators, so he ruled out the possibility of a blackout. The truth was, Israel had no idea what was going on; but he did know that David had never played, nor would he ever play, on his deepest fears. That bit of knowledge was the very thing that made Israel even more afraid. Similar to the time when he was nine, the darkness debilitated him. All semblance of calm was shattered under the heft of a vivid imagination. Israel was afraid that the monster of his childhood had returned. He could feel its presence all around him. The shadows were no longer innocent. The peace and quiet were no longer comforting. The air itself grew coarse and inimical. He was petrified that his nightmare had come back to smother him and take his *neshome*—his soul. Israel mumbled the name "*malekh-amoves*"—Yiddish for "angel of death."

He remembered his iPhone and used its flashlight to help him find his way out of his office and down the narrow corridor. The beam of light was unsteady in his trembling hand. The air-conditioning hadn't been off for more than five minutes, and yet he was already dripping sweat. Although Israel hadn't had a panic attack since his tragic event as a child, it all came rushing back, the constricted lungs and unavailable breath. The heavy palpitations of a runaway heartbeat. The uncontrollable quaking.

"David?"

Still nothing.

Just outside the main auditorium, he thought he heard something. He stopped and listened. He wasn't sure what it was, but he heard it in the distance and kept moving toward it. Whatever it was, it was faint but steady, pulling him closer.

On the other side of the auditorium, under the blanket of darkness, he heard what sounded like the low whimper of a wounded pet. As he continued fumbling his way forward, there was rustling in the corner. Israel stopped and turned when he thought he heard something behind him. "David, you know this is not funny to me. I swear to..."

He didn't finish his sentence because he slipped on something wet on the marble floor. When he retrieved his phone, the light had dimmed considerably, but he could still make out the stream of blood in which he found himself. Just as his panic started stabbing him, the whimpering in the corner grew louder, the muffled sound of words being attempted but thwarted by something unknown. The light on his phone was barely working, but as he held it in his outstretched hand, he could just make out the sight of David on the floor in full tremors, wet with blood. David's mouth was gagged, and his hands and feet had been cut off and were lying a few inches from his body.

Israel's legs suddenly felt like steel girders, unbendable. He stood frozen, his body completely numbed by paralysis. He tried to scream, but all he could do was vomit. He heard movement behind him, followed by the peculiar whooshing sound of sharp steel cutting through air in search of a solid target. It was then that he felt the searing pain of his hand being separated from his arm. Someone from behind him— someone large—gagged him and smothered his woeful cries. He felt a heavy knee in his back pinning him to the floor. Suddenly the lights turned on, and Israel saw blood, more than he ever imagined the human body was capable of producing. He saw the sizable pool from his severed hand inching toward and then converging with the river of blood that surrounded his dying brother.

Israel grunted David's name and struggled to reach him, but he was made helpless under the knee of something behemoth. All Israel could do was lie on the floor of the temple bleeding and praying to God while watching his brother close his eyes for the last time.

Israel and David were born six minutes apart: first came David, then came Israel.

They left the world in the same order.

3

Maclin had to do it in person.

Her father had been dead for almost two years now, and she was estranged from both her brothers. Including Phee and Quincy, there was less than a handful of people she felt obligated to tell.

She had first met the two partners over two years ago, when the three of them broke the now-famous Deggler case, a serial killer who was butchering clergymen. Even though she couldn't technically call them friends, what she had with Quincy and Phee was the closest thing she had to friendship. Regardless of the semantics that defined their relationship, the thing that mattered most was the great amount of respect that the three of them had for each other. These were two cops who had already proven that they would die for her if necessary, just as she would for them. That alone warranted the face-to-face.

Just as she exited the Lincoln Tunnel on the New Jersey side, she popped some Diluadid to manage the roving pain that gnawed at her insides. When she'd called Phee earlier that morning to tell him she was in town and wanted to see the two of them, he'd invited her out to the house for lunch since Quincy and Elena were staying with him for the weekend. As she pulled up to the gates of the beautiful home, she thought for a second that maybe she had somehow entered the wrong address into her navigational system. Cops didn't live like kings.

Then again, Maclin was well aware that Detective Phee Freeman was by no means an average cop. Before joining the force, he'd made millions and invested well during his eight years in the NFL. He also came from money. Though his father, Clay, was now considered a highly respected businessman and arguably the most powerful African American in New York, he'd never quite escaped his reputation as a Harlem gangster whom many still referred to as the Black Godfather. Despite the fact that shortly after first meeting Phee Maclin had read up on his football days as well as some of the things about his father's empire, she was still caught off guard seeing the detective's wealth firsthand.

Aside from the two cases they'd worked together, she really hadn't spent much time with Phee and Quincy. She'd socialized with them three, maybe four times. As the ten-foot gate opened and she pulled in, she thought about how little she actually knew the partners.

The partners' wives, Brenda and Elena, greeted her at the door with hugs and kisses as though they had known her for a while, even though it was only the second time they'd officially met. From the minute she walked into the house, she found it to be tasteful, unpretentious, and warm. It was filled with art that actually made sense. The furniture was comfortable, the kind of oversized seating that sucked a person in and made them want to stay a while. And then there was the backyard, a wide-open space with a garden of flowers and potted fruit trees and a sparkling pool. The high-pitched sound of a toddler's squeals echoed throughout the yard.

Maclin stepped outside to see Phee manning the grill while Quincy was playing with Phee and Brenda's one-and-a-half-year-old daughter, Dolicia. Bo, the family's pot-bellied, brindled French bulldog, barked and nipped at Quincy's leg as he tickled Dolicia and pretended to devour her like a hungry beast. She laughed so hard that Maclin wondered if the little girl was at risk of hyperventilating. Phee walked over to greet Maclin, offering her a cold Dos Equis that she declined. Quincy said his hellos from the ground. He finally stopped tickling Dolicia when Bo became overprotective and started barking much more aggressively. As soon as Quincy released Dolicia, Bo ran over and started licking the little girl as if they had been absent from each other for weeks. Maclin watched the girl and dog and their limitless energy. She laughed along with Phee when Bo tackled his daughter. No matter how many times the little girl went down, she popped back up and continued to chase her four-legged bestie.

Brenda and Elena came outside with plates, utensils, and cups. As the women crossed by their men, they kissed and touched them affectionately. Maclin didn't quite know what to make of it all.

Two loving couples, a joyful child, a perfect house in the suburbs where evidently happiness came in abundance. Although she didn't welcome it, a tinge of envy crept in. The couples were all so very *present* with each other in ways that Maclin knew she was incapable of being with any lover, because vital parts of her were still trapped in bitter memories of darker yesterdays. She wondered what her existence could have been like had her fiancé, Willington, not been murdered. Now that she had prematurely reached the end of her life, she realized that it wasn't much of a life that she would be leaving behind.

Maclin had no idea that Phee was so skilled on the grill. The lobster melted in her mouth with a subtle kick of spice from the homemade chipotle butter that she dipped it in. She didn't need a knife to cut the steak—Phee challenged them all to only use a fork to part the tender meat. When she did it, he winked at her and smiled. Maclin wasn't much of a drinker, but despite the pain-killers that she had taken earlier, she put away three glasses of the sangria Elena made. She needed the liquid courage, knowing that she had to tell the partners the bad news. The combination of the booze and pills gave her a nice buzz and put her exactly where she wanted to be, which was in the moment. No pain, no angst. For just a couple of hours, she let go and felt almost normal. She enjoyed being surrounded by long laughs, good food, and, most of all, people who reminded her of what love used to feel like.

Twenty minutes after the main course had been eaten, Brenda brought out a four-layer red velvet cake drizzled in a chocolate rum sauce.

"Oh my God, when you invited me out to lunch I definitely didn't expect all of this," Maclin said.

She thought the cake looked too good to eat—until she took the first bite. Although her appetite had been waning lately, she savored the meal from start to finish. She ran her finger across her plate to get the last of the frosting. Dolicia squirmed out of Phee's arms and handed Maclin her panda Beanie Baby before climbing up onto her lap.

"Wow, that's a first!" Brenda laughed. "She never just goes to people she doesn't know."

As Maclin bounced the little girl on her lap and played with her and her bear, she thought about the child she had lost. Dolicia giggled when Maclin did her best ventriloquist bit and used a squeaky voice when speaking as the bear. Bo sat nearby, gnawing on a steak bone and keeping a vigilant eye on the pair.

Just as plates were being cleared and Maclin was finishing off her fourth glass of sangria, her phone rang. Then Phee's. Then Quincy's. Brenda looked at Elena then reached over and took Dolicia from Maclin. The spouses knew that when their men were together and their phones went off within thirty seconds of each other, bad news was on the other end.

The fact that all three phones went off meant that the news was not just bad—but very bad.

4

Maclin sat in the back of Phee's black Range Rover sipping her second cup of coffee and trying to come down from her buzz before they made it to the scene. Even though she wasn't in town on official business, somehow the mayor had tracked her down and personally requested her presence. Maclin was adamant that, since she would soon be taking a personal leave from the Bureau, the most she could offer was an initial evaluation of the crime and a profile of the killer and not much else. The mayor took the offer.

As they exited the George Washington Bridge on the Manhattan side, Phee and Quincy quietly sat up front with their game faces on. They were never big talkers before a new crime scene. Both cops used the travel time to clear their heads and get into their zone.

They shot across to the East Side then zipped down the FDR Drive, exiting on 63rd Street and heading back uptown. As soon as they turned down Lexington Avenue and 73rd Street, they saw the huge crowd of people and the media circus. Phee lowered his window, but before he could flash his badge to the patrolman who stood sentry at the corner barricade, the cop recognized him and waved him through.

"Welcome to Hell, Detective Freeman."

There were close to three hundred people gathered in front of the synagogue, of whom at least 80 percent were Jewish. Reform, Conservative, Orthodox, Hasidic, even Mizrahi and Sephardim stood outside the building where their respected brothers had been murdered. The Reform followers in the crowd, both men and women, wore casual clothing, while those who were from the more conservative sects wore what was regarded as customary attire. First and foremost, their heads were covered in reverence to God. Despite the one-hundred-degree heat, the Hasidic women in the crowd wore headscarves over wigs and ankle-length skirts, while their thickly bearded male counterparts were dressed in long black coats and lustrous hats made of sable tails. *Payot*—curled sidelocks—hung just south of their temples all the way to their jawlines and in some cases even lower. They wore prayer shawls, known as tallits, over dark suits with fedoras and plain black slip-on shoes since even the knotting of shoelaces was prohibited on the Sabbath. Although they were forbidden by Talmudic law to even leave their homes on the Sabbath, the murder and possibilities of more Jewish blood being spilled were among the very few allowances that permitted them to come and be in attendance.

It made no difference that the assembled were separated by varying denominations. They were united by the murder of two of their holy men on hallowed ground, which made them all fear that it wasn't just a crime against men who were Jewish but specifically a crime on Judaism. Many in the crowd were crying, while others were visibly angry. Most of the news teams trained their cameras on the crowd in search of the perfect shot. Nothing boosted ratings more than collective pain.

As soon as Maclin, Phee, and Quincy entered the synagogue, they were greeted by one of the mayor's aides.

"Agent Maclin, detectives, the mayor would like to have a word with you."

The aide escorted them to a small conference room where the mayor, chief of police, chief of detectives (more commonly referred to as the chief of dicks or chief of Ds), and two other captains were gathered. Captain Whedon, who was Quincy and Phee's boss, was closest to the door and nodded to his men as they entered. The tension in the room was heavy—immovable. No one spoke.

Maclin noticed that the three chiefs all looked as if they'd been kicked in the groin. A tall African American woman stood with her back to the rest of the room. Her name was Rocky Henderson. New York's blue collars just called her Mayor Rocky or Mayor Rock. She was a six-foot-one, dark-skinned sista who was born, bred, and branded in the Boogie Down. Like most who hailed from the South Bronx in the '80s, she'd come up hard. She'd used basketball scholarships as her way out of the 'hood. She set records on the court at St. John's University and graduated top of her law school class. Mayor Rocky never forgot where she came from. Even though she was much more polished now, she could still outball, outdrink, outcuss, outfight, and outsmart most of those around her.

Everyone in the room waited for her to speak. She stood behind velour curtains peeking at the swelling crowd through a narrow parting. When she turned back to face the cops, her eyes were noticeably red.

"Two days after I announced my candidacy and most people wrote me off, I stood in this very room and asked Israel and David Abramovitz to help me win the Jewish vote. They told me they would endorse me under one condition: that I would never forget what it felt like to be an underdog, because those were the people in the city who needed me most."

Her husky voice cracked a little at the mention of their names. One by one she locked eyes with everyone in the room.

"I have to do any and everything I can to hold this city together. That's my job and I'm willing to bleed to do it. I just need all of you to understand that this thing is personal. I don't give a damn about protocol, jurisdiction, or any other bureaucratic nonsense; I'm looking at the people in this room to find whoever did this. And let me be clear: whether you bring them back in cuffs or in a body bag, it really makes no difference to me. Just bring them in.

We need this thing closed and we need it closed with *a quickness.* That's the only thing that matters."

While the chief of Ds worked out the logistics with the two captains, Maclin, Phee, and Quincy were led into the main auditorium, where the bodies were. Technically, there were two crime scenes. The first was on the main level, where the brothers were actually murdered. The floor was charred twenty feet in circumference. The word UMOJA was spray-painted on a nearby wall. The trio examined both the ring of scorched blood and the graffiti for a few minutes before moving on to the second scene, which was on the dais, where the twins were tied naked to a bench, facing in opposite directions. The skin of their backs was sewn together from their shoulders to their hips. Their pale corpses looked like alabaster statues.

Quincy approached Israel as Phee examined David. Agent Maclin circled the scene from ten feet back, scouring the perimeter before moving in closer. The three had worked enough murder cases to have developed an effective routine. They normally studied a scene for about forty minutes. They triangulated their approach, then alternated each position so that every detail of the scene was checked three times from three different perspectives. That eliminated the possibility of even the most minute of details being missed by all three of them.

They each noticed that the twins' severed hands had been reattached to their wrists by way of stitches. The three of them focused on not just what they saw but also what was missing. Despite the horrible violence that the two men had endured, there were no signs of blood in the immediate area. Neither on them nor in them. Not a drop.

"Exsanguination," Kravitz the medical examiner said as he placed his eyeglasses on top of his head, squeezed the bridge of his nose with his index finger and thumb, and tried to push back the massive headache that had arrived ten minutes after the bodies were delivered.

His head pounded with every beat of his heart. The big man moved slowly, his labored breathing making it sound as if he were exerting himself more than he actually was. In two years' time Kravitz had gone from being overweight to full-fledged obese. At five feet nine and not an ounce of muscle, he lugged around three hundred and eighty-plus pounds that just wasn't good for the human body. He looked like a two-legged walrus with breasts. His flesh still wobbled a couple of seconds after he stopped moving.

The twins, no longer stitched together, lay side by side on two stainless steel tables in the center of the morgue's examination room. As a coping mechanism, Kravitz had learned to detach himself from most of the bodies he worked on regardless of their cause of death. He ate over corpses, enjoyed witty banter with cops like Phee, told inappropriate jokes, and on occasion even sang irreverent songs as he worked. But as he examined the rabbis, he was all business. Kravitz was Jewish, but more so by lineage than practice. He brawled with God on a daily basis.

Very few things made a man question God's will and omnipotence more than repeatedly witnessing the senseless deaths of the
innocent and righteous. Death was Kravitz's life. In his forty-plus
years in the business he had seen things that most people couldn't
imagine. He saw firsthand death's indiscriminate reach, its insatia-
ble appetite. Children and women were usually the most difficult
for him. Even though he would never admit it, he was always less
sympathetic to those who courted mortality with pride, greed, or
apathy. But regardless of what he thought of any of them who
ended up on his table, he gave them all the best autopsy that the
state of New York had to offer.

Kravitz' headache left him moving gingerly, as if he were afraid
of having an aneurysm. He handled the twins delicately. A few
years back, he'd had the pleasure of hearing the Abramovitz brothers speak at a fundraiser he attended. They were the type of spiritual leaders who touched him in a way that actually helped heal
some of the wounds he'd endured in his many feuds with God. He
remembered thinking that if he ever got around to formalizing his
faith, he would certainly want them as his spiritual mentors.

"Their entire blood supply has been drained from their bodies,"
he said.

"You mean they bled out from their wounds?" Maclin asked.

"No, I mean that someone literally drained all the blood from
their bodies," he answered.

The sound of Maclin's phone interrupted them. She looked
down at the number, put her phone on vibrate, and let the message
go to voice mail.

"So, what are we looking at here—some wannabee vampire shit?" Phee jumped in.

Kravitz put his glasses back on. "Hardly. Textbook med school stuff. Look at the three puncture wounds on the carotid artery. It took three attempts to get it right. Despite the fact that the vics' hands were chopped off at the wrist and they would have completely bled out through the radial arteries, the killer doubled down and drained them twice. They then flushed the bodies with saline. I'm not exaggerating when I say the vics don't have a drop of blood in them."

"Oh shit," Quincy sighed.

"Unfortunately, that's not the worst part," Kravitz added.

Phee, leaning against a cabinet with his arms folded, stood up straight. "What's worse than that?"

Kravitz winced as his headache flared. "The hands don't match."

"Come again?" Quincy perked up.

"I ran tissue samples and some analysis on the cut patterns. Their hands were severed, then reattached to the wrong body."

"What kind of sick shit is that?" Phee quipped.

"Well, when you put it all into a historical context, some of the sickest we've ever seen. Agent Maclin, do you know the significance of what was done to these men?"

"I understand what you're telling us happened to them. Is there something else I'm supposed to know?" she asked.

"Since you're so well read, I was just curious about your knowledge of Jewish history."

"Just tell us what we need to know, Kravitz. We don't have time for guessing games," Quincy joined in.

Maclin didn't like the way Kravitz looked at her. She didn't appreciate being put on the spot and having her Jewishness tested like some sort of high school pop quiz. Certainly not from someone whom she had heard on at least two occasions refer to himself as "a cultural Jew." She didn't appreciate what looked to her like a hint of disappointment in his eyes.

Kravitz directed most of his speech in Maclin's direction. "The burned floor at the crime scene was more than likely used to destroy all remnants of their blood. Dr. Josef Mengele, aka Hitler's 'Angel of Death,' advocated that Jewish blood was poison and therefore needed to be completely purged from the earth to protect mankind. He ran all kinds of horrible experiments on the prisoners at Auschwitz. Jewish twins were his favorite. He sewed them together because he wanted to see if it was possible to create conjoined twins. He would also amputate some of their limbs and then reattach them to their sibling to test genetics and the degree to which the human body could be unnaturally manipulated. Looks like you guys have a helluva hate crime on your hands."

Maclin looked at the twins and the mutilation done to them. The more she looked at them, the angrier she got. Now that she was dying, life made even less sense to her. The brothers were known to be good men. Men of integrity. Godly men. Theirs was a life of purpose and grace. But despite their accomplishments, in the end none of that really mattered because when death decided to take them it came with no mercy but instead an excess of hate.

Maclin thought about the fact that she was only forty-one and lived a life dedicated to the pursuit of justice. Like the twins, even though she had done good things in the world such as saving lives and thwarting evil, it was obviously not enough to curry favors with the universe. She was angry that death was so undiscerning that it came as a gluttonous force with no logic. It tormented her that even the virtuous who dedicated themselves to the service of mankind were subjected to the cruel whims of God. It made no sense to her when the bad outlived the good.

Maclin was a realist on the subject of death. There was no beating it, and only a few temporarily cheated it. The closer she got to her own expiration, the more she realized that her life was filled with countless regrets. She regretted that she had only been in love once. That she'd never had a child. She regretted that after the love of her life was murdered, she surrendered to years of hate and loneliness. There were many more disappointments that depressed her. She conceded that one of the last regrets she would have in life was that the cancer that was ravaging her would prevent her from killing the evil that murdered the Abramovitz brothers.

5

New York stank. Literally.

The two-week-old garbage strike along with the current heat wave and civil unrest was quickly turning the Big Apple into the Big Rotting Core. The streets of the city were littered with scores of stuffed black garbage bags. Rats were emboldened by the bountiful spoils of the strike. They rummaged about as freely during the day as they did at night. Protests and marches were still going on; the Brooklyn Bridge had already been shut down twice from orchestrated sit-ins, and not even New York had enough holding cells to stockpile the hordes of angry demonstrators. Temperatures were over one hundred degrees, but tempers were registering much higher than that. New York had gone from simmering to boiling. It was no longer a question of whether or not the city was going to implode; it was now just a matter of when.

The One-Nine on East 67th Street was an old-school precinct, a lot like the 5th precinct, where Quincy and Phee worked. By the time the trio walked through the doors of the station, they were so damp from sweat that they looked as if they had been caught in a misting rain. Even though they were inside now, they couldn't feel much difference. There may have been lots of activity going on, but most of the occupants, civilians and cops alike, seemed to be moving in a slower gear. The heat was making everyone irritable; there was even bickering going on between the desk sergeant and two patrols about hogging a desk fan. The argument was pointless because the fans at the One-Nine were a joke. They were just a visual mislead for the sake of morale. The cops were simply being teased by the thought of actual air being circulated. There was no such thing. The concept of cool air was quickly becoming an urban myth. There were rumors of encounters with it on other floors of the precinct, but they were quickly proven to be as unsubstantiated as sightings of Bigfoot. It was 109 degrees and that wasn't even the expected high. There was no reprieve. Temperatures were still climbing.

The building had good bones—a neo-Italian Renaissance structure with rusticated walls of red- and sand-colored granite—but there was a lot of wear and tear. The homicide department was smaller than the one at the 5th precinct, most likely because there were fewer murders in this particular area of Manhattan.

Unfortunately, the air was dismal. The old building had a musty scent, reminiscent of damp leather in a hot gymnasium.

Maclin, Phee, and Quincy were requested to work the case from the local precinct for the sake of politics and expediency. It was a highly sensitive case that required them to work closely with the cops who knew the community and its influential constituents. None of them were happy about the temporary relocation; but, then again, if things went right they would only be there a couple of days, hopefully even less.

People had come to expect even the impossible from them. Miracles were always wished for but hard to come by. Good old-fashioned, thorough police work was all they had, all they knew. It was the one thing that had never failed them.

As Maclin, Phee, and Quincy walked into the midtown precinct, the place was buzzing with chatter about the synagogue murders. For the most part, the cops there looked like all cops. They were NYPD in a variety pack; they came in choices of fat, skinny, bald, hirsute, tall, short, male, female, black, white, Latin, Asian, and even a few *assholeans* sprinkled in for good measure.

The trio hadn't even gotten deep into the building before they started feeling the stares and smirks of haters. Half the detectives there looked at them sideways. Any cop with even a thimbleful of pride resented the very thought of strangers coming into their house to do the job that they were convinced they were capable of doing. The other half looked at the three visitors with a fifty-fifty mix of envy and empathy. Most cops wanted the high-profile cases, but not all were prepared for the burden or potential ramifications of such a case. Even though Quincy and Phee had a great rep throughout the city as being the best closers on the force, this was the case that made everyone nervous. Every cop in New York could potentially be affected by the violent backlash of exploding racial tension throughout the city. Everybody's job would be impacted by the outcome of the Abramovitz case.

The two older oscillating fans that were posted in opposite corners succeeded only in moving the warm, stale air back and forth with very little positive effect. Aside from Phee, Quincy, and Maclin there was a total of thirteen people gathered in the roll call room. Per Phee's request, everyone who had direct access to the crime scene was escorted from the synagogue in two vans to keep them isolated from everyone else. There were four detectives, two investigators from CSU, four uniforms, and two techs from the medical examiner's office along with Kravitz. Phee made it a point to look directly at everyone there whom he didn't know personally. His not-so-subtle message was that anything less than full discretion would be regarded as a betrayal to the badge.

"Okay, so this is the deal: nobody in this room says anything to anyone about what you saw in the synagogue. Not to your spouse, best friend, side piece, family, or even fellow cops. We gotta control this thing until we break it. We can't talk to the press on this one. Not a word. Let the chief and the mouthpieces handle that. The only people who know the details of what went down with the killings are the people in this room. If there are any leaks, they came from somebody here. If the specifics get out about how they were killed, we're gonna end up in a dinosaur-sized shit storm."

Even though Phee was just a visitor to the midtown precinct, he made it clear that he, Quincy, and Maclin were in charge, and since the chief of police made them the primaries on the case, there was no such thing as jurisdiction.

"I'm not really sure what I saw in there. I mean, what it all meant," said a young uniform who still looked like he was trying to collect himself from the horrible experience.

"Well, whatever it's supposed to mean, let's just hope we're past the worst of it," Quincy said, jumping in.

"What about the maintenance man who discovered the vics?" one of the detectives asked as he blotted the back of his neck with damp paper towels.

"He's an illegal from Honduras. We've got ICE holding him for a couple of days just to make sure he's not a problem," Phee answered.

He looked around the room to see if anyone needed more clarification on what was expected of them.

"Any questions? This is the time to ask. We need to leave here knowing that all of us are on the same page."

"I got a question for ya." A 210-pound Irish pug with a stump of a neck raised his hand. As was the detective's habit, he was chewing on a small wad of gum. A former Golden Gloves cruiserweight who prided himself on still being a gym rat, Egan Burns had a flattened nose that looked perpetually broken. It leaned to the left, having long ago abandoned all hope of returning to the center. The slight deformity was a daily reminder of his former aspirations.

"Shoot," Quincy said.

"So since this happened in our backyard and we were first on scene, do we at least get to run secondary on the case, or do you decide that as well?" the detective said with an obvious edge.

Before Quincy could respond, Phee jumped in. "Detective Burns, right? Look, let's squash the petty bullshit before it even starts. The case should have been yours, we agree. But it's not. You got any issues with how the mayor and chief want this played out, then take it down to 1PP. You saw what happened to the Abramovitz brothers. You know what we're up against. We're not here to offer group hugs and take a bunch of selfies with our new BFFs. We've all got a helluva job to do—it's that simple. So you can be an asset, or you can be an asshole. Choice is yours."

Phee's bluntness was a test; he needed to know right away what kind of cops he was dealing with.

"Well gee, Detective Freeman, since you put it that way, I was actually hoping to be a little bit of both because that's the only way we know how to do it here in midtown," Burns shot back with a sardonic grin. A couple of the other cops laughed as Phee and Burns sized each other up.

Phee finally broke and smiled. "We'll get along just fine. And, yes, you're our second."

It was 5:40 by the time the debriefing was done. Maclin went to work on her laptop and pulled up every hate group that appeared on the federal watch list. There were thirty-seven in

New York City alone. Quincy and Phee, along with Burns and his partner Bobby Skia, who was always called by both names, put their focus on the Abramovitz brothers. Even though the rabbis both had squeaky-clean reputations, the Deggler case had taught them all to never assume the total innocence of anyone. The four detectives scoured the financials and looked for any affiliations with controversial figures and groups. It was all a formality though, a simple process of elimination. The case had hate crime written all over it.

When Burns and Bobby Skia left for a dinner break, Phee called Brenda. After he hung up, he turned to Quincy and Maclin.

"Brenda wants to know if we'll make it back home in time for dinner. Since we're gonna end up pulling an all-nighter, I say we might as well do it at my place. It's too hot to even think here. Quincy was already gonna crash in my guesthouse. Maclin, you can stay in one of the guest rooms."

"I'd rather just keep working. I need to get as many of these profiles done as possible before I head back to DC tomorrow," Maclin responded.

Surprised, Phee looked at Quincy and then back at Maclin.

"I already told the mayor that the most I could do would be to give my assessment of the crime scene and get the two of you started on profiles of the most likely candidates. I'm not going to be able to see this one through to the end."

"You're kidding, right? Maclin, we need you so that we can close this thing as soon as possible," Quincy said, jumping in.

"I'm sorry, but I can't," Maclin said.

"What do you mean, you can't? We're not looking at some simple…"

"Quincy, I said I can't." Maclin started getting defensive.

"If you don't run point on this with us, you know how it's gonna play out. The Bureau is gonna stomp all over this thing and take twice as long because of all of their bureaucratic bullshit. The three of us working together is the best shot to put this thing down and put it down quickly," Phee said.

"Don't you think I already know that, Phee?"

"If you know it, then why the hell are we even having this conversation?" he shot back.

"I said I can't, okay?!!! I've got some personal stuff that I need to deal with."

The walls of the conference room were glass. A couple of the detectives in the squad looked in when Maclin raised her voice. In the two cases that they had worked together, Quincy couldn't recall ever seeing her get emotional. Phee's famous temper would only make things worse. Quincy jumped into referee mode.

"Okay, look, we're all on edge here. Let's just take everything down about three ticks. If we only have you until tomorrow, then we got a long night ahead of us. I think Phee is right: let's get outta this sauna and put some food in our system then spend the rest of the night spitballing about which bad actors might look good for this."

Maclin didn't give much; she just focused on her laptop as a way of avoiding Phee's stare. "Come on, Janet. We're gonna have to head out to Jersey at some point to get your car. Better to do it now than three in the morning. The drive can do us all some good.

Besides, if you thought lunch was great, wait until you taste Elena's lasagna," Quincy boasted.

Everything was shit for Maclin. The city smelled like shit. It was hot as shit, and she felt like shit. She was a half hour late taking her meds, and she could feel the rise of tiny skirmishes throughout her body. It was a transient pain that went organ hopping like it was on a shopping spree. It visited different parts of her with varying degrees of intensity. The pain felt like it was in her bones one minute, then when it got bored it camped out in her liver or kidneys and then settled into her stomach for a party of sorts, twisting it for a while before it moved on.

Maclin named her cancer Ivan, as in Ivan the Terrible. In her mind Ivan was Jewish—specifically, of Eastern European descent, more commonly known as Ashkenazim. When she was first diagnosed, she read a piece in *Smithsonian* on genomes and how hereditary mutations in BRCA1 and BRCA2 genes had infested the bloodline of her people for generations, disproportionately increasing the chances of breast, ovarian, and prostate cancer. Although Maclin often self-deprecatingly thought of herself as nothing more than a *casual Jew*, her lack of commitment ultimately made no difference. Despite the fact that she may have never been the type to boldly claim her *Jewishness*, she was discovering that it certainly claimed *her*. She visualized Ivan as a giant barbarian wielding an ancient ax and draped in the skins of his vanquished prey. She thought it only fitting that her disease should have some type of intimate identification. She needed to be able to call it something specific when it took hold of her and controlled her every move. When it was angry and uncooperative, she needed to be able to curse its name as she tussled with it with very little success. Ivan was a son of a bitch but he was hers, all hers for the remainder of her very short life.

At 7:30 it was still an unpleasant ninety-seven degrees. The city was overripe with an unrelenting funk. The air was so thick with humidity that if one breathed in too heavily through an open mouth, it was possible to actually taste the heat and stench. Maclin sat in the back seat as Phee headed up the West Side Highway toward the George Washington Bridge. The temperature seemed to slow everything down. They got stuck in traffic just two exits before 179th Street. The water of the Hudson River barely moved. The Saturday evening traffic seemed even worse. Phee's Rover crept along just a few feet at a time.

Maclin may have been the only one in all of New York who was happy to be stuck in the congestion. The slower they moved, the better. It was easier for her to hide her sickness from Phee and Quincy. She could feel Phee's eyes in the rearview mirror stealing glances at her. She pretended not to notice. Maclin just needed to buy a little more time to let the drugs take effect so she could negotiate with Ivan. The Dilaudid kicked in right away, and she was thankful that she wasn't hurting as much as she had been just twenty minutes earlier. She was waiting for the Zofran to fight back the nausea, to help her suppress the uprising. She was just hoping that she wouldn't leave regurgitated bits of her delectable lunch all over the back of Phee's SUV.

6

The drive back to Phee's house was quiet. Periodically, Maclin's phone vibrated with a text or call from the same number that she kept ignoring. The radio was turned down low, but she could still hear the voices of a host and guest on an all-talk radio station having a discussion on race in America. The guest on the show was Sheldon Grimes, an African American community activist. Phee lowered the volume even more when Grimes started shouting over the host and seemed more interested in hearing himself pontificate than having a meaningful conversation. After Phee had had enough, he turned the radio off and drove in silence.

Maclin knew Phee was still irritated with her because she wasn't going to work the case all the way through. She hated letting the two partners down, because she respected them above all other cops. She hadn't quite lied to them, but she wasn't totally honest with them either. Not telling them what she'd originally gone to see them about made her feel deceitful. Now with the synagogue murders, her visit had gone all wrong. She couldn't tell them that she was dying. She refused to be a distraction at a time when they needed all their focus on stopping whoever was responsible for slaughtering the Abramovitz brothers.

The minute the three of them walked through the front door of Phee's house, they heard hearty laughter coming from the kitchen. Maclin immediately recognized Brenda's and Elena's voices, but there was a third one that was loud, gravelly, and unfamiliar. As Maclin followed Phee and Quincy into the kitchen, she watched Elena and Brenda, who was holding Dolicia, cross to greet their men. Leaning against the onyx countertop with a glass of wine was a two-hundred-something-pound trans woman.

"Maclin, do you remember Epiphany from my brother's funeral?" Phee asked.

"Uhh, yeah," she answered.

"That's a good answer, sweetie, 'cause I am not one to be easily forgotten," Epiphany laughed.

After Phee kissed Brenda and Dolicia, he held his daughter in one arm and greeted Epiphany with a hug.

Maclin most definitely remembered her. People with personalities that were larger than life were hard to forget. Epiphany Chevalier and Phee's brother AJ had been best friends and roommates. Before AJ's murder, they were both prostitutes. Maclin thought that from the looks of things Epiphany seemed to have completely turned her life around. She wore all white: white blouse, white linen pants, and even white patent leather red-bottoms. Maclin noticed the Rolex Lady-Datejust and diamond-studded earrings and assumed that the Louis Vuitton clutch on the kitchen island belonged to her as well.

"Phee, I just stopped by to drop off the monthly statements, plus I wanted to see this scrumptious little girl of yours," Epiphany said, tickling Dolicia.

"How's construction on the second store going?" Phee asked.

"We're still two weeks behind my original schedule, but we'll be able to open on time. It'll be tight, but I'll make it happen," Epiphany answered.

Phee turned to Maclin. "Epiphany opened a little clothing boutique about a year and a half ago in the Village, selling my brother's designs. That spot did so well, she's opening another one in SoHo."

"What Mr. Modesty here left out is that he's the silent partner who's making it all happen," Epiphany added.

"Hey, obviously it's a good investment," Phee shot back.

"All right, food's ready! Let's eat," Elena said as she and Brenda ushered everyone to the dining room.

Maclin picked at her food and forced herself to eat enough to appear polite, but Ivan had taken her appetite on the drive home and refused to give it back. She thought it was a shame, because Quincy was right: what little she did eat was delicious. She had never had lasagna made with chunks of lobster and crabmeat along with Gruyère and smoked gouda. Maclin only had one glass of red because sometimes the wine and meds combined made her sleepy—which on most nights was a good thing, but tonight she definitely wanted to be sharp. Everyone listened as Epiphany told in dramatic fashion a funny story about how a couple of years ago she and AJ got booted from an audition for *American Idol*. As everyone laughed, Dolicia, just as she had done at lunch, squirmed out of Phee's arms and made her way into Maclin's lap. Bo sat at Maclin's feet, panting as he watched her every move.

"I swear, I don't know what it is about you, but she just does not take to strangers the way she takes to you," Brenda said.

"She knows you're good people. Kids just have a sixth sense about those kinds of things," Phee added. The way Phee made a point to lock eyes with Maclin along with the compliment led her to assume that it was the closest thing he would give in terms of an apology for their earlier spat. It was unnecessary but appreciated.

Maybe Phee was right. Not necessarily so much about her being such a good person as the part about kids having a sixth sense. As the little girl sat comfortably in her lap and recited all the names and biographies of all of her dolls, Maclin wondered whether children could sense death.

After dinner Phee, Quincy, and Maclin sat on the veranda with their laptops and got down to business. The spicy aroma of sweet pepperbush wafted through the air as a constant reminder of their escape from the punishing smells of New York City. Periodically the sound of Epiphany's laughter bellowed from inside the house.

There were multiple things that split Maclin's focus, and they

were just the type of minor distractions that she welcomed. Lately
the victory of her days was contingent upon how she fared through
her various battles, such as the tolerance of her pain, avoidance of
her depressions, and even more minute things like having something close to an average sense of taste or smell. She never thought
it would be a luxury to simply be able to taste a good meal; but
then again, she hadn't expected some of her senses to diminish as
much as they had over the last month. She had no idea how long
it would last, but she quietly celebrated the simplicity of being able
to smell the suburban fresh air. There were plenty of stars and the
constant chirps of courting crickets that got her attention as well.
Tomorrow could be a completely different story, but it was a small
victory that at least her five senses were simultaneously working for
the time being.

"So, I've taken the thirty-seven hate groups in New York that the
Bureau's been monitoring and I've put them into eight sets of four
and then the last bunch into a set of five. They're in descending
order of which ones the Agency feels are the real threats and which
ones are just hate talkers. The three of us need to go through and
narrow them down even more to who we think could actually be
capable of something this bad. I'm already forming a spin, but I'd
like to go through everyone on the list before I share it."

Quincy sat with his elbows on his knees and both of his
thumbs tapping the bridge of his nose, deep in thought, while
Phee researched the criminal history of each group on his laptop.

Brenda carried Dolicia out in her pink Dora the Explorer paja-
mas. After the little girl kissed her father and godfather, she scur-
ried over to hug Maclin and kiss her goodnight as well before
Brenda wrangled her back into the house. For the next four hours,
Maclin, Phee, and Quincy meticulously went through the files of
the thirty-seven groups.

Maclin thought better when she moved. She stood and walked
ten feet forward, then ten feet back. Her phone still vibrated every
now and then, but she continued to ignore the calls. The tiled
deck felt cool underneath her bare feet. She was surprised at how
relaxed she was and pleased that the partners had convinced her to
leave the city to come work from the house.

"Okay, so I still think the most likely would be the top four
on my list. We've got Black Muslims in Harlem, an Aryan group
in Vinegar Hill, skinheads out in Canarsie, and neo-Nazis in Fort
Greene. We've arrested members from all four of these groups on
federal charges from arson to murder. Let's start with the most
obvious: the word 'umoja' that was spray-painted at the scene."

"It's a Swahili word that means 'unity,'" Phee said.

Maclin nodded, then countered, "It's also one of the names
that the group up in Harlem goes by."

"If they're so badass, how come we've never heard of them?"
Quincy asked.

"They're relatively new to New York. Started in St. Louis
almost fifteen years ago after a few members broke ranks from the

New Black Panther Party and converted to Islam. They started off simple enough—their philosophy was 'unity through community.' They became more radicalized four years ago after their founder, Hasan Bluridge, was shot in the back by a cop who said he was resisting arrest after a simple traffic stop. The cop was never indicted, and two months later he ended up killed in an ambush by unknown assailants. A week after that, the prosecutor who wouldn't indict was killed the same way. Both were shot multiple times."

"Yeah, I remember hearing about that," Phee added.

Maclin pressed on. "We assumed the group disbanded until we discovered that some of the newer members relocated to New York six months ago and started heavy recruitment in Harlem. Their current leader is a guy by the name of Shaka Zaire-Ali. Outside of a couple of petty crimes several years ago, we really don't have that much on him. He just kind of popped up out of nowhere."

"Are they top of the list just because the name of their group was spray-painted at the scene? Feels pretty convenient, doesn't it?" Quincy asked.

Phee stood up and stretched his lower back. "I agree with Quincy. I can see the motivation for them killing the cop, if they did it. By the same token, I could even see them doing the prosecutor. But why would they kill a couple of rabbis who were well respected in the black community?"

Maclin leaned forward and set her glass of water on the grass. "I've cross-referenced all known members of Umoja and even some of their recent recruits and came up with at least a person of interest by the name of Jared Harris."

Phee perked up when he heard the name.

Maclin struck a couple of keys on her laptop and then turned it around so that the partners could see the photo she pulled up.

"Shit," Phee hissed.

"You know him?" Maclin asked.

"Yeah, I grew up with him. We called him Spider. Both of you met him at my brother's funeral. So why did he come up as a POI?"

"His sister's kid was Devon Timmons," Maclin answered.

"The same Timmons who was chased to his death two weeks ago by a Jewish mob?" Quincy jumped in.

Maclin looked at Phee when she answered. "Yeah, the same. Right after his nephew's death, Jared Harris was recruited by Umoja. Maybe it's circumstantial and maybe it's not. Probably won't buy us a warrant, but if we're looking for motive, how about the oldest in the book: an eye for an eye. Maybe Spider and his new friends are just taking it one step further: 'They take one of ours; we take two of theirs.'"

7

Maclin had worked with Phee and Quincy until just past two in the morning. She woke up at 5:14 but lay there for a half hour trying to convince her body it was time to move.

She started the first few moments of each morning waiting for her body to catch up with her intentions. In the last month of dawns, she couldn't help feeling like a vintage Chevy, her engine needing warming up before any type of acceleration. Movement for her required thought, negotiation even. When she was finally able to move, she did so like a thief careful not to alarm her pain. Her arms felt as stiff as wooden telephone poles, with a radiating sensation that left her hand strength so depleted that it was impossible for her to perform even the simple task of unscrewing the cap of her pain pills that she needed to start the day.

Mornings were usually the roughest for her. All she could do was stay motionless while the pain traveled from one end of her body to the other. On good days, the journey only lasted five minutes or less; on bad days, it took up to thirty. With nothing to do but lie there, she took in the room. Maclin winced from time to time as the pain relocated itself, shifting course on its tedious expedition. She distracted herself as she stared at the pair of Pierre-Marie Brisson paintings, the glass-domed Tiffany clock on the nightstand, and the raw silk valance and drapes that hung to just an inch above the Brazilian dark wood floors. She entertained herself for a few seconds by trying to find the seams in the herringbone pattern in the wallpaper. She couldn't. Although she was just an overnight guest, the room made her feel as though she belonged.

The muscles in her left arm were the first to release her fleeting paralysis. By 5:35 she was sitting up and popping pills. When she checked her phone she saw that she had several missed calls from the same number. She didn't bother to shower because she wanted to be out of the house before Phee or anyone else woke. Maclin wasn't good with goodbyes; she found them more cumbersome than not.

Just as she headed toward the front door, Bo appeared from nowhere and started barking at her.

"Bo, shhh." Brenda emerged from the kitchen and snapped her finger. Bo stopped on cue and sat at his mistress's feet. Brenda was in a pair of gym shorts and wearing an oversized Giants jersey with her husband's number on it. The jersey hung low on her but was snug across her protruding belly.

"Bo's a trip. He's all bark and no bite, trust me. You're up early," Brenda said.

"Yeah, I uhh, wanted to get back to the city before morning traffic started."

"It's Sunday. It won't be bad. Elena and I were just having some coffee and biscuits. Come on in and join us."

"Thank you, but no, I need to get back."

"Oh come on, just one cup before you head back into the jungle."

"I'm fine, I…"

Brenda hooked her arm in Maclin's and directed her toward the kitchen.

"I was raised in the South, where it's sacrilege to let a guest leave your house on an empty stomach."

Maclin had no choice but to like Brenda. She was just *likable*.

As the two of them walked back into the kitchen, Elena was standing in a corner pouring coffee. She was wearing a wife-beater and yoga pants. CNN quietly played on a twenty-four-inch flat screen that was mounted high in a corner near the fridge.

"Morning," Elena said. "You're up early, considering how late you all worked."

"Yeah, I'm not a big sleeper. Do the two of you always get up this early on the weekends?"

"My little terror wakes up at six fifteen every morning. I just like to have some me time before she starts running me ragged," Brenda laughed.

"How do you like your coffee?" Elena asked as she opened the cupboard and pulled out a mug that was bigger than most soup bowls.

"Cream, no sugar."

As Maclin looked oddly at the large mug that Elena set in front of her, Brenda laughed. "If you haven't already guessed, we do things big around here."

Maclin hadn't had a morning appetite in quite some time. She picked at the hot cheddar biscuit that Brenda set before her. Melted butter ran down the sides of the warm, puffy bread with sticky apricot jam in the center.

"Forecast says it might get up to 110 degrees in the city," Elena said.

"I'm definitely not missing living there," Brenda sighed.

"How could you miss Hell when you've got a piece of Heaven?" Elena teased.

Elena was right: the home was heavenly. They stood in the middle of the Tuscan-style chef's kitchen complete with birch-paneled Sub-Zero fridge and freezer and a vintage La Cornue stove. The kitchen wasn't just a cook's playground; the large, open space was designed to accommodate larger as well as intimate gatherings. Maclin looked around and thought that the kitchen was almost half the size of her entire apartment in Langley. Her domicile was like most things in her life: much more about function and sustainability than anything else. Her lifestyle wasn't the kind that included impromptu dinner guests or late-night sleepovers. It certainly didn't include early morning coffee and homemade biscuits with girlfriends and chats about children and weather. Maclin had spent so many years in obsessive pursuit of the serial killer Deggler that once she, Quincy, and Phee finally killed him, it only further exposed how void her life had become of, well, living.

Brenda heard sounds from the baby monitor that sat in the center of the kitchen island. She saw her daughter restlessly stirring. The sound of the little girl's voice was as loud as a baby rooster ushering in the start of a new day. Dolicia, in her pink pj's, stood and held the bars of her crib like a mini convict plotting her escape.

"That's my cue. The reign of terror begins," Brenda said as she sipped the last of her coffee and turned to exit. Elena intercepted her by putting a hand on her shoulder, "You stay. I'll get her."

As Elena went to retrieve Dolicia, Maclin took a sip of coffee. Even though her taste buds were still slowly waking up, the warm fluid felt good sliding down inside of her.

"You really do have a beautiful home, Brenda."

"Thank you. You're always welcome here. Phee and Quincy always speak so highly of you."

"They're the best I've ever worked with."

Brenda opened the fridge and took out some Greek yogurt, along with some fresh blueberries and strawberries. After she mixed all three in a child's bowl she poured some carrot juice into a Little Mermaid sippy cup.

"You mind if I ask you a question about your work?"

"Not at all, as long as it's not about the case."

"No, nothing like that. I just wanna know what's it like?" Brenda asked as she finished preparing her daughter's breakfast. "I mean, doing what you do? Phee never talks about his work. He thinks he's protecting me from the big bad world."

Maclin chewed on Brenda's words and stared at her as though

she was trying to decide which early morning truths were palatable and which were not.

"He is protecting you. Be thankful for that. The thing you might not understand is that the protection goes both ways. Cops deal with the kind of darkness that most people can't even fathom. The only way to survive that intact day in and year out is by knowing there's some light waiting for you at the end of your shift. Otherwise it grinds you up so much that it owns you, and you end up lost somewhere between the shadows of who you think you are and who you really are."

Maclin sipped her coffee and got quiet as though she had inadvertently said too much. Brenda felt a little awkward because she couldn't quite read her. As she drizzled honey on her daughter's yogurt, she wondered if she had accidentally opened a can of discomfort that struck much too close to home.

Elena came into the kitchen carrying Dolicia. As she handed her off, Brenda blanketed the little girl with morning kisses, which made both of them laugh.

"Good morning, my little mama," Brenda said.

Maclin looked at the exchange between mother and daughter and saw firsthand how they were the light that got Phee through. Phee was right to protect Brenda from even the slightest detail of the darkness they pursued case after disturbing case. Maclin saw purity in Dolicia and Brenda. It was a purity that was worth protecting at all costs even if it meant hiding certain truths from his wife. Even if it meant telling permissible lies that fathers tell their daughters, such as there were no monsters in the dark and there were happy endings aplenty because the world was a good and decent place. Although it had been a very long time since she had had anything in her life resembling such innocence, fortunately she hadn't forgotten how to appreciate it. It wasn't envy that she felt but rather an unfinished longing. She wasn't certain, but she thought for just a moment that she saw a similar longing in Elena's eyes as they both looked at Brenda, who was completely smitten by her pint-sized angel.

Dolicia insisted on sitting in Maclin's lap so that her new best friend could feed her from the bowl of yogurt and berries. Maclin laughed and obliged, thankful for the opportunity. Bo sat nearby, jealous of their union. Just as the night before, as soon as the two settled into each other Dolicia proved to be a more powerful palliative than the daily meds Maclin relied on. Even if only temporarily, she felt repaired by the infinite smile of Brenda and Phee's little terror. However, the side effects were somewhat bittersweet. She couldn't help but think about the child she had miscarried shortly after Willington was murdered. Although there were voids in Maclin that no other child could fill, she at least allowed herself the moments to enjoy how perfectly Dolicia fit in her lap, much like a lost puzzle piece unexpectedly found. She enjoyed it so much she ended up not leaving the house until almost 7:30.

The second she crossed the George Washington Bridge, it felt like the temperature jumped twenty degrees. Again her phone vibrated, and again she checked the incoming call and chose to ignore it. There were now thirteen voice messages on her phone. At 7:45 the thermostat in her dash read eighty-nine. Even with the windows closed and the AC turned up, Maclin could sense the city simmering like an overnight stew in a Crock-Pot.

As she drove down Broadway, she passed block after block of undeclared refuse stuffed in giant blobs of black plastic bags that ate up half of the sidewalks. She pondered which would end first: the garbage strike or the heat wave. The city could survive one at a time, but Maclin wondered how long New Yorkers would hold it together when things really started boiling over.

It was only 8 o'clock on a Sunday morning, but she started seeing the first cracks of the day. Cabbies laid on their horns at the slightest provocation. She actually saw two come to blows at the intersection of 66th and Broadway, just in front of Juilliard. Even though one was bloodied from the pummeling he took, no one came to his aid; instead, several pedestrians just stood by and filmed the fight on their phones in hopes of it becoming the day's viral sensation.

Maclin was a woman of habit. She found efficiency in routine. By the time she made it to the hotel where she always stayed when she came to New York, it was just after 8:15. The Richardson was a boutique hotel near St. Mark's Place and 3rd Avenue with small rooms and low ceilings but the type of hospitality that made each guest feel like they were the one and only priority. By the time she parked her car and walked a half block to the hotel, she was sweating and thinking about a long, cool shower.

"Janet."

Just as she reached to open the lobby door of the hotel, she heard her name called. It was the same voice that had left several voicemails for her. It was the one voice that she had hoped she would live the rest of her life, however short that might be, without ever hearing again.

8

Spider Harris hated white people. Maybe not as vehemently as did his father, grandfather, and even great-grandfather, but the racism and xenophobia that he had been weaned on all his life were deeply planted in him with bottomless roots. Such were the results of being raised under the bilious rants of lifelong racists.

That loathing was a revered family heirloom that had been carefully passed down, generation after generation. His father and grandfather taught him that whites were vampires, feasting on the souls of all whom they deceived. Accordingly, he avoided them as much as possible. Spider was born and raised and worked and lived his entire life in Harlem. Even now, in his midforties, it was still the rare occasion that he traveled south of 110th Street. Harlem was his world, and not enough people seemed to be concerned that it was being choked under the stranglehold of gentrification.

It broke his heart that far too many blacks insisted on walking through life blind and weak. Spider was woke, and he hated what he saw. Every day he mourned the slow and steady death of black consciousness. He was thankful that he had such strong men in his family who had set examples for him. Besides his family and the brothas from Umoja, nobody seemed particularly alarmed by the cryptic writing on the wall.

Spider especially hated Jews. It was a new distinction for him that had started only two weeks before, after a dozen or so Hasids out in Borough Park chased his seventeen-year-old nephew to his death. Not one person was charged. Not even Ezra Pearl, who was caught on video leading the deadly chase. Before that tragic event, Spider's view of Jewish people had been much more complex. On one hand, he felt about them the same way he felt about all whites: they were not to be trusted. Although he would never openly admit it, as a self-proclaimed history buff he secretly admired them for being great survivors. Spider actually envied them and how after the Holocaust they turned their greatest tragedy into their greatest triumph: Israel. It pissed him off to no end that African Americans had no sovereign state; there was no Israel that existed for Spider and his people. Slavery had all too brilliantly severed the umbilical cord between African Americans and their motherland. The sad truth was that at best, the vast majority of blacks felt only an obligatory connection to the Dark Continent.

Spider saw his generation, as well as the half dozen previous ones, as a nation of the disenfranchised. As far as he was concerned, the closest thing to a motherland were the dissected pockets of black life that were scattered around the country in the form of urban sections of the American landscape. The consolation prize for him was that atop the cultural food chain for black people was his beloved Harlem. It was the black holy land. This was the one place in the world that he would fight for, bleed for, and willingly die for, if it came to that.

Spider woke up in a warm pool of blood. He couldn't remember a damn thing. No idea where he was or how he got there. All he knew was that he hurt. The only good thing about his pain was that he felt so much of it that he knew he couldn't be dead. That was it; that was the best confirmation that he had that he was still alive. His hands hurt the most, but his neck wouldn't support him enough to see why. Any attempts at movement left him feeling helpless from his total lack of control. The inside of his head felt like pounded meat. He floated in and out of his fugue, which only left him operating at about 20 percent. A sharp pain in the back of his skull jump-started his senses just enough that things slowly started becoming a little clearer.

His body still wouldn't move, but his focus, eyesight, sense of smell, and hearing crept back at a snail's pace. The temperature in the room was at least mid-90. A softball-size hole in the roof allowed a thin ray of morning light to shine in. Its glow was so weak that it lit only a small portion of the room.

Because of his lack of mobility, the ceiling was the only thing he could see. There were large brown water stains on corroded tiles that threatened to come crashing down on him at any moment. The corners of steel rafters were covered in peeling lead paint that exposed an ugly mass of what was probably asbestos. Thirty feet above the center of the pit were the broken remains of an ancient pulley system. Several groups of water pipes in varying sizes spread across the ceiling like a headless gang of metal snakes. The room was clammy from the humidity, and there was a heavy stench of sulfur that reminded him of a batch of rotted eggs.

Spider lowered his eyes to the large, faded graphic that was embedded high into the brick wall. He was looking for any clue that might tell him where he was. The harder he stared at the wall the more he could just make out the broken lettering of the name HOZINGER'S MEATS. The building trembled a little as a train rumbled by in the distance. Although he had never been there before, Spider knew exactly where he was: Hozinger's was a major meat supplier from the early '50s through the late '80s before going out of business in '91. He'd heard horror stories about the building throughout his childhood. The name Hozinger on the wall of a well-known factory not far from passing trains told Spider two things. One, he was on the northern tip of the Bronx. Two, he was being held captive in an abandoned slaughterhouse.

As the fog cleared in Spider's head, he started feeling the full measure of the pain in his hands and arms. The more conscious he became, the more aware he was of the pain in his hands. He'd never felt anything like it. Once he regained enough strength to finally lift his head to inspect himself, he saw the horrible reason: all ten fingers had been severed at their knuckles.

He screamed when he saw his missing fingers and the cauterized stubs that had been left in their place. He yelled something low and primal, a sound similar to the uncountable number of cattle that had been slaughtered in the same place years before him. His desperate screams bounced back and forth off the brick walls until all that was left of them were faded mutters.

Although he had no idea how long it was, Spider yelled until everything was siphoned out of him. As he eventually quieted down, he heard movement in a nearby corner. Someone or something was in the room with him. As he listened more intently, he recognized a familiar sound that he hadn't heard in years. It brought him back to when he was a child growing up in the grant housing projects on Morningside Avenue and 123rd Street. There were far too many nights that he went to sleep hearing the same thing he heard now. It was the unmistakable ruckus of rats fighting for food.

Spider raised himself up a bit until he was resting on his elbows. His head was spinning, and it took real effort to keep his eyes open. He was still groggy from an assault that he could only vaguely remember. He couldn't make sense of anything. He tried to think clearly, but his efforts only led to more confusion. There was a residual tinny vibration ringing in his head. The skin just above his left ear felt stretched from a swelling bump that was about the size of a golf ball. His eyes were slowly acclimating to the dark room with its faint streaks of light peeking in from the small hole up top as well as under the door or the random cracks where the walls separated from the ceiling.

The more his hearing improved, the better he could hear the

increasingly violent shrieks of the brawling rats. There was a shrill screech from one of the rodents that was obviously in severe pain. A second later, Spider saw a medium-size rat weakly hobble past him. The creature's fur was matted in blood, and it was presumably the defeated side of the battle. A couple of seconds later, a much larger rat passed within two feet of Spider. As he looked closely, he saw that the rat was carrying half of a familiar-looking finger.

Spider's head pounded as if his skull were a half size too small for his brain. It wasn't just that the slightest movement made things worse; even the simple act of thinking hurt. Regardless of the pain, there was no stopping the deluge of thoughts that flooded his mind. He wondered. He second-guessed. He replayed things over and over, trying to figure out how he ended up where he was. Spider knew he needed to figure shit out if he was going to survive.

He should never have trusted the phone call from the stranger who said he had irrefutable video evidence of Ezra Pearl pushing Spider's nephew just before a passing car killed him. The last thing he could recall was entering Central Park on 110th Street at Bone's Valley to meet the person who said they "wanted to set the record straight." He could clearly recollect waiting on the same bench where, as a kid, he and his boys used to watch the best dominoes players in Harlem throwin' bones. All he could remember was waiting there at the designated rendezvous shortly after sunrise. That was all.

There were tangible consequences to his senses returning. Every nerve ending in his hands felt as if it had been doused with gasoline and set on fire. The rotting smell in the air made him want to throw up. As if he didn't already have enough things threatening to break him, he started hearing sounds that, despite the horrendous heat in the room, chilled him to his core.

Someone in another part of the building was screaming in utter agony. Spider heard pain-filled decibels that he never even knew the human voice was capable of reaching. Each scream was preceded by the sound of something striking flesh. He counted seven exchanges. Seven blows and seven cries. He wasn't exactly sure if he imagined it, but it seemed to him that each strike was louder than the one before. Even when the cries suddenly stopped, the sharp pitch of skin being struck reverberated throughout the large building. Blow, silence, blow, silence, blow, silence, and so on. Spider counted fourteen blows even after the crying had stopped. Then it was quiet. A long, empty, ominous silence that made him think of death.

9

"Not saying you owe me an explanation or anything else, Janet. You said up front what you wanted and didn't want. But I just thought in addition to whatever it was that we were doing for the last two years that we were at least something resembling friends. Twelve phone calls and texts and nothing? I gotta stalk you at your hotel just to beg you for five minutes of your time? The funny thing is, the reason I was reaching out to you had nothing to do with us. I'm here because of your case."

Losher Saum leaned against a waist-high white lacquered dresser drawer, never taking his eyes off of Maclin as he spoke to her. On the other hand, her guilt made it difficult for her to even look in his general direction. She grew more self-conscious by the second in his presence. If anyone could detect the illness she was hiding, she assumed it would be him. He would see it in her eyes, in her skin, in the almost imperceptible way her clothes were beginning to fit just a bit more loosely. Even though her body was covered, he would know that she was beginning to lose millimeters of muscle mass. No matter how subtle, her life was now in atrophy.

She knew he was angry, but what she heard most in his voice was pain. It was a low, dull sound brimming with disappointment. This was completely new territory for the two of them. They had never argued before, because that type of thing was a luxury that their encounters simply couldn't afford. There were specific rules to their arrangement. Number one on the list was anything approximating "catching feelings" was strictly prohibited. They got together once every three weeks in the same hotel and usually in the same small room with white lacquered furniture. They ordered room service, ate naked on the floor, and occasionally talked, as long as the conversation didn't get too touchy-feely. But mainly, they fucked. Long, hard, and with varying degrees of violence.

These were the Maclin rules.

She was always cautious when she dealt with Losher because he was different from the others. He wasn't in the same pool of random men whom she used for sex and remembrance. In contrast to his pseudocounterparts, his function in her life was more than a temporary reminder of her part-time need for pleasure and— despite her fierce independence—the confirmation that a man's touch still made her feel more alive than anything else. Losher was the only one since Willington who consistently stimulated her deeper than the flesh. He was a good man whose only weakness that she could see was that he couldn't control his feelings for her.

Even though he did his best to mask it, Maclin knew he'd broken the rules very early into their fling. It was supposed to be sex and nothing more. Unlike her, he wasn't adept at keeping such things in their proper perspective. Maclin knew she was stronger than him and obviously more proficient at steering clear of love and similar liabilities.

She stood in a corner and leaned against the window, because the room was so small that there weren't many other options. The cramped box wasn't suitable for much besides sleeping and fornicating. It was all she had known with him in the room. It was a sacred space for her. The three hundred square feet gave her what she needed, nothing less and certainly not much more.

Everything was about proficiency for Maclin. She appreciated the boutique hotel mainly because it was a convenient place for her and her accommodating lover, a place where she could rest her demons and indulge her kinks. She loved the thick concrete walls and the containment that came with them, both aurally and physically. At almost six hundred dollars a night, it was worth every cent to her. Before her sickness came, her semimonthly excursions to New York were what she looked forward to most.

Losher was an ER doc who had treated Maclin when she'd been injured during the Zibik case two years earlier. He had hazel eyes that looked like a pair of honey-colored marbles. There was a hint of an Eastern European accent that still lingered twenty-five years after he'd emigrated with his parents and twin sister from Prague. A small chai dangled from a gold necklace three inches below his neck. His hair was mud brown with thick waves that just touched the top of his shoulders. He was a CrossFit enthusiast with a thick, muscular upper body and long, lean legs. At thirty-seven, he was four years younger than Maclin.

"You're right. I could have handled things better. But I've just got a lot going on right now. Things you wouldn't understand," Maclin said.

"You could always try me."

"There are things we do and things we don't do."

"Because of your precious rules?" Losher asked.

"Because some things are better left just the way they are."

"Got it."

"Look, I just came to get my stuff. I'm headed back to DC this afternoon. What was it about the case you wanted to tell me?"

"Yeah, I uhh… This could all be related. The head rabbi at my sister's synagogue thinks his son is missing."

"He thinks?"

"Well, he's pretty sure, but we don't have any hard proof."

"So why exactly does he think his son is missing?"

"Because his son is Ezra Pearl."

Maclin perked up a little at the mention of Pearl's name.

Losher saw it and felt a bit more encouraged by her reaction.

"Ezra and his father have dedicated the last ten years of their lives to creating a new Holocaust museum in Brooklyn. They were both being honored last night by one of the most respected yeshivas in New York because the museum opens in a few days. Ezra was a no-show, and no one has heard from him. There's no way he would have missed one of the proudest nights of his life. Cops seem to be dragging their feet because it hasn't been twenty-four hours yet."

"I'll make a phone call."

"I was hoping you'd do more."

"I'm not actually working the Abramovitz case. I'm headed back to DC."

"But I saw you on TV at the synagogue. That's how I knew you were in town."

"I was just there in an advisory capacity."

When he lowered his eyes, Maclin thought about how she'd felt when she'd let Quincy and Phee down by informing them that she wouldn't be seeing the case through with them. Losher looked similarly stung, as if by an act of betrayal. It was even more indicting because of their past intimacy. Although Losher never said it, Maclin knew that he expected more of her. It had only been two days since getting the dreaded confirmation of her diagnosis, and yet the dying game already had her letting down the few people who actually mattered in a life that was woefully short on connections.

His voice was her undoing. It was the one thing about him that reminded her most of Willington, who had been her truest love. There were times in the dark when Losher fucked her that she pretended that he was her murdered fiancé. It wasn't that the two men sounded exactly alike; it was more in their shared intonation. They both lifted the end of their phrasing, which made most of their sentences sound like questions. Losher's voice was deep and easy to lean on, even for Maclin, who wasn't used to leaning on much of anything or anyone. In the rare times that she inadvertently dropped her guard, Losher's voice and touch reminded her of what it meant to belong and what it meant to be celebrated.

They stood quietly across from each other, nothing more than intimate strangers. With just six feet between them, Maclin could smell him. She inhaled the subtle whiff of the Creed cologne that she was fond of him wearing. It was a light, spicy musk that only complemented his natural masculine scent. The fragrance reminded her of the ocean during warm spring rains. Smelling him had always been foreplay for her. Even though the cancer had robbed her of sexual desires, her nearness to Losher at least reminded her of the raw connection they used to share.

She was careful not to give him anything that might be misconstrued as an opening. Aside from the brief conversation regarding Ezra Pearl, Maclin's body language communicated that she was unreceptive to anything personal he might have to say. She kept her distance in more ways than one. Even though the room was small, their separation seemed best measured not in inches or feet but acreage. It wasn't her intention, but the distance seemed to leave him subtly floundering and even shrinking bit by bit before her. Maclin could see him fighting the invisible battle of whether to stay longer or go. She assumed whatever weakness he had for her kept him there leaning against the white lacquered dresser, feeling uninvited but too embarrassed to leave. Finally, when he seemed to tire of the obvious chasm he forced himself to stand, he headed toward the door, stuffing both hands into his pockets.

"Anything that you can do as far as Ezra Pearl goes, I'm sure his family would appreciate it. So would I."

Maclin didn't bother to speak because she didn't want anything she said to be interpreted as a promise. She watched him shift his weight from his left leg to his right. He seemed to be stalling.

"Are you taking care of yourself? You look a little under the weather."

"I'm fine. Just a migraine," she lied.

He turned, opened the door, then stopped. He kept his back to her. He stood there. No words. No movement. She allowed the moment. Endorsed it even. She felt it was the least she could do, knowing that she would never see him again. They heard a couple from somewhere down the hall. There was distant laughter that was muted then swallowed by a closing elevator. Even when Losher found his voice, he still kept his back to her.

"I'm sorry, Janet, that I wasn't enough to make you wanna give us a real try."

As he left, the hollow clanking of the closing door bounced off the walls and then through her as though she were nothing but air. The deep quiet left her feeling alone, until she quickly realized that she was anything but. Losher had left his scent behind as if it were a trained pet whose sole purpose was to remind her of his absence. Even as she stood by the window, she could still smell him, while his final words tumbled in her head like a damp load of laundry just beginning its cycle.

After Maclin took a shower and finished packing the few clothes she brought for the trip, her cell phone rang. She sat down on the bed and answered without looking at the caller ID, but she recognized the voice immediately.

"This is one of those phone calls that I've been hoping to make for some time now."

She couldn't ever remember him calling her directly. There were things that powerful men like him just didn't bother to do. The two or three times that he had called, there were seconds for her to prepare because an assistant always connected them. Maclin automatically stood because although he couldn't see her, his voice alone commanded that type of respect.

"Sir?" was the only thing that Maclin could squeeze out.

When her stomach twisted and made strange gurgling sounds, she wasn't sure whether it was her nerves or the cancer. It was an understatement to say that when Percy Tuttle, the director of the FBI, called, it was definitely a big deal.

"I wanted you to be one of the first to hear it directly from me instead of a newsfeed. In an hour the president is going to announce that he's selected me to become vice president."

"Congratulations, sir. That's incredible news," Maclin stammered.

"Thank you, Janet, but this phone call is more about your future than mine. I've had my eye on you for quite some time now. I wanted to assure you that your dedication, work ethic, and skill set have not gone unnoticed or unappreciated. I remember the first time I met you and I asked you what made you want to work for the FBI, and without missing a beat you said because one day the Bureau would be ready for its first female director. Unfortunately, I can't give that to you just now, but I can give you the next best thing—a path to making that goal a reality. I've convinced my predecessor to come out of retirement and replace me during my first term. I'd like to appoint you general council. It'll give you four years to be groomed. I'm sure you'll be bored to death, but at least you'll get to learn the paper pushing and the bureaucratic crap, not to mention make the politicians more comfortable with your eventual appointment. I'll be the first to admit that this will be an unorthodox path, but both the president and I want to see you as the eventual first female director of the FBI, because we feel it's high time that things are done differently."

Maclin was still breathing but not much else.

"Janet, are you there?" Tuttle asked.

"Uhh, sir, I don't know what… I mean yes, sir, I'm here. Yes, I'm here."

"I know it's a lot, but I'm sure this is the call you've hoped for your entire career."

"Of course. Why… I mean how…?"

"The old-fashioned way: you earned it. The president loves your record. Loves your squeaky-clean background, and to be totally candid, he loves the fact that you're a woman. He thinks you're just the type of progressiveness the Bureau needs going forward. I couldn't agree with him more."

"I uhh, I don't know what to say, sir."

"Your work and rep speak for themselves. Trust me, four years will go by in no time. I'm not going to sugarcoat this: things will get a little bumpy at times, the closer we get to you actually getting appointed—especially during the Senate approval process. It's just a part of the game. You shouldn't have much to worry about, though, because your record is pretty damn impressive. You'll be able to get enough bipartisan support to make it through. Everything we do from this day forth needs to be strategic as hell, starting with what's going on there in New York."

"How's that, sir?"

"I want you to end your days as an agent on a big enough win that people will remember it even four years from now. I got a call from Mayor Henderson, and she practically begged me to have you run point on the rabbi murders, strategically speaking. I think if you keep working the case and manage to break it by the time your promotion to general council is announced in two weeks, that would be a huge feather in all of our caps. I'd leave with a big win, and you'd be promoted with a big one."

Tuttle went on about a few of the logistical things that needed to happen, but by that time Maclin was only half listening. Her head was swirling, and she started feeling as though her insides were in a giant vise grip. She knew immediately that Ivan the Terrible had returned right on cue. He stood beside her and whispered in her ear that not even good news could keep him away. At times Ivan was like a spoiled child who, when ignored too long, threw a tantrum in order to get attention. He had an incredible ego and often felt the need to remind her which one of them was in control. Ivan let her know that she was not deserving of the one dream that had always mattered most to her. It was a dream dangled before her but never meant to be fully realized. It was just the sort of thing that God and Fate did to remind everyone that the universe had a cruel sense of humor. Ivan was the messenger, the physical confirmation that even though she had gotten close, time was not on her side.

After Maclin hung up the phone, she rushed to the shoebox-size bathroom, fell to her knees, and kissed the porcelain god. Bent at the waist, she felt as if she was heaving out every organ. Once she emptied herself, she stood and leaned on the corner of the sink until she regained her bearings. Maclin popped some of her medication and then cupped her hands with cool water from the sink to wet her face. As she stared at her reflection in the mirror, she started laughing. It was a steady and committed laugh, the kind that gave her something solid to clutch. It was the grandest of "fuck yous" to Ivan. Laughter and determination were the only weapons she still had with which to fight him.

Although she had conceded to losing the battle between life and death, as long as there was still breath in her body, she was resolute that her final victory would at least be going out on her own terms. She couldn't control how or when she died, but being the fighter that she'd always been, she knew no other way but to live the rest of her life in motion and not stasis. In pursuit, not retreat. Dreams, even the most improbable ones, lured both the foolish and sagacious alike with the shimmer of hope.

Maclin crossed back into the bedroom, threw her suitcase on the bed, and started unpacking.

10

Quincy and Phee were at their temporary desks banging on keyboards as they researched the hate groups on their list.

"This political correctness bullshit is killing me. It would make a whole lot more sense if we could work this thing back at our own precinct. Shit, at least we have air-conditioning there," Phee lamented.

"No point in bitching about it. Everybody from the loo all the way up to the commissioner wants it run this way, so we just gotta deal with it," Quincy replied.

"Yeah, well loo-tenant ain't the one sweatin' his balls off in this pizza oven. And I'll bet you my lunch money that the air-conditioning is working just fine at 1 PP."

"I say we run the investigation from your house. I could get used to all the home-cooked meals."

Both Quincy and Phee turned to see Maclin standing behind‑ them.

"I thought you were on your way back to DC," Phee said.

"Evidently, I'm not."

Phee looked at her and nodded. "Are you in?"

"Looks that way. I'd like to see this case closed within the week."

"We'll do our best to accommodate your schedule," Quincy said with a smile.

"So who are we talking to first?" Maclin asked.

"The black Muslims up in Harlem. Figure we'd start with them, since their name was spray-painted at the scene. Glad to have you back in lead, but from what we've read on Umoja so far, I think it would be best if I run point on the interview. Let's just say they have some old-school notions on what a female's role is. The idea of a woman with authority—and white, at that—questioning their leader might not be our best play. They're not gonna wanna talk to us, especially not about a pair of rabbis, trust me," Phee said.

"Like I just told you, Detective Freeman, we ain't in the business of killin' Jews," said Shaka Zaire-Ali, the group's leader.

Quincy jumped in. "What about cops? Or prosecutors for that matter?"

"We ain't in the killin' business. Not even racist cops or crooked-ass prosecutors. Look, you asked me if I knew where Spider Harris was, and I told you I don't. Now, I got a rally in

Brooklyn to get to. Since you ain't got no warrant, I ain't really got shit else to say to you."

The Umoja headquarters was a recently refurbished storefront mosque. Having decided that Phee would run point on the interview, Maclin lay back in the cut, more or less a fringe observer. She chose to stay close to the door as though she were only half invited in. It was the first time she could ever remember attempting to make herself less significant. She couldn't take her eyes off the group's leader. Shaka Zaire-Ali looked more lion than man with his mane of tightly coiled, shoulder-length dreads and a bushy nest of a beard. He was a dark-skinned brotha, a Serengeti Maasai kind of dark. He reminded Maclin of some of the behemoth linebackers she imagined Phee had played against in his days with the Giants.

Most people in Harlem called Shaka "B-Mo," a nickname for Black Moses that stuck to him because he looked so biblical.

He was huge, a hill of a man just a few pounds shy of a full-fledged mountain. The beige leather wingback chair that he sat in drooped to one side, as if it were in pain under his massive weight. Not all of him fit in the chair. Parts of him spilled out, uncontainable. At six feet four, 297 pounds, there was a lot of him. His chair squeaked—or, more likely, cried—when he leaned back and toked on his e-cig. The secondhand oak veneer desk that he sat behind was peeling at the seams. A piece of furniture that should have been discarded long ago, it was an underdog of a desk. The entire office had an old-school, '70s revolutionist vibe. There were framed posters of Malcolm, Huey, Farrakhan, Garvey, and Selassie. Gil Scott-Heron's famous track "The Revolution Will Not Be Televised" played softly over unseen speakers. The word *umoja* as well as the Arabic spelling of the word *unity* was displayed on an eight-foot-wide red, black, and green banner.

Phee and Quincy didn't bother to sit. They stood near the desk surrounded by four members of Umoja who, like Shaka, were all dressed in long, white flowing *thobes* over baggy cotton pants called *serwals*. Each of the five men wore a knitted white skullcap.

"Okay, so you won't tell us where Spider is. Maybe you can tell us how the name of your group ended up tagged at a murder scene?" Phee asked.

"First of all, Umoja is not a group, brotha. It's a movement. Second, do you really think that if we had done it, we would be stupid enough to sign our name to a murder scene?"

"In our line of work, you can never underestimate the ignorance and/or arrogance of criminals," Quincy said matter-of-factly.

"That's funny, because I've learned to never underestimate the incompetence and/or stupidity of cops," Shaka quickly shot back, causing three of his men to snicker.

Phee smiled. "That's a good one. You got jokes."

"I assumed this whole conversation was a fuckin' joke." Shaka sucked on his vapor cig.

"You really think a murder investigation is a joke?" Quincy asked.

"Well at the very least, your double standard of justice is, Detective Cavanaugh. Y'all got every cop in the city fallin' all over themselves 'cause a couple of Heebs got bodied up." Shaka took another toke and looked directly at Phee.

"Where was all this *investigatin'* last month when brotha Devon

Timmons was chased down like an animal by these same devils that you actually expect me to give two fucks about? So yeah, I'd have to say this shit is all a big joke. The saddest thing of all is that there are niggas like you who put others before his own people and are too ignorant to know you're the punch line."

As Phee took a step closer to the desk, Shaka stood to meet the confrontation. Maclin and Quincy rested their hands on their holsters when the four guards shifted into a more defensive position. The old air-conditioning unit groaned in the window as though it had been wounded in battle by its hapless war with the heat. The air in the room had gotten stiff, a lot less comfortable, and damp with humidity. The sweating was contagious. It moved from body to body, baptizing them all. Phee felt his shirt sticking to him as he crossed around to the side of the desk and stood toe-to-toe with Shaka. He could see tiny beads of perspiration sliding down the sides of the man's big face like black fruit shimmering in the sun. Phee was close enough to smell the sour green apple vapor mix on his breath, along with the fading hint of breakfast lox and capers.

"You really wanna play this out? Because I guarantee you that it doesn't end well for you and your boys. The only thing you need to know about me is that if you're guilty, I'm the one that's either gonna take you in or put you down," Phee threatened.

Shaka stepped an inch closer. "Is that right?"

"Yeah, it is. So if you were half as smart as you'd like to think you are, then you would realize that if you're actually telling the truth and you didn't do it, we're the only two cops in this city who are even entertaining the possibility that you all are being set up."

"Oh, so now we're supposed to think that y'all actually give a damn about us?" Shaka shot back.

"Not at all. Because we don't. I've just known Spider all my life, and I know he ain't a killer."

Maclin kept her hand planted on the tip of her holstered weapon while sizing up whether the threat was rising or dissipating.

"My partner is right," Quincy said. "Evidence against you right now might just be circumstantial, but how much time do you think you have before that changes? All of you are poster boys for this crime. Do the math: we've got big black scary Muslims who preach separatism and two dead rabbis who did work in Harlem. So if you know where Spider Harris is, you need to tell us so that we can get to the bottom of it all."

Shaka looked from Phee to Quincy then back to Phee. He even shot a quick glance over at Maclin. He and Phee stared at each other like two heavyweights waiting for the bell to sound and give them permission to knock each other's head off.

Phee was the first to speak.

"You can either do what's best for your ego, or you can do what's best for your organization."

Shaka finally turned away and went back to his seat.

"Spider called me late Friday night and said he was gonna meet somebody yesterday morning who had video evidence that Ezra Pearl was responsible for his nephew's death. I asked if he wanted me to roll with him, but he said no. Ain't nobody seen him since then," Shaka relented.

"Did he say a name or anything else?" Phee pressed.

"Nah, just that he was meetin' them in the park over at Bone's Valley near 110th."

"Yeah, I know the spot. Spider and I used to play dominoes over there when we were coming up." Phee took his card and placed it on the desk as Maclin and Quincy finally took their hands off their weapons.

"You hear from Spider, you tell him we gotta talk," Phee said more as a command than a request. Shaka just stared at him, neither agreeing nor disagreeing. Phee took a couple of steps toward the door then turned back to Shaka. "And another thing. You ever disrespect me again, I'm gonna show you just how much Harlem I still got in me. Don't get carried away with your size, brotha. I've chopped down bigger."

As they approached their car, Maclin asked, "Now what?"

"Next on the list are the skinheads in Canarsie," Quincy answered.

Maclin shook her head. "Let's put somebody else on that. Give it to Burns and Skia. We need to take a look into Ezra Pearl. His name is popping up too much to be a coincidence."

The small elevator in Ezra's apartment building rattled precariously as it plodded toward the ninth floor. It was a vintage Otis with brass grating and a honey-streaked, marbleized light fixture. The walls were a rich mahogany and shone as if they were polished every hour on the hour. Maclin could imagine photos of the elevator featured in some expensive coffee-table book on prewar architecture and design. She thought it would be better suited to a museum or anywhere other than still in use, as it was having obvious challenges just delivering its passengers in one piece. Maclin wasn't normally claustrophobic, but the six-foot-square interior coupled with the few bumps along the way made her a little nauseous. It was a tight fit with Quincy, Phee, and Solomon, the octogenarian landlord who seemed to find her discomfort humorous.

"They don't make them like this anymore. Don't let her fool you; she's as sturdy as they come," Solomon said as he looked at Maclin and winked. He held his yarmulke with one hand as he bent to pick up a piece of gum foil with the other. She noticed a line of fading numbers tattooed on his forearm, peeking out from underneath a half-rolled shirtsleeve. As he stood up straight, he sighed as though the litter was a personal attack on his reputation. When he caught Maclin staring at his tattoo, he just nodded his head and turned away.

They were all so close to each other that they didn't have room for conversation. It was a silent, long climb. Her nearness to Quincy and Phee made her the most uncomfortable. She was afraid of the exposure. She was convinced that if the ride didn't end soon they would see or smell it on her. They were the best detectives in all of New York. Sooner or later they would detect what was wrong with her and know the secret she had been trying to hide.

The minute the landlord let them into Ezra's apartment, Maclin saw it. It greeted her in the foyer and welcomed her in. She wasn't sure if Quincy or Phee recognized it or even if the old man who had been in Ezra's home many times saw it, but it was there. She couldn't deny the familiarity if she wanted to. Ezra's tiny apartment was just like hers, despite the different furniture and floor plan. There were no similarities whatsoever in how the sunlight brightened their respective spaces; Maclin lived in the back of her building, where very little light crept in, and Ezra lived in the front of his building, where sunlight was annoyingly abundant. She was in a modern DC townhouse, and he was in a typical New York City prewar brown-brick apartment building. On paper, they were in completely opposite dwellings, but Maclin saw beyond that.

Like hers, Ezra's was a life of solitude. There were no plants or pets and only a handful of personal photos. They were both minimalists whose lifelong possessions could easily be packed away or even discarded in under an hour. She felt the loneliness waiting in the apartment as though it were hoping for Ezra's return. It was there, quiet and patient. Even though it attempted to be invisible, Maclin saw it in all of its edacious glory. It was no different from what she went home to each night.

After looking around for twenty minutes, none of them found anything that could shed light on Ezra's whereabouts.

"When was the last time you saw Mr. Pearl?" Quincy asked the landlord.

"Yesterday morning I ran into him down in the basement when he was in his storage space. That was around eleven."

"Would you mind showing it to us?" Phee asked.

As the old man locked up the apartment, Maclin, Phee, and Quincy headed back to the elevator. Phee read an incoming text.

"Shit," he said under his breath.

"What is it?" Quincy asked.

Phee spoke quickly and quietly enough that the old man couldn't hear him as he trailed behind them. "It's from uptown. The patrol that we sent to the park to canvass Spider's photo found blood in the vicinity of where he was supposed to be having his mystery meeting."

It was a typical apartment basement, complete with narrow pathways and winding trails of overhead pipes and concrete walls that were painted in the requisite phlegm green with an eggshell-white trim. The basement and the rest of the building reminded Maclin of its caretaker: old but neat. The two of them were survivors of horrendous storms. The old man and the building were both still sturdy.

As the four of them approached the caged storage space that tenants paid extra for, Solomon reached for his key but noticed that the door to Ezra's unit was already slightly ajar.

"That's strange. Mr. Pearl never leaves this unlocked."

Maclin, Phee, and Quincy, who were behind him, looked at each other and immediately stopped the old man from moving any closer.

"Sir, would you mind just staying out here please?" Maclin requested.

Quincy and Phee followed Maclin in single file. As soon as they entered, they saw an overturned box, a smashed cell phone, and broken glass lying in the shadows. Quincy reached up and pulled the fraying string of the dangling light bulb above. And there it was, in the back near the corner: enough blood on the floor to fill a tea cup.

"Crime scene," Maclin called out.

"Shit just got even more interesting," Phee said as he surveyed the scene.

11

Ezra Pearl awoke choking—mouth full of blood. Every time he coughed, he could feel the pain in different parts of his body. As he lay motionless on the ground, he knew even without moving that things were broken in him. He was worried most about the internal damage. The aching was everywhere—throbbing, knifing random organs and muscles. He could feel each of the millions of neurons burning throughout his central nervous system reminding him of the incredible damage done to his body.

The worst of it was the unrelenting burning sensation in his eyes. Even his tears felt like lava rolling down his cheeks. It wasn't the pain or even the multiple fractures that launched him into a crying fit. It wasn't the fact that he was terrified of what additional torture awaited him.

Ezra couldn't *see*.

The horrible burning in his eyes had left him blind. He couldn't stop crying because of all the things he knew he would never behold again. He would never see his father or the other people who mattered to him most. He would never lay his eyes on the things that gave his life meaning—like his students at Yeshiva University or in Israel, where he went twice a year. There were things—some great, some inconsequential, some that he cherished, and some that he took for granted. He would not be able to stand on the roof of his apartment building in Borough Park to watch the sky change to orange, then red, then purple when the sun dropped in Brooklyn. There would be no more mitzvahs or readings of the holy Torah. None. Whether he would die that day or the next or even if somehow he miraculously survived, Ezra Pearl had seen the last of anything he treasured—because the first thing his abductors had done was to take his eyesight.

His mouth was a mess. Both his upper left incisor and canine had been knocked out, leaving a gap that created a low wheezing as he gulped and sucked in air. He pricked the tip of his tongue on the edge of a broken tooth. As he lay still in the utter darkness, the back of his throat was warmed by his own blood each time he swallowed.

Even though he never saw them or heard their voices, he knew right away who took him. It didn't require a degree in rocket science to figure out who would target him this way. Ezra considered himself to be a good man. He was a beloved father, a teacher, and a highly respected person in his community. He honored God and was proud to be a direct descendant of the Chosen People; those were the things that were most important to him. He certainly had no great desire to become a martyr, but if he was being victimized for protecting his people and if that was going to cost him his life, then he just hoped it would happen without further brutalization.

He could wish and pray for it, but he wondered if his hopes were ultimately in vain. There would be no reasoning with them, because they had proven long before his kidnapping that they were incapable of such things. They weren't designed for it. Reasoning required intellect and objectivity. Animals didn't reason. The more Ezra thought about it, the more doomed he realized he was, because they were even lower than animals. They were people without souls. Ezra didn't need to see them or hear their voices to confirm who they were. There was no doubt in his mind who was behind something as heinous as what they were doing to him. Ezra Pearl knew that it was the blacks.

He first saw them for what they really were when he was an eighteen-year-old freshman at Yeshiva. Ezra remembered the night back in the early '90s when he and Rebecca, a nice Jewish girl from Queens, were on the subway coming home from a party in Washington Heights. As they were riding the A train around one a.m., it suddenly went out of service at 125th Street. Ezra and Rebecca were the only whites amongst the two dozen disgruntled passengers. There were furtive glances in their direction but nothing that lingered longer than a New York minute.

After they had waited on the platform for around twenty

minutes, Ezra heard some loud and obnoxious Yo-boys starting to harass people just for kicks. As they approached and started making lewd gestures toward his date, Ezra stood up to the four of them. He was promptly sucker punched in the face. His lip busted open and he was immediately dizzy, but he stayed on his feet. He had never been a fighter, but neither had he ever been a coward. He swung back, but it only made things worse: he soon found himself on the receiving end of a vicious beating. As they took turns punching him, Ezra went down and tried to protect himself as much as possible. When they couldn't sneak more blows in they stomped him. His head bounced off the concrete platform, leaving him bleeding and concussed. Although his hearing was muddled, he still heard the distant cries of Rebecca over the laughter of the animals who showed him no mercy. When he looked in their eyes and pleaded with them to stop, all he saw staring back at him was their soullessness. Although he tried his hardest not to, Ezra cried. Besides the pain, he was scared that they would kill him that night while all the other blacks standing on the platform did nothing.

When his assailants grew bored with beating him, they walked off laughing at how "the punk-ass Jew boy cried like a bitch." Ezra ended up in the hospital that night with two broken ribs, a concussion, and a fractured collarbone. After the incident, he refused to speak to Rebecca, much too ashamed to answer any of her calls. Although he never talked about what happened to him that night in Harlem, he still thought about it almost every day. How the animals broke him that night and made a coward of him, then left him to live his life in unamendable pieces. It was impossible for him to shake the memory of the things the blacks took from him twenty-two years ago.

His kidnapping had to be connected to the death of Devon Timmons. Ezra was accused of being the ringleader who chased the black kid to his death after Devon and another man were spotted spraying graffiti on the side of his father's shul. As far as Ezra was concerned, he'd done nothing wrong. Even though Devon hadn't attacked him directly, Ezra still viewed his actions that day as self-defense. Self-preservation, even. The blacks were a constant threat in one way or another. He'd seen them deface property and pollute the ears of children with their foul language. He hated when they drove down the street blasting their loud rap music and regularly disrespecting the holy Sabbath. Devon Timmons had no business being in the neighborhood. Ezra was no longer just a scared eighteen-year-old bleeding on the platform at 125th Street. He and a couple of the other men from the shul had chased the trespasser. Ezra wanted to beat the boy the same way he had been beaten twenty-two years ago, but he never got the chance to. The only thing he regretted about that day was that he never got the opportunity to take back the piece of him that was stolen on the platform at 125th Street.

Ezra rolled over onto his stomach to stop himself from choking. Once the coughing subsided, he patted the area around him in a feeble attempt to locate his missing teeth. He just needed to put things back the way they were, and maybe it would somehow stop the nightmare. He didn't know how long he had been unconscious. The beatings could have ended an hour ago or a few minutes ago; he really had no idea.

Even though he couldn't see, he thought there had been two people in the room earlier: one the punisher, the other the observer. Neither one of them spoke, but in between the blows there were times that Ezra could hear their separate breathing. Ezra lost count of how many times he blanked out from being brutalized. It felt like it went on for hours. The punisher took breaks then started again until finally Ezra lost consciousness.

After Ezra finally gave up hope of finding his teeth, he heard movement coming from the opposite side of the room. As best he could tell, there were still at least two people nearby. He could feel them watching him, studying his every move as though he were a wounded lab rat. He could still smell the bleach that he had been doused with. His eyes continued to burn as he stumbled about in complete darkness.

"Please let me go," Ezra cried.

He continued to plead for his life just as he had done the moment he was kidnapped.

Someone in the room let out a clipped laugh, as though the pleas were one of the most ludicrous things they had heard in a while. Then there was more silence.

They were watching. Just watching. His helplessness and suffering were entertainment for them. His begging fell on the deaf ears of people with no souls. No humanity. When he calmed down and finally sat still, he thanked God for the quiet. Not only did it give him time to think, but at least they weren't still torturing him. He replayed every detail in his mind, from the time of his abduction, through the multiple beatings, up until his present moment. No matter how minute, there had to be some bit of information that he could somehow use. Ezra was an academic, a mathematician by trade. If there was one thing that he had relied on his entire career, it was the fact that there were always solutions to be found.

In his mind, he listed everything he could remember.

A) The echoes of his cries told him that he was in a large, cavernous space. Based on the fact that they never showed any concern over how loud he screamed, they were either somewhere private or far enough away so as not to worry about neighbors hearing.

B) They hadn't killed him yet, which meant one of two things: either they just wanted to torture him as long as possible, or they had other plans for him.

C) Ezra had no physical defense against his captors. He was blind, injured, and naturally much weaker than the large man who had kidnapped and beaten him. However, since they were less than animals, the one advantage that he had over them was that he was smarter than they were. He just needed time.

Ezra listened as the floorboards creaked under the weight of his abductors. Based on the two distinct pitches and the vibrations that followed each movement, he got the confirmation that not only were there two people in the room but one weighed a lot more than the other. He heard faint whispering, but none of it was loud enough for him to decipher.

The larger of the two grabbed Ezra by his ankles and started dragging him on his back down a long corridor. His body was too fragile to be manhandled the way that it was. There was no regard whatsoever for the numerous injuries he had already suffered. His back was snagged and punctured by splinters from the rotting wood floors.

"What are you doing? Please, stop. Where are you taking me? Just listen to me. Please, I didn't do anything. Just listen to me!!!"

He was dragged a good sixty feet before his captor stopped and Ezra heard the clanking of keys followed by the unlocking of a heavy door. After he was tossed into a room like an open bag of garbage, he felt a heavy metal clasp placed tightly around his ankle followed by the rattling of a chain. He then heard the door close and then the heavy clink of it being bolted. He raised himself up on his elbows and listened for sounds that might tell him where he was.

The room was hot and silent. Ezra listened for even the tiniest bit of information. He let out a high-pitched whistle to try to gauge the size of the room based on how the echo bounced back to him. The room didn't feel nearly as big as the space where he had been tortured. Whether or not there would be any way for him to use it, he was determined to gather as much intelligence as possible until they snatched his final breath from him.

He could feel his pant leg sticking to his thigh, wet from God knew what. When Ezra felt the ground around him, his hand was covered in something sticky and thicker than water. As he rubbed his fingers together, he knew right away what it was. A small puddle of blood that was already too gummy to be his. It was quiet, just the sounds of an old building settling.

12

Phee drove down 13th Avenue near 50th Street in the Jewish pocket of Borough Park. In honor of the Swedish diplomat who had saved a hundred thousand Hungarian Jews during the Holocaust, 13th Avenue had been renamed Raoul Wallenberg Way.

More than any other place in the world, turning onto a New York City block could feel like crossing the border into a completely different country. Brooklyn was considered by many as the American epicenter of Judaism because it had a higher concentration of Jewish people than anywhere else in the United States. Parts of Bensonhurst and Borough Park out-Tel Aviv-ed Tel Aviv. There were synagogues adjacent to Jewish community centers, yeshivas, clothing shops, dentist's and doctor's offices, bakeries, tailors, and kosher groceries as well as other eateries. Large Hebrew lettering appeared on awnings and signs on the various commercial

buildings. In accordance with *halakha* (Jewish law), married orthodox women hid their hair under various types of wigs, or *sheitels*,
as they pushed baby carriages and navigated their broods while
encountering the tribes of others. The streets were crowded with
families and rich in customs and traditions.

Maclin rode shotgun while Quincy sat in the back of their
taxpayers' mobile. Blue Gypsies were the standard-issue vehicles
for NYC detectives. It made no difference the color or even the
make of the car; they were all referred to as blue because of the
cops who drove them and gypsies because they were as easy to
spot as gypsy cabs looking for fares. The department had a handful of Chrysler 300s, which Phee preferred but instead ended up
with a horrid pea-soup-green automobile that Buick must have
been giving away for free to its two favorite causes: underfunded
police departments and PETL—People for the Ethical Treatment
of Leprechauns. He joked about how the car handled like a bulky
piece of furniture, with a chassis and suspension system that must
have been built by Lego. On the bright side, it had four wheels and
good AC, so for the time being the three of them were rollin' like
ballers in their honorary Bentley.

Halfway up the block, they saw a thick crowd of chanting
protesters, armed with placards, directly across the street from the
Beth Israel Synagogue.

"The blood of Devon Timmons is on your hands!"

"We value the lives of our loved ones just as much as you do yours!"

"Does Judaism condone murder?"

Along with four uniformed cops, there were twelve *shomrim*, a Jewish citizens watch group that was sanctioned by the NYPD. They were dispersed among the three dozen Hasidic men who stood across the street from the protesters, guarding their house of worship. The protesters maintained a lawful distance and were well versed in the ways of conducting a legal demonstration. There were of course a handful of troublemakers and opportunists amongst them, but the vast majority of them were young, black, hungry foot soldiers just cutting their teeth on matters of social activism. They saw themselves as rabble-rousers in a broken system that desperately needed rousing. The police presence had been reduced due to the shortage of manpower, and because the protests had gone on for eleven days without incident. Although none of the major news outlets were present, there were still a couple of second stringers circling the field for scraps. A two-week-old story about a black kid being killed didn't exactly rank high on the scale of relevance or commodification.

It ultimately made very little difference to the protesters that most of the news crews no longer felt that their cause was worth covering, because they had a powerful game changer nonetheless: the internet. The revolution would most certainly be televised, at the very least on YouTube.

As Maclin exited the car with Phee and Quincy, she saw Losher walking toward them.

"Losher, thanks for meeting us on such short notice," Maclin said.

"I'm glad you called. I'd like to help in any way that I can."

"Phee, Quincy, this is Dr. Losher Saum. His sister is the

executive assistant to the rabbi here. If we're going to get Ezra Pearl's father to open up to us quickly, I thought he might be helpful."

As Quincy shook Losher's hand, he looked at him hard, as though he was trying to place where he had met him before.

A big voice deep with thunder boomed in front of the crowd. It had a familiar bottomless bass that was still fresh in the ears of Maclin, Quincy, and Phee from just a few hours earlier. As they flashed their badges to the patrolman guarding the front entrance, the trio turned to hear Shaka Zaire-Ali address the protesters.

"When does it end? When does the open season on black people in this country end? Do you think for one second that if the situation was reversed and a bunch of us chased one of them to their death, we wouldn't be in jail charged with every type of murder they can come up with? Press would have been writing about it and showing it on every station there is for weeks and weeks about how 'a pack of animals' descended upon some helpless white youth. Whenever they want to, they can chase us down like dogs, just like the cops who are supposed to serve and protect all citizens can shoot us at will and nothing ever changes. Nothing. Jews or white gentiles, makes no difference. They're just devils by different names who won't be happy until we're all dead. That's who they are. Devils only understand two things in this world— and that's force and subjugation. Just ask any Native American. Japanese American. Just ask any Palestinian. Ask the family members of the countless brothas and sistas who have been murdered at their hands in this country in just the last year alone. And all we do is bitch, moan, and cry while choking on words like 'injustice' and 'accountability.' When do we wake up and realize that the so-called justice system was never built with us in mind? We rally, chant, and go to funerals and then rally and chant and go to even more funerals. And even while the tears are still warm on the cheeks of mothers and fathers, sisters and brothers, and orphaned children, the cycle of violence against us is claiming its next victim. How many more do we lose before we stop chanting that we've had enough and start showing it in the only language they truly understand?"

As Maclin, Quincy, and Phee entered the synagogue, Maclin saw Losher huddled in a corner of the vestibule with his twin sister. Yael was the shorter, thinner, more pious version of the two. They shared a strong resemblance, magnified even more as they stood side by side. From the way they interacted with each other, Maclin could tell that they were connected by more than just title and blood; they were each other's favorite. Although Maclin had been sleeping with Losher off and on for two years, she had never met any of his family or friends—and neither had she a desire to.

After Yael exited through two large oak doors, Losher walked over to Maclin and her partners.

"My sister says they're ready to see you. I know you all know this, but a word of advice before you go in: just keep in mind you're dealing with a very conservative culture. Even though most of them consider me to be more secular than they'd like, they're still more comfortable with me here as a liaison since I'm the one vouching for you all. Despite the fact that they're asking for your help, they're not used to answering to outsiders. Might not always make sense to you, but they are guided by very old and deeply rooted beliefs. They even have a thing called *mesirah*, which is an interpretation of the Torah that dictates exactly what you're allowed to inform on a person of Jewish faith to non-Jewish authorities. Look, I'm not saying they've got anything to hide, because I wouldn't know that one way or the other. I'm just saying that these are their ways. Oh, also keep in mind that Ezra's father is an Auschwitz survivor as well as a war hero who fought for Israel and is now one of the most revered rabbis in all of Brooklyn."

The office was hot but not unbearable. In unison, two portable cooling units hummed a reverberant drone of white noise. Even though the office was a good size, Maclin had expected it to be even larger. There were two tall windows segmented by multiple panes. On the wall behind the old handcrafted desk hung an ancient Torah in a beautiful display case. She thought the artifact and its owner were very similar in a few ways. Although they were each in their own way frayed around the edges, they had each, against considerable odds, outlasted generations and survived the Holocaust and at least two wars.

Rabbi Zon Pearl wasn't exactly what Maclin thought he would be; she almost felt cheated. From the little bit that Losher had told them about the rabbi, she was expecting someone more *giantly*. His skin was paper-white, which only accentuated the tiny islands of age spots and intersecting veins that looked like a network of purple wires just beneath the surface. She put him at no more than a buck twenty-five, and it was possible that the thick, white cloud of a beard that eclipsed most of his face accounted for at least half of his weight. He was a small man of big import. If Brooklyn had been Oz, he would have been the Wizard behind a fortress of velour curtains, dwarfed under the vastness of his own mythology.

He sat at his desk flanked by understudies who stood by his side like obedient children in anticipation of his every move. The room was more or less evenly divided, with Losher and the cops on one side and four rabbis and Yael on the other. Outside, the chants of protesters rose and fell like the cheers at a soccer match in sudden death.

Losher made the introductions: "Rebbe Pearl, these are Detectives Cavanaugh and Freeman and FBI Agent Janet Maclin."

It didn't go unnoticed by Maclin that even though she was FBI, she was introduced last. She could tell that the rabbis in the room were surprised—that she wasn't what they were expecting. Rabbi Pearl looked at Losher and Yael as if he were somehow disappointed in them. Yael lowered her eyes as she walked toward the exit, no longer welcome to sit at the grown folks' table.

The reception was neither warm nor cold; it was just an introduction, a necessary formality. Both sides of the room teetered on a balance scale with a few pounds of wariness on one side and a few more pounds of mutual need on the other. Even though *The Wizard of Oz* was one of Maclin's favorite stories growing up, she couldn't remember if the Wizard was supposed to remain untouchable. She was unsure whether to extend her hand as she greeted the rabbi, so she decided not to.

"Despite the unfortunate circumstances, it's an honor to meet you, Rabbi Pearl," Maclin led with. He never looked at her directly, just in her general direction. There was an odd gleam in his eyes that confused her. She couldn't tell if her presence bemused him or if it was some type of affront to his antiquated customs that in return was an affront to who she was as a modern woman. Although she was the one who greeted him, he looked past her and rested his eyes on Quincy.

She heard it on the first word he spoke. His voice was as comforting as a cool glass of water. Words trickled from his mouth with a soothing ease. When he spoke, he made people want to listen.

"We may have lost valuable time when the police chose not to take our claims seriously," Pearl responded.

"I apologize for that, but the police typically can't consider a person missing until twenty-four hours have passed."

Although Maclin was the one speaking to him, the rabbi continued looking at Quincy. She and Phee were designated *personas nonvisible*. She couldn't help but wonder whether this was isolated behavior reserved for outsiders or if sexism trumped racism in such a segregated, patriarchal community.

"There is nothing typical about my son or his disappearance." Rabbi Pearl still looked at Quincy.

"When was the last time you spoke to your son?" Maclin said, pressing on.

"He was here yesterday morning."

"What time?" Quincy lobbed.

"Seven thirty. He was here for about fifteen minutes. Said he had some errands to run and that he would see me at seven last night at a banquet where we were being honored."

"And that was the very last communication you had with him?" Maclin asked.

As Rabbi Pearl opened his mouth to address Quincy once again, Maclin cut him off. "Rabbi Pearl, I'm the one addressing you. I mean no disrespect, just as I'm sure that neither do you, but I'm the lead investigator on this case, and like you, my primary concern is the safe return of your son."

Rabbi Steiner took a step forward and started to speak but was shut down from a subtle head turn from Rabbi Pearl. Pearl turned to Maclin and looked her in the eyes for the first time since her entrance into his office. He looked at her without speaking for a second or two, as if he was sizing her up.

"I'm sure you *mean* no disrespect, Agent Maclin. So, to answer your question, yes, that was the last time I communicated with my son."

"How did he seem?" She pressed on, ignoring the unapologetic slight.

"He was fine, relaxed and happy."

"Did he mention where he might be going or specifically which errands he was running?"

"No, he didn't, and I didn't ask."

"Had your son received any direct threats after the death of Devon Timmons?"

"Pretty much every day, which is what we tried to tell..." Rabbi Steiner, who was second in command at the synagogue, spoke out but was once again quickly silenced by the simple gesture of Rabbi Pearl raising a single finger.

"We certainly felt that he had received valid threats, but unfortunately the police department didn't agree. This is a printed list of emails that we received on the synagogue's website. The same ones we showed the police last night but were told that insults did not constitute a threat."

Maclin watched Rabbi Pearl sift through the small pile of emails. His fingers, although fully functioning, were bending out of sync from what she assumed were the advancing stages of rheumatoid arthritis. The two dozen pages tilted his hands downward as if they were too heavy for him. As he put on a pair of magnifying glasses masquerading as eyewear, his eyes nearly doubled in size. They were a warm heather gray with charcoal pupils. Maclin thought they were gentle and immediately understood how people could trust and unburden themselves to such eyes. There was history, deep and winding, that had helped mold the eyes that Maclin couldn't stop staring at. They had seen him through the atrocities at Auschwitz as well as the birth of Israel. She wondered about both sides of the incalculable tragedies and triumphs that such eyes had been witness to. And although they still twinkled with a benevolent glint, she also recognized a very familiar weariness to them. Like hers, Quincy's, and Phee's, the rabbi's eyes sagged with the heaviness of having seen the worst that man had to offer.

"Would you mind if we took those with us while we conduct our investigation?" Phee asked.

"No, not at all," Rabbi Pearl responded, but he did not look at him.

"Do you happen to know the password to your son's email?" Maclin asked.

"No, I don't. Before we start considering invading his privacy, let's keep in mind that my son is the victim here, Agent Maclin."

"I assure you we are not looking to invade his privacy; we're looking for any and all information that can help us to find him. Based on evidence that we collected at your son's apartment building, we believe he was abducted. As horrible as I know that sounds, it's not all bad news."

Even before Maclin could finish her sentence, she saw water pooling in the wells of his eyes.

The chants outside were now louder and more constant. *"Justice for Devon. Justice for Devon. Justice…"*

Rabbi Pearl removed his glasses and placed them back on his desk. He wiped his eyes and squeezed the bridge of his nose between his thumb and index finger.

"How can you tell me that my son was abducted but that it's not all bad news?"

"Because, statistically speaking, most kidnappings don't end in murder. And even the ones that do rarely occur within the first forty-eight hours of abduction. This all might just buy us a little more time to find him."

"In that case, why waste time on things like my son's emails when I already know who took him?"

Maclin shot a quick look at Quincy and Phee. "Who…?"

"We all know." His eyes floated past Maclin and landed on Phee. "The blacks took him."

"Justice for Devon. Justice for Devon. Justice…"

The tone of the crowd was shifting. Their voices rose in furious harmony as they grew drunk from the cheers of endless anger. The peaceful protesters started devolving into a boisterous lot, feasting on each other's rage and all the while growing hungrier for more. The distant cries of approaching sirens underscored the soundtrack of a brewing riot.

"We'll start by examining the emails more closely as well as exploring every potential angle until we get a break," Maclin said.

"I've already told you, Agent Maclin, that…"

Crash!!!

Shattered glass rained into the office as three bricks in quick succession smashed through a stained-glass window, one of them striking Rabbi Steiner on the back of the neck, knocking him to the ground. His eyes went white as they rolled back in their sockets. He looked possessed. As soon as he went down, his body started twitching. Instead of going to the aid of their fallen colleague, the other rabbis hovered over Rabbi Pearl, using their bodies to shield him from potential harm. Losher knelt over the bleeding Steiner and tended to his injury as Maclin, Phee, and Quincy drew their guns and crossed to the smashed window.

"He's in a full seizure! I need someone to help hold him down so that he doesn't choke on his tongue," Losher barked.

"Move Rabbi Pearl to the other side of the room away from the window," Quincy said as he holstered his gun and crossed back to assist Losher.

Maclin and Phee stayed at the window, taking in the escalating mêlée outside.

"Shit. This thing is about to get completely out of control real fast. I gotta do something," Phee said as he started making his way to the door.

"Phee, there's nothing you can do. Backup is on its way. You can't go out there." Maclin tried to reason with him.

"She's right, Phee," Quincy added as he continued holding Steiner down.

"I can't just stay in here. At the very least, we gotta make sure that none of the protesters get inside," Phee said as he bolted out the door.

"Phee!!!" Maclin called after him.

There was lots of pushing and shoving. Then scuffling. Punches flew freely. The sea of black fists swinging far outnumbered all that was white. The handful of cops were no match for the angry crowd. They were stripped of their weapons and beaten with their own batons. Blow after blow rained down on broken noses, busted lips, and swollen eyes. The crowd was a whir of black, white, and red. Once the blood started flowing, the angry youths were immediately hungry for more.

The twelve members of the Jewish citizens watch group as well as the neighborhood men were the easiest targets. They were out-numbered and out-pissed. Although a couple of them ran back into the safety of the synagogue, the crowd swallowed most of them whole, kicking and punching them into submission. The first wave of backup cops arrived, and before they were even completely out of their vehicles, they were promptly greeted with pelts of rocks, bottles, and other throwables. Soon there were over thirty cops on the scene, assembled in riot formation. They stood shoulder to shoulder, shields extended, marching forward in an attempt to push the crowd back. However, the script was flipped when the police were attacked from behind. Their formation was quickly broken, and soon it was every cop for themselves. They went to work on the mob with clubs, pepper spray, and even tasers. Even though they deployed half a dozen canisters of tear gas, the crowd still man-aged to fight back with bottles, bricks, sticks, and anything else that could pass as improvised weaponry. They didn't scatter; instead they fought back, fueled with the insistence that they would be denied no more. They would be unheard no more. Unseen no more.

The normally peaceful Brooklyn street was now filled with smoke, glass, and blood. Maclin stared through the window and flinched when she heard three gunshots ring out. Her stomach knotted and her lungs felt clamped. She bit her bottom lip and drew blood. Maclin searched the crowd looking for Phee amongst the bedlam, her eyes intently roving the carnage. Two more shots followed, and as the protesters scattered she was just able to catch sight of Phee, whose face was covered in blood. Maclin saw him stagger. She screamed when she saw him go down and not get up.

13

There were streams of blood slicks in the street just outside the synagogue. White sheets covered the dead bodies of two rioters and one highly respected cop. Paramedics tended to a dozen people with assorted injuries: broken bones, cut skin, taser burns, and two gunshot wounds. Some of the people had been taken out by the heat, felled by sunstrokes and dehydration. Many sat in what little shade there was while recovering on the sidewalk amongst the debris of the violent clash.

Scores of news vans descended upon the scene like a school of hungry fish. They were bottom dwellers that mined the crowd in search of the lowest common denominator. Although rivals and competitors, they collectively constructed the same, singular narrative. They came under the guise of covering the news, when in actuality they were much more adept at crafting it. The reporters showed up with a typical presumption of who was cast in the roles of guilty or innocent. Their cameras were strategically trained on anyone white, bleeding, and sympathetic-looking while, conversely, they made sure to include the prerequisite footage of scary, handcuffed blacks being led away to face warranted punishment. "Truth and impartiality" was an outdated slogan that didn't generate the same type of ratings that the capturing of savages did.

By the time Mayor Rocky arrived, for the most part, order had been restored. The dead had been carried away, and the wounded were being tended to. Maclin was just outside the synagogue and at the mayor's side as soon as she stepped out of her vehicle. Rocky came as quickly as she could after getting the news that one of New York's Finest, whom she knew personally, had been killed in the line of duty. All the brass was there, as was customary whenever there was an officer-involved death. The battalion of cops ran eighty deep, as no fewer than six hundred neighbors and spectators flooded the streets.

There were a couple of isolated skirmishes between blacks and whites that amounted to nothing more than pushing and shoving with a few hurled insults. After Mayor Rocky paid respects to the assembled cops who were mourning a fallen brother in blue,

Maclin urged her to seek safety in the synagogue until the situation was completely quelled. Even though Maclin pleaded with her not to, the mayor made her way to address the large gathering. Maclin stayed at her side. The two of them stood in the same spot where Shaka Zaire-Ali had stood just two hours earlier. Maclin stood sentry, constantly scanning the crowd.

It took a few tries, but Mayor Rocky finally got the restless crowd to quiet enough for her voice to be heard. "We lost today. Every one of us. And if we're foolish enough to continue down this path, then we'd better be prepared to lose everything we hold dear. The cover of this morning's *Post* said that this was the 'City of Hate.' Even after all that happened here today and over the last couple of weeks, I still believe that the city we all love and all the citizens in it whom I care deeply for will ultimately not be defined by some cheap headline."

A young black man no more than twenty-two heckled her from the center of the crowd. "That's bullshit. You don't even care about your own people. Where were you when Devon Timmons was killed?"

Those nearest to him whooped and hollered in agreement. Maclin tensed, fearing that the capricious crowd would be stirred by the slightest provocation. She watched two cops wade through the sea of bodies in the direction of the man until Mayor Rocky waved them off.

"Leave him alone. He has a right to speak his mind. But if we're going to have open dialogue, it will be done with respect. For the record, you might wanna check yourself on a few things, young brotha. First of all, *all* New Yorkers are my people. Anybody who loves this great city, then I got nothing but love for them. Anybody who bleeds for New York, I'm right there bleeding with them. So to answer your question about where was I the night Devon Timmons was killed, I was hugging and crying with the family until four in the morning. Just like I'll be doing the same with both black and white families who lost loved ones here today. Just because I don't play out everything in front of the press, don't ever presume that I'm not here for any New Yorker in need. No matter what our differences are or the difficulties ahead of us, I still believe we're bigger than hate."

Maclin escorted the mayor inside the synagogue, where some of the wounded, both Jews and gentiles, were being treated. Although bloody gauze and torn clothes littered the makeshift triage center, all was relatively calm. The more seriously wounded victims had already been dispatched to the hospital. Maclin trailed behind Mayor Rocky and her chief of staff, who was quietly bragging about how the mayor had gone viral faster than a Kardashian scandal. He told her she was trending quite well on Instagram, Facebook, Snapchat, and Twitter just a matter of minutes after addressing the crowd. Maclin heard pure delight in his voice as he told her how the numbers kept growing on the likes and retweets of her impromptu speech, which was accompanied by the handle #BiggerThanHate. He whistled an enthused pitch as he tracked how many thousands of hits she was getting on social media.

"We haven't had this kind of traction since you were sworn in," he beamed.

"So you got what you wanted?" Mayor Rocky asked.

"Absolutely, exactly what we needed."

"I'm assuming you planted the kid in the crowd. You might have given me a heads-up."

Although she said it on the low, Maclin was close enough to hear their semiprivate conversation. The chief of staff was just two ticks short of being giddy. "We just boosted your favorability and kept you noncomplicit in the process. I'd call that a grand slam."

The mayor nodded her head in approval and moved past him. Maclin walked beside her.

Mayor Rocky was hard to keep up with. She blew in and out of rooms with the force of a two-legged hurricane. Maclin noticed that she had big feet for a woman yet moved with the quickness of an athlete. After checking on Rabbi Pearl, she made her way to a back room that normally functioned as a learning center for children. There, a stocky Dominican paramedic was stitching up a nasty gash on the top of Phee's head. He was seated on a small table because the miniature chairs weren't an option. Quincy stood nearby, interviewing a heatstroke victim whom Losher was rehydrating with an IV.

"How is he?" Mayor Rocky directed her question to the paramedic.

"I'm good. Some idiot mistook my head for a bottle opener," Phee said.

Mayor Rocky shook her head and sighed. "I know how hardheaded the Freeman men can be. That's why I'm asking the paramedic."

"He's fine, ma'am. No concussion—just a head laceration," the paramedic responded.

As the paramedic finished up with Phee and walked off, Quincy and Maclin approached.

"Lou Pendle was a good cop. I had him on my detail my first three months in office. I met his wife and kids a couple of times. Now just like that, he's gone. That's what all this craziness is doing, snatching the lives of innocent people. We lost a good cop today and two more citizens. This thing has already gone sideways on us. We gotta stop it before this city gets completely turned upside down. So, where are we?" Mayor Rocky asked.

"We've got at least two possible abductions: one black, one Jewish. We're still sifting through the most likely players. Shaka Zaire-Ali so far is the lead actor, but at best it's circumstantial. I wish we had something more concrete, but we don't," Maclin said.

"Circumstantial or not, Shaka Zaire-Ali is a hatemonger who needs to be shut down. If we're not careful, he could single-handedly rip this city apart. Pretty speeches and good tags only go so far and last so long. No matter what I say or do, nothing really matters until we start making some arrests and showing this city that we're in control," Mayor Rocky rallied.

"We'll pick him up on inciting, but it won't stick," Quincy said. "Supposedly he left fifteen minutes before the riot actually broke out. We got seven witnesses, including two of the injured, that said they saw someone up on a roof throw the first brick that set things off."

"Bring Shaka in. I don't care what you have to do. Hold him as long as you can. You all have to buy me time to help keep this city together," Mayor Rocky instructed.

While her chief of staff approached and whispered in her ear, the mayor looked at her watch. Her chest heaved and was followed by her releasing an elongated stream of frustrated breath.

"I've gotta go convince the governor that calling in the Army Reserves is a bad idea. I'll spare you all the pep talk because everyone here knows what's at stake. We gotta find a break."

Mayor Rocky walked toward the door then turned back. "Phee, tell your father I send my regards. And try not to catch any more bottles with your head. Okay?"

Maclin walked back over in Losher's direction as a young black patrolman, still wet from the Academy, walked up to Phee and handed him a plastic bag containing a clean top to replace his white polo, which was heavily spotted with blood. When Phee removed it from the bag, he discovered a New York Jets T-shirt.

"This the best you could come up with?" Phee snipped.

"Sorry, Detective."

"You do realize that I played for the Giants for eight years, right?"

"Yes sir. My partner kept this in the trunk of our cruiser. I'm sorry—it was the only thing we had," the young cop said as he walked away.

"Thank you, but if I were you I'd get a new partner!" Phee yelled after the cop before taking off his shirt and putting on the tee.

Maclin stood next to Losher while he disengaged the empty IV from the heatstroke victim.

"I just wanted to thank you for everything today. I really appreciate it," Maclin said.

"No problem. Just glad I could be of help." Losher pulled her a few feet away from the victim for privacy.

"My sister would like to talk to you about Ezra Pearl, but she said she doesn't want to do it here. I'll text you her address."

"Thanks," Maclin responded.

"Janet, we got something," Phee called from across the room.

"I gotta get going," she said, hesitating before actually walking away, as though there were unfinished words between them.

Losher called after her. "Janet, I uhh…"

When she turned back to face him, he looked as if he had misplaced the words he had for her. "I uhh, I just wanted to wish you luck on the case."

"Yeah," she smiled. "We could use all we can get."

As Maclin walked away, she was very aware of how Losher's scent escorted her across the room like a faithful shadow.

"So, looks like we don't have to worry about bringing Shaka Zaire-Ali in," Phee said to Maclin.

"And why's that?" Maclin asked.

"Because he just walked into the One-Nine and said he wanted an immunity deal and a sitdown with the three of us."

14

The chair was too small for Shaka. Even though there wasn't one in the entire precinct that could have adequately accommodated his massive size, he was intentionally placed in one of the smaller seats in the building, an armless metal deal with a busted cushion.

The discomfort was deliberate. Cops enjoyed every opportunity for throwing something, no matter how small, into the mix that could possibly leave suspects off-kilter. Even the most minuscule bits of leverage were, after all, still leverage. The art of the interrogation was often measured by one ounce of shrewdness at a time.

Shaka remained Zen-like, seemingly unfazed by the cops' feeble attempt to shake him in any way. He sat calmly at the table looking like a circus bear invited for noon tea. Maclin, Phee, and

Quincy stood in the hall looking into the room through a large observation window. Maclin looked down at her watch for the third time within a minute.

"DA's office won't be here with the paperwork for another twenty."

"I gotta say that I'm surprised you got the DA *and* the U.S. Attorney's office to sign off on this."

"The only way it works is if both of them are on board," Maclin replied.

"We really gonna cut a deal with him?" Quincy directed the question at Maclin.

"I'm afraid we don't have much choice. If he's got information that we need, then we gotta do what we can to get it," Maclin responded.

Phee paced a few times. "I just don't want this full immunity thing to bite us in the ass. Who knows what kind of dirt is in his closet? I don't trust him any farther than I can throw his big ass."

"Am I the only one who finds it strange that he's doing this without an attorney?" Maclin asked.

"Doesn't surprise me. It's all about his ego. He's arrogant enough to wanna show us that he doesn't need anyone to beat us," Phee shot back.

"I'm just not buying it. From everything I've read about him and everything the two of you have told me, something about him is not adding up," Maclin said.

Quincy stared through the glass at Shaka, trying to detect even the thinnest of cracks in his calm demeanor.

"Whatever's he's got, he must be pretty certain that it's good. He knows that we need him more than he needs us. There might be a way to get what we came here for and still control the situation. I say we make a run at him before the suit gets here." Quincy said it much more as a statement than a suggestion.

"We don't want to compromise ourselves by breaking procedure. Shaka will only use it against us," Maclin offered.

"Fuck procedure. We're making an audible. You in or out?" Phee pressed as he and Quincy walked toward the door.

Shaka stared straight ahead when Quincy, Phee, and Maclin entered the room. Shaka lightly bobbed his head, groovin' to a beat that only he could hear. When he finally decided to acknowledge the trio, he did so with the smug look of a man who knew he had more power than his adversaries. He relished having them come to him on his terms. Shaka looked at Phee's T-shirt and smiled. "I thought you used to play for the Giants, brotha."

Phee ignored the jab. Quincy sat directly across from Shaka. "All right, so let's hear it."

Shaka burst out laughing. "Thought the DA was supposed to be here in these situations."

"What's the matter, Shaka? Don't you trust us?" Quincy smirked.

"Trust is a relative thing, Detective Cavanaugh," Shaka fired back.

Maclin pulled out her phone and took a step forward. "The DA should be here in twenty minutes."

"Well I guess that doesn't give us a whole lot of time for us to get better acquainted, does it?" Shaka smirked.

Maclin pressed the "record" feature on her phone and placed it on the table in front of Shaka.

"Turn it off. I ain't with that," Shaka protested.

"Doesn't work that way," Maclin responded.

"It works whichever way I say it works. We talk on my terms or I bounce, and y'all can sit around and wait for more bodies to pile up. I know for a fact that the synagogue murders were just a warm-up."

As Maclin reached for her phone, Quincy stuck his hands in his pocket.

"That means you too, Detective Cavanaugh. Why don't you and Brotha Phee turn your phones off and put them on the table?"

As Quincy pulled out his phone, he turned off the recorder. Both he and Phee placed their phones on the table beside Maclin's.

"Hey, I ain't mad at you. It's good to know that your reps are real and that the three of you are willing to go down swinging. I like to know whose hands I'm putting my life into," Shaka added.

"Why don't you stop with the bullshit games and tell us what it is you know," Phee said.

"Relax, Phee. We all ultimately want the same thing."

"What the fuck are you talking about?" Phee started getting heated.

Maclin crossed over, leaned on the table, and looked directly at Shaka. She sniffed the air in front of him like a wolf on the hunt. "This whole plea deal is just a front, isn't it? Phee, do you remember the first thing you said when you met me?"

Phee looked at her and nodded, realizing where she was going. "Yeah, that you smelled like a Fed."

Shaka smiled at them. "That's pretty good. I was wondering which one of you would figure it out first. I'm ATF—and the three of you just crashed into my investigation."

15

've been under for two years on a deep op that we started after seeing an influx of military-grade weaponry popping up in the hands of hate groups. I was recruited from gang infiltration out in Compton 'cause nobody knows me on the East Coast. I infiltrated Umoja to build up some cred to chase the one lead we have."

Maclin was off to the side on her phone.

"Look, we get it, brotha. But the riot today? A cop got killed. I could have gone down as well," Phee said.

"We've found out the hard way how many secret supporters these groups have. That includes cops as well as Feds. I've already lost two friends who were agents because their covers got leaked from the inside. That's how big this thing is. We don't know how deep the dirt runs in any of the agencies. I couldn't let you know anything sooner because it took my handler the last two days to run the three of you top to bottom. He hit me a couple of hours ago and said you all came back cleaner than rain. That's when I turned myself in. Look, I'm sorry about not being able to tell you from the jump. But the fewer people who know who I am, the better my chances are of staying alive. Besides the three of you, the only two people in my agency who know what I'm doing are the supervisory special agent that Maclin is talking to and the ASAC who's handling me."

Shaka sat back in his chair, crossed his arms, and rested them on his wide midsection.

Maclin hung up her phone after confirming with Shaka's superior. She nodded at Quincy and Phee and then turned toward Shaka.

"You couldn't give us a heads-up?" Maclin asked.

"Look. I know the position that this put the three of you in—trust me. But the only thing I've got is a pocketful of tough choices and worse choices. If we're not willing to do whatever we have to do to stop this thing, more bodies than we can count are gonna start piling up. I'm really sorry about how shit went down today—that's some blood on my hands that will never come off. But we were being auditioned."

"Auditioned?" Maclin asked.

"Yeah. Looks like somebody is auditioning groups and rewarding the most radicalized of them with weapons."

"So what made you decide to trust us now?" Quincy asked.

Shaka's militant façade had all but disappeared; he was quite the opposite of his angry doppelgänger. Phee saw the beginning cracks of the battle-weary soldier reassessing his options.

"I got no choice. There's a whole lot of bad shit that's about to jump off. The brothas at Umoja got people up in Harlem saying that if Spider is not returned safely, then the first thing that needs to happen is that a different Jew is shot every day he's missing. I couldn't blow my cover, so I put the word out that nothing was to happen for the next two days. I just tried to buy some time. If we don't hurry up and find Spider and Ezra, the streets of New York are gonna bleed way more than what happened today."

"What kind of progress have you made in identifying who the bad actors are?" Quincy asked.

"I got an email three weeks ago that said the only way I could get a sit-down was if we showed how committed we were and whether we were willing to take the fight to our enemy's front door. We were given three different dates with three different instructions: *Desecrate. Agitate. Eliminate.* The email said as soon as we completed all three assignments, we would have an immediate face-to-face. Phee, your boy Spider volunteered to desecrate the synagogue two weeks ago. I didn't know he was gonna bring his nephew Devon Timmons with him. When they were chased, they got separated, and we all know what happened after that. The next morning there were about a dozen automatic weapons left for us in a storage unit on Eighty-Eighth and Third. Just like clockwork, right after the riots today we got more weapons—and something even worse."

"What was that?" Maclin asked.

Shaka hesitated. For the first time he looked timid, as if he were weighed down by an anvil of regret. He lowered his head, avoiding their stares. When he finally spoke, the words tumbled out of his mouth in clunky blocks of information.

"A fifty-gallon tank of a…chemical compound…called Zyklon B. I looked it up and…it's the uhh…same nerve gas that was used in the showers in the German death camps."

"Oh shit!!!" Phee blew the words out more than he spoke them.

Maclin drooped her head. Quincy opened his mouth, but only silence and air spilled out.

"There had been rumors for years that neo-Nazis peddled this stuff on the black market, but we always thought it was just urban myth. Their email said that if we did something big with the nerve gas, we'd get ten weapons for every Jew we killed." Shaka said.

The room was silent for several seconds. No one quite knew what to say. Phee leaned against the wall and closed his eyes, taking some of the necessary weight off of his uncertain legs.

"So when is this all supposed to go down?" Quincy found his voice.

"In two days."

Maclin wasn't quite sure whether it was the cancer or Shaka's words that left her having to fight the urge to vomit. The room swayed, leaving her feeling as if she had just stepped off of a dizzying ride at an amusement park. She gripped the edge of the table until the spinning slowed, then subsided.

"Nothing in your investigation has come up with any names or possible leads?" she asked.

"No. Just that they had been reaching out to different radical groups, both black and white. Everything comes through an email with a spoofed IP address that's been rerouted to Russia. We haven't been able to hack the origin yet. These sick motherfuckers are on some serious Holocaust bullshit."

"I agree with you. But what if it's even worse than that?" Phee posited.

"What could be worse?" Quincy asked.

"Think about what's happening throughout the city. Shaka just told us how people in Harlem are making serious threats against the Jewish community. We also know that whoever we're chasin' is giving guns to both sides. What if the reason they're using groups like Umoja to do their dirty work is to start a full-on race war? It makes sense now. Spider's and Ezra's abductions are gonna be used as the gasoline that starts the fire. The more immediate question we need to focus on right now is, what happens when you can't deliver bodies in two days?" Phee asked.

"I can guarantee you, brotha, you're not gonna like my answer."

"Let's hear it anyway," Quincy insisted.

For some strange reason, when Shaka finally stood he seemed slightly smaller. His shoulders were hunched forward, and there was a bend in his knees as if he were carrying an unbearable load.

"They said that they would start sending body parts of random brothas and sistas every hour on the hour starting with one of our own. I think you're right about Spider and Ezra being used to start the war." Shaka pulled out his cell phone and showed them all a photo of Spider's battered face and fingerless hands.

Phee sucked in an audible breath and clenched his jaws until the muscles made it look like he had a rock in each cheek.

"What the…?" Phee grabbed the phone.

As Phee continued to torture himself by staring at the image, Shaka directed his words at Maclin and Quincy.

"They said if we don't do *what* we're supposed to *when* we're supposed to, then they'll be sending Spider back to us in eighty-eight pieces."

16

As Spider looked at both his butchered hands, at the ten useless stubs where his fingers used to be, he couldn't help but cry.

He had always been taught by his father and grandfather that real men never cried. Especially those who saw themselves as warriors. Spider was nine the last time he shed tears. He gave up that childish habit after his mother was beaten into a coma by a white cop for stealing hamburger meat to feed her family. He ran out of tears and prayers in the two weeks she clung to life before leaving him to go meet her maker. It was right after her funeral that he gave up crying, as well as the myth of God.

Weak black boys grew up to become weak black men. Warriors raised warriors. Those were the inculcated lessons of his youth. Even though it tore him up inside, Spider thought that the most fitting tribute at his father's funeral seven years earlier was that he honored him with no tears. He hoped that he had made his old man proud in the afterlife if in fact there was one.

As he became an adult, he flip-flopped regularly on the question of God's existence. On the one hand, he hoped there was such a thing; but on the other, if God turned out to be white, then his father was fucked and so was he. He wondered whether his hero was somewhere looking down at him or even looking up to him—and whether he was disappointed at the fact that there, in the bowels of the abandoned building, Spider sobbed like a frightened child.

After the crying stopped, he could feel sleep tugging at him to surrender. His eyelids drooped mercilessly from fatigue. Spider didn't go peacefully; he fought the slumber war as long as he could until he was defeated. He didn't know how long he was out, but the whisper of a familiar voice gently shook him. Spider heard his father call his name. When he looked over at one of the darkened corners, he saw him huddled there in the shadows facing the opposite direction. He was lying on his side in the fetal position gently rocking himself. Even though he whispered his son's name a few times, Spider couldn't answer because his voice was lost somewhere in the bewilderment of it all. As absurd as it was, his father was there nonetheless. In Spider's moment of despair, his hero had returned to him to remind him that he was the son of a warrior. There was no time for tears and cowering. Each time he heard his name he felt himself getting a little stronger. Spider crawled over to his father, who was still facing the wall while rocking back and forth.

Nothing made sense anymore. The room was no longer the room. They were suddenly in the green, lush field of Central Park's Sheep Meadow. All around them, white people were picnicking, flying kites, and reveling in the sun without a care in the world. His father lay on the ground, blanketless in the cool grass, reading to Spider from Ellison's *The Invisible Man*. They were the only two people of color there. They ate cold roast beef sandwiches from Blimpie and chased them down with lukewarm Mountain Dews. "No matter what you do in life, Spider, don't ever let 'em make you feel that you're invisible. People find a way to knock you down; you find a way to get back up even stronger. That's what a warrior does."

Spider listened to his father read to him until they both fell asleep.

The echo of a door slamming woke him. When Spider opened his eyes and saw that he was still imprisoned in the slaughterhouse, he knew that he had only been dreaming of his father. He was disoriented from his deep sleep. The room was a black sea of impenetrable heat. The air was as dense as a cotton cloud, pressing down on him until he felt as if he were suffocating. He coughed when he got a whiff of himself. He smelled foul and inhuman: a combination of wet dog and burned funk. Spider could feel the lightlessness gulping him whole as if he were prey in the throat of a hungry shark.

He heard the clanking of a door's bolt just down the hall

followed by someone walking away. As he pressed his ear up against the brittle plaster of the dividing wall, he listened to the heavy, retreating footsteps that slipped through the cracks and compromises of the decaying building. They weren't the thudding strides of an average man. The floorboards whined under the girth and weight of someone big. Each step lost a bit of its boom until the fading sound was completely muted in the distance. Spider forced himself to try to remember more specifics about his abduction. He had a vague recollection of feeling drugged, then thrown over the shoulders of a large man. His memory still wasn't much, but for whatever it was worth it was creeping back in ruins like the rest of him. The best he could do was wrestle with the stingy bits of detail in tracing how he had ended up in his current situation.

He sniffed harder. The room was tangy and smelled of wood rot and mildew. Even though he was still groggy, he could sense right away that something was different. He could feel that he was no longer alone in the room. If his mind wasn't still playing tricks on him, he thought he saw the silhouette of a man's form in a sliver of light.

He stayed as still as possible, despite the fact that he grew more and more anxious. The warrior in him was still asleep. His panic was starting to strangle him. The sweat that pooled beneath him cooled his lower back. He tried to slow his breathing, but the effort only made him more afraid that whoever was in the room with him would hear how loud his heart was beating. He wondered what they would do to him next. What else would they take? Toes so that he couldn't run? Eyes so that he couldn't see? His tongue so that he couldn't scream? What about larger limbs? What about his life? He had questions for the person in the room with him, but he didn't call out because his throat was swollen shut with fear.

The faint scent of bleach snuck into the room somehow. The rustling in the corner was now more obvious. When Spider looked in the direction of the noise, he could just make out the blurred outline of a man lying on the floor. Once they became aware of each other's presence, neither one of them moved or made even the slightest of sounds. He had no idea how long they played the silence game. The old building periodically creaked and groaned as its lumber swelled in the heat.

Spider heard the one thing that began to lessen his fright. It was a welcome sound because it came with no threat. The familiarity brought with it a certain sense of ease. It was something that he knew firsthand.

Spider was no longer, afraid because whoever was in the room with him began sobbing, just as he had done earlier.

17

Maclin couldn't shake the horrible images of the violence done to Spider's hands. It pained her to see the devastating blow dealt to Phee. She waited nervously for the detonation. In the two years that she'd known him, she'd quickly learned that his go-to was to greet negativity with his temper. Properly provoked, he could easily go from zero to sixty. She was certain that the mutilation of his childhood friend would send him to the dark, deep end. But instead, he just sagged in the corner, brokenhearted. Maclin saw glimpses of vulnerability in him that made her feel like a nosy neighbor intruding at the most inopportune time. Quincy hugged Phee and whispered something in his ear while Maclin and Shaka stood awkwardly by. Maclin saw how the effects of the case made even the strongest of men teeter.

A few minutes later when an attorney from the DA's office

knocked on the interview door, Maclin met him in the hall with a bag of lies. She told the chubby shark with the thinning hair and unpolished wingtips that the information Shaka was offering wasn't worthy of immunity. She saw his jaw tighten and thought his knockoff designer suit suddenly looked a size too big after his deflation. Maclin watched a bead of sweat get swallowed by two rolls of fat where his chin should have been. He complained about his time being wasted then stormed off, mumbling his indignation.

She crossed to a nearby water fountain and swallowed two of her pills while she glugged at the small arc of water. Even though it wasn't cold, it cooled her as it went down. She didn't know exactly how much she drank, but it felt like a gallon. She tried to will the expediency of the medicine coursing through her body. Maclin was angry with herself that she hadn't made better efforts to keep herself hydrated. Her system was too vulnerable to neglect in any way. After a brief addiction to Vicodin two years earlier, she'd steered clear of taking medicine—not even so much as aspirin. She was now dependent on drugs not for recreation but for general function. The only thing that mattered to her was staying vertical and moving forward. Even though her body was in steady decline, her mind still had valuable contributions to make. The pills made her feel relevant. They at least lulled her into a fragile truce, not just with her nausea but also with Ivan and the havoc he was capable of wreaking.

She looked at a text on her phone and walked back toward the door with renewed purpose. When she reentered the room, the air was still laden with defeat. She knew that in her brief absence no progress had been made, no miraculous solutions born. Each man hovered in his own space, in deep contemplation while wrestling with himself in hopes of finding valid suggestions. She was certain there was some tasteless joke to be made on how long it takes four alphas in one room to stop a holocaust and prevent a full-on race war. Just as she opened her mouth to speak, Phee broke the silence. "Let's give them what they want. It's the only play we got."

No one quite knew how to respond. His words were delivered with such indifference that they immediately felt orphaned from him as soon as they fell from his lips. Although he said them, he did so with little to no proprietorship. Phee gave up very little in terms of expression. His voice was hollow and his gaze was downcast, as if he wasn't quite ready for direct eye contact.

Shaka was completely dumbfounded. "What the hell are you talking about??? We can't kill innocent people."

"I never said anything about killing anybody. Whoever is behind all of this wants to know that you did what you were ordered to do. If that's what gets you a meeting with them and saves lives, then that's what we give them. It's like you said earlier: all we got is a pocket full of bad choices and worse choices."

Quincy stepped forward and nodded to his partner. "Go ahead and run the play for us."

Phee finally looked up at the three of them and spoke. "With everything that's been happening lately the city would implode from a hate crime of this scale, right? I mean, there is no way we could handle that, right?"

"Of course not, but I'm still not following," Shaka said.

"The mayor and all the way up to the governor are gonna do

whatever they can to avoid full-on civil upheaval—maybe even if that means media suppression for a day or two to try to get ahead of the situation."

Maclin nodded at Quincy as the two of them started understanding Phee's plan at the same time.

Shaka spoke up. "I see where you're going. But that's a very big maybe."

Quincy joined in. "But he's talking about suppressing a *supposed* crime and using it to our advantage."

Maclin was constantly impressed with how the two partners thought outside the box. Even though they often clashed with her more conservative approach, there was no denying that they all made each other better cops.

Phee continued explaining the plan to Shaka. "Brotha, we're in the golden age of fake news. Doesn't take much for rumors and supposition to spread like wildfire. We stage a crime scene and then anonymously leak just enough info to a couple of alt-right sites and let the conspiracy theories blow up enough to get you a face-to-face. Once they start bitching about how a democratic mayor and governor ordered the liberal press to cover up a potential massacre, the word will get back to who we need it to get back to. As far as the legitimate press goes, we don't confirm anything. If we're lucky, maybe we get forty-eight hours before the truth comes out that there really was no crime. We just gotta hope whoever we're after keeps responding as quickly as they have been."

"So the question is, will the mayor go for it? This could put her in all kinds of vulnerable positions," Quincy pondered aloud.

The weight of the question silenced the room. The four of them were momentarily left feeling as though they had been thrown a lifeboat with possible leaks in it.

Phee pulled his phone out and started dialing. "We'll find out soon enough. My father knows her better than anyone. He'll tell us the best way to go at her."

By the time Phee got off the phone, there was a new energy in the room. Although the game plan was dependent upon several variables all aligning at the right time, it was still something. Even the most anemic hope was exponentially better than no hope at all.

Maclin spoke up: "I got a text from Losher's sister. Says she wants to speak with me one-on-one. Said it was important."

"Mayor doesn't get back from Albany for another hour and a half, so now might be the best time to go do that. Quincy and I should put Shaka in lockup on a bullshit obstruction just to cover our tracks. He can post bail in a couple of hours; hopefully by then, we've got the mayor on board and we'll have an even clearer game plan."

"Yo, Phee, let me holla at you for a quick sec," Shaka said, pulling Phee off to the side. Even though they spoke a little quieter than normal, Maclin could still just overhear their heavy voices.

"We both know the risks that go with the job, brotha, and I'm cool with that. But we're dealing with some next-level shit here. All I'm asking is that at every step along the way we make sure we're swinging as smart as we can on this, 'cause I'm the first one who gets burned if we don't."

"I know you're puttin' your ass on the line, but we got your back. *I* got your back—and that's bond, brotha."

Shaka nodded at him in appreciation. "On the shit that really counts, there ain't a whole lotta difference between you and me. At the end of each day, I'm trying to make it back to my wife and little girl just like you."

The two men gave each other a fist pound and 'hood hug.

Maclin sent a text as Quincy walked her to the door.

"I'm hoping Yael might be able to give us some better insight into Ezra and Rabbi Pearl. I'm sure your gut is telling you that there's more going on there than what the old man led on to. I shouldn't be gone more than an hour."

She wasn't certain, but she thought she caught Quincy staring at her after she finished sending her text. It was subtle, but just enough to make her feel a bit self-conscious.

"Who knows—maybe we get something useful there," Quincy said, still stealing glances at her.

Just as Maclin opened the door, Quincy blurted out, "Phee and I have been wondering—are you okay?"

When she turned to him, she saw obvious concern in his eyes.

"Yeah. Why?"

"You look a little pale and you just haven't really been yourself. I know you said you were dealing with some personal stuff and we certainly don't mean to pry, but we're just concerned."

She refused to turn away like she had something to hide, even though there was plenty that she didn't need her partners knowing under the current circumstances.

"I guess the thought of genocide has a way of wearing on me," Maclin covered.

Behind them, Phee continued talking to Shaka. Maclin glanced back at Quincy to see if she could read any more suspicion in his look.

"Yeah, I'm sure we're all gonna be a lot worse for wear after this one."

"You and Phee don't have to worry about me. I'm all right."

"Good. Go see what you can get on Ezra. I know we're grasping at straws here, but if we don't hurry up and find him and Spider, this city's gonna burn," he said before walking back over to join Phee and Shaka.

18

Despite the fact that he could no longer see, Ezra felt someone's eyes on him. Examining him. He could hear them breathing. He was a prisoner two times over: not just by the confines of his cell but also by the imprisonment of his blindness. There was nothing he could do about the inescapable blackness. It was his now, despite the unwanted ownership.

The pain in Ezra's eyes was pitiless. It felt as if fragments of glass were slicing him deep from cornea to retina. It made no difference how much he blinked or teared; nothing he did soothed or washed away the chemical burn. The aching buried itself so deeply in him that no matter what he did, it only reminded him of how inseparable they really were.

Someone was still watching him. He moved his head in every direction, scanning the room with useless eyes. He could feel them hiding there in the silence, casually deciding his fate. Whatever their intent, Ezra accepted the daunting fact that he was at their mercy. He stayed motionless and tried to will himself into being unseeable. Broken as he was, there was no defense he could mount other than invisibility. For once in his life he wanted to be nothingness, as transparent as the breaths he sucked in and released. Ezra prayed that God would keep him still. He managed to ignore the sweat that itched as it rolled down both sides of his face. It was difficult, but he didn't move when what he assumed was a large rat sprinted across one of his legs. His nose was singed from the bleach that had been used to blind him. His eyes were still on fire.

Tears slid down his cheeks like tiny toboggans trying to outrun the avalanche that threatened to overtake him. Try as he might, there was no escaping the deluge. It was what he felt as the inevitability of his tragic ending that undid him. It shattered his fantasy of being able to disappear into the warm air around him. That was when the hopelessness took over. The thought that his life would end in such a violent and insignificant way made something inside of him burst. The crying came without warning or dignity. He had no control over it. It was the ugly kind of cry that was full of facial contortions, snot, and girlish timbres. Ezra cried even more than he had when he was eighteen and was beaten on the platform at 125th Street. He cried so long that the muscles in his face became sore as his skin tightened across his cheeks.

It wasn't until he emptied it all out that he finally spoke.

"I know you're in here. What do you want me to do? Beg? Just tell me. Say something. Please. Are you going to kill me? This is all just a game to you, isn't it? Why don't you say something?"

His words were stillborn. They fell lifeless to the floor, dying in the ether as unceremoniously as fumigated flies. All he could do was listen. Even in the silence, he still *heard* someone watching him. Although he did his best not to show it, Ezra was growing increasingly unnerved by the muteness of it all.

Then finally, "I ain't the one you gotta worry about. I'm locked in here just like you," a man's voice spoke.

As soon as he heard the man, Ezra knew he was black and not to be trusted.

"Who are you? What are we doing here?" Spider asked.

"You tell me. You know who I am. Where I live. Is this just a part of the game?"

"What game? What the hell are you talking about? I'm just trying to figure this shit out."

Be smarter than them, that's how you beat them. Ezra put that thought on replay. He had to keep telling himself to lead with his head and not his fear. As he moved to wipe the sweat that streaked down his forehead, he realized that his fingers were slightly stuck together with drying blood from a gash on the palm of his hand. He couldn't quite keep up with the number of injuries he had accumulated. When he finally moved his legs, he realized that one of them was shackled.

"How did you end up here?" Ezra said, pretending to go along with the man's claim.

"I got no idea. One minute I was in the park waiting to meet someone, then the next I woke up here."

That was exactly how Ezra felt. One minute he was in his basement rummaging through his storage space; the next, he woke up blind and clueless as to where he was.

"What is this place?" Ezra asked.

"Sign on the wall says Hozinger's. It's an abandoned slaughterhouse up in the Bronx."

"Who are you?"

"My name's Jared Harris, but everybody calls me Spider. What's yours?"

What the hell—give them only what they already know, Ezra thought. "Ezra Pearl," he said.

Ezra never thought that real people gasped. They did it in books and old movies, but even then they were mostly women sprawled across divans sipping absinthe just before receiving news that was so shocking it literally made them inhale a large gulp of dramatic air. It was possible that he had forgotten, but he couldn't remember it as being something he ever experienced in real life. Although he couldn't see him, Ezra heard the man suck in air in such a way that it could only be classified as a good old-fashioned gasp.

Somewhere in the distance, the faint sound of a train's horn could be heard. When the man spoke again, his voice hovered just slightly above an angry whisper. All Ezra heard him say was "Oh shit!"

19

The entire city smelled like rotting cabbage. The simple act of breathing was an assault on the senses.

As soon as Maclin exited the precinct, she was hit with the unpleasantness of the stagnant heat. In the two hours that she had been inside, it had only gotten worse, like a horrible sequel to an already bad movie. As she crossed the street to her Chevy Tahoe, all she could smell was the acrid scent of burning rubber, as if the tires of the parked cars were actually melting. The inside of her vehicle reminded her of the one and only hot yoga class she'd taken and hated—simply because it was too damn hot. She had to suffer through the furnace-like air that blew on her from the air conditioner before it eventually cooled and made her world a bit more tolerable.

When Maclin looked in the rearview mirror, she saw the

paleness that Quincy had spoken of. She wondered if the investigation, which on one hand had filled her with energy and determination, was also exacerbating her decline. The specter of death left Maclin questioning pretty much everything.

She turned the radio off after feeling inundated with nonstop reports of scattered outbreaks of violence and vandalism spreading throughout the boroughs. She didn't need the secondhand accounts of what she was witnessing firsthand. By the time she made it to Brooklyn, she counted five interracial arguments, three shoving matches, and two full-on fistfights. The seams of the city were fraying like thinning twine. Maclin saw it all unfolding in real time, the bitter tally of animus festering. New York was coming undone. Sides were now being chosen and battle lines drawn. She didn't know which was the greater threat, the violent-minded scrappers or the do-nothing enablers. There had been very few instances in Maclin's life when she had been truly afraid, but by the time she arrived in Losher's sister's neighborhood, she was petrified by the rage and apathy that were intent on devouring all of New York. Maclin lamented that the days of hate were now upon them.

She made it to Borough Park in less than twenty minutes. As she turned onto Yael's street, the first thing she noticed were the flowering dogwoods that ran from one end of the block to the other. The three things that stood out to her the most were how beautiful the brownstones were, how spotless the block was, and how there was not one person outside. As soon as she exited her SUV, she was mugged by the 114-degree temperature. Her eyes looked upward, as though she was asking for relief that she knew wouldn't come.

There were puffy cotton clouds suppressing the heat, keeping the air trapped. The patches of sky were a bright July blue, encircling a golden dot of sun whose sole purpose seemed to be to punish the citizens of New York. The thickening air necessitated calculation and effort even for the thoughtless act of breathing.

She'd only walked a few feet before she felt sweat slithering across her skin as it meandered on parts of her body that she seldom thought about. She dawdled more than she walked, slowed in part by the cumbrous heat. Maclin could feel various eyes on her from behind slightly parted window sheers in the buildings on both sides of the street. Just as she reached the top of the stairs to Yael's brownstone, she noticed the tiny prayer scroll tacked to the inside of the door frame. In fact, there were mezuzahs adorning every doorway on the block.

Yael opened the front door before Maclin had a chance to knock. She greeted her with a curious look and an uncommitted smile.

"Thank you for coming over, Agent Maclin."

When Yael reached out and grabbed Maclin's hand to lead her into her home, Maclin felt scrutinized under the unblinking stare of her lover's sister. Even as Yael closed the door behind them, Maclin could still feel that she was being inspected.

Having never been in one, Maclin didn't know what to expect in regard to the home life of Orthodox Judaism. The brownstone was inviting and even smelled of freshly baked bread. It wasn't particularly large, but it was airy enough to make it feel more spacious than it actually was. There wasn't a lot of furniture, which was seemingly more by choice than circumstance. Maclin noted that the few pieces that were in the home were more expensive and had better craftsmanship than the bare essentials that she had in her own apartment. The house was cluttered with coloring books, dolls, puzzles, toys, and even small furniture complete with pink plastic tea sets. It was a place that had been surrendered to the reign of small children.

There were no fewer than thirty photos, either hanging on walls or perched atop cabinets and other pieces of furniture with flat surfaces. There were color photos as well as sepia-toned and even vintage black-and-whites in a variety of beautiful wood, metal, or ceramic frames. The one that stood out immediately to Maclin was a picture of Losher with longer hair than she had ever seen him wear. He was standing next to a pregnant Yael, who was being hugged, presumably by her husband. Rabbi Pearl along with his son Ezra were also in the photo that was taken in front of Yad Vashem, the Holocaust museum in Israel.

Maclin thought the overall feel of the home was that of a living museum honoring, not just the cherished moments of more current times but also a pictorial history of ancestors several generations deep. Everywhere she turned, she was reminded that the primary purpose of the home was the celebration of family, both past and present.

She saw something hanging on the living room wall that she hadn't seen or even thought about in years. It was a framed *ketubah*, which was a Jewish wedding contract. It reminded Maclin of when she was a child and her mother would hold her in her arms and read a similar type of contract aloud in Hebrew. Although she had long forgotten the words and their correct pronunciation, the happy memories of their private lessons came rushing back.

As Maclin followed Yael into the kitchen, the scent of warm bread grew stronger. Four-year-old twin girls, followed by their two-year-old sister, came racing toward them, screeching for no apparent reason. Yael feigned being startled, which sent the three girls into an even louder fit of laughter. The girls were each dressed in not identical but very similar navy-blue jumpers and white knee socks. Despite the blistering heat outside, they each wore a long-sleeved cotton blouse with a rounded collar. Maclin thought they looked more appropriately dressed for a cool autumn day than for the current heat wave that was baking the city.

Yael made the introductions. "The twins are Hannah and Miriam, and the youngest is Shoshana. Girls, say hello to Miss Maclin."

"Hello!" The twins belted out in near unison as Shoshana, who was the shyest of them all, hid behind her sisters, staring suspiciously at the stranger.

"Shoshana, are you going to say hello?" Yael pressed her. Overwhelmed by the pressure of having all eyes on her, the little girl turned and ran down the hall, followed by her giggling sisters.

"Welcome to the house of who knows what comes next!" Yael laughed as she crossed to the small kitchen island, where she resumed separating a hardened wheat flour ball into pebble-sized morsels. Maclin just stared at her.

"I'm making farfel. Have you ever had it?" Yael asked.

"No, I can't say that I have."

"It's a noodle dish that we usually only have for Passover—but my husband has been craving it for the last week, so I wanted to surprise him."

As Yael poured an extra glass of a kosher Syrah, Maclin raised her hand and declined.

"I would love to, but I'm still working."

"How about just half a glass then? I promise not to report you," Yael said with slightly forced laughter.

The more Maclin looked at the woman, the more she realized that Yael was trying to mask her nervousness. Maclin still felt as though she were being dissected. Whether it was just her imagination or not, she felt as though Yael was trying to look through her.

Under more normal circumstances, Maclin would have taken at least half a glass, if for no other reason than to disarm her host. But she thought about how the sangria at Phee's house, mixed with her medication, had caused her to feel a little more sleepy than usual. She graciously declined.

"Thank you, but I'm not much of a wine drinker," she lied.

As Yael poured more for herself, she stared at Maclin's necklace.

"I noticed your *hamsa* earlier. It's beautiful. Do you wear it for religious purposes?"

"No."

"Are you a religious woman?"

"By religious, do you mean am I a religious Jew?"

"That wasn't the question, but now that you bring it up..."

"I wear it to honor my mother, who gave it to me when I was a child."

"Is your mother Jewish?"

"Was, by way of conversion. She passed away when I was seven."

"I'm sorry to hear that."

"Thank you."

"And what about your father?"

"Are you asking me whether he is still alive, or whether he's Jewish?"

"Both."

"No, he passed almost two years ago. My father was half-Jewish and half-indifferent."

"And you? What are your views on God, Agent Maclin?"

"Cautiously optimistic. And please call me Janet."

Yael smiled and raised her glass in a toast, then walked toward the doorway listening for her children.

"Excuse me for a second—I need to check on the girls. You learn the hard way that when they are too quiet for you to hear them, that's when you need to be the most afraid."

As Yael exited the kitchen, Maclin took in the space. There was a single redbrick wall filled with more framed photos of the three little girls. Crayoned artwork hung on the refrigerator door from plastic magnets in the shape of Disney-themed characters. A herd of stuffed animals were corralled in a small pen in the corner, as if it were an improvised petting zoo.

Maclin had never been in the home of a devout Jewish family, Hasidic or otherwise. As she scanned the kitchen she was a bit

surprised by how much it differed from some of the precon-
ceptions she'd entered with. Even though she was expecting all
things Jewish, there wasn't a surfeit of menorahs or other religious
symbols. The shelves and cupboards weren't overflowing with
Manischewitz products like matzo and sweet wine. There were
glass canisters of nuts, dried fruit, and honey-glazed sesame sticks
neatly arranged on a counter. Aside from a couple of Shabbos
candles and kosher cookbooks on a small metal rack, the kitchen
was not much different from any other family kitchen she had
been in.

Maclin concluded that the kitchen was horizontally divided in
half: anything below four feet fell under the chaotic realm of three
rambunctious children, but everything above had the obvious
touch of an organized and domesticated woman. Although they
were both intelligent, professional women, Maclin thought about
how different she and Yael were. Maclin was married to her job.
Her cases were her children. Each time she solved one, the triumph
of good over evil was the closest she ever got to being religious.
Yael, on the other hand, was blissfully heavy on family and faith—
the two things that Maclin was light on.

After Yael breezed back into the kitchen, she sipped her wine
and started kneading more dough for the farfel as though she had
never been interrupted.

"They're coloring in their books. Should buy us all of ten minutes before they start fighting." She took another sip and savored

the liquid courage slowly going down as she completed her kneading. She turned on the faucet to wash her hands.

"I just have to be clear with you up front that there are some things that I can't tell you, at least not directly. I don't know if my brother told you, but I am bound by a code of *mesirah*, which is…"

"I know," Maclin said. "It prohibits you from informing on a person of the Jewish faith to a non-Jewish authority, although technically I am Jewish."

Yael smiled at Maclin. "Anyone who has to lead with 'technically I'm Jewish' is missing the point." She took yet another sip of wine before continuing. "I've known Ezra Pearl since we were kids. He was always the class clown. The funniest kid I knew. Something changed him his freshman year of college."

"Changed him how?" Maclin asked.

"He just became bitter. Angry, even. I never knew what it was, but he became as different as night and day. Even when he got married a few years later to someone I knew, she left him shortly after the birth of their son because, she said, she was afraid his dark soul would corrupt their child. In our culture, it's very rare for a woman to leave her husband, especially if he's the son of a rebbe."

The more Yael talked, the more courage she seemed to gain from the momentum of the conversation, though Maclin had the distinct feeling that she was still skating around what she really wanted to talk about.

"So how do you think this might be connected to his abduction?" Maclin tried to steer her.

"I'm just… I don't know." Yael finished off her glass of wine and walked over to the other side of the island to sit next to Maclin. "Ezra and I are both adjunct professors over at Yeshiva; I teach Judaic history. One of my favorite eras to study is the Roman Empire. I've just always found it fascinating. Most people don't know this, but back in the times during the Roman occupation of the Middle East there was an extremist splinter group of Jewish zealots who belonged to a secret order of assassins. This group of rebels was called the Sicarii, which was the name they took on from the ancient daggers they used to kill the Roman soldiers. They attacked their enemies wherever they could, but mainly on the roads outside Judea as well as in crowded marketplaces or at rallies. They'd slip in and out of the crowds, kill their targets, then disappear. The Romans branded them one of history's first terrorist groups. The odd thing about the Sicarii was that they didn't just target Roman soldiers; they even killed other Jews who they didn't feel were radical enough."

As Yael poured herself another glass, Maclin noticed how the bottle trembled ever so slightly in her hand. She waited patiently for the woman to continue.

"There have been whispers in our community for the past six months that there might be a neofaction of the Sicarii. I had always assumed it was nothing more than rumor. But the day before Ezra went missing, I overheard him on the phone asking someone that if in fact Sicarii was real, then what did he need to do to join."

"So do you have any idea who he was talking to?"

"No, I don't. And to be honest, even if I did, I don't know that I would be at liberty to tell you. For the record, I'm simply a professor who invited a friend of my brother's over for a glass of wine and a bit of Jewish history."

"But…"

From the way Yael stared at her, Maclin knew not to press for more.

"…I'm appreciative of the invite," Maclin offered.

"You're welcome. I'm assuming that I can count on your full discretion."

"Absolutely."

"I'm afraid that's all I feel comfortable saying at this point."

"I understand."

The two women looked at each other in awkward silence for several seconds.

"Would you mind if I switched gears and asked you a personal question?" Yael asked.

"If it's about your brother and me… I would prefer not."

"Understandable. You know the funny thing is, from the time Losher and I were kids, everyone was convinced that I would be the doctor because they all said God had given me a very rare gift."

"What gift would that be?"

Yael reached out and grasped both of Maclin's hands, staring at her the same way she had when Maclin first arrived.

"I wasn't being rude earlier when I was staring at you. It's just that when I look at people hard enough, I can see things in them. Sometimes I can feel them. I don't always understand this thing that I have, but I've learned to trust it."

Maclin tried to hide her discomfort as she took her hands

from Yael, who continued staring at her and speaking just above a whisper.

"I don't mean to make you nervous in any way."

"No, you're not. I just really should be getting back to the precinct."

As Maclin crossed through the kitchen doorway, Yael blurted out, "My brother the brilliant doctor doesn't know, does he?"

"Know what?" Maclin asked as she turned around.

"That you're ill. Very ill."

"I really do need to get back. If you think of anything else that might help our investigation, please let me know," Maclin said as she walked toward the front door without looking back. Yael followed closely behind.

"You *have* to find Ezra, Agent Maclin, and quickly. If the Sicarii is real and he's a part of it, there could be horrible consequences should any violence befall him."

20

Ezra felt as if he were drowning. He was having challenges breathing under the combination of stifling heat and blackness—two oppressive forces competing with each other for dominance of the room. They both looped in tormenting replay. And then there was the maddening silence.

Even though Spider and Ezra sat just twenty feet apart from each other, it felt more like miles. Each ignored the other while awaiting his uncertain fate. Spider's hand throbbed, but he was determined not to let his pain defeat him. With each passing moment, he grew more resolved to be the warrior his father raised him to be.

The one good thing about the quiet was that it began to calm him. Now that his fear had lessened its hold, Spider's anger started tugging at him. It was the thing that redirected his anxiety and replaced his feelings of weakness with sheer will. The thought of revenge was empowering, to say the least. As he sat on the floor with his back against the wall, Spider told himself over and over that not only would he survive, but he would have his retribution. No matter what, there would be blood for blood. All the devils would pay. Not just his captors, but Ezra Pearl as well.

Ezra wondered if it would have been more merciful if they had gouged his eyes out and been done with it. The burning was so unforgiving, so constant, that he wanted them gone. What good were eyes that didn't see? They were as dead as stones. Nothing more than useless orbs whose only function was to remind him of his torment. He listened for the man named Spider but heard nothing, not even the soft rustling of movement. Even though they were both prisoners, Ezra still had strong apprehensions about his cellmate. The black man was not to be trusted. None of them were. No matter the situation, they were deceptive by nature. It had been hours since they had last spoken to each other. Once Ezra had shared his name, there was an obvious shift in Spider's reaction to him: there was an immediate tension.

Ezra knew Spider was near because he could smell him. The stench of his sweat wasn't quite human. It made perfect sense that the black man smelled like something feral. Not only could he smell him, but Ezra could also feel him thinking. Plotting. Periodically, he heard a slight shift in the man's breathing pattern—the steady exhalation of someone lost in deep thought. Ezra had no idea what it was, but he knew Spider was planning something. His captors had already proven their brutality. The threat of gruesome possibilities at their hands terrified Ezra. He was just beginning to find a small reprieve in temporarily being locked in the room away from them. Now he had to reconcile the fact that only a few feet away from him, reeking like a wild animal, was a different threat that happened to be named Spider.

21

Relative to the madness that had seized the city, Maclin's drive back to Manhattan was uneventful—or at least it appeared that way on the surface. The momentary reprieve by no means alleviated her mounting concerns. The air was still septic—permeated by piles of rubbish and festering hate. She saw one possible skirmish that could have easily been nothing more than a couple of young Brooklynites roughhousing.

In a city of growing assumptions, she tried to keep an objective eye. It was becoming increasingly difficult to ignore the darkening clouds hovering over New York, filled with the threat of anarchy. She saw it in the restless faces of the pedestrians as well as those in the cars around her. She even felt it growing in herself like an unwanted pregnancy. Fear was swelling, a shape-shifting specter spreading like an ever-growing shadow. The more she looked, the more she saw evidence of the great divide. As she was leaving Brooklyn, she noticed groups of blacks and groups of whites carrying on their day in segregated clusters like a snippet of Mississippi circa 1959. Imperceptible lines were being drawn—sharp lines with jagged edges.

After crossing the bridge back into Lower Manhattan, Maclin could feel the tension even more. As she pulled up to a red light at the corner of Essex and Canal, she glanced at a text from Phee. "The Mayor wants to see us at her office in forty minutes. Swing by the precinct and pick us up."

When she looked up, she was greeted with threatening stares from a group of black teenagers hanging in front of a bodega. She gave them a cursory once-over, quickly assessing them in true cop fashion. Once she summed them up she looked straight ahead, avoiding direct eye contact with them even though she could feel their undivided attention on her. The tallest of the boys, who didn't look to be any more than seventeen, sported long Knicks basketball shorts, a pair of Jordans, and a Biggie Smalls tank top. His skin was cinnamon brown and shone in the sun under a mist of sweat. He sported an old-school Afro that was three to four inches high. He was long, lean, and at least a year or two from filling out his wiry frame.

When he stepped off the curb and stood six inches in front of her car, Maclin knew she was being tested. If she looked away, she was labeling herself a weak mark. If she stared back at him, she was directly challenging him in front of his boys. Both reactions had potentially dangerous repercussions.

Maclin looked at him but made sure she didn't linger. Her face was blank, showing neither fear nor entitlement. The depth of contempt staring back at her left her feeling injured. She wondered why a boy so young was filled with so much disdain toward someone he had never met. Even though they were strangers in the purest sense, he looked at her as if they had a history of animosity between them. It was as though they were members of rival gangs or feuding clans raised on generational hatred. She could feel that he despised her long before ever setting eyes on her. This was now what New York was becoming, a city teeming with random hate that was inching closer and closer to full contagion.

Just before the light turned green, three more boys stepped in front of her car, preventing Maclin from moving. She no longer heard the New York traffic or city clamor. All of her focus was on the four potential threats and her preparedness for however deep their bad intentions might run. The thing that alarmed her the most was the emptiness in their eyes. She found it tragic that, when she looked at them, she saw four boys hurtling toward manhood seemingly void of basic compassion.

They eyed her as if she were inconsequential, something worthy of loathing but not much else. Though their stares were filled with rage, Maclin neither feared nor pitied them. Instead, she wondered how her mere presence was now somehow partly accountable for the tragic cycle wherein the boys played the typecast roles of self-deprecating bit players in a long-running farce.

That was the moment that an interesting paradox dawned on her. They were strangers, and yet coconspirators. Their chance encounter had been years in the making. It was born of a history nurtured by suppositions and falsehoods. She embraced the unspoken truth that they were all equally guilty of the same offense: presumption. If reason was to prevail, it was that murky acknowledgment that had to at least be her starting point.

The boys were now just an inch in front of her vehicle, daring her to touch them. Maclin considered the very real possibility that they were only an inch away from full escalation, from bloodshed and maybe even worse. Although her right hand was in her lap, just inches from the 9mm on her hip, reaching for it was something she refused to let be an option. She raised both of her open palms in front of the steering wheel. She continued looking straight ahead in the direction of the first boy, whom she had designated as the leader.

When she finally looked him in the eye, she did so with more empathy than anything else. She capitulated just enough so that he could walk away feeling empowered, which was what she thought was the very thing he wanted most. Needed. Even though there were no words exchanged, volumes were spoken between the two—and precious requisites were both given and taken.

When he finally waved her on, Maclin nodded and then pulled off, never looking back.

There was something about the encounter that Maclin just couldn't shake. As she thought about the current tensions in the city and its surging tribalism, the boy's aggression left her taking stock of things—namely, how little her life had previously been affected by the racial chasm in the country. She'd grown up in a white neighborhood, she'd attended white schools, and now she worked in a disproportionately white field. Just like the strangers she passed on the street, most people of color in her life were nothing more than pedestrians. Temporaries who very rarely rose to the rank of anything close to cultural intercourse. They were blurs at best, but more often than not they were simply invisible to her.

Phee was the only African American whom she had actually spent real time with. She respected the hell out of him, as both a cop and a man. She even secretly harbored a harmless schoolgirl crush on him. He was the exception. The one black friend she had. She was far too pragmatic to ever be mistaken for a racist, nor was she fashionably consumed with the banality of white guilt. She was pretty much a loner who kept people of all colors at arm's length.

Oddly, after being confronted by the skinny black boy, she thought about how the world that she had created for herself professionally, as well as what little personal life she had, was conspicuously lacking in diversity. For the most part, the extent of Maclin's racial miscellany consisted of random encounters, certainly nothing remotely approaching immersion. Just like that of most of her white colleagues, her ascension didn't require much in the way of cultural inclusiveness. She had risen to the top of her field, and yet she could count her association with minorities on one finger.

Maclin had spent so much of her career smashing glass ceilings that she'd somehow become oblivious to the walls of racism, which, although scaled, were still in need of complete dismantling. She'd found herself more preoccupied with thoughts on race in the last two days than she had her entire life. Not having to think about such things on a regular basis was in and of itself a privilege, one that was not afforded the angry boy or even Phee for that matter.

On her way back to the precinct, she got another text from Phee saying that the mayor had to push their meeting back two hours. After she parked in front of the station, she sat still in the cool sanctuary of her Tahoe, despite the pile of work that waited for her upstairs. As she sat in stillness, her mind went from one random thought to another. She ran the mental gamut, from the most pressing to long-forgotten tidbits that no longer mattered. Her reveries ranged from the current case, to the murder of her fiancé, to the sour green apple and peanut butter snacks her mother made her as a child.

She thought about her time at the Academy as well as her teen years in high school. There had been something in the stare of the angry boy that even made her think of having read Ellison's *Invisible Man* in the eleventh grade. She remembered being absorbed in the writing for the most part, although the book ultimately left her feeling as if she was missing something. The young boy made her feel like she finally knew what it was. The last thing she wanted to do was romanticize the notion that all the recent events in her life had awakened in her a deeper consciousness, but she did genuinely feel a greater hunger for an understanding of how easily the city was being ripped apart.

As Maclin pictured the hardened image of the boy's face all ripe with bitter indictment, it dawned on her that the heart of his confrontation was his refusal to be counted among the *invisible*. When she looked past the swag and forced bravado, she understood that what he really wanted most—actually, what he demanded— was to be *seen*.

22

Ezra had the shits. He barely got his pants down in time. The length of his shackles was only ten feet, allowing him to move only so far from where he had posted up after being locked in the room. His cramping stomach was a result of the severe dehydration that was wreaking havoc on every part of him. First came the vomiting, then a few hours later the runs.

His body was suffering from the collective damage both inside and out. He crawled back to his original spot, but there was no putting distance between him and the stench that hovered in the room. He had endured Spider's sickness, so as far as he was concerned, one good turn deserved another. As he leaned back against the wall, he heard a sound that caught his attention.

He didn't know exactly where it was coming from. There was no way of telling from how deep in the building's cavity it was emanating. It was faint but constant. There was the low, distant echo of water dripping. He timed the drops in his head and counted them falling in intervals of six seconds. Not that he needed it, but the sound of water reminded him even more of how thirsty he was. He couldn't quite remember the last time he'd had something to drink. His throat was so dry that he was all but certain if he coughed, clouds of dust would literally float out of his mouth. Three to five days, that was on the high end of how long the human body could survive without water. He remembered that from high school biology. It could actually go weeks without food, but only days without water. Each drip was a reminder of every precious second that was steadily evaporating. According to Spider, the building had been abandoned for years, so it was highly unlikely that there was still a water supply.

Not only was it the hottest summer on record, it was also the driest—which eliminated the possibility of there being any type of runoff from rain. The sound hadn't been there earlier, when he'd listened for hours for every bit of info he could gather about his new environment. Ezra wondered if it was all being orchestrated. It was possible that it was nothing more than some perverse strategy intended as another form of psychological torture. *Plop...plop...plop...plop.*

He and Spider still weren't speaking, so he had no distractions. He had nothing to do but focus on his pain and yearning. Even though it ultimately did nothing to relieve his thirst, he periodically tasted his sweat as it rolled down his face, one salty bead after another. He made sure to breathe through his nose so as not to dry his mouth any more than it already was.

Ezra was growing more and more lethargic from his lack of water. Headaches came and went. He wondered how long it would take for the sound of the dripping water to drive him completely mad. *Plop...plop...plop...plop.* His captors were winning. They had already defeated his body. Even though there were additional victories for them to claim, Ezra kept telling himself that he had a fighting chance as long as he was thinking clearly. As difficult as it was for him to admit, he was no good on his own. Whether he trusted him or not, if he stood any real chance of survival, he would need an ally in Spider.

Three days and not a crumb of food or a drop of water. Spider's stomach alternated between grumbling and full-fledged roars. He adjusted his body position, as if that might somehow stop his hunger pangs. He couldn't tell which was worse—the thirst or the hunger. His insides twisted tightly from the ongoing duel within. Some of his organs felt swollen. Not that he knew which ones specifically; he just knew that his guts were sore and inflated with nothing in them but contaminated air. Somewhere outside the room he heard the rhythmic tapping of water dripping: *Plop... plop...plop...plop.*

He started having the strangest cravings. Things he hadn't thought about in ages. Spider was a twenty-year pescatarian who would proudly tell anyone who asked how he no longer fucked with swine or red meat. Maybe it was because he was locked in the belly of an old slaughterhouse and hadn't eaten in days, but he kept having vivid images of ribs and hot links the way his father used to grill them when he was a kid.

The hunger and thirst scared Spider—the implications, even more than the physical toll they were taking. The fact that he and the Jew hadn't been given anything to eat or drink raised a very troubling question: Why bother to give prisoners the basic needs to stay alive if the game plan was to kill them all along?

Spider didn't know how much longer he had before he became too weak to be either defensive or offensive. Even though everything in him was depleted, he still managed to throw up bile twice more. Time wasn't exactly on his side. He looked over at Ezra, who was sitting in a ray of light and appeared to be licking sweat off of his upper lip. Spider thought he looked pathetic and despised everything about him. Ezra's eyes were still puffy, surrounded by pink skin from some kind of chemical burn. Spider didn't know all that they had done to the man, but he hated them for taking his eyes because when he killed the Jew, he wanted to be the last thing that he saw. Even if it took the last ounce of strength he had, Spider was sending Ezra Pearl to hell, or wherever his people went when the world was done with them.

23

Langley doesn't have anything on any group calling themselves Sicarii. Maybe it's just a start-up. If they were real players on the stage of radicals, we would have something on them. Maybe Ezra was lured the same way Spider was," Maclin speculated as she continued drumming the keys on her laptop, her fingertips damp with effort. She could type quicker than she could think. She worked a desktop and her iPad at the same time while Quincy and Phee sifted through piles of files on hyperradical Jewish organizations. Unlike Maclin, the two detectives were unapologetically old-school. They both connected to cases more from the feel of files in their hands.

Phee answered his phone and had a brief conversation. After he hung up, he pushed back his chair and stood up in frustration. "That was Shaka. He said Harlem is getting restless. He doesn't know how long he's gonna be able to keep a lid on things if we don't hurry up and find Spider and Ezra. This thing is getting harder and harder to get some traction on. Just when we think we're making a little sense of it, we gotta switch up and go left." Phee's tone straddled the fence between sarcasm and confusion.

"The sister didn't give you anything else?" Quincy asked.

"No, she was afraid she was saying too much as it was. It may not be much, but it's more than what we had."

Though there was nothing accusatory in his tone, Maclin imagined it nonetheless. The implied disappointment that she couldn't get more concrete info from the sister of her sometime lover made her a little more defensive than she intended to be.

"I already ran Ezra's phone on the day before and day of his disappearance. Besides his father and a couple of calls from the synagogue, there was only one other call that came in. Unfortunately, it was from a burner," she added.

They needed a break and they needed it quickly. Every minute that Spider and Ezra were missing brought the city closer to its own destruction. New York was running out of time—and so was Maclin. The hollow toll of fading time was a constant echo ringing in the back of her mind. Everything for her needed to happen *now*. The uncertainty of tomorrow crept toward her void of promise, bringing with it nothing more than an unrenewable warranty nearing its expiration.

One of her many torments was that she was no longer in

control. Maclin loved being in control. Although she believed in God, she struggled with the theory that no matter what choices she made in life, it was all somehow a part of a narrative that had been pre-scripted by an invisible yet omnipotent author. One thing that she couldn't deny was that it had started—the reexamination of long-held convictions. She no longer had the luxury of ignoring that the only true guarantee in life was the incommutable sentence of death. She was on the final legs of her goodbye tour. The last of things had already started for her. It was her last case. It was the last time she would work with the two men whom she admired most in the world. There were people and sights that she would never see again. There were feelings that she would never experience again. No matter how slowly she tried to read the pages, there was no extending the final chapter of her life. As much as possible, she was determined to at least close the book on her terms: doing what she was born to do.

She had no idea how close she would get to fulfilling what she saw as her destiny. She was now running on the fumes of possibility, being promoted to her dream position even though she knew it was a job she would never be able to actually take. She had to lower the bar on the height of her dreams. She would never serve as the director of the FBI; but maybe, just maybe, she would at least accomplish what had never been done in being the first woman named to that title. Her name would forever be there in the annals of history. She would at least be remembered for that. She could take that to the grave with her.

Maclin threw herself into the many tasks at hand to keep as

active as possible. She loved the work because it was the closest thing to making her feel whole. She savored it all—the repetition, the boring minutiae, the interminable research, and the haystack's worth of files. She was invigorated even through the overwhelming tedium of sorting through such a complicated case.

Television and the movies got it all wrong. There was nothing flashy about good police work. It was neither glamorous nor sexy. It was monotonous and nitpicking. The immersion in work at least afforded her the luxury of temporary amnesty. There were fleeting moments, albeit thin and nonredeemable, when Maclin wasn't consumed with thoughts of sickness and death, but just a good cop doing what she loved. She needed the work and all that it demanded of her: attention, intelligence, and tenaciousness. Cops soared or sank by their ability to dissect, digest, and disseminate information. Maclin took her time reading and rereading every detail. She sat at her desk for hours surrounded by Phee and Quincy, the three of them working meticulously in search of the thinnest of needles amongst large bales of hay. The case was too important, too horrific to risk missing anything. The thought of her taking an "L" to the grave terrified her. Maclin had nothing left, save her legacy.

The air in the precinct didn't move. It just hung around the room dense, lazy, and unemployable. It no longer had a function other than misery. She saw the frustration in her partners' faces when no breaks revealed themselves, even after scanning every bit of info multiple times. The more frustrated they got, the more determined they became. The three of them worked with a manic obsession with stopping the evil that was being inflicted upon New York. They were all of the same opinion—the entire city was at stake. They needed to find Spider. They needed to find Ezra Pearl. They needed to stop the madness that had already been set into motion. The synagogue murders as well as the abductions were the kind of case that scarred not just everyone involved but countless others who fell under the purview of collateral damage. Hate was never a spectator sport; no one could escape its affliction unchanged. Undented.

The last time either of them had been in the mayor's office was over two years ago, shortly after closing the Deggler case. As soon as they were ushered in by an aide, Maclin heard Phee say under his breath, "Damn, sista brought some flava up in here."

It wasn't just the administration that had changed; the whole look and vibe were different. Under the previous mayor, the office had felt staid. Predictable. Bureaucratic. Now, under Mayor Rocky, the office was filled with vibrant art from the likes of Romare Bearden and Kerry James Marshall as well as black-and-white photos from Roy DeCarava along with Shona sculptures and a couple of bronze pieces from Robert Graham. An ivory-colored Japanese silk and multipatterned kente cloth were used as a coffee-table runner and sofa throw, respectively. The mayor utilized her background as an art history minor to transform the city's most powerful office into something warm and homey. It was both a very comfortable room to talk politics and policy and the kind of place that made a person, no matter their station in life, feel welcomed.

"You have got to be kidding me!!!" Mayor Rocky fumed.

"About which part: Shaka or our plan?" Phee asked.

"How about all of it. People were killed today and you're telling me the ATF was involved. They send him to my city to do some shit like this, and they don't even give me the professional courtesy of a heads-up?"

Maclin watched the vein throbbing in the mayor's neck. The room was by no means comfortable anymore. Mayor Rocky had a big voice that filled every crevice of the office and left no room for doubting just how pissed she was. Maclin thought she saw glasses rattle on a nearby credenza.

Phee didn't back down. "I agree with you, but it was a tough call on their part. We're fighting this thing, and we don't even know who the enemy is. Shaka says protocol was broken because these people are plugged in everywhere."

Mayor Rocky stopped pacing and looked at Phee as if she were seeing him for the first time. When he saw her anger turning into confusion, he took a step toward her.

"Yeah—cops, Feds, maybe even people here at City Hall. Trust me: I hate how things went down today as much as you do, but whatever we've seen, it's just scratching the surface of what's to come. I know it's a heavy price to pay, but Shaka playing it the way he has is giving us the closest thing we've got to catching these assholes." Phee caught himself. "Excuse my French."

Mayor Rocky leaned against the front of her desk and folded her arms. "Agent Maclin, you've been quiet on this."

"Because I agree with Detective Freeman."

Quincy jumped in, "We're all on the same page, ma'am."

The Mayor shook her head in frustration, as if they weren't seeing the big picture. "We've had nine bomb threats at both mosques and synagogues in the last three weeks, and you all really think staging some fake extermination at one of their sites is our only viable option? That's a pretty vile option to me."

"We agree, but it's still the best we've got. We have to do something quick and bold. One of our working theories is that the abduction of Ezra Pearl and Spider will be exploited to incite a race war the likes of which would rip apart New York and even beyond," Maclin said.

Maclin noticed how the invisible weight hefted upon the mayor's shoulders caused her to slouch a little.

"Have the three of you thought about the fact that if this thing goes sideways, we lose the city?"

"Yes, we have," Maclin answered. "Considering the current racial climate in this country, if we don't try this, there's a good chance that we'll lose even more. There are no easy answers—but we feel this gives us a solid shot at getting Shaka inside."

"What about the other angle—this Sicarri group?"

"We just got this info about two hours ago, and I'm having my colleagues at the FBI look into it. But we have no way of knowing if it will yield anything. And even if we do get something, it might not be enough and it might not be in time. You have to trust me, ma'am. We're looking at this from every possible side, but we have a small window to halfway control this thing."

"I need some time to think about this."

"We don't have time," Phee said sharply.

"If it gets out that I signed off on staging some scene from the Holocaust as well as suppressing the press, I'm done."

"I say let's save some lives and think about our jobs later," Phee retorted with an unapologetic edge.

At six feet one, when Mayor Rocky stood up she was almost eye to eye with Phee. She had no problem squaring off with any man, Phee included. She waited before she spoke, knowing that the awkward silence reminded everyone in the room who held the power.

"Like I said, I need time to think about it."

Phee didn't back down. "If we get stuck on bureaucracy here, a lot of innocent people will die—and that will be on everybody in this room. We gotta all be willing to do whatever we need to as long as we stop this thing—and if there are consequences, we deal with them later. No disrespect, but saving lives should be the only thing that matters."

Mayor Rocky's eyes had fire in them. The harder she stared through Phee, the more she struggled to restrain her initial instincts. Even though her voice was relatively calm, it was clear to all just how furious she was.

"Let me guess, you called your father before this meeting and you all decided that challenging my priorities would guilt me into going along with this? So that we're clear on a couple of things, don't *ever* think you can overstep your bounds with me because of my relationship with your father..."

"I wasn't..."

She stopped him with a look. "Don't ever try to play me, Phee. I assure you, I'm not the one."

Even though the mayor was addressing Phee, Maclin had the distinct feeling that her warning was directed at all three of them. Phee wasn't the wilting type, but he did take it down several notches.

"I know you're not. I apologize, and I promise you it won't ever happen again."

Quincy used the brief silence as an opportunity to jump in. "With all due respect, ma'am, you put us on this thing because you felt we could close. Take the cuffs off, and let us do what we do."

Maclin had worked with Quincy and Phee enough to know when to lay back and let them play their roles. Phee was the provocateur, the hot-headed one with a talent for pushing people's buttons. He was certainly not above using guilt or shaming the mayor into action. Quincy was the calm after the storm, the voice of reason and assurance.

Mayor Rocky looked at the three of them expressionless, playing her hand close to the vest. She turned back to her minibar, poured herself some Japanese whiskey, and looked out the window as if they were no longer in the room. She was good at taking her time. She kept her back to them as she swirled her drink and stared in the glass as if the answers to difficult questions might be floating amongst the smoky, brown liquid.

When she finally got around to speaking, her voice was a bit dull. It sounded like an impostor had snuck into the room and was doing a weak impression of her. The voice lacked her usual confidence and even hit very subtle notes of fear.

"This thing wants to swallow us whole, along with everything that we love and honor. We are just one mistake away from New York being turned inside out. So whatever you see as my hesitation, it's not about protecting my job. It goes way deeper than that. Are we clear?"

Phee opened his mouth to speak, but Maclin went off script and cut him off.

"Yes, very much so." She walked over to Mayor Rocky and stood by her side. It was a simple gesture that suggested an intimacy of friendship. Maclin spoke in a temperate tone, less as a cop and more as one woman confiding in another.

"The only way we are going to stop this madness is to be bolder and more aggressive than they are. We're going to have to risk more than them because we have more at stake. This only works if we all trust in each other. The only thing more dangerous than someone willing to kill for a cause is someone willing to die for one. The three of us will die if we have to, to stop them. If that's what it takes to protect you and this entire city."

Maclin stood erect offering up the type of reassurances Mayor Rocky needed. There was no wavering. The Mayor looked at

Maclin hard, moved by her dedication. The two women were quiet, staring at each other for a while before Mayor Rocky finally relented and nodded her consent.

"Let's just hope it doesn't come to that. I need the three of you to go save my city!"

"Yes, ma'am." Maclin squeezed the back of the mayor's hand.

As the trio headed for the door, Mayor Rocky called after them. "Phee, for the record, what exactly did your father say to you?"

Phee smiled like a child caught in the cookie jar. "He said if I tried to play you, you would chew me a new one—but then you would listen to your heart."

The mayor sipped her whiskey and turned back toward the window.

24

The entire block surrounding the Brooklyn Congregation B'nai B'rith Community Center had been evacuated. The normally quiet Jewish neighborhood now looked like something out of *Close Encounters of the Third Kind*. Yellow flashing lights from Con Edison trucks and a few other emergency vehicles lit the night. Police barricades lined the perimeter as twenty or so cops kept a restless crowd at bay.

Maclin stood discreetly behind the corner of the building, scanning the hordes of looky-loos. She searched the faces and body language with the slim hope that something, anything would stand out. The only conclusion that she came to was that the vast majority of New Yorkers looked suspicious in one way or another. She couldn't help but wonder if somewhere, hidden amongst the crowd, was the very evil they were pursuing.

The front entrance of the Center was tented off, obscuring all interior activity. There were sporadic glimpses of workers in white hazmat jumpsuits emerging then quickly disappearing, resembling a band of shy ghosts. The night heat didn't help. Agitated neighbors shouted at the cops, demanding details on what was going on. Maclin lay back in the cut and kept an eye on all of the activity at the halfway point between the building and the crowd. Finally, at around 10:30 a police sergeant, accompanied by a younger cop, addressed the gathering with a bullhorn.

"Folks, everything is fine. It was just a gas leak that we didn't want to take any chances with. Con Ed has everything under control. We appreciate your patience. We should have this all wrapped up within the next hour." Even as people in the crowd continued shouting questions, the sergeant abruptly turned without answering and walked off with his underling.

"I don't get it, Sarge. I've worked gas leaks before and there's definitely something weird about this one. And what's up with the lady Fed? What's really going on here? I know you know."

"The only thing I know, Hitchens, is that we're here to keep our mouths shut and do our jobs and control the crowds."

"Come on, Sarge. You can tell me, I mean…"

The young officer was cut off by Maclin's voice directly behind them. "You should listen to your sergeant."

As the two cops turned to face her, she kept her eyes glued to the young cop, deliberately making him feel uncomfortable under her scrutiny.

"Officer Hitchens, am I right?"

"Yes, ma'am." His sphincter tightened a little.

"Well, Officer Hitchens, like your sergeant said, you're here to do your job. Let's make sure that's your only priority, okay?"

"Yes, ma'am."

She nodded at the sergeant, then walked to the rear of the building. Because Quincy and Phee had somewhat of a rock star status in New York from all of the high-profile murder cases they had closed, the trio decided it was best that the two partners stay clear of the Center since the scene was supposedly a random gas leak and not a murder investigation.

Maclin was the eyes and ears on the ground, the conductor of the ruse, as it were. As she reached the cordoned-off area of the courtyard far from the prying eyes of the crowd, where not even police were allowed, she took out her phone and started taking photos of the secret activity. She nodded at Kravitz and snapped two photos and a short video of him directing two of his workers dressed in hazmat suits to wheel a couple of gurneys, with stuffed body bags, out through an alley.

"All right, let's wrap it up," she said. "By the way, Kravitz, Phee says you have a couple of Rangers tickets coming your way for doing this."

Kravitz waved, mumbled something incoherent, and waddled off.

"This is good. This is really good," Quincy said as he and Phee looked at the photos and video on Maclin's phone after she returned to the station.

"So who do we start with?" Maclin asked.

Quincy handed the phone back to her. "First thing we gotta do is raise the question of whether the gas leak was really a cover-up for something worse. Our best bet is to play an alt-right conspiracy card. We leak the video to a Breitbart-wannabe site like 180-USA that would love to implicate the mayor in a major cover-up. Nothing will get people screaming conspiracy theories quicker and louder."

"Shaka posted bail an hour ago. We gotta figure out a way to keep a close eye on his back, 'cause once the shit starts rolling, things can happen pretty quickly," Phee added.

"I'll have our New York office send over an RFID kit," Maclin responded.

"You mean like the tiny chips they put in pets?" Quincy asked.

"Same principle, except ours actually has GPS monitoring for up to two miles. One of the bonuses of being a Fed is that we get better toys. It's put in with a needle. It's pretty simple, but effective."

"All right. I'll call Shaka and see if we can meet him somewhere on our way home. Quincy and Elena are staying with us until the heat lets up. You should come back with us?" Phee suggested.

"No, I couldn't," she answered instinctively.

"Why not? You could leave your car here and ride with us." Phee looked at her.

"Well, I just…"

"Come on. You know it's a hundred times more comfortable than your hotel, and we can continue to brainstorm. Besides, you'll help me score some bonus points with my daughter. Come on home with us, Maclin."

She heard an echo on the word *home*. Whether real or imagined, it rang loudest in his speech. The truth was, she was hungry for inclusion. It had been years since she felt any connection to even the simplest routines of something resembling a family structure. Her father was dead, and she wasn't close to her brothers. She had grown used to the aloneness, the sole citizenship on an island of an existence. Maclin loved Quincy and Phee because they reminded her that she was needed. They made her feel that she belonged.

"Yeah sure," she relented. "Drop me by my hotel so I can pick up some clothes."

They met up with Shaka just past midnight on the Jersey side of the George Washington Bridge. They parked in an empty lot of an abandoned diner. Shaka climbed in the back seat of Phee's Rover next to Maclin.

"How'd it go?" he asked.

Phee looked back over his shoulder from the driver's seat. "We'll find out soon enough. We sent out the leaks. If all goes right, the shit should hit the fan first thing in the morning. We gotta be prepped for any and everything now. Agent Maclin's got a tracker for you."

"If they contact me to meet, I'm not going in with a bug," Shaka protested. "If they're smart enough to stay off all of our grids, then we can't underestimate how cautious they are."

"We already thought of that. We can track you with an RFID chip," Quincy joined in.

Maclin opened a small black case and donned a latex glove as she pulled out a tiny metal capsule and a large needle.

Shaka looked at her uncomfortably. "What the hell is that?"

"It's just the chip," Maclin responded.

"I'm not talking about that. I'm talking about that big-ass needle."

Maclin loaded the chip into the syringe. "That's how we put the chip in."

"Oh hell, no!!!" Shaka protested.

"What's the problem? We gotta know your whereabouts at all times," Quincy said.

"Yeah, I get that part. But I don't do needles."

"You gotta be shittin' us, right?" Phee chuckled.

"Yo, it ain't funny. I've always had a thing with needles."

Maclin chimed in, "It'll only sting for two seconds and then it's done. I just need to insert it into the skin in between your thumb and index finger. Just trust me, okay?"

Maclin grabbed Shaka's left hand and was a bit surprised by how substantial it was. It was a heavy hand, weighted with might and possibilities. The knuckles were marred from old adversities and victories. The palm was mercilessly calloused, she assumed from life and toil. As she stared at it she saw deep, uninterrupted imprints. Like his namesake, he had the hands of a warrior. Maclin felt a twinge of envy from the inherent power embedded in such hands. She wasn't sure he fully appreciated what he had. With hands like his, she would have no fears, certainly not of needles or Ivan and possibly not even of death itself. If she had such hands, she knew she could fight anything. What could she possibly fear with hands big enough to box with God?

"All right, all right! Just don't look at me when she does it, okay?" Shaka half demanded, half pleaded to Phee and Quincy.

"All right. Cool." Phee cut his eyes at Quincy and stifled a laugh. As Maclin brought the needle closer, Shaka closed his eyes tightly and contorted his face as though she were about to perform an amputation. She caught Phee's eyes in the rearview mirror and fought off a giggle attack from Phee silently mocking Shaka. The big man flinched much more than was necessary when she inserted the needle.

"Okay. We're all done. See? Told you it wasn't that bad," Maclin said.

"Hey Quincy, why don't you look in the glove compartment and see if we have a Band-Aid to put on our brave little big man's boo-boo," Phee teased. Quincy laughed. Maclin held it together.

"Fuck you, Phee," Shaka roared. "When all this is finally over, I never wanna hear about this damn needle thing again, okay?"

"Can't make any promises there, Shaka. I mean, it ain't every day you get to see a three-hundred-pound brotha whining like a little schoolgirl who scraped her knee at recess."

Maclin finally caved in and started laughing.

Even though it was Shaka's habit to play the role of the indignant tough guy, he too eventually joined in the chorus of cackles directed at him. It was a much-needed release from the horrors of the past couple of days and the even greater threats that awaited them. They were like four giddy teenagers drunk from silly banter.

Maclin laughed so hard that she felt tears rolling from the corners of her eyes. Her stomach hurt, not from her illness but rather from one of the best prescriptions of all.

Maclin looked around the vehicle and couldn't help but think that they were the preamble of a bar joke: "So two black men, an Irish-Italian American, and a Jewish woman were all sitting in a car..." They were the best line of defense in more ways than one— and although it was unspoken, their laughter and union were a collective act of insurrection in the face of hate. They sat in Phee's truck for another forty-five minutes hypothesizing, strategizing, and laughing boldly.

25

S he couldn't believe how hard she slept in Phee's guest room. Harder than she had in quite some time. After they'd gotten back to the house at two in the morning she, along with Phee and Quincy, had hit the proverbial wall. It didn't happen often, but she actually managed to fall asleep without her mind engaging in combat with itself.

When Maclin awoke, she felt renewed. She felt energy coursing through her body. She got out of bed with no hesitation or need of pharmaceutical assistance. It had been a while since she had felt so *alive*. She threw on her clothes and raced downstairs to catch the sunrise.

There was a small gazebo in a garden at the edge of Phee's property that sat on a knoll facing east. The garden was filled with potted fruit trees, columbine, Russian sage, and at least ten varieties of daylilies. Because the sun had yet to rise, most of the flowers were still sleeping. Maclin wanted to start her day there welcoming the infinite possibilities that accompanied each dawn. She longed to bask in the first rays of sunrise and be inspired. She wanted her face warmed with hope and appreciation of even the most infinitesimal reminders of life.

Maclin thought about God and wondered if, after all this time, He still found beauty in things as simple as the dawning of another day. Her low-heeled pumps sank a little in the soft grass, damp from the early morning dew that cooled the sides of her feet. As she reached the edge of the garden and approached the gazebo, she was surprised to find Quincy there under the dim skies, his face aglow from the light of his laptop. He was so preoccupied with his work that Maclin's arrival seemed to startle him.

"I see I'm not the only early bird," Maclin said.

Quincy jumped a bit and quickly closed his laptop.

"Morning." He recovered.

"What are you working on this early in the morning?" she asked.

"Nothing much. Just another case I was looking into before we caught this case."

"You mind if I sit out here?"

"Of course not," he answered.

As Maclin sat, she noticed that Quincy seemed to intention-ally place the laptop off to the side as far away from her as possible. It was the first time she could ever remember him not looking directly at her when he spoke to her. Cops tried not to *cop* each other, and certainly not their partners. Conversations needed to be just that, not a constant assessment bordering on interrogation. The gift and curse of good cops such as Maclin, Quincy, and Phee was that they were always in various stages of *cop-ness*.

The morning light wasn't yet perfect. It was still unfolding and swallowing the shadows bit by bit as the sky was getting bluer by the moment. When Maclin finally caught Quincy's eyes she wasn't certain, but it looked as if he may have been crying or at the very least been on the brink. Even though something felt slightly off to her in his behavior, she looked away from him as a gesture of immunity from prying.

"This place is amazing," she offered.

"Yeah, it is. During the summer Elena and I come out almost every other weekend. It's like a staycation. Phee and Brenda actually thought they had to convince us to come stay more until the heat wave breaks, but we said 'Hell yeah' before they could even finish the suggestion. This spot right here, first thing in the morning, is hands down my favorite. Not a bad way to start a day," he responded.

The two of them grew silent as the sun peeped out over the horizon revealing itself inch by inch, like a timid child gaining confidence. Neither of them spoke because they both seemed to share the same thought: that not all moments were quantifiable. They quietly enjoyed their front-row seats to a private showing of the world awakening before them. Two privileged beings no more than the size of specks under an infinite sky that changed color multiple times—yellow, orange, plum, red, then finally blue. Although it was a sun of humble beginnings, Maclin knew that within the hour they would begin to feel its might. By noon they would swelter under its rage.

She breathed in deeply as though she were trying to stockpile some peace for the imminent tumult. After the sun had risen and the sky had turned a lighter shade of blue, Quincy stood at the edge of the gazebo and stretched as Maclin stayed seated.

"Supposed to be hotter today than it was yesterday and then even hotter tomorrow. Heat's not gonna break for another three days."

"Well, we just have to hope that we don't break before the weather does," she smiled.

As they continued talking, the conversation became more interesting, not for the things they talked about but for the things they didn't. They steered clear of the case and any reference to anything connected to it. It was just a matter of time before they would once again be fully immersed in their investigation, but for a few precious moments at sunrise they both embraced the short reprieve. They kept to safer subjects such as the weather and Phee's magnificent home and beautiful daughter.

"Do you think you and Elena will have children?" Maclin asked.

"We've talked about it a lot, but just talk."

"Which means she wants to and you're on the fence," Maclin said with a smile.

Quincy smiled back. "This is a rough world to bring a child into. What about you? Do you think about having any?"

For some reason, even though she was the one who initiated the topic, Maclin felt thrown by the question.

"I uhh… I used to think about it before but not anymore."

"For what it's worth, I think you'd make a really good mother, seeing how you are with Dolicia. My mother used to always say that people with big hearts can never hide them, especially not from children. It's great seeing that part of you, Janet. You've got a lot of love in your heart."

Maclin was left speechless. All she could offer was a smile and an appreciative nod. She noticed that after mentioning his mother, Quincy once again looked as sad as he did when she first joined him. She looked out on to the garden at the rows of different-colored daylilies. She could feel him staring at her as she kept her eyes on the beautiful flowers, careful not to encroach in any way.

When he finally spoke, his voice was different, a bit disembodied.

"My mother always had this thing for violet daylilies. I heard it started on the first date with my father fifty years ago."

"Yeah, they're my favorite as well."

When she turned to him, Maclin saw the effort in his smile. The masking. He stood and moved closer to the edge of the gazebo. As he continued speaking, he directed his words more in the direction of the horizon than at her. She just sat silently and listened as he talked more at her than to her.

"Although Brenda has never come out and said it, I'm pretty sure she planted all these daylilies in honor of my mother. Every time I'm here, she cuts a dozen of them for me to bring to the cemetery. A few times I've gone and there were already a dozen of them placed on her grave just waiting there."

Although Maclin couldn't see his face, she heard the brief snort of a half-committed laugh.

"I've gotten into this weird habit when I'm there. I always end up just sitting in the grass and watching the other families that come and go. I look out at all the rows of tombstones and try to imagine how each person came to be buried there. Disease, illness, natural causes, human error, or acts of God? I can't help but wonder how many of them got there like my mother. How many of them got there the hard way? The kind of way we politely avoid talking about, even with partners. Did you ever read the report on my mother's death?"

"No, I decided not to."

"There were pieces of her that were never found. Important pieces. Next day, patrol came across a meth-head that had OD'd in Central Park with my mother's blood and jewelry on him. They ruled her death a robbery gone bad. Two days later, they said my brother Liam was so broken by her murder that he jumped from the GWB. By the time they finally recovered his body a week later, it was so badly decomposed that we had to ID him through DNA from stuff found in his apartment. You, me, and Phee—that's one of the things we all have in common. The three of us know firsthand that when you lose loved ones like that, to violence, there are parts of you that break that never really get fixed. But the thing that fucks with me the most, the thing I just can't let go of, is knowing there was no way in hell my brother killed himself over a mother he despised."

He kept his back to her and stared out at the field of daylilies that were just awakening, their petals stretching and yawning at the low-hanging sun. Maclin wasn't sure if he had more to say or if he wanted her to stay or go. She walked over and stood ten feet behind him. Just enough distance not to crowd him and enough to remind him that he wasn't alone.

By the time the two of them made it back inside the house, Brenda, Elena, and Dolicia were in the kitchen already into their routine. The local news played quietly on the television in the background. Dolicia's eyes widened at the sight of Maclin. Brenda, attempting to feed her uncooperative daughter, stopped as Maclin approached and greeted the little girl. Dolicia started laughing as Maclin made funny faces at her.

"Perfect timing. She's been feelin' some kind of a way from the time she got up. She slept with us, but neither one of us got much sleep because Phee tossed and turned most of the night having nightmares."

Quincy sighed and momentarily lowered his head. He sagged a little under the burden of an invisible tax. When he looked up and caught Maclin looking in his direction, his body language changed, albeit with an insincere effort. Brenda and Elena were preoccupied with Dolicia and missed the shift, but Maclin definitely saw the sudden unease.

Brenda continued negotiating with her daughter to eat her breakfast. Dolicia seemed much more interested in Maclin than her mother's pleas and a bowl of Greek yogurt, honey, and fresh fruit.

Maclin thought of her own mother and the dramatic lengths to which she'd often had to resort to get her children to eat.

"Brenda, would you mind if I tried to feed her?" Maclin asked.

Brenda handed Maclin the spoonful of yogurt. "Be my guest."

Maclin made a performance of eating a blueberry as though it were the greatest thing in the world. Dolicia laughed at the theatrics as Maclin traded turns doling out spoonfuls to the toddler and popping blueberries into her own mouth, as though every bite were a competition. Even Elena got involved as she grabbed a sliced strawberry from a bowl on the counter and tossed it in the air and caught it in her mouth like a hungry seal. The kitchen was noisy and full of life by the time Phee ambled in.

"Ahh, there's my grumpy bear," Brenda said as she poured herself another cup of coffee. Phee mumbled a *good morning* to no one in particular.

"Dada," Dolicia said loudly.

"Hey, Yummy!" he responded.

"Ate food, Dada."

"That's good, baby."

The usual spark in Phee's eyes whenever he looked at his daughter seemed oddly dim to Maclin. It wasn't just that he was fatigued. Maclin saw something weighing even heavier on him. Had it been anyone other than Phee, she would have sworn it was fear. As she continued playing with Dolicia, Maclin kept an eye on Quincy and Phee as they faded back closer to the entrance of the kitchen speaking to one another quietly enough so as not to be heard by anyone else. After a terse exchange, Quincy once again lowered his head and sighed.

Phee suddenly tensed as he looked past Quincy. Maclin followed his stare to the kitchen television, where she saw some of the video footage she'd shot the night before. The breaking news caption flashed the words GAS LEAK FATALITIES AT JEWISH CENTER—HOAX OR COVER-UP? Phee moved quickly to the island and grabbed the remote, turning the volume up.

The anchor read, "...reported gas leak at the Westside Jewish Center in Brooklyn is the focus of growing controversy as to whether there were actual casualties as suggested by a video that was acquired by the alt-right site 180-USA. The New York City police and fire departments have yet to confirm or deny that there were in fact fatalities at the site. However, secretly shot footage of what appears to be bodies being removed from the facility is raising great alarm throughout the city, particularly in the Jewish community. As of this hour, the mayor's office has yet to weigh in."

As the anchor droned on, the three partners looked at each other in silent affirmation. Phee grabbed his car keys off the counter. "Looks like we're back on the clock."

Maclin watched Phee cross to Dolicia and kiss her on her forehead. "Bye, Yummy."

"Bye, Dada."

Brenda gave him a hug and a quick peck, but as she attempted to turn away he held on to her hand until she turned back and gave him a more significant kiss. Quincy hugged Elena tighter than a simple goodbye. Maclin couldn't name it, but starting with Quincy the seconds before Phee's arrival and somewhere between the hugs and goodbye kisses, she thought something was off in her partners' usual demeanor.

The perfectly white gravel in the driveway crunched underneath their footsteps as the three made their way to Phee's SUV. Maclin broke the silence just as they reached the vehicle. "Somebody wanna tell me what the hell is going on with the two of you?"

Phee dug into his pocket and pulled out his wallet. He palmed a twenty to Quincy, who just looked at him with smug satisfaction, which only confused Maclin more.

"Phee said we wouldn't make it out of the house. I said we would at least make it to the car before you asked," he explained.

"Okay, so now that I'm asking, which one of you is going to tell me?" Maclin pressed.

"All right, so first thing is, you can't laugh and you can't call us crazy," Phee bargained.

"Well, that's an interesting opening," she responded.

"He's serious, Janet. It's gonna sound like some crazy superstition or bizarre coincidence, but it's real. You gotta trust us, because we've seen it happen too many times," Quincy joined in.

Even though she considered them usually serious men, she now found them extra serious.

Phee twirled his keychain around his finger as if the act would help him to better explain things to Maclin.

"Before we officially met, you did your homework on us. You know in the six and a half years that Quincy and I have been partners, we've closed a helluva lot of cases. Last time I counted, we were at a hundred and forty-nine. Twenty-seven of them were national headlines, like the Deggler case." Phee sighed and looked a little embarrassed as he continued. "I've got this weird thing about snakes. I don't know what it is, but whenever I get crazy nightmares about them a day or so into a case, I know we're about to go from bad to worse."

Quincy jumped in. "The first time he told me about this, I didn't put a whole lot of stock into it either, because there was really no way to explain it. But since then, on twelve different cases he's told me about the nightmares—and twelve times he was spot on."

"Spot on about what exactly?" Maclin asked.

"First the nightmares, then some really bad shit happens."

"Like what?" Maclin asked.

Phee hesitated, as if holding the words in might somehow change the outcome of his premonition. Even the partial admission depleted something in him. Quincy intercepted, possibly to help shoulder his partner's burden.

"Like we lose one of our own."

26

But the delay in announcing the deaths was only for the benefit of taking time to notify the next of kin. Four of the seven deceased were rabbis from three different countries, which, as you all can imagine, complicated things quite a bit. This is a horrible tragedy that I felt needed to be handled with the utmost respect and discretion." Mayor Rocky Henderson hovered over a podium addressing a roomful of zealous press.

Maclin stood in the back of the conference room with Quincy and Phee, listening to Mayor Rocky's press conference.

A reporter from the *Times* pounced with a question as soon as he sniffed an opening, "Mayor Henderson, don't you feel the public had a right to know immediately that there were fatalities, and was there any concern on your part that your silence sent a message of denial of the full magnitude of the situation?"

"As far as claims of denial go, like I just said, I made the call not to publicly confirm anything until we reached the families. It's not any kind of a conspiracy; it's called compassion. The gas leak was an accident, plain and simple, that was completely contained within twenty minutes after it was reported. Since there was no threat to the public and there was no criminality involved, I and I alone made the decision to not go public with it until we had the opportunity to contact the immediate families of the deceased."

The mayor played her part well. Like all politicians, she was an accomplished liar. Maclin was impressed with her unwavering poise as well as her deflection skills. She particularly liked it when the mayor strategically floated the word "conspiracy."

Maclin stood between her two partners, who seemed equally pleased with Mayor Rocky's performance.

She heard Phee's phone buzz and felt his entire demeanor change when he read the incoming text. When he showed the text to her and Quincy, they immediately made their way out the back door.

The mayor entered her office full of steam and edge as Maclin, Phee, and Quincy waited for her.

"Just so that everybody in this room is crystal clear: my ass is officially on the chopping block. We're not gonna be able to play this hand for too much longer. The only possible win here is if we apprehend who's been behind all of this and then come clean to the public as to why we had to lie to them. This thing doesn't go our way, I lose all credibility. I'm done. We all need to…"

"Shaka's been contacted," Phee interrupted.

"What? When?" the mayor asked.

"Three minutes into your news conference," Maclin jumped in. "They want a face-to-face with him today at three."

Mayor Rocky sat on the corner of her desk and folded her arms. "Do we know where?"

"No. They said they'll reach out again an hour before the meeting," Quincy added.

"So, what's the game plan?" the Mayor asked.

"We stay on the low," Phee warned.

Maclin stepped a little closer. "We promised Shaka that we wouldn't do anything to jeopardize his cover, so we'll put together a small unit, no more than a dozen. Just people we know we can trust. We already put a chip in Shaka to monitor his whereabouts at all times. We've notified NSA that we are tracking an unnamed domestic terrorist group, so once we get an address on the meeting, hopefully they'll give us an assist on surveillance."

"One of you will be on the phone with me directly when this goes down. This insanity has to end." Mayor Rocky's tone occupied the rarefied space between a desperate plea and an unbreakable command. Maclin was used to being in rooms filled with true powerhouses. She, however, couldn't recall being in a room with such powerful people whose fear was so plentiful.

Hers was arguably the most encompassing. As Quincy and Phee continued talking with the mayor, Maclin grew quiet because the fear that she was feeling swelled and threatened to explode as she questioned not just the outcome of the case but if over the course of her career she had accomplished nearly enough. If her life had been enough.

Detectives Burns and his partner Bobby Skia made the cut. They were the first two to be cleared for the twelve-man unit to raid Shaka's meeting. Burns, married to a sista for almost twenty-seven years, had four biracial children; Bobby Skia was half-Jamaican and half-Cuban—so it was a safe assumption that they were not secretly in cahoots with the mysterious hate group. The two detectives then selected three others from their unit whom they trusted with their lives. Quincy and Phee pulled in two cops from their own precinct that they could unequivocally vouch for. Maclin brought in a local African American agent named Gerald Suggs, whom she didn't know personally but who had a great reputation. His addition was more for bureaucratic correctness than anything. The SWAT unit was placed on standby under the premise of a potential hostage situation. The details on the operation were given on a need-to-know basis to control who had what information and when.

By noon, everything was ready to be set into motion. Waiting was the hard part. Although they were sitting on their biggest lead, they were left with very little to do until Shaka was actually contacted. Bobby Skia made a sandwich and soda run to Katz's deli on 69th and brought back some Reubens and thickly stacked pastrami on rye. Phee and Quincy tore into their lunch as soon as it arrived. Maclin had forgotten that none of them had eaten breakfast. She didn't bother to unwrap her sandwich; she just looked at the small white bundle with a quartered dill pickle skewered by a toothpick on top. Not only did she not have an appetite, but her stomach felt as if it was in shambles. Just as she thought the twists and knots were subsiding, the uncomfortable churning started cycling again. Maclin retreated to the bathroom and found at least a little solace in a tiny stall with a broken slide lock. She leaned her back against the door until a bout of abdominal cramping left her bent slightly at the waist as the first round of dry heaves came. Despite the fact that she hadn't eaten anything since the night before, she could feel the rumblings of a riot within. A few seconds later, she threw up.

As soon as she made it back to her desk, Maclin went fishing for more info on radical Jewish groups that might give her some insight into Sicarii. She needed to pass the time doing something. Anything. Wasting even a second was no longer an option. Maclin needed to keep moving. Phee and Quincy busied themselves with repeatedly going over every detail of the raid, even though they were operating off of very limited intel. They were reduced to prepping hypotheticals.

Maclin gulped down one of the two cold cans of Coke that Bobby Skia had placed on her desk when he brought back the sandwiches. She hated Coke, thought of it as nothing more than gut rot. She drank it for two reasons: because she hoped the carbonation would help to keep her stomach settled and because the soda felt like the coldest thing in the entire city. She hadn't had any type of soda in over twenty years, but as she finished off the first can she immediately reached for the second. It was nothing short of cold joy going down. Aside from the brain freeze, she relished every drop of the guilty pleasure. The thought of Coke eventually killing her was the least of her worries.

Even though she tried to distract herself with her work, she was very aware that every time Phee reached for his phone the room seemed to slow a bit. She couldn't help but periodically check her watch with the hope that Shaka's phone call would come soon. Time seemed more foe than friend. It crawled by at a cruel pace, with no regard that lives hung in the balance.

Over an hour passed, and she still couldn't find anything useful regarding any current group calling themselves Sicarii. Not even on the dark net, where she looked up fringe factions of hate groups. The most she found was a one-line reference from a little-known site called the Eyes of Justice—they debunked the group's existence as nothing more than a rumor.

She had just started rechecking all calls to and from Ezra's phone within the last month when Phee's phone finally rang at 1:47. The raid team stopped what they were doing, and Phee was on his feet immediately. All eyes were on him as he did more listening than speaking. He nodded his head a lot as if the caller could actually see him acknowledging instructions. Just before hanging up, the only thing Phee uttered into the phone was, "We got your back, brotha."

As she followed the rest of the team out the doors, Maclin fought to suppress another round of dry heaves.

27

Up until a year and a half ago, the Gungerman Building on 37th Street and 9th Avenue was home to the biggest furrier in the city. After a hugely successful seventy-five-year run, it took just over two years for the founder's grandson to bankrupt the business with his addiction to gambling and fentanyl.

The three-story building, which had for years been a jewel of neoclassical architecture in the heart of the Garment District, sat abandoned for a year in probate. Two statues of lions flanked the front steps, their mouths gaping open in frozen roars while eyeballing the steady stream of midtowners. Even though the streets were overcrowded and bustling as usual, there was a not-so-subtle difference. The city felt off, as if it was lagging a beat or two behind its usual rhythm. The majority of pedestrians seemed to be slowed a little by the heat and stench, not to mention the menace of a race war. People were nervous and much more suspicious of those they passed by. The crowded streets of Manhattan had become nothing more than a city of side-eyes.

Maclin, Phee, and Quincy posted up in a stationery shop directly across from the Gungerman Building. Maclin, who for the last thirty-seven minutes had been on the phone with NSA haggling for support, was becoming increasingly more frustrated. Phee slipped the owner a couple hundred bucks not just to close the shop but also to stay off of her cell as well. Detectives Burns and Bobby Skia sat in a loading alley in the cab of a tow truck that belonged to Burns's brother-in-law. Since they'd had less than an hour to set up surveillance, they improvised. They put eyes on every entrance of the Gungerman Building. Agent Suggs along with SWAT was kept at the ready one block over. All team members were in play with fifteen minutes to spare. Quincy both manned his laptop and tracked Shaka on a city grid on Maclin's iPad. He watched a red, pulsing dot turning onto 37th Street.

"I've got Shaka pulling up," he said.

Phee raised a pair of binoculars as he spoke into his walkie. "All right, everybody, we're in play. Let's make it count."

Shaka pulled up in front of the Gungerman Building in a shiny black Escalade driven by an Uber driver. In the short walk from the curb to the entrance, passing midtowners stepped out of the way of the big scary-looking black man with flowing dreads. A few beats after he climbed the building's four steps and banged on the entrance, the blur of a figure in a dark hoodie opened the locked glass doors and quickly ushered him in. Phee watched as the figure turned and secured the doors with a thick, padlocked chain.

Maclin finally ended her phone call and walked over to her partners. "NSA won't give us any support in midtown this late in the game."

"We need ears in there. Who ran the schematics on the building?" Quincy asked.

Phee, on his cell giving Mayor Rocky the play-by-play, responded.

"Janet had Agent Suggs do it. He just shot 'em to me, and I forwarded them to you."

Quincy picked up his laptop and looked at the blueprints while Phee looked over his shoulder. Maclin hovered over her iPad for indeterminate stretches without blinking as she stared at the red dot as if all their lives depended on it. She called out the details as the dot started descending beneath the first floor.

"Looks like they're headed to the basement. What are the access points that they would use?" she asked.

"According to this, there are just three. A freight elevator in the center and two stairwells, one on the northeast side and one on the southeast," Quincy answered.

"Okay, then it looks like they're taking him down the northeast stairwell." When Maclin glanced up she noticed that Phee couldn't stay still, his breathing slightly heavier than normal. He alternated looking at Maclin's and Quincy's devices as he put his phone on speaker so that Mayor Rocky could hear directly what was happening. "Looks like they're taking Shaka down to the basement. We can't just leave him in there by himself too long."

Mayor Rocky's voice was heard over the phone's speaker.

"We've gotta be patient on this one, Phee. We have to go in at the right time. We don't want any of them getting away."

Phee, growing more anxious, started pacing. "We've got at least one bad actor in there with him. I say we swoop in and take whoever's there, and press as hard as we can until we break them for useful intel. We don't control the situation. I think we gotta take what we can get. I got a fucked-up feeling on this one."

"I hear you. But playing devil's advocate, if we go in prematurely and if the person at the door won't or can't give us something useful, then we blow everything and end up with nothing. That also means the last two years of Shaka's life. Not to mention we could end up pushing them off the grid. Phee, Shaka knew going in it wasn't going to be a perfect operation. He understood the risk, but he still wasn't going to let anything or anybody stop him," Quincy countered.

Mayor Rocky's voice floated in the air, "Phee, I agree with Quincy. Stand down."

Phee raised his voice. "We all know the risk, but that's not…"

Maclin interrupted the conversation. "Are the plans showing any subbasements?"

Quincy scrolled down on his laptop. "No. According to the prints, we bottom out one level below the first floor."

Maclin's entire demeanor shifted into obvious alarm. "Then we've got a problem. Shaka just went two levels down, and his signal is getting weaker."

Phee clicked off his phone, hanging up on Mayor Rocky. "Fuck this. We go in *now*!" Phee grabbed his walkie and burst through the front door, Maclin and Quincy trailing behind. Outside was a blanket of heat, enveloping them as soon as they exited the shop. They were sweating within seconds. Phee shouted into his walkie, "Everybody in. Repeat, everybody in!"

Just as they reached the street, Maclin saw Phee heading on a collision course with an oncoming motorcycle and shouted after him, "Phee!!!"

Phee managed to pull up three inches short of certain tragedy as the motorcycle roared past him. As he approached the front door, he drew his gun and fired twice, shattering the glass. People on the street scattered everywhere as Maclin, Quincy, and the rest of their team descended upon the building. They came in fast and hard announcing their office over the crumpled sounds of broken glass, "NYPD! NYPD!" They broke into pairs and trios as they fanned out into every direction of the building.

Maclin, Phee, and Quincy headed straight for the northeast stairwell with detectives Burns and Skia closely behind. Maclin shouted over her shoulder at both, but neither of them in particular, "Tell SWAT to seal the perimeter high and low and sweep every alley in a four-block radius. Make sure nobody gets out."

When Maclin looked down at her iPad, Shaka's signal had completely disappeared. "I've lost him!" She and Quincy took the stairs two and three at a time while the more athletic Phee, who was ahead of them, jumped down a whole flight. Maclin was suddenly lightheaded and slipped on the last two steps. She went down hard. Quincy and Burns quickly lifted her up to her feet.

"You okay?" Quincy asked.

"I'm fine. Go!"

She didn't know which was more bruised, her ego or her scraped knees. Although both her legs were sore, she followed behind her team as quickly as she could.

The basement was large, running half the length and width of the entire building. In addition to Maclin, Phee, and Quincy, Bobby Skia and Burns along with four other members of their team spread out and searched the dark, cavernous space. It took them ten minutes to find a hidden panel, the size of a small door, behind a seven-foot furnace. The door led to a set of narrow stairs and a steel plank. They crossed it and entered into an empty room that was roughly forty by forty feet. Their mini xenon flashlights lifted the blanket of darkness all around them. An antique chandelier draped in cobwebs dangled from the mirrored ceiling. Faded Art Deco murals decorated the walls, and a ten-foot curved mahogany bar, covered by decades of dust, took up a small area near the entrance. They all stood in the middle of a forgotten speakeasy hidden deep in the lower innards of the old building. The room was a dead end with no signs of Shaka.

As the team shone their flashlights in various directions, Maclin was the first to see it: two small pools of fresh blood, glistening under the beam of her light.

By the time proper work lights had been brought in and set up, Shaka had been missing for close to twenty minutes. Now that the room had been lit up and designated a crime scene, Maclin, Phee, and Quincy were the only ones allowed to walk the space before CSU arrived. They eventually found a hidden latch door in the floor beneath the bar that led to a subway tunnel. Maclin waited as Phee and Quincy disappeared on the tracks in opposite directions, only to both return ten minutes later with their heads bowed in failure.

"Prohibition tunnels. We got played from the start. They knew that signals would be jammed underneath all the steel and concrete and that by the time we even figured out this little maze, they would be long gone," Quincy said.

Maclin looked at Phee, who stood near the pools of blood. Even though he was deathly still, she could sense the anger churning deep within him. She took a step in his direction but then thought better of it. Phee was beyond solace. They all were. Maclin didn't go in much for things like premonitions. She was too much a woman of reason to surrender to what she deemed coincidental occurrences. Whether there was some ominous connection to Phee's foreboding vision or it was all just inexplicable happenstance, there was no denying that Phee's dream of snakes was absolute. Just as he had prophesied, they had lost one of their own.

They walked the crime scene with such precision and efficiency that it only took them half their normal time. One worked the core and the other two the periphery, and then they seamlessly alternated positions to make sure nothing was missed by whichever team member preceded them. When they were at the top of their game, they were three meticulous hawks surveying a field and finding even the most minuscule clues. Losing Shaka completely debilitated them. They autopiloted through the scene, each in their own world tottering from the loss of their colleague. Other than Phee taping off the area surrounding the blood on the floor, they simply went through the motions, each failing miserably at pretending that Shaka's abduction hadn't completely gutted them.

They halfheartedly toiled under a heavy veil of silence. Save the vivid ramblings of their imagination of Shaka's ordeal, none of them had any real focus. Ultimately, Maclin was rendered useless from the evisceration. So too was Quincy. So was Phee. There were no uplifting phrases about hopeful possibilities. There was only the truth, and the truth was cruel and ugly.

CSU canvassed the subbasement of the Gungerman Building for fibers and hair and ran a screen of samples from the two pools of blood, which in a matter of minutes yielded two different blood types. The discovery was the single ray of hope in an investigation that was short on leads. Maclin, Phee, and Quincy stayed at the scene for hours after Shaka went missing. They stayed after they had dismissed the last two members of their team and even after the last tech had gone.

They hung at the site not because they thought they would find something that had been overlooked but because they had no idea what else to do. Even though Maclin pulled every string she could to get a quick turnaround on the DNA of the blood samples, they still wouldn't have results for another twenty-four hours at the earliest. They were left with nothing to do but mourn the unconfirmed death of their newest partner. Their collective guilt filled the hall and left very little room for anything else.

They were a disjointed trio that occupied separate areas of the speakeasy, careful not to infringe on each other's personal space. Maclin sat on the floor with her back against the bar. She wasn't certain if the onset of a migraine was Ivan's doing or if it was just a result of the incredible stress that was swallowing them all. Her head pounded. Had she been a betting woman, she would have played the odds that her aching was nothing more than Ivan at play. The pain blurred her vison. Maclin stayed still, just hoping to ride it out. She took refuge in the silence. She found a sliver of solace in the fact that the three of them had no words for each other and were seemingly reluctant to interact in even the simplest of ways. The only thing Quincy and Phee commented on was how Shaka went out using his head. He knew to draw blood when things got rough. He left a trail that would hopefully lead them down the road to avenging him.

By the time they finally exited the building, the sun was dropping, but unfortunately the heat was holding steady. Maclin regretted it immediately when she made the mistake of inhaling the stench in the air that was now twice as strong. When she asked Phee to drop her at her hotel, there were no protests or attempts at persuading her to stay in New Jersey as had been the case just last night as well as two days ago. A few seconds later, Quincy said that he would be staying in the city as well. He called Elena and asked her to meet him back at their apartment without giving her any explanation. Phee just responded to their requests with a half-assed nod.

Even though it wasn't articulated, it was there all around them—the unspoken need to grieve on their own terms. They were all quiet on the short ride to the hotel. None of them knew what to say. There were no words to change the fact that not only had they missed their opportunity to make an arrest in one of the most frightening cases any of them had ever investigated, but more importantly they had all failed Shaka in the worst way possible. Though none of them could voice it, Maclin knew they needed the distance from each other because together their mutual guilt only feasted on itself at an alarming pace, threatening complete consumption. Quincy and Phee felt it also, Phee possibly the most. There were no dishonest pep talks. The heavy burden of truth left the three of them, each in their own way, sinking in the unfillable holes left by the loss of one of their own.

The three of them were racked with incredible pangs of guilt as they pulled up and parked in front of Maclin's hotel. Although the storm in her head had weakened, there still lingered the threat of the return of her migraine. Maclin remained quiet. In fact, they all just sat in the car in silence. Although she wanted to exit the vehicle—needed to— she was unable to move. When the quiet became much too jarring, Maclin finally spoke, offering up the desperation of a feckless lie that she felt they all needed to hold on to. "If they wanted him dead, then that's what we'd be looking at right now. There's still hope."

Although he didn't bother to look in her direction, Phee's flat intonation killed whatever fraudulent optimism she was earnestly trying to promote. His unwelcome truth cut her. Cut them all. Pierced them to their cores with a sobering finality. His simple words were an unintended coup de grâce that slayed them one by one.

"We've seen what these fuckers are capable of when they take their time. If he *is* still alive, that's probably the worst thing for him."

28

Both Spider and Ezra were struggling to stay awake. They alternated nodding in and out of consciousness. Spider could see Ezra fighting it as much as he was. Not that either one of them could offer much in the way of defense if their captors came to do further harm to them. However, both men wanted to know what was coming and when.

Spider looked up at the tiny piece of sky through the hole in the ceiling. Just a few feet away from the open space, there was an overweight pigeon perched on a beam, resting comfortably, looking down on the two men. Spider thought that unlike him and Ezra, the pudgy bird had what they could only wish for; freedom was still an option.

Based on the sunlight, Spider's best guess was that it was late in the afternoon. He was thankful that his injuries weren't the same as Ezra's. As horrific as it was losing his fingers, Spider thought, at least he still had his eyesight. He still had the power to behold things in the world like sunlight, portly birds, and even the hope of seeing his son's smile again. He was still alive. They were still alive. As much as he hated Ezra, he certainly hated their captors more.

"Don't make sense for both of us to try to stay awake when we can just take turns nappin'. Go 'head. I'll wake you up in about an hour," Spider offered.

Ezra didn't say anything in the way of accepting or rejecting the suggestion, but five minutes later the low rumble of him snoring was confirmation enough.

Spider kept himself awake by documenting the tiniest of details of their prison. He watched the shadows in the room expand in the afternoon sunlight. Dust particles slow-danced in the air, clinging to the golden rays of their spotlight. Spider smelled death in the room. He looked around until he spotted the carcass of the rat that had been wounded days earlier. There were a few flies now feasting on its corpse. A wolf spider crawled near the rat and the happy scavengers. The spider slowed as it came within a centimeter of an unsuspecting fly preoccupied with its abundant meal. There seemed to be contemplation and then the moment passed. The spider found its own spot on the carcass, joining in on the feast. The fly and spider were within touching distance but focused on a much greater offering.

When it was Ezra's turn to stay awake, he listened to the darkness. He deciphered the sounds that presented themselves. He still heard life in the old building. The wood occasionally whined as it swelled then shrank in the humid air. High above him he heard the coo and wing flaps of a pigeon that had somehow found its way into the building. Ezra heard flies buzzing in the room and the soft thudding of rats traveling inside the walls. The thing that he was most grateful for, though, was the sound that he didn't hear: he didn't hear human movement. There were no approaching footsteps echoing a prelude to another round of torture. He was safe, at least momentarily, with all that he heard and didn't hear. Death wasn't coming for him in that instant. It was just him and Spider.

Although he and Spider didn't agree on much, Ezra did think it was a good idea for the two of them to alternate when they slept. At least one of them always needed to be thinking of any potential ways to help with their predicament. The two men were at least in an unspoken understanding that they would hold on to hope with everything they had left in them.

Spider slept. He snored. He mumbled an incoherent conversation in his sleep. Save for a few desperate "no's," Ezra couldn't make out much else. He wasn't positive what haunted Spider, but he certainly had a good idea. Although the two of them were polar opposites in so many ways, Ezra started thinking of the tangible commonalities between them. They both breathed and bled and snored and tussled with demons that invaded their dreams. What if he and Spider were in fact not that different, at least on the things that mattered most? What if they were both just dutiful sons who idolized their fathers as well as being proud fathers who worshipped their sons. There was no exclusive claim over pride, love, and faith.

They were each public domain not delegated by color, gender, or religion. Ezra thought of the factual links between them. How they both carried within them the genes of slaves. They knew a little more intimately than most the scars of oppression. Even though they were raised in extremely different worlds, they now found themselves beaten, shackled, and completely at the mercy of a shared enemy.

Ezra tried waking Spider twenty minutes later, but his shouts were unheard under the heavy barrage of snores. He pounded the floor a few times with the chained heel of his foot. Spider woke with a start.

"What's wrong? What are they doing?"

"Nothing's wrong. I uhh… I just wanted to talk," Ezra clarified.

"Talk about what?"

"Stuff."

"What kind of stuff?"

There was hesitation on Ezra's part, his pause gravid with ambiguity. When he finally responded, his words spurted out with frail conviction. His voice was abstract, uncommitted to any specific emotion.

"Your nephew and what happened that night."

Ezra could hear Spider's shackles rattle, presumably as he sat up. There was even more of an awkward quiet that fell between them. A black hole filled with both contrition and anticipation.

Ezra finally blurted out what he was struggling to say: "I didn't touch your nephew the night he died."

"Yo man, I ain't tryin' to hear your same lies and bullshit."

Spider sounded disappointed—that after all he'd been through, he was still denied something as simple as the truth.

"Hear me out," Ezra pressed. "I didn't say that I didn't kill him. I said I didn't *touch* him."

"What the fuck is that supposed to mean?"

"I *wanted* to kill him. Trust me. I wanted it with everything in my being. I chased him like the animal that I thought he was. You say you want the truth, so I'm giving it to you. I was the first one to catch up to him. Couldn't have been more than a few inches away from him when he was trapped between us and the parkway. I was so close to him that all I had to do was just reach out and push— but I couldn't do it."

"You really expect me to believe that?"

"No, I don't. But whether you believe it or not, it's the truth. I really don't expect you to believe any of it. But that night I realized something that I'd been denying my entire adult life."

"And what's that?"

"I'm a coward. Have been since I was eighteen. I didn't push your nephew because I was too scared. I would have just been pushing myself because that night, in that moment, there wasn't a whole lot of difference between us. I know that might sound crazy to you, but it's not when you think of it in terms of fear and apathy. Because that's what I saw on him. That was the recognition. The thing that stopped me from pushing him. He probably saw the same on me. And if you were there, you would have seen it too. I know it's easier for you to pretend that you don't know what I'm talking about, but if you had looked at him hard enough you would have seen it, not just that night but a long time ago. I don't know you and can't even lay eyes on you. But I suspect it's on you as well. I didn't have to push your nephew that night in order to kill him. All I had to do was be all the ugly things he'd spent his life running from. I just had to be the hate, to be the man who didn't value him as the same. That was enough to make him run into traffic. Enough to kill him."

Spider stewed for a few seconds before speaking. "You can dress it up any way you want to, but at the end of the day you're the one who's responsible for him being killed."

"I accept that. But I wasn't the only one. *You* killed your nephew just as much as I did. Be honest. You brought him with you so you could teach him everything you knew about hating Jews. And I chased him with everything I knew about hating... niggers. Neither you nor I put a hand on him that night, but we both sure as hell pushed him in front of that car."

"Fuck you!"

Spider didn't think. He just surged forward. His anger adrenalized him. He didn't give his body time enough to think about weakness, dehydration, or fatigue. He charged at Ezra with everything he had until his shackle stopped him abruptly. Spider tried his hardest to get at Ezra, but his constrained leg kept him ten feet away. He saw Ezra scurry away with his own burst of energy.

Spider could see Ezra's silhouette quickly slide across the floor on his ass until he backed into a wall. There was only ten feet of separation between them. The fact that Spider couldn't get to him only incensed him more. He was breathing like an angry dragon, full of fire and rage.

Fifteen minutes later, after he finally calmed down, Spider discovered something: he had more fight left in him than he thought.

They didn't speak. They didn't sleep. They stayed on their respective sides of the room in mutual isolation. The earlier exertion drained them both and left them struggling to stay awake. It became an undeclared competition between them that neither wanted to be the weaker man who yielded to their lethargy first. Within the hour, they were both snoring loudly.

Ezra wasn't sure whether or not he was dreaming. He felt a stream of water being poured about his face and neck. Even though it wasn't cold, it felt good on his parched skin. It was the loud, drunken laughter that woke him. Someone was standing above him and urinating. He recognized the laugh immediately. It was the same heartless cackling he'd heard during his torture.

"Thought you might be a little thirsty," the voice said.

Ezra used the dirty sleeve of his shirt to wipe away the urine from his face. He suddenly felt the tip of a hard boot crashing into his rib cage. Ezra yelled and tried to suck back in the air that had been knocked out of him. The man put his face closer to Ezra's. "You need to be more appreciative. I own you; you understand that?"

Ezra got a pungent whiff of alcohol on the man's breath and felt flecks of spittle land on his face.

"Yes."

"Then let me hear you say it."

"You own me."

"So, if I decided it was time for me to end your useless life right now there ain't a damn thing you can do about it, is there?"

"Please don't…"

The man shouted, cutting him off, "Answer me!"

"No, there's nothing I can do about it."

The man grabbed Ezra by the throat. "Say it the way I wanna hear it."

Ezra coughed as the man released him. "If you decided it was time to end my useless life there's not a damn thing I can do about it."

"That's better." The man laughed as he crossed over to Spider. "What about you, my nigga? Whatchu got to say?"

Spider kept his eyes on the man standing over him. Almost daring him. Along with the surge of anger coursing through his veins, he felt a swell of energy. The man was five ten max, knocking on the door of a hundred and ninety pounds fully clothed, fully fed, and two pockets full of sand. He was a textbook skinhead, complete with the predictable buzz cut and hate art tattooed over his arms, neck, and what could be seen of his chest. Under normal circumstances, Spider had no doubt that he could have beaten the man senseless. The thought of having to kowtow and beg for his life meant swallowing a boulder-sized lump of pride.

It was counterintuitive to what growing up on the streets of Harlem had taught him. *Brothas don't take shit from nobody, especially not white boys. No matter what, don't ever get punked, 'cause once a bitch, always a bitch.* He had to think about his son and what was really at stake. All he had to do was bend to fight another day. The victory was in seeing his boy again. Nothing could get in the way of that. Spider had to keep reminding himself that prisons and cemeteries were disproportionately overflowing with brothas undone by pernicious pride.

He lowered his head in a subservient way.

"If you decided it was time to end my useless life there's not a fucking thing I could do about it."

The man kicked him twice, then spit on him. "Next time I ask you a question, don't take so long answering me. If it was up to me, I'd kill the two of you right now. But looks like I'm gonna have to wait one more day. At least that lets you think about how I'm gonna take my time and make it hurt."

The man pulled Shaka's silver medallion from his pocket and dangled it in front of Spider. He laughed at Spider's surprise.

"Yeah, your boy Shaka thought he could outsmart us. Did you know he was working with the cops? Shit, more than likely he's a cop himself."

Spider opened his mouth to protest but then thought better of it. Instead, he just sat there in shock.

"Cop or no cop, makes no difference—it all ends the same."

A much larger man appeared in the doorway. Spider put him at a solid two twenty to two thirty. Even though he stood hunched over from bad posture he was easily six three but not much more than that.

"We need to get on the road now if we're gonna get to the celebration on time," the big man said.

The smaller of the two men looked at his watch. "Yeah, you're right." As he crossed to the door he turned back and looked at Spider and Ezra. "You girls have fun tonight. If I was you, I'd find a way to make the most of it. We'll be seeing you tomorrow."

The door slamming closed echoed in the room. Spider and Ezra listened to the receding footsteps, followed by a door closing down the hall. Although there was still daylight, the scattered boom of premature fireworks could be heard off in the distance. As the city was warming up for the nighttime celebrations, Spider and Ezra sat silently in the old slaughterhouse. Their thoughts were both on the same thing: tomorrow was their end.

PART II

29

God outdid Himself. The bucolic village of Eagle's Hill was only two hours north of Manhattan, but it felt like a different world and different era entirely. From the natural springs and rolling hills to the 360-degree never-ending vistas, it was immediately clear why the tribe of Iroquois, the first to settle in the area, called it "the land of a thousand wonders." There were at least thirty shades of green from the various species of trees and ground cover outlining dozens of horse ranches and farms. The homes had big yards and the type of affordable acreage that made a man feel richer than the confines of his bank account.

Eagle's Hill was a valley of languid fields. It was Heaven without the dying part. A place where one could lie on their back and smell the fertile earth while touching drooping skies. Neighbors delighted each other with rumors of God winking down through the clouds at their chosen community, assuring them that their existence really was a part of a master plan. There were long stretches of pure silence, but when the wind swept across the water and got tangled in the branches of the great oaks, some folks believed that they could hear the distant laughter of angels at play. Here, reasonable men felt humbled by that which was greater than them. The population of Eagle's Hill was just under two thousand. The locals dubbed their quaint existence "Heaven by the Hudson."

It was a beautiful Fourth of July celebration that brought families from as far away as Pennsylvania, Connecticut, and Delaware, as well as the five boroughs of New York City. They came for the annual Heritage Pride Picnic sponsored by Ellis Brock, a retired, wealthy Wall Street trader turned part-time evangelical preacher. He owned 240 acres of good land and privacy. The event had started years before as a family reunion but quickly grew in size each year. It was by invite only, and only a few select locals were permitted to attend.

Ellis Brock loved the peals of children's laughter echoing through the valley. He stood by and took it all in: the chasing, the catching, the tumbling. There was kickball, apple bobbing, face painting, and even sack races. Parents were much more lenient and actually took small delights in the grass stains and dirt that covered their children's clothing. Fathers manned the grills as mothers and grandmothers piled plates high with smoked ribs, pork links, and barbecued chicken with potato salad and corn on the cob. It took two large picnic tables to hold all of the cakes, pies, and numerous other sweets. The event was a throwback to more innocent times, an environment where kids spent the day without a worry in the world. No video games or phones or computers of any kind were allowed, not even cameras. The kids used their imaginations to entertain themselves, and the parents used the day as confirmation of what America could be.

Just before sunset, Brock addressed the nearly two hundred people in attendance as he stood on a raised platform under a banner that read THE ALLIANCE FOR A BETTER TOMORROW. He was a tall man in his late fifties and carried a certain regality—not the kind that one is born with but the kind that was leased but never truly purchased. He was a rich man from humble beginnings—the son of a cobbler who now spent more money on a one-day picnic than his father ever made in a year. At six feet four, he cut quite an image with flour-white hair and sky-blue eyes framed by pink pigmentation in the corners and lower lids. He sported a Band-Aid on his neck to hide the scrape and cut he'd sustained in an earlier altercation. His skin was as pale as virgin snow and glowed still in the fading sunlight.

Ellis Brock was an albino—and a rather imposing one at that. The crowd silenced as he took the stage. From the youngest to the oldest, all eyes were on him. When Brock spoke, everyone listened.

"I love this country. My country. My father's country and his father's before him. Know your history, people. Our ancestors cultivated this land and developed the technology and created a nation of greatness. And each time the welfare of this nation was threatened, did we not rise to its defense? From the Civil War to the Gulf Wars, we are a people who rise to the defense of our nation.

"Well, I stand before you this evening to tell you that our glorious nation is in peril. Threatened with inevitable destruction. Destruction of the values and the morals that have become the very fiber of our existence. Destruction of our land and of our homes and of our dreams and of our future. Destruction of the dreams and the future of our children and our children's children's children. The greatest nation in the world, and we turn our backs on our farmers. We foreclose on the homes of our mothers and fathers. We steal the jobs from our most qualified. We undermine the potential of our best and our brightest. We... No, not we...*them*. The impotent liberal. The hypocritical conservative. All the puppet politicians. The soulless Jew. The amoral nigger. The parasitic immigrant and all the other innumerable undesirables that have infested this great land.

"These days they say it's not considered politically correct to denounce another group of people. Well, I'm here today to tell you that if being pro-Christian means that I'm anti-Semitic, then so be it. If being pro-white is anti-nigger, then so be it. In times of war, political correctness is an ineffective weapon. Don't be fooled, people; regardless of which puppet sleeps in the White House, these are most certainly times of war.

"I call upon each and every one of you to proudly defend all that we love. Onward, Christian soldiers, that we may eradicate the evil that is destroying our great country. Only then will we be able to create an ethno-state for all that is white, pure, and good. We must fight like the brave soldiers of the Phineas Priesthood. Let them call us what they want. The only title we need concern ourselves with being worthy of is the title of American. God bless America!"

All those assembled cheered loudly as they applauded. Even though the small children had no true comprehension of the context of Brock's speech, they followed the lead of their parents and grandparents and clapped enthusiastically. As Brock stepped down off the platform to a warm reception, bluegrass music began to play.

For the next hour or so the night air was filled with merriment. They danced. They laughed. They ate and drank all that they could. Daylight in Eagle's Hill was indescribably beautiful, but the nightfall was absolutely breathtaking. It was a place where there were far more stars than sky. The moon in all of its wondrous brightness hung low enough to give all who gazed upon it the optical illusion that it was in fact reachable. Touchable.

Fireworks lit up the night. It was all so very perfect. And still there was more entertainment to come. As Brock and sixty of his most trusted male followers stayed near the barn, the women, children, and even a handful of the newer male recruits were loaded and transported in open-wagon hay rides to a giant tent about a quarter of a mile away at the other end of Brock's property. There they were greeted by clowns, dancers, and men on stilts. Once inside the tent, they were treated to a life-sized puppet production of *David and Goliath*. Their eyes were aglow, awed by how realistic the wooden figures looked and moved.

Far from the laughter of the children, the main attraction for Brock and the sixty men who accompanied him started promptly at 9:30.

Shaka, whose head was completely covered and whose hands

were tied behind his back, was led out of the barn by three equally mammoth guards. The burlap sack that covered his head was soaked in a couple of areas with dark, red spots that shimmered under the light of the pale moon. Two of the three men who escorted him had scrapes and bruises on their faces as well, just enough confirmation that Shaka got off a few good blows of his own. Each time Shaka slowed, he was struck across his buttocks with an oak two-by-four as though he were an uncooperative field mule.

The crowd of men followed the foursome to the northwest corner of the property, just outside a large converted barn that served as a church. There, they assembled around a giant red oak that was at least two hundred years old. Its lowest branch was twelve feet high and three and a half feet in diameter. It was a good hanging tree.

As Shaka's hood was removed, all the men jeered him. One of his eyes was swollen shut, and streams of blood had left crimson streaks that looked painted beneath his nose and mouth. Not that it would have done much good, but he was unable to scream for help because behind his broken teeth his tongue had been burned useless with a branding iron. The coarse rope that was tightened around his neck scraped his skin like rolled sandpaper.

Shaka stood as tall as his injuries allowed. It was his final act of rebellion before the cruel mob. He didn't bend under the sentence of a grim fate. He was determined that he would at least coauthor his end by denying his enemies the thing they hungered for most: fear. He tried his best to look at them all with his one good eye. He singled them out in the crowd as much as he could, indicting them all on their *soullessness*.

Though muted and seemingly outdone, he was intent on taking a few casualties of his own. They would talk about him in years to come as the ghost who robbed them of tiny bits of peace. He would hold hostage their dreams with a hefty enough ransom to wake them with the reminder that they were unable to break him with their hatred as they had done so many before him. He kept staring, even as the rope choked him more and he felt his bare feet leave the earth, his soles still cooled from the evening dew. He kept his mind off of his woman and child because he knew those were the things that compromised a man most in the desperate moments just before his death. Instead, he thought of the trail he left behind. The trail that he was certain would lead Phee, Maclin, and Quincy to avenge his death.

As he was suspended six feet from the ground, his legs violently kicked for life, spasmodically dancing on air. He fought off death longer than any of the assembled thought humanly possible. Finally, when there was no fight left in him, Shaka stopped resisting. A lazy evening breeze whispered the vile echo of his neck snapping like winter kindling. The split second before his death his bowels released, causing some in the crowd to frown as though they were personally offended that his body failed him.

Ellis Brock, beaming with pride, stood front and center next to his thirteen-year-old son Ellis Brock, Jr. Although it wasn't the first lynching that the young boy had witnessed, it was still considered a rite of passage for him since he was pawing at the brink of manhood. He was being prepared for a future inheritance of hate and entitlement. Because he was his father's son, it was both his birthright and his duty.

Although at times he burned with disapproval, he was still obedient in all filial expectations. While Shaka's limp body swung back
and forth like a pendulum, Brock, Jr., flinched and tried to turn
away. Ellis Brock turned his son's head back in the direction of the
swinging corpse. Even though he hated his father for forcing him
to watch, he knew he was bound to honor him and play the part
of the dutiful heir.

Brock, Jr., thought the killing was senseless, nothing more
than savage sport. He heard snickers and the occasional pockets of
laughter coming from the crowd. Some even hurled unreceivable
insults at the dead man. The younger Brock stood transfixed at the
sight of the humongous tree and the swinging of its strange fruit.
The boy had seen other bodies hung. He'd borne witness to the
last bit of life seeping from scared black men. He had never seen
one like Shaka, not just in size but in resolve as well. Unlike all the
others, Shaka showed no signs of being afraid of death. Ellis Brock,
Jr., had been caught in his stare. It was a stare he would never
forget. He watched the body slow its swing until it came to a stop.
The thick and unmovable branch creaked just enough to make the
boy wonder if, even in death, Shaka might have some small victory
in breaking what had always been regarded as unbreakable.

Ellis Brock, Jr., thought of all the lives the tree had taken.
Those murdered even before his birth. He thought of the generations that had been cheaply traded for what amounted to a few
minutes of twisted delight for a voracious crowd. Although he was
regarded as nothing more than a young boy, he saw through his
father and the rest of the men who basked in the senselessness of

their violence. They were all pathetic and weak. He was certain of this even as his father pulled him closer and rested his large hand on his small shoulder. He knew his father beamed not just because of the day's events but because he was actually buoyed by the fact that he felt surrounded by what he saw as hard-working, faithful Christians who shared his vision of what America could be.

30

Shaka was dead.

Even though there was no physical evidence, Maclin knew. Through her entire career, she had been taught that nothing was conclusive in the absence of hard-core proof. Knowing what his abductors were capable of, Shaka's death was as certain to her as the unfathomable torture she assumed he endured. She had no material confirmation of his death, yet she was as convinced as she had ever been. Maclin knew Shaka was dead simply because the fragmented pieces in the center of her chest told her so.

Her room was a cool sixty-five degrees, with only occasional whiffs of the foulness that reeked in the streets and now buried itself in the pores of her clothes and skin as well. As soon as she entered, she started undressing as she went straight to the minibar and grabbed her third Coke of the day. The cold drink helped to cool the faint fire of a waning migraine. She stood naked in front of the mirror staring at old battle scars from long-forgotten wars, some professional and some recreational.

Her shower was longer and cooler than normal, and she didn't bother to dry off when she was done. As the fireworks boomed and lit up the night, she crossed to the window in hopes of catching a glimpse of the Fourth of July celebrations. She was wrapped in a towel, her hair wet and tickling her shoulders and upper back. As she pressed her face close to the window, the most she saw was a tiny piece of the sky glowing over the steady, distant thuds of exploding fireworks coming from the direction of the East River.

After the show ended an hour later, Maclin stayed by the window, tussling with thoughts of Shaka and the various roles he'd played. In just a matter of days he'd gone from perceived enemy to incredible ally to true martyr. She didn't know much about him, but she was nonetheless profoundly affected by his loss. She knew he had loved ones, a wife and daughter stashed away in New Haven. She knew he was dedicated to good and willing to make the ultimate sacrifice. As far as she was concerned, those were the most important things about him.

Maclin heard the fading echo of a drunken street quarrel falling off somewhere in the dark. She felt alone, accompanied only by loud thoughts and the quiet hum of the minibar. She still felt the weight of Shaka's impossibly big hands smothering hers as well as the vibrant laughter that shook his large frame. It was the tiny details about him that both saddened and uplifted her.

Maclin hated how useless she felt. She sent off a couple of

midnight emails to both colleagues and superiors at Quantico to see if they could assist in pressuring the New York branch to expedite the DNA testing of the blood samples even more.

She thought about Quincy and Phee and how they were managing their grief. They both had what she didn't: the comforting shoulder of a loved one. Phee in fact had multiple choices. Maclin wondered in such times of pain whether it was Brenda or Dolicia whom he held tightest, or whether he just alternated between the two, consoling himself amongst his embarrassment of riches. She envied Quincy and Phee on one hand and pitied them on the other. The very thing that fortified them simultaneously exposed them and left them weak. They had unconditional love, but they were also weighted with the hefty ransom that it demanded of them. She saw them as two honorable men forced into deception. Maclin wondered how each night when they made it home they were able to wear the masks and play their respective roles. How did they hide their fears and pretend to be what their loved ones needed them to be—strong and optimistic?

Even though they were two of the bravest men she'd ever met, the more she got to know them and their families, the more she saw love make cowards of them both. If the definition of a coward was a person whose every action and reaction was dictated by fear, then surely her partners fit the description. Every day that they went to work, Quincy and Phee heard and saw things that made them afraid. Each night that they returned home, they pretended to Elena, Brenda, Dolicia, and even a bit to themselves that the world was a little safer and that good always triumphed over evil.

Stronger than any lies they told themselves was the irrefutable truth that they were living in fearful times. Although her partners pretended to be more hopeful than she, Maclin knew that deep down—like all of those who fought on the front lines—the skepticism grew more on the debate over whether or not their efforts really mattered in the big scheme of things. They all saw on a daily basis the horrible things that man was capable of. Whatever lies her partners perpetuated to those they loved, there would always be certain cases that mired them all in the ugly truth. The Deggler case, or Zibik, and even the current evil that they hadn't yet identified left all who wore the badge questioning whether they were fighting a winless war.

Maclin had gone so long without the supplement of love that she was no longer clear on the muddled distinction between living and merely subsisting. It had become relatively easy for her to spend her days shielded by the diversions of work and denial. Her normal routines kept her busy enough to maintain the suppression. It was the nights, when she wrestled with a multitude of needs, that proved to be the more difficult challenge. The daytime tactics that she used to get from point A to point B were ineffective in the midnight hours. Her nights were much more honest than her days. She was humbled most when the quiet took hold and kept her from sleeping, and her truths were born in darkness.

A night of mourning Shaka stripped away her façade even more. She felt alone and empty. Because she had no one to help alleviate her pain, she opted for the much simpler task of satiating the carnal.

Maclin reached for her phone and dialed.

A man's groggy voice answered after three rings.

Losher was knocking at her hotel door at just past 2:15.

The preestablished rules of engagement were that there were no casual conversations until after sex. Kissing was only permitted if Maclin initiated it. Touching was never to be construed as tenderness. When she summoned him, it was for one purpose, which was to please her. Her pleasure was pain.

She was already naked when she greeted him at the door. She crossed back to the queen-sized four-poster bed and sat in its center as she watched him set down a medium-sized black satchel with drawstrings, then take off his jeans and a tight white V-neck tee that helped show off his obsession to fitness. His body did things to her. Uninhibited, primal things.

Her arousal was quick and base. She appreciated that Losher was always hard even before he got his underwear off. She leaned back and reached for her handcuffs, which were on the nightstand next to her gun. Losher rummaged through his bag but used his body to shield her from the things he took out. It was his ritual to tease her by not allowing her to see what kinky toys he'd brought with him to please her. He always fucked her imagination first, making her wonder which torture and ecstasy he had in store for her. She thought about how she loved the feel of his strong hands firmly wrapped around her neck squeezing pleasure and life from her as she toyed with death until she climaxed long and hard. She wondered if she would feel the sting of the tasseled whip or the firm clinch of the nipple clamps she enjoyed so much.

He stayed with his back to her a little longer than usual, which only made her more curious. More excitable. She had no idea if he would start slow and then incrementally increase her punishment, or if he would start like the last time they got together, when the first thing she felt was the aching thud of a studded leather paddle.

"Lie back and close your eyes," he ordered.

His deep voice was strong and resonated in the most erogenous parts of her body. Maclin rested her head on two pillows and obeyed his command. He finally crossed to her and blindfolded her with a satin sash. He cuffed her wrists to the head post, then secured her ankles to the footboard with two more sashes. She stretched her mouth open wide after he parted her lips and teeth with his fingers, then inserted a leather ball gag with a tight-fitting strap, which he attached behind her head.

Even though she lay in complete blindness, she could feel him step back, staring at her as though he was memorizing her body from head to toe. She listened for the shift in his breathing that let her know he was masturbating as he sometimes did after cuffing and blindfolding her. She got off on how desired he made her feel. That her just *being* turned him on.

He was quieter than normal. Maclin listened for it, but she couldn't hear the elevated breathing or even the rustling of his body moving closer to her. She lay spreadeagled on the bed, waiting.

And then he made her wait more.

Maclin waited for the pain to come. Her skin was aching for

it. She needed it to take her away from the hollowness she felt. Her mind needed rescuing from tragic thoughts of Shaka as well as the inevitability of her own plight.

So, she waited.

His delay both increased her arousal and simultaneously tortured her. Losher had gone off script. He was holding back the very things she needed. She couldn't speak, she couldn't see, and she could barely move. She was at his mercy and still he said nothing, did nothing. Maclin waited for blows that never came. Even though her body needed the liberation that she derived from pain, Losher seemed unwilling to oblige her.

She couldn't tell how long she waited. When the prolonged deprivation finally turned her arousal first into irritation, then anger, her body wriggled against her restraints while her cries of protestation were muffled by the gag ball. She bucked wildly in mutiny against whatever power he may have assumed he had over her. She continued fighting even after she tired herself out. The sheets beneath her were damp with her sweat, and the only sounds in the room were the minibar and the heavy sucking in and exhalation of air from her labored breathing.

The quietness was her anguish. She needed him to say something. Anything.

And still Losher waited.

By the time he finally touched her, she was caught off guard and her body twitched from the surprise. He ran his fingers the length of her inner thigh from knee to pelvis. His touch was much softer than she liked. The more she struggled against it, the more he exerted his will over her. The more she rebelled, the longer his strokes lingered. She fought the long, hard fight because she needed to remind him at every turn that she was indeed untamable. She exhausted herself until she had no struggle left in her.

Only after her body started cramping from fatigue did she finally stop resisting. Even when she had nothing left, she still held on to what little opposition she could. Losher waited her out until she accepted the futility of her efforts. He waited for the capitulation, the realization that she no longer controlled him. Her body was his to do whatever he wanted with.

Now that he was completely in control, Maclin was afraid of what he might take from her. When she was physically at her most helpless point, she wondered if him coming to her in her time of need was nothing more than a ruse. She trusted Losher and couldn't understand the sudden treachery. There was never any safe word between them because one was never needed. Even if there had been, she was now unable to scream it.

Losher lowered his face to hers and she could feel his warm breath on her as she smelled the faint remnants of mouthwash he'd used before coming to her. She could feel the stubble on his cheek against her soft flesh. It was a prickly caress with a coarseness that started arousing her despite her objections. She tried to pull away when he put his lips on her neck, but there was nowhere for her to go. As she lay cuffed and powerless beneath him, he began kissing her in previously unpermitted ways, knowing full well that she was staunchly opposed to whatever tenderness he offered.

Maclin tried to zone out, to shut her body down so that it

wouldn't respond to him—but he persisted. The act of foreplay became nothing less than a war of attrition between them, a war in which Losher outlasted her. She hated the fact that every time he put his lips on her he made her feel as though he were taking small parts of her, even though they were parts she no longer valued. Bits of the hidden, forgotten, and discarded. Undeterred by her resistance, he patiently waded through all the debris masquerading as indifference.

Losher endured.

In denying her the routine of their violence, the only thing she was left with was the softer side of his touch. He laid hands on her in ways he had never been allowed to before. Only after she had fully submitted did he give her the things she had lost the courage to claim.

Losher finally removed all the restraints and granted her the choice of fight, flight, or immersion. Her instincts were to move, to get up and kick him out for breaching the verbal contract she had dictated to him two years ago on the first night they had sex. She wanted to punish him for violating her trust and, in doing so, waking things in her that had been safely dormant for years. She wanted to—but she couldn't muster the will. Instead, she lay there offering herself to him like cornered prey. She spread her legs and pulled him inside of her. She felt a shift immediately after welcoming him in. It was a different type of equilibrium for her, one in which she no longer straddled what she had come to define as the thin line between love and decimation.

Long after the final fireworks had lit up the New York skyline in celebration of the fight and victory for independence, Maclin surrendered after losing her own battle. Losher proved himself to be more than a worthy adversary—simply because he loved her more than she loved herself.

After the surrendering and the reaping that followed, Maclin finally did what had of late become at best a sporadic event: she slept. Peacefully. Soundly. Heavy, uninterrupted sleep. Even deeper than the sleep she had enjoyed at Phee's house.

Her eyes were still closed, but she could feel the faint light of dawn on her face. As Losher's leg brushed against hers, Maclin thought about being too proud to ask him to stay but how pleased she was when he'd instinctively known that she needed him to.

She hadn't made love in years. She had of course had her fair share of survival sex and cathartic fucking, which for her was mostly of a violent nature. Although she had long ago convinced herself that it sustained her, it was nothing close to how Losher had left her feeling. She kept her eyes closed and thought back on the night. She could feel him studying her. She listened to inaudible whispers that sounded like he was either praying or counting to himself. When she finally opened her eyes and turned to face him, his head was propped against the headboard staring at her and counting to himself.

"What are you doing?" she asked.

"Trying to count the freckles on your arm," he answered.

"And how's that going for you?" she smiled.

"I was just finding my rhythm. I made it to 127 before you rolled over. Now I'm going to have to start again."

As Maclin laughed, her phone vibrated on the nightstand with an incoming call. As she reached for it and saw that it was Quincy, she immediately threw her legs to the side of the bed and sat with her back to Losher.

"Janet, they just found Shaka up in Harlem in Morningside Park. It's pretty bad."

Even though the news came as no real surprise, the actual confirmation still managed to leave her winded. She sighed or at least something like it and hung her head low. Wordless.

"Are you there?" Quincy asked.

"Yeah, I uhh… Did you call Phee?"

"Yeah. He's… Like I said, it's pretty bad. I'll pick you up at your hotel in fifteen."

Maclin didn't know if she managed a goodbye before hanging up. She just stared at the phone in her hand until Losher's getting out of bed reminded her that she wasn't alone. By the time she turned back toward him, he was already standing by the foot of the bed and slipping his jeans on.

"I've gotta…" Maclin started.

"I know," Losher cut her off.

"Look, I uhh… When this is all over, maybe we can talk then?"

"It's okay, Janet, we don't have to pretend anything here. Both of us needed last night for different reasons. It is what it is, and I get that," he responded.

"No, that wasn't the way I meant it. I'd really *like* to talk to you when this is all over," she said.

Losher heard something in her voice that he couldn't recall

ever hearing from her before: vulnerability. He studied her. He took in not just her nakedness but what he thought—actually, hoped—was exposure of a different kind.

"Sure, I'd like that too," Losher said then put on his T-shirt and sneakers and picked up his bag. Maclin trailed behind him as he crossed to the door. There was an awkward silence in the tiny entryway. They both fumbled with goodbyes that were laden with the dilemma of saying either too much or too little. Just before she closed the door behind him, she managed to say the one thing that she had wanted to tell him after his previous visit.

"For the record, you weren't the one who wasn't enough."

31

I t wasn't just bad; it was worse than bad. Much worse.

It was the kind of cruelty that only heartless men could dream up. The level of brutality reeked of hate and antiquity. It made no difference that it was New York, or even Harlem for that matter: Shaka's naked body dangling from a tree in Morningside Park was reminiscent of a good old-fashioned Alabama lynching. He had been castrated and his mouth stuffed with his own genitals.

In the hard angles of the morning light he seemed fake, more of a fabrication of a man than actual flesh and blood who had lived a real life filled with laughter, love, and aspirations. It was the only possible justification for such a senseless disregard of human life: somehow, he had to have been mistaken for a worthless inanimate object and therefore unqualified to be deemed a desecration.

Despite the fact that he now left behind a husbandless wife

who would be broken and swallowed in her mourning of him, as well as a fatherless daughter who was now sentenced to live her life consumed with questions related to the reasons and details of her father's tragic end, he could not have possibly been seen as human in the eyes of his executioners. He looked like he was hanging in effigy, put on display to remind all who saw him that America's dark and racist tendencies were still violently alive in the hearts of some.

By the time Quincy and Maclin showed up to the scene, Phee was already there. He had already cried. Though his eyes were still susceptible to more tears, he had graduated to a darker place. Maclin recognized the look immediately. She had seen it once before when his own brother was murdered. It was manic. Singular. Obsessive. The unis had cordoned off a forty-foot perimeter around the body by using yellow tape with bold black font declaring, "POLICE—DO NOT CROSS" tied to the trunks of bent oaks. It was a simple enough deterrent to keep potential spectators at bay, but there would be no control when Harlem was fully awake and came to see the horrors done to one of their own. A patrol car slowly approached and parked directly under Shaka's body.

"What the hell are they doing? They're compromising the scene!" Maclin was pissed.

As she made a move to intercept the uni getting out of the car, Phee stepped in front of her. "I ordered them to cut him down."

"We gotta run the scene, Phee, same as we always do," Quincy interjected.

"No, we gotta get him down as soon as possible. News crews

monitoring our radios will be here any minute. The witness who called it in said that Shaka wasn't here at five thirty when he started his run. It wasn't until he was jogging back twenty minutes later that he noticed him. Rigor has already set in. He's got lividity in his fingers and feet, not to mention secondary ligature marks that are much fresher than the original. He's been dead for a lot longer than an hour, and he sure as hell wasn't killed here. This is just for show, to get Harlem up in arms. We caught a break that we only have one witness. We gotta control him. The longer Shaka stays up there, more people will see him—which is exactly what whoever did this wants."

The uni who drove the cruiser stood on its hood and used a utility blade to cut the rope as three others lowered Shaka's large body to the ground. They stumbled but never fell. Even though Maclin stood just ten feet from Shaka's body, she couldn't bring herself to look at him. She refused to let the heinous things done to him be the lasting image of her brother in blue. The best cops were the objective ones; egos and feelings only got in the way. Over the course of her entire career, the Deggler investigation had been the only time that the case became more personal than professional. She'd been blinded by what she felt. It chewed at her a little each day until eventually it devolved into ravenous consumption. She breathed it. She ate it. She dreamed it.

As she turned away from Shaka's corpse, like Phee she could feel a darkness taking hold of her. It wasn't exactly the same thing she'd felt when Deggler killed her fiancé, but it was close enough for her to recognize: Maclin felt rage.

She wondered how obvious it was. Phee and Quincy were much too busy grappling with their own feelings about Shaka's death to notice her descent. She saw Phee staring at the witness, a heavyset brotha in a Brooklyn Nets jersey filming the scene on his cell phone.

"We gotta do something about the witness. Erase whatever's been recorded. Grab the phone if we have to," Phee said.

"On what basis?" Maclin asked.

"On the basis of trying to keep this city from imploding," Phee responded.

"I get it, but we still can't violate his rights like that," Maclin countered.

"The hell we can't," Phee snapped back. "Whether we like it or not, we all know we ain't gonna stop this thing by playin' by the rules."

"The rules are all we've got, Phee." Maclin refused to back down.

"Yeah, well whether that's true or not, Harlem ain't burnin' down today. Not on my watch. We already know that people are ready to start random kills if we don't hurry up and locate Spider and Ezra. What do you think people up here will do if they find out Shaka was lynched? We gotta run this as a John Doe suicide."

"Phee's right, Janet." Quincy finally spoke up. "I don't know if we can stop this war that's being started, but I do know that we have to at least do whatever it takes to delay it as much as possible. If Shaka's death is one of the things that finally tear this city apart, then he died for everything he hated and not what he loved. We owe him more than that. Phee, do what you need to do. Just try to keep it on the DL as much as possible."

Phee nodded and glanced at Maclin, who just stared back at him in obvious disapproval. As Maclin and Quincy watched Phee walk over to the man with the cell and pulled him away from the officer who was taking his statement, Maclin turned to Quincy.

"It's right around the time that we start cherry-picking which laws to protect that we need to ask ourselves whether we've already lost the war."

"I don't disagree with you, but unfortunately wars are never that simple. My first day on the job I had this old-school field-training officer who'd seen it all at least once and done it all at least twice. He told me the hardest day in a cop's life was the day he'd have to make a decision on whether he can live with sacrificing the needs of the masses for his code of ethics or sacrificing his code of ethics for the needs of the masses. We're wading in very murky waters, Janet. Believe me, I get it."

Maclin's phone vibrated as Quincy's words tumbled in her head.

"Is this Agent Maclin?" the male voice on the other end asked.

"Yes, it is," Maclin answered.

"I'm Agent Michael Danvers. I work at the lab here in New York, and I was told to give you a call as soon as we had something. We ran the samples you requested from yesterday's crime scene through the CODUS DNA data bank and got a hit on a con recently released from Attica. His full file is still downloading; you should have it in five."

"Thanks, Agent Danvers. By the way, what'd you do—pull an all-nighter?"

"Yes, ma'am, those were the orders."

"Orders or not, I owe you. Thanks again."

The surveillance van smelled of Doritos, stale coffee, and indecipherable meat. The air-conditioning was temperamental at best: it burned for twenty minutes, then puttered for twenty. It was the only thing available out of the One-Nine under such short notice.

Dyker Heights, a middle-class Brooklyn enclave better known during the holiday season as "the King of Christmas Lights," was a small suburb that was considered one of the safest neighborhoods in all of New York. Maclin, Quincy, Phee, Burns, and Bobby Skia were all packed into the hull of the van, which was parked across the street from a two-story, single-family Tudor. The four men looked over Maclin's shoulder as she sat in front of a bay of three monitors pecking away at a laptop. She pulled up a mug shot and rap sheet as well as the suspect's Army record. His neck was a collage of crude prison tats and Aryan symbols.

"Darren Lyles. Twenty-nine, six five, two hundred and seventy-nine pounds. Served a year in Afghanistan but was dishonorably discharged from the Army for assaulting an African American superior in '09. He's been affiliated with at least four known hate groups but just short stretches in each of them. Three prison sentences since his stint in the Army, mostly for agg assault. He was just released from Attica, where he was a guest for the last eighteen months. He did seven of those months off and on in solitary confinement."

"We pinged him here from the number he has registered with his PO. This is also the address he has listed on file. We got any deets on the house?" Burns asked.

Maclin pulled up a photo of a middle-aged blond. "Belongs to a girlfriend, Maggie Squiero, forty-two. Husband died three years ago. Comes from money. Seems like she's on some bored rich girl trip. She may have started off as a prison pen pal. Based on what little we can gather on her, she comes off more like a sympathizer and white pride tourist than hard-core member. Lyles picked a good one. He comes out of prison living like a prince with a sugar queen."

"So how do we wanna move on him?" Bobby Skia asked.

Quincy continued reading over Maclin's shoulder. "Hard and smart. There's a good chance that we only get one shot."

"Copy. He's Army and did seven months in solitary in the Terror Dome, which means he might not be easy to break," Burns added.

Maclin continued pulling up info on the monitor. "I ran him through Lexis-Nexis and Faces of the Nation on all family and known associates. Both parents are deceased. There's an older brother, Cameron Lyles. Pulled him up, but didn't come back with much other than he and his brother have always been pretty close, which is reason enough to look a little deeper. No record. Actually did a year in med school but dropped out after two semesters. On paper, Cameron is clean, but take a look at his DMV photo. The tattoo on his neck. Can't see the whole thing, but does that look like the top of two zeros or two eights just beneath his collar?"

Quincy bent over to get a closer look. "Can you blow it up?"

Maclin hit the keyboard a couple of times, magnifying the photo. "This is the best I can do before it starts pixelating."

Quincy stood up straight. "Can't say for certain, but I'd bet the farm that those aren't two zeros and that it's the number eighty-eight."

"I'd have to agree with Quincy," Phee said as he looked closer at the photo.

Maclin clicked back on Darren's mug shots. "Okay, we'll look deeper into Cameron, but right now let's focus on Darren. What we do know for certain is that aside from his brother, our boy Darren is a loner and an outcast. The intel analyst gave us his school profile and even his sealed juvie records. He's been in and out of trouble since he was eleven, when he was remanded into a psych evaluation facility due to his violent behavior tendencies. He's definitely not the sharpest knife in the drawer—low IQ and hot temper. My gut is, he's nothing more than muscle, a foot soldier in this whole thing. I don't see him as smart enough to have orchestrated everything and managed to stay five steps ahead of us. We need the brains behind all of this if we really want to stop it," Maclin responded.

"So what's the move?" Bobby Skia asked.

"Well, let's play it out. If he really is a badass, what do we do if we roll on him full force and he decides to go out swinging on some kamikaze, suicide-by-cop shit? Even if we bring him in, there's no guarantee we get him to talk. His people then know that we're at the very least circling them. Does that make them escalate even sooner?" Phee speculated.

Quincy picked up as soon as Phee finished. "We can't afford to just sit on him, 'cause who knows what these bad actors are planning next?"

"A real fuckin' conundrum," Burns lamented.

"What if we tickle the wire and let him know we're coming for him? Maybe he runs in the direction that we need him to. Even if he doesn't, we got a track and trace on his phone, so we just need him to make contact," Bobby Skia proposed.

Quincy mulled it over and then shook his head. "That's too big a gamble. If they're on burners, we end up with jack. I say we take him in and take our chances on breaking him for useful intel. I'm not crazy about any of our options, but this seems like our best play."

There were collective nods from the team.

Maclin stood up. "Burns, you got a taser?"

"I've got a little bit of everything in my trunk."

"Good. We get in any kind of standoff situation, don't hesitate to hit him with it."

"Copy that," Burns responded as he put two fresh sticks of gum in his mouth.

The five cops checked their weapons and grabbed their vests.

Maclin finished putting on her vest as she continued laying out their approach. "Burns, you and Detective Skia take the side and back. Quincy and Phee will come through the front with me. Even if it all goes south, under no circumstances do we shoot to kill."

As everyone started heading out, Maclin and Phee were the last two in the van. She kept her voice low when she spoke to him.

"I know you're running hot on what happened to Shaka—we all are. But Lyles does us no good if he's dead."

"That's much more on him than me," Phee responded as he grabbed the battering ram and exited the van.

They were damp with sweat even before they made it to the stairs. Maclin and Quincy posted up on either side of the front door as Phee came straight up the center swinging the ram back as far as he could, then smashed the front door open with such force that he almost took it off its hinges.

"NYPD! We have a warrant!" Quincy shouted out.

They came in loud, hard, and strong with the clear objective of disorienting and instilling fear.

Two seconds later there was a crash from the rear of the house, followed by Burns bellowing the same battle cry.

The couple, who had been sprawled out on the living room sofa naked and wet from a midmorning tryst, immediately jumped up, startled. Darren was tall, thick, and cut—body by Pen, as in penitentiary. Dozens of tattoos illustrated most of his body. The largest of them were the five block letters AFABT across his chest. The "T" at the end of the acronym was in the shape of a cross with a drop of blood at its base.

Darren snatched up a 9mm from the nearby coffee table as Maggie grabbed a nearby throw to cover herself as she stood in front of him.

"Put your gun down," Maclin said at an even keel.

"Fuck you!" Darren spit back at her.

"Considering that I can see what you're working with, I'm going to have to take a pass. Once again: put your gun down."

"Ma'am, step away from him," Quincy commanded.

"Leave him alone! He hasn't done anything!" Maggie yelled.

"Step away from him now, ma'am!!!" Quincy repeated.

Burns inched a little closer, trying to get a better shot with the taser. The team formed a semicircle around the couple, essentially boxing them into a corner. Maggie stared at the five weapons aimed in their direction and started breathing hard, on the verge of hyperventilating. Just as she took a step forward, Darren grabbed her by the hair and snatched her back toward him, putting her in between himself and the weapons pointed at him. "Stay right here."

"Darren, what are you doing? You're hurting me. You can't beat them, but I can get you the best lawyer there is," Maggie pleaded.

"Shut the fuck up! You said you were down with the fight. You don't get to walk out now."

Maclin took a half step forward as the voice of calm and reason. "Listen to her, Darren. That's the only way we all walk out of here."

"No, the only way we all walk out of here is if you back the hell up before I pop this bitch!"

Maggie started crying and pleading with Darren.

Phee stepped to his side, trying to get just enough of an angle to get a clean shot.

"That's not gonna happen. Now you need to put the gun down before we put you down," Phee warned.

As Darren adjusted his body to shield it from Phee, he exposed himself a little more to Burns and Quincy, who were on the opposite side. Maggie's constant squirming compromised a clean shot for Burns.

Maclin, seeing that Darren was becoming increasingly more agitated, slowly lowered her gun.

"Everybody, we all need to just take a sec and breathe before we all do something that we can't undo. Darren, just listen to me. You help us out—just give us a little information—and we can help you out."

"I said back the fuck off! I ain't no snitchin' bitch, and I damn sure ain't being put back in no cage," he yelled.

Darren pulled Maggie back to the corner of the room and put his back against the two walls. Since he was more than a foot taller than she, he wrapped his free arm around her midsection and picked her up to make her a more effective shield.

"Well then, we got a problem," Phee said, trying to get Darren to face him, which would expose him more to Burns.

"Yeah, you do got a problem 'cause if you ain't out this house in ten seconds, I'm doin' this bitch right in front of you. Her blood is on your hands."

Maggie's crying eyes went wide. Even greater than the fear etched on her face was the wounded look of betrayal. She was all tears and snot. In the midst of her repeated cries of "Why?" she added a few "But I love yous."

Maclin raised her hand to her team. "Everybody stand down."

"But Agent Maclin?" Bobby Skia kept his weapon pointed at Darren but looked at her.

"I said stand down!"

Bobby Skia and Burns looked at Quincy, then followed his lead as he lowered his weapon. Phee kept his weapon on Darren.

"Phee, I need you to lower your weapon," Maclin insisted.

"I lower mine when he lowers his. We've shown him enough goodwill, now he needs to show us some by letting the woman go," Phee responded.

The team members each played their part, ranging from the obedient to the reluctant to the defiant. The command was a ruse to help deescalate a spiraling situation. Veteran cops knew to feign resistance to make it all feel more credible. A team leader ordering their team to stand down in a dangerous hostage situation was code for *Lower your weapon but if the offender offers up a clean target, hopefully woundable, take it.*

"He's got a point, Darren. Show us some goodwill and let her go, so we can talk this whole thing out," Maclin said.

"We ain't got shit to talk about. You think I'm scared to die? I ain't. One dies. Twenty rise. My daddy didn't raise no bitches. I'm good to die for what I believe in. Are you?"

"Nobody here needs to die. That's not what you want, and that's certainly not why we're here." Maclin remained calm.

"You're wasting your time and your bullshit speeches. Don't try and handle me. You ain't the one that's in control here. I am. You can't stop us, and you sure as hell can't beat us. You got ten seconds to get the hell outta here, or I swear I'm gonna do her."

Every time Darren referenced Maggie, she squirmed with a new jolt of fear. She whimpered like a scared pup. She was laid low by how little she knew the man she thought she loved.

"You know we can't leave," Maclin tried to reason.

"Well then, have it your way." It took Darren less than a second to take Maggie's life with a shot to the back of her head. He still used her lifeless body as a shield, only offering up small targets. Maclin and Quincy both hit the massive arm he had wrapped around Maggie's torso. Bobby Skia winged him in the side. Phee took out his legs with a shot to the shin. The big man fell awkwardly, still clutching his gun with Maggie's body on top of him. As the team moved in closer, Darren made contact with Maclin and offered up something close to a smile.

"Put it down! Drop your weapon!!!" Maclin shouted.

"You don't get the privilege," he said just before swallowing the barrel of his weapon and pulling the trigger.

32

They tore Maggie's house apart but failed to find any game changers to the investigation. Nothing hidden in the backs of closets or the bottoms of drawers. Techs found nothing of significance on the two cell phones, desktop, or laptop that they went through. Maclin came across a two-page program for the Lord's Blood Church. There was no address or contact number, just a boring table of contents of the previous week's service. The only thing of substance that was found were ten unopened burners in an office cabinet. The find only complicated the case, because the takeaway was that whatever group they were tracking was thorough enough to constantly switch to untraceable phones.

Maclin and the team had nothing of value to report to their superiors. The progress they had hoped to make now lay scattered amongst the ruins of Darren Lyle's suicide.

It was rare to see all the bosses at a crime scene that didn't involve a fallen cop. They came out to Dyker Heights in full force: Quincy's and Phee's boss Captain Whedon, Burns's and Bobby Skia's boss Captain Danny Winslow, along with the chief of patrol, chief of Ds and the police commissioner, followed by the mayor's right hand. Maclin even got a call from her boss in Quantico. No one was happy. There were no outright admonishments, but the flat tones in their voices and looks of disappointment were reprimand enough. The only real lead in the case had blown his head off and taken a semi-innocent woman with him. Even though everything had been done by the book, the fact that there were no gains in the case rendered everything else moot.

Maclin and team would have preferred a proper dressing down. You don't make it as a cop without having thick skin. Having their asses occasionally handed to them went with the job. Getting chewed out only lasted so long. Anger came with expiration, but fear felt eternal. Although some of the superiors attempted to mask it more than others, there was fear in abundance. Every misstep brought them that much closer to losing the city. New York was about to detonate, and yet every move they made was ineffective at stopping it. They were left holding nothing but the inevitability of things to come as the day was getting hotter and the fuse was getting shorter.

What Maclin saw in the eyes of the brass was the worst thing cops could ever show: defeat.

She watched the bosses as they walked to their separate cars, on cell phones calling whoever bosses call when shit rolling downhill turns into an avalanche. Maclin stood on the lawn wiping sweat from her brow as the coroner's crew wheeled out Darren's body. Quincy and Phee joined her first, then came Burns and Bobby Skia. Although no one voiced the question of *what next*, it was apparent that it was the only thing that everyone was thinking.

Maclin finally looked up at the team. "Quincy, reach out to Kravitz and let him know we're on our way and I'll call him from the van, but in the meantime he's not to touch Darren's body, and tell him to notify the brother. Phee, I need you to do what you do best."

"What's that?" Phee asked.

"Piss somebody off."

Victims of violent deaths were always granted every effort at making them more presentable to the loved ones who came to claim them. It was not just the professional thing to do; it was the humane thing. The desperate times/desperate measures equation left Maclin recalculating the burden of her humanity. She got an earful from Kravitz when she called him from the car to clarify that there were to be absolutely no such efforts made on Darren Lyles's behalf. Kravitz reminded her that in all his years of service to New York, he had never done anything as reprehensible as what she was asking of him. It went against every ounce of professional pride he had. He let her know in no uncertain terms that it was bad enough how overwhelmed he and his team were from the piling up of bodies; now she was asking him to break unofficial vows of his craft? When she'd heard enough, Maclin cut him off by clarifying their respective roles in the case and the different demands it made on them. He served the dead, and she served the living. End of conversation.

Maclin, along with Quincy and Phee, came through the doors of the morgue midconversation with a little steam in their stride. They were completely caught off guard by the sight of a dark brown woman with flowing dreads who wept inconsolably over the body of Shaka. Maclin immediately noticed the wedding ring. The only thing that interrupted the woman's cries were the tiny pecks she planted on his cheeks, lips, and forehead as though she were trying to kiss him back to life. Even in devastation, she was a sista of dignity. A weeping lioness mourning the loss of her king. She was much too preoccupied with her grieving to notice the trio. Still, they seemed stuck in place trying to decide whether they should stay or leave. Although neither of them knew her name, there were still sufficient grounds for kinship. She had after all married herself into the tribe of blue.

Without the slightest hint of warning, the three were pierced by the bloodcurdling shriek that bounced off the walls and sent shivers through them. Maclin felt her heart breaking all over again. She wanted to comfort Shaka's woman and assure her that his death wasn't in vain. That no matter what it took, he would be properly avenged. She chose instead to respect the privacy of a bereaving wife. Maclin looked at Phee and Quincy, and the three of them quietly tipped back out of the room.

Even though they all knew that Shaka was dead long before seeing him strung up in the park, the visual confirmation left them a bit unhinged. Maclin could see how differently the three of them processed their pain. Phee's anger was fed. Quincy's fear was eating him. She was an equal combination of the two. They were all so obsessed with finding Shaka's murderers that they hadn't been afforded the luxury of peace to properly mourn him.

Waiting outside the doors of the morgue, listening to the excruciating wails of his wife seemed to hit—actually, more like stab—them all at the same time. They bled in the hall and then they cried. They cried for a man they hardly knew, an adoptee who believed in the job as much as they did. They cried for the new brother they'd lost.

Quincy leaned against a wall with his chin to his chest. Phee turned his back to his partners as though he were trying to hide his tears, but it was obvious that the crush of losing a blue sibling had overtaken him. Maclin sat on a long wooden bench and wept openly at the crescendo of earsplitting screeches slipping through walls and doors too weak to incarcerate the pain of a bereaved wife.

She couldn't remember the last time she'd prayed. Or even attempted to. She mumbled a few words but stopped because she wasn't sure which would be the more compassionate of her two Gods. Judaism was the religion of her childhood, while Christianity was her occasional go-to as an adult. At best, she teetered on the fringe of two faiths, which placed her in the precarious position of being unfaithful to both. Now that she wanted to beg God to ease the pain of Shaka's widow, she questioned whether or not she was qualified to ask Him for anything.

The one time in her life that she'd felt the most connected to God and/or religion was when she was a small child and attended the temple of her mother's lap. She could still remember having her hair brushed by her mother as she sang sweet *zemiros* to her and quoted favorite passages from the Torah. Although Maclin was never one to broadcast her Jewish roots, unlike her father and brothers she at least never denied them. She may not have considered herself religious, but it was what she saw as their sins of self-loathing to the point of apostasy that greatly contributed to her distancing herself from them.

Maclin could count on three fingers the times that she had actually attended a proper Jewish service after her mother's death. She knew the Bible more than she knew the Torah—the slight distinction was that she had committed to memory three passages from the Bible and only two from the Torah. The more Shaka's wife's voice echoed in her head, the more one brief passage in particular came to mind:

"Any man who has caused a Jewish soul to perish has caused a whole world to perish."

Shaka wasn't Jewish, but Maclin hoped the God of Abraham wasn't a god of semantics. In mourning him, she mourned the world that perished with him. He was a good man who paid the ultimate price trying to do more good. She bowed her head and prayed to the God of her mother. Surely, no just God would value a righteous man any less because of a minor technicality. Although she may have not considered her soul to be the most qualified for mercy, Shaka's had to be.

Ten minutes later after they had somewhat collected themselves, Shaka's wife exited the double doors that led to the hallway. Maclin introduced herself as well as Quincy, who approached the two women. Phee kept his distance—because of guilt, Maclin assumed. After expressing her condolences and hugging the woman, who was named Ghana, Maclin held her hand and whispered something in her ear. Ghana wiped her flooded eyes, attempted something of a polite smile, and thanked Maclin before walking off.

Darren Lyles was wheeled in on a gurney, still cocooned in his body bag. Once he was removed he was placed in the center of the room. He had a gaping exit wound in the top of his head: clumps of pinkish brain matter sprinkled with shards of skull. The hole was the size of a tangerine and gave the illusion that one could actually see the last thoughts on his mind. The right side of his face was swollen and distorted in a way that made him look like a Halloween mask. Other than removing Darren's clothes by cutting them away, Kravitz couldn't touch him, not even to shield the wound in anticipation of their expected visitor. He wasn't even allowed to wash the heavy streaks of black-cherry-colored dried blood that covered half of Darren's face. Maclin was adamant that nothing was to be done that in any way made him more presentable. She was unmoved by Kravitz's repeated declaration that the morgue was supposed to be a room of unconditional compassion.

He had no idea how deep her compassion ran. Although it was boundless, it was most certainly not without conditions. As she glanced over at Shaka's body, which was less than ten feet away, she felt herself drowning in a sea of it; when she looked back at Darren, she couldn't muster enough to fill a thimble. She was perfectly fine with the fact that between the two men, her compassion was directed at the only one who was deserving of it.

She thought about the fact that although they could not have been further apart on the matters that defined them, they were now sharing the same room in the same morgue on the same day. Maclin thought it ironic that in life the two men had been separated by hate, race, and ideology. Now they were separated by not much more than the length of a gurney. Even though she had conflicting thoughts on the existence of Heaven and Hell, she was crystal clear in her hope that the soul of Darren Lyles burned for the rest of eternity.

Maclin got a text from Detective Burns, then nodded at Quincy and Phee.

"He's here."

A few minutes later, Darren's older brother Cameron Lyles came through the doors of the morgue. Cameron was roughly thirty pounds heavier and an inch or two taller than his brother. He was a tree—a sequoia to be exact. He was easily six feet seven, with broad branches for arms and a trunk of a torso. His tight tank top showcased years of obsessive gym work. His muscles were redundant.

The second Maclin saw him, she knew he was dirty. In Maclin's eyes, people were either civilians or offenders. Cameron was no civilian. He was grade-A white supremacist. A 283-pound canvas of unadulterated bigotry, he wore his hatred with pride. She could see that Phee felt it too by the way he tensed and slowed his breathing like a lion in high grass waiting to pounce. Maclin didn't know if it was the heat, or the fact that Cameron left in haste to claim his brother's remains, or simply that he gave less than two fucks, but he showed up having made no attempt at covering the collage of offensive tattoos that adorned his upper body.

He was obviously addicted to ink. As far as Maclin could tell, there were more tattoos on him than virgin skin. He had the same block letters—AFABT—that Darren had. And like his brother's, the last letter was a "T" in the shape of a cross with a drop of blood at its base. The only difference was that Cameron's was on his right shoulder instead of his chest. There were swastikas, SS initials, twin lightning bolts, and other popular Nazi insignia. Maclin saw the fully exposed number 88 tattooed on his neck, which in the world of white supremacists was the numerical representation of the letters HH, which in turn was synonymous with Heil Hitler.

Any second-guessing she had about whether her orders to Kravitz had gone too far disappeared. It was the purple bruise and abrasions on his cheek, presumably souvenirs left behind by Shaka, that filled her even more with anger and mercilessness. She wanted Cameron to bleed the same way she, Quincy, and Phee had when they saw Shaka hanging from a tree. She needed his heart to break into tiny bits of agony. Her goal was simple enough: get him to feel the way she and her partners felt—demolished. If they got that much from him, then it was worth everything, even the forfeiture of basic decency.

Cameron was only a few feet into the room when she saw the water in his eyes tipping their lids and wetting his cheeks. He stopped midstride and buckled, pulling up five feet short of Darren's body, unable to turn away. Even though he had walked in alone, Maclin could easily see the specter of hate that walked beside him like a conjoined twin. She wondered if Phee and Quincy saw it as personified as she did.

Cameron looked bitter. Confused. Cheated, even. Younger brothers were not supposed to be buried by elder kin. Cameron didn't move; he just stared at his brother as if he were standing over the body of a mythical god that had been assumed to be impervious to death. Maclin could see him struggling to compute the fact that Darren was undeniably human and was now nothing more than a corpse with a huge hole in his head. When she saw what she needed to see—the brokenness—she assembled just enough composure to sidestep her instant loathing for him and move in his direction.

"Mr. Lyles."

His eyes were still glued to Darren. If he heard her, he gave no indication. His body trembled a little every time he inhaled. His head hung so low that from her angle he looked neckless. He tried to move closer to his brother, but his feet seemed rooted in place. The best he could do was sway. Cameron was a big man who became woefully smaller by the second.

Maclin waited for her opening, for him to sink deeper. She waited for the right moment to exploit the liability of his sorrow. For him to be reduced to crumbs. When he started to cry she felt nothing. Her only concern was opportunity. Maybe it was one of the lowest of blows—grief interrupted. She gave less than two fucks.

She spoke again a little louder. "Mr. Lyles, I'm FBI Agent Janet Maclin. I was wondering if I could talk to you about your brother."

When he finally looked at her, it was with alternating incredulity and contempt.

As he opened his mouth, only one blurred word stumbled out. "What?"

"Unfortunately, your brother's suicide has compromised our investigation. We believe he was involved with others who…"

He found his voice and cut her with it. "Are you fucking kidding me? You wanna stand over my brother's still-warm body and talk to me about compromising some bullshit investigation and who he hung out with? You don't even have the decency to show some fucking respect or even offer condolences."

Phee jumped in. "She didn't offer because you don't deserve it. I mean, let's keep it real—your brother was a piece of shit, and you don't smell much better."

Cameron's entire body tightened. His swollen veins bulged beneath the skin. His face was flushed a darker shade of rage. He was instantly an angry bull who grunted and advanced toward Phee and Quincy, who stood their ground. Phee didn't blink.

He rested his hand on his weapon and spoke calmly. "Bring it. There's plenty of room in here for you to join your brother."

Maclin saw Cameron do the quick math: three cops, three guns. Even though he was on the verge of going full apoplectic, he had enough sense to recognize the ramifications of being outnumbered and outgunned. He pulled up three feet in front of Phee. As Cameron stood seething before them and contemplating his next move, Maclin wondered if he had the same suicidal tendencies as his younger brother.

Phee's voice was calm as he pressed more. "Just so you know that I'm not some insensitive asshole, I kinda feel for you and your brother. I mean, for all his belief in white power and supremacy, your brother knew at the end of his insignificant existence that I, a black man, held the real power over him—the way you'll come to realize the same thing the moment just before I end you."

Maclin saw the effort, the furious restraint in Cameron. The deliberate rearrangement of his scowl into a grin. He then started laughing. Although it was strained, he did it long enough until it turned into something real.

"You really think I don't know what you're trying to do? You're not even good at it. It's not your fault. We both know what you are. A gun and a badge doesn't change a fuckin' thing. Once an animal, always an animal. You ever wanna handle this—I can't even say man-to-man because that's only a half-truth—but if you ever wanna step to me when you're not hiding behind being a cop, you just let me know. My father ain't raise no bitches."

Phee smiled at him. "That's the same bullshit your brother tried to claim before he blew a hole in his head. Funny thing is, a couple of my boys who are CO's up in Attica who knew your brother told me how he would intentionally get into trouble so that they'd throw his punk ass in solitary confinement to avoid gen pop—because the first week he got there, a couple of brothas pulled a train on him. Probably didn't get around to telling you about that, did he? So technically speaking, your father raised a helluva bitch. As far as you go, there's only one of two ways I see it playing out. Either I end up putting you down or, if you're lucky, you get to spend the rest of your miserable life ass-up for a bunch of brothas who like to nut up to the sight of a bloodied swastika. Either way, you're fucked. You should leave now."

"I have a right to be here with my brother."

"The only rights you have are the ones I decide to give you. You've ID'd him and you have nothing to help us with our investigation, and we still have to process the body. So there's no need for you to be here anymore."

Cameron made no attempt to move. He just stood staring at Phee, unblinking.

Quincy took a step closer to his partner. Maclin unsnapped her weapon's holster, keeping her hand on her waist next to her gun. Phee made a subtle gesture as though he were waving off both Maclin and Quincy. He took two steps closer to Cameron, stopping just inches away. Although Cameron towered over him, Phee had no fear. When he spoke, it was quiet and deliberate. "We're done!"

Cameron sized up both Phee and the unwinnable situation he found himself in. He stared back at Phee for a long, hard beat before finally responding.

"Not by a long shot. *Brotha.*"

Cameron walked back over to Darren's body, squeezed his hand, and muttered, "I got you."

He then walked out without looking back.

33

Maclin didn't understand why they weren't moving faster. She hurried out into the hall of the morgue thirty seconds after Cameron left. When she turned around, she was surprised that neither Quincy nor Phee was right behind her. As they walked toward her, she was confused by their seeming lack of urgency. By the time they joined her in the hall, Phee was on his phone to Bobby Skia. "He's on his way out."

"If we're going to tail him, we have to move," Maclin said.

"We're good, Janet. Let's give him a five-minute lead," Quincy responded.

"In five minutes, we won't even know where he is."

"It's cool; we got it handled," Phee said, hanging up the phone.

"What does that mean?" she asked.

"We've got a lock on him."

"How?"

"I'm not sure you wanna know."

"I'm pretty certain I do."

"While Asshole was in here, I had Skia and Burns plant some ears and a tracking device in his car. They duct-taped an open burner under his seat."

"What are you talking about? We don't have a warrant for that."

"I know we don't—that's why I didn't tell you. We get any blowback on this, it's on me. I'll take the heat."

Maclin was dumbfounded. "So, Quincy, I'm assuming you knew about this."

"Of course I did. Phee and I are on the same page. We knew you wouldn't agree, so we wanted to give you plausible deniability."

Maclin exploded. "I don't give a damn about deniability! But what I *do* care about is that we're straight up with each other. Do the two of you understand that?"

Phee faced off with her. "Yeah, we understand it—we heard you twice the first time. You wanna be straight up, how's this? You need to back up what you told the mayor earlier— or was that just a pretty speech? Whatever the fuck it takes to put these assholes down, I'm willing to do. Quincy's willing to do. Even Burns and Skia. You know I got mad respect for you, but you're willing to allow yourself to be handcuffed by rules that will only keep us ten yards behind. That may work for you despite everything that's at stake, but as long as you know, nothing is gonna stop us from saving this city. Not even you, Janet. If that means I burn, then so be it. We all looked into both of those motherfuckas' eyes and saw nothin' but evil. I'm not going home and looking at my daughter and my woman knowing that I had a chance and I didn't do everything I could, right or wrong, to stop that evil that I know will one day come for them. So, I'm willing to lose my job, my name—shit, even my life if I have to—to stop that. You might not know how far *you're* willing to go to end this, but the rest of us are crystal clear."

"You don't think I want to stop them as badly as you do?"

"He didn't say that, Janet," Quincy jumped in.

"Well that's exactly what it sounded like. You want clarity, Phee? Well how about this: neither one of you gets to stand here and dismiss how much I want to put these assholes away just because I don't want us to end up compromised. If we have to put these animals down, fine, so be it. If we lock them up, then I want them to stay there forever. I damn sure don't want to run the risk of them getting off on some technicality because we thought we were above the law or decided it was okay to be sloppy cops. We stop them, we stop them the right way."

Phee looked at her, much more calm and deliberate. "Us doing *whatever* we need to do *is* the right way. We play strictly by the rules on this one, we lose by the rules. We've got a good tail to follow. You're welcome to come or not."

Phee turned and walked off. Quincy hesitated for a second or two, looked at Maclin as if he had more to say, but then turned abruptly and followed Phee.

It was hard to tell if it was hotter outside or inside the van. The air-conditioning was still on an ill-timed sabbatical. Hot air circulated through the whining vents, making the van a hot box on wheels. Maclin was the last one in. The residual tension between her and Phee cooled things a bit, but not in any way that was useful. She, Quincy, and Phee settled in around the surveillance equipment in the back. Bobby Skia, who was at the wheel, took off as soon as the door was closed. Burns followed closely behind in an older model Crown Vic that at least had a slightly better air-conditioning situation.

Bobby Skia looked back over his shoulder. "Whatever you did, Phee, you sure as hell poked the bear. He started making calls as soon as he got in the car. We caught a break—he used speaker-phone, so we got both sides of the convo. Hit the playback button on the bay."

As Quincy pressed the button, the sound of a phone ringing was amplified through the van's speakers.

After three rings, a voice answered: "Hello."

"It's me," Cameron said.

"I'm assuming you're on a burner."

"Of course I am."

"How did it go? You holding up okay?"

"I want these fuckin' cops to bleed for what they did to my brother. Especially this nigger detective who, I swear to God, I'm smokin' before the sun goes down."

The voice on the other end was firm. Commanding.

"Listen to me. I know you're emotional right now, but we all have to stay focused. We're too close to getting what we want to stray from the script. You can take all the revenge you can handle after tomorrow. But right now, I need you to stick with the plan."

Cameron tried to interrupt. "But…"

"No buts! Stick with the plan. Do you understand me?"

There was silence.

"I said do you understand me?"

"Yeah."

"Let me hear you say it."

"I understand you."

"Good. Send Wallis and Jesse up to the spot, and kill the nigger and the Jew and plant them like we talked about. While the cops are chasing their tails, it's time for us to start putting all the pieces into play. Meet the rest of us upstate. Make sure you're not being followed."

"I'm good. I'll see you in two hours."

The team listened as Cameron hung up the first call then immediately made a second call. The voice that answered was monotone and had the dull drone of a worker bee who simply did what was demanded.

"Yeah?"

"I need you and Jesse to head to the meat plant and take out the garbage. Kill 'em both. Do it as soon as possible. Cut the Jew and dump his body in Harlem near Umoja, then call it in. Burn the nigger and leave him at the temple. Make it look like payback."

"Jesse's out in Queens with no ride."

"Tell him to take the subway, and meet him at the station. He should be able to get there in forty."

"Will do. I'll call you when it's done."

After Cameron hung up, hard rock music blasted from the car stereo.

"Those were the only two calls he made," Bobby Skia said.

Phee had a habit of cracking his knuckles one by one when he was nervous or deep in thought. In this moment, it was hard to tell which one he was experiencing.

"They have to be talking about Ezra Pearl and Spider. What if we run Lexis-Nexis to see if there are cross-references and if any known associates named Wallis or Jesse pop up?" Quincy suggested.

"Cameron doesn't have a record. We don't have that kind of intel on him," Maclin shot back.

"I'm not talking about Cameron. His brother Darren would have known them as well."

"Even if we did find the connect, we've only got forty minutes. We can't ping their phones because they all use burners—not to mention we can't get any kind of warrant because everything we've heard, everything we know, has been illegally obtained. No judge is signing off on that. This is not an I-told-you-so moment, but we're on our own. They're going to kill Ezra Pearl and Spider, and there's not a damn thing we can do about it."

Phee finally spoke: "Skia, let Burns know we need his car. The two of you stay on Cameron, but use the tracker to keep a mile back. He'll be checkin' for you."

He then turned back to Maclin and Quincy. "We may have one shot. I ain't gonna lie. It's a helluva Hail Mary—but it's all we got."

34

Just like the hordes of animals that came before them, they waited in fear for the slaughter to come.

With each passing hour, the room seemed to get smaller, morphing into a tomb where animals and unfortunate men came to die. Spider Harris couldn't escape the irony of ending up at Hozinger's, a childhood breeding ground for ludicrous urban legends. When he was a boy, he spun twisted tales of mutilated children whose remains were supposedly found in the lunch meat and hot dogs that he and his friends enjoyed so much. Spider terrorized the other boys with threats of bringing them to the slaughterhouse and locking them in amongst the doomed creatures. He embellished the story by telling them if they listened hard enough on a still night in Harlem, the unanswered cries of stolen black boys could be heard coming from the Bronx.

Thirty years after the last of the livestock was butchered and the doors of the slaughterhouse were closed forever, a slightly altered but equally horrifying version of his nightmare came back to haunt him. While he waited in the dark, bathed in heat and silence, humbled in the company of his enemy, he started thinking of his regrets.

He lamented the fact that aside from history books, he'd never read enough. Traveled enough. That for all his self-proclaimed black consciousness, his feet had never touched the dark soil of his ancestors. He had never kissed Africa. He had never seen the world beyond the myopic lens of his own bigotries.

Malcolm X had always been his childhood idol. Spider randomly thought about Malcolm's spiritual renovation after his famous pilgrimage to Mecca, when he renamed himself El-Hajj Malik El-Shabazz. A black Muslim who left Harlem, only to return transmogrified into a global spiritualist and a much more woke revolutionist. Spider now felt like he had failed his hero because he had become nothing more than a misguided soldier who never quite comprehended the war he was fighting. Unlike Malcolm, Spider had to accept the fact that he merely played the role of the wannabe revolutionist and now was forced to question whether his life had been, for the most part, fraudulent. He knew that if given the time, he would have found a way to make his family and people proud; but the encroachment of death put an end to the fruition of potential. All that he would take to the grave was a world of unrealized possibilities.

His father often grumbled that one of the worst things a black man could be was some "self-pitying, coulda/woulda been nigga," blaming all but himself for his failures. He'd also once told him, "A man's distorted truths in the course of his life are much less faithful on the eve of his death." His father was right on both accounts.

Spider no longer had a need to bend truths to conform to his narrative. He now saw things in a much different light. They were much more illuminated to him. Truth and light were inseparable. He saw even the simplest of things with vivid clarity. He stared through the shadows at the faded redbrick walls that would be the last to confine him. The concrete floor was the last thing that he would feel beneath him. The smells, though sickening, would be the last he inhaled. The stale taste of fear would be the last meal he consumed. He wondered if he screamed whether the sound of his voice—even if reduced to a wounded whisper—would miraculously make its way back to his beloved Harlem. He wanted at least some part of him, no matter how obscure, to live on in the streets, alleys, parks, buildings, and people whom he loved so much.

He wondered now if he had it wrong. Instead of pitying Ezra as he did earlier, he now questioned whether or not he should envy him. The Jew was better off than he because when death came for them in all its vicious fury, his blindness would at least spare him the visual horror of a violent demise. They would die not with the dignity afforded most men but unceremoniously, with the lowness of beasts.

Ezra Pearl was fresh out of hate. Amongst the clutter of fear, regret, and seeping hope, there simply was no room left in him for something that now felt so banal. He'd always taken for granted that when death came, it would find him retired and nestled in the bosom of Mother Israel. He saw himself dying as an old holy man, a warrior, and a hero of his people. He'd always assumed that at the end of his long and fruitful journey, he would be revered as the author of a purposeful life. He wanted most of all to have lived a life that did the motherland proud by upholding his responsibility as a "good Jew" in protecting the safety and well-being, not just of his generation but also of their progeny.

Ezra Pearl knew he was a good man, his loathing of the blacks notwithstanding. After all, it was justifiable, or so he'd convinced himself; animals were never to be judged by the same standards as men. Especially men of the Chosen People. Ezra Pearl knew hate, both intimately and historically. When Egypt was still young, he'd felt the sufferings of persecution that his forefathers endured, even though he was nothing more than mist in the universe. As the world wrestled with its humanity, he'd cried at least six million tears, decades before his conception. He knew anti-Semitism long before his arrival. He ingested a steady dose of it in embryo. When he came into the world and suckled his mother's teat, he choked at times on the bitter sorrow he tasted in her milk.

He knew all about bigotry. Prejudice. Anti-Semitism. Bias. Xenophobia. He knew all too well the tired tropes of preconceived hatred. Even though the knowledge in his DNA went back thousands of years and should have filled him with compassion and insight, he still managed to leave enough room for the ogre of racism to occupy the hollowest corner of his heart.

Ezra Pearl never saw God so clearly as he did after losing his sight. In the darkest moment of his life, his instincts still led him to surrender to faith rather than despair. Though he may not have felt he deserved it, he knew that HaShem, the God of Abraham, was a forgiving God. Despite the staggering bleakness, the abundant fear, deliverance was still real. That was, after all, the cornerstone of Judaism. Even when all was lost, there still existed the unbreakable thread between God and man. All his life, Ezra had been taught to never think in terms of what was possible or impossible—because all that really existed was God's will.

Even though there was just a sliver of light in the room, Spider saw Ezra gently rocking with his head bowed. It all started quiet, voiceless, nothing more than an over-sibilant whisper. At first Spider wasn't sure what his cellmate was doing, but after a while Ezra's words became incrementally clearer. He was praying.

"...and I beseech you, HaShem, to forgive me for my sins as I beg my brother to forgive me for the trespasses that I've made against him. Protect and deliver us from any further evil while you strengthen us with your mercy. Give us both the confidence of faith, for all things are with you. Amen."

When he finished, the room was quiet again—at least for twenty seconds or so, before Spider started laughing.

Ezra turned his head in the direction of the laughter. "You mind if I ask what's so funny?"

"I was just thinking that you're the first person that I know of besides my mother to ever pray for my black ass."

"Well, I didn't exactly describe you to God that way, but if you think that's more accurate... Dear Lord, please protect Spider's black ass along with my not-so-black ass."

Spider laughed, then Ezra followed suit. Spider laughed harder and then so did Ezra. Both men seemed to welcome the amnesty of it all. A few precious seconds of peace. It wasn't much, but even the most fragile of truces carried at least a single seed of possibility.

After the laughter faded, Spider asked, "So you really think God is gonna get us outta this?"

"His will is invincible if we believe."

"Look, I ain't really into the whole God thing. So even though that kind of thinking may work for you, what I believe is that the only way we get outta here is if we make it happen ourselves."

Ezra thought before he spoke. He needed to circumnavigate the tenuous negotiations of a temporary ceasefire. The peace between them was at best inchoate, still fragile in its infancy. It was certainly not the time for sermons or attempted conversions of nonbelievers. Not the time for alienation.

"I just choose to believe that God will show us a way," Ezra said.

"You mean the same God that put us here in the first place?"

When Ezra didn't respond, Spider pressed the matter. "That's my point. If he's all omnipotent, then that means he's responsible for every fucked-up thing that happens as well as the supposed miracles. Can't have it both ways, brotha. So you can stay on your knees praying to who-really-knows-what, but I'm going out fightin'—'cause that's what *I* believe in. If we do end up making it out of here, you can call it God or whatever you want to, but bottom line is we either fight together or die together. It's on you."

Ezra listened to Spider. It wasn't much of a plan, but considering how dire their situation was, it was the most they'd had since their abduction.

They waited. They didn't know if it was an hour or two or three. It was a long, nonnegotiable wait. They tried not to be swallowed in the shadows by their fear and imagination. It helped when they focused on the things that meant the most to them: another chance to see the ones they cared about and who cared about them. Harlem and Brooklyn, Africa and Israel. The laughter of their children and the embraces from all who loved them. Both men wanted to live more than anything. That primal desire nourished them. Strengthened them. Depluralized them. It robbed them of ego as well as the luxury of discord. The only thing that really mattered was a singular purpose. There was no room left for anything else.

They heard the clanking sound of a metal door opening somewhere in the distance, followed by the ricochet of heavy footsteps. Then came the jangle of keys and the muffled voices of two men in conversation coming toward them. Spider was standing. He had been doing so for the last five minutes, feeling the blood circulating in his legs. Summoning in them whatever strength he could. He'd heard of panicked mothers lifting cars to save their children. That's what he hoped for, that his fear would empower him and remind his legs of what they were capable of.

He wasn't expecting the impossible. He didn't even need them to be the legs of his youth. As long as they didn't fail him, he stood a tiny chance of living. He was too weak for anything prolonged. Spider had felt his anger energize him earlier. That's exactly what he needed now, a well-timed burst of adrenaline. Thirty seconds. He would win or lose in thirty seconds. Live or die. Everything depended on his legs. He had no God to turn to. No miracles to cower and beg for. Ezra had his God, and Spider had his legs. All he needed was a couple of lucky breaks for things to fall his way. As far as he was concerned, luck trumped God every time.

Ezra prayed for strength. He thought about the story of Samson and how he begged God to grant him enough fortitude to destroy his enemies in his one last hurrah. Ezra didn't need the power of Samson—just enough stamina to hold on and not let go. Ten, twenty, thirty seconds, however long it took.

Spider told him he had to hold on with everything he had. If they worked together, they stood at least a minute chance. Unlike Spider, he had never been an athlete; so if he was going to be successful, he was definitely going to need God's help. His eyes still burned, and darkness was all around him. He tried in vain to slow the heart palpitations that increased with every outside footstep as they got closer. Thump, thump. Thump, thump. Thump, thump. His heart didn't simply beat: it bounced in his chest, sending reverberations throughout his entire body.

He sat shirtless on the floor following Spider's instructions. Ezra's skin was slick with sweat, and he could smell the squalor in the room as well as what was coming from him directly.

When the footsteps were still about forty feet away, Spider sat back down on his side of the room and started arguing loudly.

"You're a fucking liar! He didn't do nothin', and you killed him anyway."

"I didn't kill anyone! It was an accident. He ran because he knew he was up to no good," Ezra yelled back.

"Even if he did what you said, he still didn't deserve to be murdered by a bunch of fuckin' racist-ass Jews."

The door suddenly opened and the two men from earlier stepped inside. Spider continued arguing with Ezra.

"He was my nephew!" Spider yelled.

"Hey!" Wallis, the smaller of the two men, hollered. "Shut the fuck up!!!"

As the light from the hall poured into the room, Spider peeped at them and saw that they each carried a machete; but fortunately he saw no signs of guns. He'd survived two knife fights in his life, but he'd never had to try to take on a gun. If Spider had his full strength and the use of his hands, he'd give them both a run for their money; but since he only had his legs, he needed Ezra to do his part.

"Before he dies, this piece of shit needs to admit that he killed my nephew," Spider demanded.

"Didn't he tell you to shut up?" Jesse, the taller man, stepped in Spider's direction.

Spider was unrelenting in his plea. "Look, I know you're gonna kill us. I ain't even trippin' on that anymore 'cause I ain't scared to die," he lied. "I'm just askin' you—beggin' you—do whatever the fuck you wanna do to me, but just let me kill him first. What difference does it make to you? Dead is dead."

"You don't get to ask for shit. How many times do we have to tell you to *shut the fuck up?*" Wallis crossed over to Spider and was just about to kick him when Jesse stopped him.

"Leave him alone. He's right—what difference does it make to us if they kill each other? But how do you plan on killin' somebody when you only got half your hands?"

"I got my legs and feet—that's all I need," Spider responded.

"Shit, this should be fun," Wallis laughed. "As long as you know this doesn't change anything: whichever one of you is left standing still dies."

"I know that. I just need him to admit he killed my nephew." Spider stood. He saw the machetes resting at their sides, the blades flickering in the afternoon sunlight that peeked through the door behind them. There on the walls he saw more clearly the row of rusted meat hooks that were securely embedded into the four walls. The hooks were three feet apart from each other and almost seven feet from the floor. Although he couldn't see them all, Spider estimated that there were twelve hooks in total, at three per wall. He didn't know much about slaughterhouses, but he knew enough to deduce that they were in a bleeding room. The place where gutted carcasses were hung on hooks and bled dry. He now knew why the floor was uneven and sloped toward the large drain in the center of the room.

Jesse crossed to Spider and unlocked the shackles that bound him. He then crossed to Ezra and did the same. Spider watched as both men rested their hands on the hilt of their machetes. Ezra resisted when the man pulled him to his feet.

He protested loudly, "This is not right! Please don't do this. I didn't kill anyone. It's not too late to let me go. I don't even know what you look like. I swear I won't say a word. Please. Don't do this."

Wallis turned to Spider. "You got five minutes. Better make it count before you die."

Spider exaggerated his weakness and exhaustion even more. He wobbled in Ezra's direction and threw a halfhearted kick that just missed its mark. The second kick landed but not with much force; still, Ezra helped sell it by stumbling backward a couple of feet.

The two guards laughed.

Ezra used the sound of their laughter as a chime to let him know of their exact position. He circled just in front of them, pretending that he was trying to avoid Spider's menace.

"If that's all you got in you, I might as well kill him for you and just get it over with," Wallis said.

"No, he's all mine," Spider objected.

Ezra twisted and turned his body toward the sounds in the room, his ears his only weapon. He listened for direction from Spider. He had no choice but to trust the language they'd developed for their plan to work. Any number mentioned in a sentence informed him how many steps to take. *Ahead* meant to move forward and *behind* meant to move back. The three cue words that they came up with told him exactly what to do and when to do it. *Nephew* meant move to the left. The word *racist* meant to move to the right. When Ezra heard the word *Jew*, he knew it was an order to charge and grab.

All he could do was listen and act as instructed. Spider was not only his eyes but his hope as well. In the latter regard, both men were equally reliant upon the other. Never in a million years could either one of them have imagined that he would ever be so dependent upon an enemy who now wore the mask of an ally.

For the most part, Spider pulled his kicks and took a little steam off of them, but he made sure they in no way looked fake. He grunted a little just before each attack, which allowed Ezra to tense his body to better absorb the impact.

"If I could kill you three times I would, you racist piece of shit!"

"Hey, if you're gonna kill him, then kill him. Fuck all the talk," Jesse said.

Spider stumbled toward Ezra but didn't put him down when he kicked him in the back of his quads. Ezra recovered and took three steps to his right. Spider was trying to line him up perfectly with the smaller of the two men to give Ezra a fighting chance. Unfortunately, the men took a couple of steps back as Ezra got closer to them. Spider now had to improvise. He positioned himself between Ezra and the men.

"My nephew had his whole future to look forward to, and you and those other eight bastards took that from him!"

"Enough with all the talk! You don't wanna kill him, I will!" Wallis yelled.

"No! The Jew is *mine!*" Spider shouted the cue to Ezra. Just as Wallis took a step closer, Spider turned quickly and delivered a full-force roundhouse kick to the groin, which immediately keeled him over and made him drop his weapon.

At that point, everything happened simultaneously. Ezra followed Spider's voice to his target with his arms outstretched before him. He only needed to take seven quick steps forward before he collided with the bent-over body. He found the man's neck and hooked his arm around it from behind and squeezed with everything he had.

Even as they toppled backward, Ezra held on and wouldn't let go. As soon as Spider kicked Wallis, he saw Jesse raising his machete. Spider bent at the waist, lowered his shoulders and bull-rushed him, driving his adversary back the way he had done so often in his younger years as a linebacker. He wrapped his arms around the larger man's waist and kept pushing him backward. Even when the man brought his machete down on Spider's back and the blade parted his skin like soft butter, the searing pain didn't stop his legs. They just kept moving forward.

When Spider felt that he was a few feet from the door, he used what strength he had left to wrap his arms even tighter around the man's hips and lift him off the ground by about eight inches. They crashed into the wall with full force.

"*Arrrhhhhh!*" Jesse's yell filled the room.

There was a loud clank of the machete hitting the concrete floor. Spider could feel that the man was no longer resisting him. Instead his body twitched in violent tremors as he stuck to the wall. His feet dangled several inches above the floor. A rusted meat hook impaled him, suspending him in the air like the thousands of slaughtered animals of so many yesteryears.

When Spider stepped back, his body was spent. He could feel the burn of his wound and a warm trail of blood running down his back. All that he asked of his legs was that they not fail him—and they didn't. He followed the daylight through the half-opened door and stumbled toward it.

Even though he heard Ezra calling for him, pleading for his help, Spider exited without looking back. He didn't owe the Jew anything. His only debt was to himself and making sure that what little energy he still had left was saved for his own survival and not wasted on a man who, at the end of the day, was still his enemy. He was certain that if the situation had been reversed, Ezra would have abandoned him as well. Each man's fate was now in his own hands. Spider had done his part. The only thing that mattered now was that each step he took he was that much closer to freedom.

Ezra should have known that blacks weren't to be trusted. Spider never came for him, never answered his pleas. He and Wallis were still in their grappling match, their movements slow and deliberate. They looked like two overturned turtles piled atop each other. Ezra was on his back on the bottom and, even though his arm was still firmly wrapped around Wallis's neck, he could feel his strength being depleted.

Wallis pawed at him but was unable to grab hold of his sweaty skin, just like Spider had said. Unfortunately, it was a short and insignificant victory. Ezra felt the sharp pain of two elbow blows landing in succession on the side of his stomach, which momentarily emptied the air in his lungs.

And just like that, Wallis was on top of him, punching him about the face, then choking him. Ezra struggled, but Wallis was the stronger of the two. Wallis repeatedly kneed him in his ribs until there was the distinct sound of something breaking and Ezra yelled out in pain. Wallis then straddled him and put his knees on Ezra's forearms, successfully pinning him down in a helpless position.

"You fuckin' piece of shit! You get to die hard, and then I'm gonna track down that nigger and do the same."

Ezra was done. He couldn't even muster enough strength to resist. As Wallis's grip tightened even more around his neck, Ezra's airway narrowed and he felt his life being squeezed out of him. As he lay dying he thought of three things: his soon-to-be-fatherless son, his would-be sonless father, and finally the Almighty Father of all men. If his death was God's will, then Ezra was taking with him the final conviction that at least his parting was not in vain. Ezra lived by faith; he was now ready to die by it as well.

The thought of seeing his son again fueled Spider more than anything else. It carried him forward, even though his body was weak. He kept his mind on his boy and grew more determined to make sure that he was around to help mold his son's future. Among other things, he thought about the type of man he hoped he would grow up to be. Like most fathers, he wanted his son to be honorable. He wanted him to be a man of unimpeachable rectitude. Someone who was ethically fearless. He wanted his son to be a better warrior than he had been. At the very least, he needed his son to know which wars were truly worth fighting and which convictions were still worth dying for.

There was no explanation. Certainly not one that made sense. His legs, ever so faithful, now betrayed him with a mind of their own. His feet carried him, not by his will but rather by their own.

They carried him back to the very place he was trying to escape.

Although he couldn't rationalize it, he still wasn't ready to concede that it had to be the omnipotence of a God he no longer gave power to.

Spider was weary and weak, but he still hoped he had something left in his legs. As he stood in the doorway and saw Wallis sitting on top of and choking a motionless Ezra, he knew he was too late. His fear had caused him to break his word—enemy or not—and Ezra had lost his life as a result of it.

Spider felt the rage swell inside him so much that he feared it would lift him off his feet. He snuck up from behind and surprised Wallis with a vicious kick to the side of his head that not only knocked him off Ezra but also busted his ear drum in the process.

Once he had him dazed, Spider stomped him twice, once in the chest and once in the face. Both men collapsed, one from his injuries and the other from sheer exhaustion. Unfortunately, Spider couldn't finish him off because he couldn't move.

He had absolutely nothing left. His muscles were jelly. Sweat dripped from him as if he had been hosed down with it. His legs were now immovable beams that were impossible to lift. His arms were numbed from dehydration. Even breathing was a formidable challenge. It all collided—the exertion, the lack of water and food, and the loss of blood from the nasty slash on his back all conspired to defeat him.

Just a few feet away from him, Wallis moaned in pain. Spider knew it wasn't over. It wouldn't truly end until one of them was dead. The final outcome depended on which one of them recovered first. Even though he tried his hardest to will himself up, his body refused to move. There was nothing he could do to reverse the fact that he was temporarily paralyzed with fatigue. As he lay there, sentenced to a helpless stillness, he found the answer to why, against all logic, he had returned.

Three of the most memorable things Spider ever heard were the countless *I love you*s from his mother, the bold cries of his son entering the world, and now the sound of Ezra coughing his way back to life.

Spider was still too weak to lift his head; all he could do was turn it to the side facing Ezra's direction. They lay less than ten feet from each other, both on their backs, trying to recover.

"I can't move," Spider confessed.

"Neither can I," Ezra responded. "I thought you had left me."

"Me too."

"So why'd you come back?"

"If I ever figure it out, I'll let you know."

The two men laughed. Nothing hard or loud—neither had the energy for it—but it was an earned laugh nonetheless. When it subsided, Spider heard rustling and turned his head in the direction opposite from Ezra to see Wallis army-crawling away from them. Spider's eyes widened once he realized that Wallis was dragging himself in the direction of the discarded machetes just twelve feet from him.

"Ezra, listen to me. You gotta get up. You gotta get up now!" Spider commanded. Ezra tried his hardest but he too was in pretty bad shape. Not only was he weak and exhausted, his cracked ribs made any movement on his part terribly painful.

"Get up, Ezra. Follow my voice. He's trying to grab the blade."

Ezra tried to do as he was told. When he couldn't lift himself, Spider yelled, "Crawl!" As Ezra yelled out in pain from movement, Wallis's pace started picking up as though he were getting stronger the closer he got to the weapon. Spider, who was still between the two men, realized that it was all too late. There was no way Ezra could get to the machete first, and neither one of them would be able to stop their would-be killer. Ezra had only made it as far as Spider's legs before he ran out of what little energy he had.

Wallis grabbed the handle of the machete then rested for a beat. Both sides were quiet. There was only the sound of the three men breathing heavily. It was a most peculiar impasse. Fates were now decided and roles were cast. One would kill and two would be killed. As Wallis struggled to his feet with the machete in his hand, Spider looked at Ezra and spoke. His tone was plain, conciliatory to a degree. "Hey brotha, we went out fightin', ain't no shame in our game."

He tried his best to hide the fear in his voice so that they could die with at least some semblance of both victory and dignity.

Ezra returned the effort, "No shame at all."

Wallis staggered toward them, his equilibrium still fucked up from the busted eardrum. Blood streaked down the right side of his jaw onto his neck, then shoulder. He reached Spider first. As he hovered over him, he swayed. It took quite a bit of effort for him to raise the weapon up to his shoulder, but he used gravity to do the rest.

As Wallis brought the machete down, Spider instinctively put up the stub of his hand to shield his face. The blade sliced his palm down to the bone. Spider yelled in pain. Ezra yelled in anguish. Wallis grew stronger by the second, bolstered by the sheer defenselessness of his enemies. He raised the machete high above his head. High enough to sever flesh and bone. High enough to split Spider in half. Spider no longer resisted. He chose to no longer fight. Instead, he lay there, blinded by his own sweat, the salt burning his eyes. His vision was so foggy that all he could make out was the faint silhouette of Wallis above him. Spider didn't need the full faculties of his sight to know that death had come to claim him. In his final seconds, he thought about the son he would never see again.

If there was such a thing as God, he hoped his mother would be on the other side to welcome him. He surrendered to the peace of accepting his fate. There was still a triumph of sorts to be had: his final act of defiance was that even though he would be killed like an animal, he could still at least die like a man.

There was a muffled yell, followed by a violent noise. The sound jolted Spider. It was the sound of death echoing off the walls. As he wiped his eyes, he could just make out Wallis's fallen body, facedown on the ground beside him. Spider saw the blurred image of three people standing near the doorway. When they moved in closer, he was relieved to see that one was his childhood friend Phee along with two others, guns in hand, trained on Wallis's still body.

35

Maclin was no longer so apt to dismiss the possibility of miracles. It wasn't that she ran out of logical counterpoints challenging their validity; it was just the simple fact that she no longer felt the inherent need to dispute what might reasonably qualify as an act of God.

There were eight abandoned meat plants in New York and New Jersey, four of them in the Bronx. Just going off the intel that the slaughterhouse was somewhere north of downtown and not far from a subway station, somehow Phee led them to a place that he had never visited but had known of by reputation. His Hail Mary was a house of urban legend that had haunted him in his youth.

It was possible that the greater miracle she witnessed was the sight of a tortured Spider and Ezra laughing together and wishing each other well as they waited for the paramedics to arrive.

Neither one of them was able to tell them anything about the case that they didn't already know. The singular victory was that they were alive.

Maclin and Phee addressed their wounds as best they could. Even when there was nothing more he could do, Maclin watched as Phee stayed by the side of his childhood friend as an older brother would a younger sibling. She saw it in Phee's face, the immense relief. The exoneration. She never considered him a particularly gentle man, save for his interactions with his daughter and wife, but she saw something different in him as he consoled both Spider and Ezra. When the release came, the emotional totality of how close they had come to being killed, the two men broke down and cried. Phee was there between them offering what comfort he could.

After Maclin reached out to Rabbi Pearl, she called Losher. "Ezra is safe."

There were just a couple of exchanges between them, mostly about the details of Ezra's status and which hospital he was being taken to. Even though she was the one with all the info, she listened intently to the few words that he did speak. She had always thought her name—Janet—was common. Simple. Functional. Yet when Losher spoke it, he made her feel as though it were something more. He held on to it. He spoke it with the same deliberateness and savoring that he did when they first met. It had been there all along, but Maclin felt like she was no longer just listening to him but finally hearing him the way he wanted to be heard.

Losher loved her. Truly loved her. She heard it all in his voice.

"Janet, I've never once doubted what you're capable of. Thank you for being your usual amazing self. When this thing is truly over, I hope you and I get to celebrate what you all have accomplished."

Quincy was on his phone when the paramedics and patrol arrived. He rushed over to his partners as soon as he hung up. "We gotta go. Now." Phee patted Spider on the shoulder, and Maclin said goodbye to Ezra as they hurried off.

As they exited the room, Maclin asked, "What's up?"

Quincy kept moving, not bothering to look back. "Skia and Burns tracked Cameron to a spot upstate called Eagle's Hill. They said they found the game changer we've been looking for."

Skia brought the team up to speed. "Even though it's a private residence, it's run through an LLC. We thought that was kinda weird, considering that there are a whole lot of horse ranchers and simple folk out here who don't usually make that much effort to hide their identity. Did a little more diggin' and found out that this same LLC is listed as the controlling entity of some organization called Alliance for a Better Tomorrow. This place is listed as the address of operations."

Maclin glanced back at Quincy and Phee before responding. "AFABT—the tattoos on the Lyles brothers." She then turned back to Skia and Burns. "This is all great intel, but we still don't have the name of the owner for the LLC?" Maclin asked.

"I didn't say that."

Maclin looked at him oddly.

Skia smiled. "It's a lot less dramatic for me to just come out and tell you that we were able to track the info down. Can't waste an opportunity to show you how hard we actually work for our underwhelming compensation."

Burns jumped in, "The owner's name is Ellis Brock. He was a bigwig broker on Wall Street. Made a shitload of paper before he retired ten years ago. Since then, as best we can tell he became some kinda alt-right evangelical preacher. Get a hold of this: there is a registered church on the property, and it's run through the same LLC. The church angle could just be a front for tax exemption status. They could launder a whole lot of money that way."

Maclin was instantly on her iPad accessing the FBI database.

"Any known ties to white supremacist groups?" Quincy asked.

"Well, sorta," Skia responded.

"What the hell does that mean?" Phee asked.

"Me and Burns busted this old-school broker in a hooker sting a couple of years ago. We cut him some slack but use him as a CI every now and again. We called him—he'd definitely heard of Brock back in the day. Said that he was good at what he did but was also known as being arrogant as fuck about it. Made almost as many enemies as he did money. At the height of Brock's Wall Street days, the *Village Voice* ran a story on his father Dellwood Brock. We pulled up the article. Back in the late '60s, Dellwood was a big-time segregationist and supporter of George Wallace. Ellis Brock reads clean though. Looks like he started out as an attorney before going the Wall Street route. We ran him on local and state, and we got no bumps on him. Looks like he's..."

"I got a hit on him on AFIS," Maclin said, cutting him off as she scrolled her iPad. "FBI's got fingerprints on him even though his case was expunged, which is why you've got nothing on him from state and local. Looks like he was down in Charlottesville when all hell broke loose. He caught a felony agg assault on an African American protester."

"I wonder how he got it expunged," Skia posited.

"He's rich, white, and connected. Take your pick," Maclin shot back. "By the way, good work digging up his father."

"Well it gets even better." Burns was on a roll. "Besides Cameron's car, there are eight vehicles on-site. We ran the plates on them all and came up with two felons with bench warrants for no-shows on parking violations and one with multiple run-ins with the law but no convictions. All three have deep ties to hate groups."

The five cops were crammed around the computer monitors of the surveillance van. The van, along with Burns's Crown Vic, which Phee commandeered earlier, were both parked behind an overgrowth of bushes, slightly obscured from the road. With a pair of binoculars, Maclin looked through the windshield of the van at the Brock ranch, which was almost three hundred yards away.

"How'd you see all the vehicles on the property? The gate's too high to see the driveway from the road."

Burns looked at Maclin as if he was deciding whether or not to answer her. She turned more directly toward him, waiting for a response. Burns glanced in Phee's direction.

"I asked *you* the question, Detective Burns, not him."

Burns looked back at Maclin. "You sure you wanna know?"

"If I didn't want to know, I wouldn't have asked."

"We hopped the gate and did a sneak-and-peek."

Maclin didn't bother hiding her frustration.

"And in so doing, any observations that you made are now inadmissible—not to mention this compromises us getting on that property legally."

The van got smaller. Her frustration shifted to anger. The mounting tension between Maclin and Burns started sucking the air out of the already cramped space.

"So now we're in a *fruit of the poisonous tree* situation," Maclin declared.

"I respectfully disagree." Burns tried to defend himself.

"Certainly your right to do so, but if we all respected the law more, there would be no disagreements." She kept her eyes locked on him, shaking her head, all the while growing more exasperated.

Burns was red and getting redder. His cheeks were approaching a deep plum color. His jowls drooped, making him look like an indignant bulldog. Maclin may have been FBI, but Burns came from a long line of blue-collar, Irish cops who didn't take to being talked down to by anyone. Not even their superiors.

"We've been busting our asses and hoping to get a break on this case, and me and Skia get us right to the front door—and instead of figuring out a way to make the most of that, we gotta get a lecture?"

Bobby Skia put his hand on his partner's shoulder to try to calm his Irish temper. "Come on, Burns, chill."

Burns shrugged away. "Fuck chill. I'm a hunnit degrees past chill."

Maclin, never one to back down, clapped back, "You being pissed doesn't change the fact that you…"

Quincy stepped between them. "We all need to take it way down and figure this out. Everybody just take a breather. Janet, let's step outside for a sec, get some air."

"I'm fine! I don't need…"

"Well, I do. Come on. It'll do us all some good."

As she finally relented and exited the back door, Quincy gave a subtle nod to Phee to join them.

Quincy was right. The country breeze felt good on her skin. It was ten to fifteen degrees cooler than Manhattan. Much more bearable. Downright pleasant. There was certainly no denying how beautiful the rolling hills, perfect skies, and giant trees of Eagle's Hill were. Her lungs gulped in the clean air, and for just a second she almost forgot how pissed she was.

Almost.

The fact that Phee had joined them meant that they were going to attempt to work her. Maclin was definitely not in the mood to be worked. Not even by the best of them.

She went offensive instead of waiting to be the defense. "Before the two of you try to convince me that I'm…"

"We're not trying to convince you of anything. We wanted to apologize to you."

"Excuse me?"

Phee jumped in. "You're right. We can't do things that're gonna compromise putting these assholes behind bars for the rest of their miserable lives. But we gotta use every and any advantage we get. One of the most fucked-up things about this job is knowing that everything that's legal ain't always right, and everything that's right ain't always legal. For the record, we're all in agreement that *how* we arrest them has to be by the book. But this deep into the game, how we gather intel has to be by any means necessary. I know you have problems with that, and we get it. We may not always be on the same page, but we are definitely always on the same side. We all want the same thing, Janet."

"You're the senior investigator on this case, but Burns was right about one thing: he and Skia got us to the front door. The question is, what do we do now that we're here? You tell us how you want us to play it, and that's what we do," Quincy added.

Maclin looked at the partners, definitely not expecting the words that she was hearing. She took her time and thought about the question.

"So, most of what Burns gave us, even though it's useful, would be chewed up by a halfway decent defense attorney. Not to mention Brock himself was an attorney, so whatever we do has to be to the letter of the law. No holes to let them slip through."

Maclin pursed her lips together and paced in a tight formation. Four steps forward, then four back in the direction she started. She did that a few times; then she suddenly stopped and looked at Quincy and Phee.

"We have to find our freedoms through our limitations," Maclin said partly to herself and partly to Quincy and Phee.

"Okay, so how do we do that here?" Phee asked.

"Burns may have already given us enough useful intel," Maclin responded.

"Yeah, but you said yourself it wouldn't hold up."

"We wouldn't need to worry about what would hold up if we gained access with consent. That would change everything."

Phee laughed. "So what are you suggesting—that we just knock on the door and they'll invite us in?"

"Actually, that's exactly what I'm suggesting."

They brought Burns and Skia up to speed on how they planned to gain access to the property. Burns was a bit skeptical at first but came around after Phee pulled him aside and spoke to him privately. Although it was faint, there was still residual tension between Maclin and the detective. Just as they were leaving, Maclin noticed Burns placing something in Phee's hand—she couldn't quite see what it was. But she was able to see clearly that Burns then reached into his pocket and handed Phee a pack of his chewing gum.

It was an imposing gate. Cold and unwelcoming. The only one of its kind in the tranquil enclave. It looked out of place in a community where one's closest neighbor, on average, was a half mile away. Special measures to ensure privacy felt both aggressive and unnecessary.

Maclin caught a bad vibe the closer she, Quincy, and Phee got to the driveway. In every pore of her body, she felt that she was approaching a place where bad things happened. She rolled down the window of the Crown Vic and pressed the button of the intercom.

Twenty seconds later, a dry voice answered, "Yeah."

"Ellis Brock, please," Maclin responded.

"He's busy. You wanna leave a message?"

"Well, you might want to ask him to get *unbusy*, and tell him that I'm Special Agent Janet Maclin of the FBI and I'd like to speak with him, please."

"What is this about?"

"That would be between Mr. Brock and me, and I would venture to say that he would want you to let him know as soon as possible that the FBI is at his front gate to see him."

The intercom went silent. Maclin looked at both Quincy and Phee but didn't speak. Thirty seconds later, a much deeper voice came over the intercom. It was rich and full of authority. It was the same voice they'd heard Cameron speaking to after leaving the morgue.

"This is Ellis Brock."

"Mr. Brock, I'm Special Agent Janet Maclin along with Task Force Officers Freeman and Cavanaugh. We were hoping to have a word with you."

"About what exactly?"

"Well, a few things, but let's just start with the fact that we have credible reports of two felons on your property with outstanding bench warrants."

"Do you have a warrant?"

"Not at all, and we're hoping one won't be necessary because at this point we're much more interested in a conversation with you than a confrontation over unpaid parking tickets. But if you feel a warrant is required, then I'm sure as a former attorney you are fully aware of legal terms such as inevitable discovery or exigent circumstances; but if perchance you've somehow forgotten, it means that if we come in with a warrant, then we are obligated to search every inch of your property and belongings and detain all persons present during the course of our investigation, including you. I assure you that we are not interested in such a disruption of your day. But make no mistake: if I do call it in, in the next three minutes all bets are off. It's your choice, sir."

The intercom was quiet. Maclin listened for even the faint sound of breathing on the other end but heard nothing. All was still. The only thing she heard was the sporadic chirps of Eastern Kingbirds in a nearby tree. After a full minute of no response, Maclin threw the car in reverse and started backing out of the driveway. As she looked over her shoulder, she said to Quincy and Phee, "Well, that didn't quite go the way I would have liked."

After she had backed up ten feet down the driveway, Quincy, who was riding shotgun, interrupted her. "Don't underestimate your ability to be very convincing."

When Maclin looked at him, Quincy nodded in the direction of the imposing gates as they parted.

"I think you had him at *perchance*," Phee chuckled.

36

Maclin parked in a gravel lot next to the nine vehicles already on the premises. Three cars, one of which belonged to Cameron, were parked alongside five pickups and an HVAC van. All the vehicles had an AFABT bumper sticker on them. The trucks all had rifle racks in the rear window, and one sported a pair of Confederate mudflaps. As soon as they got out of the cruiscr, Phee reached back in and unlocked the shotgun, loaded it, and then pocketed some shells.

"The rifle racks in all the trucks are empty. We are not about to show up to a possible Klan rally without a little eye candy to help keep the good ole boys humble."

As Phee took a step toward the house, Quincy stopped him with a hand on his shoulder. "Phee, you know they're gonna come at you. You're on Cameron's turf now. Don't let them provoke you.

Because we all know they're gonna say some insulting stuff that's gonna piss you off. You gotta stay cool."

"I'm cool."

Maclin looked at him somewhat skeptically.

Instead of Phee getting defensive, he put a couple of sticks of gum in his mouth and looked at her with an ambiguous grin. "I said I'm cool."

As they approached the house, the front door opened. The three of them were surprised when a young boy no older than thirteen stepped out on the porch to greet them.

"Hello, I'm Ellis Brock, Jr. My father is out back in the church. If you don't mind, he asked that you join him there."

Maclin smiled at the polite boy with sad, ocean-blue eyes. His hair was golden and buzzed on the sides and heavier on the top. He reminded her of images she'd seen of the Aryan Youth Movement in the days of Hitler. He had a stout, abbreviated chin with droopy cheeks that hung like two full sacks of grief. As he led them around the corner of the house, she thought about how she had never met a child who looked so burdened.

The red church was a large, converted barn. It came complete with white shutters and beautiful stained-glass windows depicting images of Jesus and his twelve disciples. Maclin thought she had stepped back in time. The church was a slice of pure Americana. It looked like a Billy Graham and Norman Rockwell collaboration. Just in front of the beautiful church was a forty-foot flagpole with two flags waving proudly in the light breeze. The flag at the top was the original Stars and Bars of the Confederacy. The second, which was known as the Stainless Banner, was the more popular, revised version. Maclin wasn't sure why, but she found it a bit curious that the American flag itself was nowhere in sight. The white painted letters just above the front door spelled out CHURCH OF THE LORD'S BLOOD. There at the roof's apex was a large, white cross with a painted drop of blood at its base.

The boy opened the large doors to the church and welcomed them in. The sun glimmered through the stained-glass windows, prism-like, creating rainbow-colored rays. The space was larger than it looked from the outside. The church could comfortably accommodate a couple of hundred congregants. Maclin could easily imagine the type of soul-stirring that went on in the converted barn that proudly flew not one but two banners of hate.

Ellis Brock, Jr., ushered them toward the pulpit, where an imposing twenty-foot walnut table with a dozen chairs was in the center of the small stage. There was a huge pipe organ just to the side. Seated at the table thirty feet in front of them were thirteen men, four of whom were armed with rifles and shotguns, shoulder to shoulder with an albino man, who sat at the center of the table. Maclin saw the desired optics right away. It wasn't happenstance that the albino was flanked by six men to his left and six to his right. The intended theme seemed to be something feebly reminiscent of Jesus and his twelve disciples. Some distorted interpretation of the Last Supper.

Phee lagged behind, taking up a defensive position as he sat in the second row of seats, where he had a more objective perspective of the stage and all who were assembled there. He rested the barrel of the shotgun over the top of the pew in front of him, pointing in the direction of the men. As one of the armed men shifted his weight and in so doing raised his weapon ever so slightly, both Maclin and Quincy instinctively inched their hands toward their holstered guns.

"Welcome to the house of the Lord." It was at best a perfunctory greeting accompanied by a stingy smile. Although unwarm, it still technically qualified as something passing for civility. His voice, booming under the support of the great acoustics, sounded even deeper in person than on the intercom. It was the type of voice that herded men, women, and children and made minions of them.

"Ellis Brock?" Maclin clarified.

"Yes, Agent Maclin. Exactly how can I help you?" He took a final inhale of his cigarette and then extinguished it in the ashtray in front of him.

Cameron took a step forward and pointed his finger at Phee. "He doesn't get to come in here."

Brock raised his hand. It was nothing more than a small gesture, but it stopped Cameron on the spot.

"I invited them in; therefore, they will be treated like guests. Even though we all know they've come with prejudice and to bear false witness, we will still treat them with graciousness."

Maclin walked up three steps onto the stage. Quincy used another set of stairs so that they were more spread out—in case things went south and they found themselves in any sort of a firefight situation, they wouldn't be easy targets standing in tandem. The closer Maclin got, the more she could see Cameron, who was closest to Brock, fighting to restrain himself as his focus stayed locked on Phee. The rest of the disciples were exactly what she would have expected them to be: large men with small minds. There was nothing subtle about them. They were offensively tatted hatemongers whose eyes burned with enmity.

"I assure you, we're not here with prejudice or to bear false witness against anyone."

"Of course you are, but then again I would expect no less from the government. So why don't you just ask what you came here to ask, so we can both get back to our day."

"Well for starters, I'd love for you to tell us exactly what Alliance for a Better Tomorrow is?"

Brock affectionately pulled his son in closer to him by putting his arm around the waist of the young boy.

"Well, it's exactly what it says it is: a group of concerned Americans who are dedicated to making this country better for our children. The last time I checked, it was still our constitutional right to do so, Agent Maclin."

"Well, that would depend greatly on how you and your colleagues are going about doing that. Murder and hate crimes are not a constitutional right."

"Well I assure you that we are peaceful, law-abiding patriots."

"Hopefully, you can understand my skepticism with your claim when Darren Lyles, our lead suspect in a murder investigation, seems to have been associated with you and your lovely church."

"Many people attend our church. Sometimes more than I can keep count of, let alone classify as a true association."

"Are you saying that you don't know Darren Lyles?"

"I'm simply saying that many people attend our church."

"Since his brother is standing right next to you, would that classify Darren as at least an associate?"

"Ahhh, yes—Darren Lyles. Now I remember. A strong, Christian man who only wanted what was best for his family and this country. From what I remember of him, he was a true patriot. America certainly needs more men like him."

"I hope you don't mind if I beg to differ."

Brock looked at Maclin's *hamsa* necklace. "Not at all. That's what this great country is all about: our constitutional right to disagree. These fine young gentlemen and I feel it is our honor, duty, and privilege as Americans to dissect and challenge accepted norms and misconceptions—so much that we were actually thinking of forming our own private debate squad. We could randomly get together, choose opposing sides of the factual as well as the hypothetical. Before you interrupted us, we were just having a constructive debate on what is the greatest threat to America and why."

"And have you reached any conclusions?"

"Well, the discussion was getting interesting just before you arrived. Keep in mind the dialogue was only hypothetical in nature. Some took the position that the infestation of immigrants was the greatest threat, while others thought the growing influence of black culture was potentially the most detrimental to our society. Strictly for the sake of creating a more dynamic debate, I disagreed with both."

"Oh really? So, in your opinion—of course only from a hypothetical perspective—what *is* the greatest threat to America?"

Brock smiled as if he'd been waiting for a cue. He turned to his
son. "Please forgive my obvious bragging, but my son here is quite
the gifted child. He's only thirteen years old but with an IQ of 167.
He'll be starting Harvard in the fall. Since he's clearly the most
intelligent person here, why don't we let him answer the question?
Junior, would you share with Agent Maclin a hypothetical perspective of what is the greatest threat to our country?"

Maclin wasn't sure if the boy's hesitation was from reluctance
or shyness. She was equally uncertain if Brock's nod to his son was
a nudge of encouragement or an unbreakable command.

Ellis Brock, Jr., addressed Maclin, speaking to her with a tone
of apathy as if he were giving a weekly book report on global
warming and its effect on burnt toast.

"Immigrants are certainly a serious threat, particularly to our
economy. They extract well over sixty billion dollars each year to
send back to their places of origin. Although this is one of the
several ways they compromise America, they are still considered a
manageable enemy through tougher policy and diligence. As far as
African Americans or blacks—or as they are so apt to call themselves, niggas—are concerned, statistically speaking, they pose a
much more serious threat to themselves based on their collective
divisiveness and perpetual self-disenfranchisement. Fortunately,
they're morally and mentally enslaved enough to mitigate any real
danger to our country. Case in point, did you know that in the
seventy-three years between 1877 and 1950, there were just shy of

four thousand documented lynchings, but in 2016 through 2017 alone, there were well over five thousand black-on-black murders nationwide? Although they breed at an alarming rate, niggas will self-implode long before they pose any organized threat to the most powerful nation in the world."

Maclin couldn't help but notice the twinkle in Cameron's eye as he stared hard at Phee. She saw the dawning of a grin spread across his face. It was as if every word spoken by the young boy seemed to inflate him more and more. Ellis Brock, Jr., took a dramatic pause, letting his words float in the air in the direction of his intended target. Maclin could see Phee in her periphery. Considering how annoyed she herself was becoming, she was a bit surprised that he remained quietly sitting. Her irritation only grew as the boy continued speaking. The focus of his delivery went from Phee back to her.

"Adolf Hitler, who was one of the most brilliant men who ever lived, knew that in his day the greatest threat—not just to Europe, but the world—was without question the Jew. He knew that throughout history they have always been the consummate interloper, bent on world domination. In fact, just at the end of the nineteenth century, there was an actual doctrine created by them called the *Protocols of the Elders of Zion* that laid out their plans for Jewish hegemony. Unlike immigrants and niggas, Jews wield a far greater power economically, which in turn affords them political clout to influence policy that bends toward their Zionist goals. As dictated by their protocol doctrine, they've already accomplished this through media, entertainment, banking, and other industries that they've strategically overtaken. They won't stop until they have dominated every cornerstone of our society, even the sanctity of our Christian beliefs. This is why the Jew is unassailably the greatest threat to this country."

When he finished, he looked in his father's direction as if he was seeking approval. Ellis Brock, Sr., flashed a self-assured smile as he patted the shoulder of the boy. His cronies were a bit giddy as they nodded their heads and nudged each other as if they had just won the national debate championship. Maclin couldn't quite get a solid read on the younger Brock. When he glanced back in her direction, he looked the part of both a gifted junior hatemonger and a brain-washed puppet simply bent on serving his father/master. When he seemed unable to hold her gaze, she leaned toward the latter.

She saw the smugness in the faces of the men who smirked at her and her partners. She despised them, not just for what they represented but for their heinous ability to poison the minds and hearts of innocent children. For the better part of her career, she had managed to not let her emotions compromise her objectivity in a case. She'd fallen short of her standard the minute she laid eyes on the slaughtered rabbis. She'd hated the senior Brock long before she met him.

"He's quite the orator; wouldn't you agree, Agent Maclin?" Brock asked. It was a rhetorical question more than anything because he didn't bother to wait for any response from her. He lit another cigarette and puffed on it as he spoke. "He's always been able to present those kinds of compelling arguments."

Brock took another deep drag on his cigarette. "If I'm not

mistaken, you're a Jew, aren't you, Agent Maclin?" He asked as he savored the nicotine in his lungs.

"Yes, I am," she said with edge.

"I thought so. When many of the Jews fled Germany, they adopted various altered versions of the names of their hometowns. I'd wager good money that your people were from Mecklenburg. I'd go even further and say shortly before or after they emigrated to this country, in an effort to Anglicize themselves, they bastard-ized the name Mecklenburg and made it Maclin. One could easily make the argument that your very name is a denial of who you and your lineage really are. The funny thing is, unlike blacks and most immigrants, who you can identify a mile away, a self-loathing Jew can very easily assimilate into a decent society. I think that's what my son meant by 'the consummate interloper.'"

Brock savored one final, long pull on his cigarette before extin-guishing it and smiled at her as he exhaled. He stared at her as if he was challenging her restraint.

It started in the soles of her feet. Hot blood traversed its way through her entire body until she was flush with anger. Her mouth was so dry that the back of her throat felt as if it were cracking. She felt pain somewhere in her midsection. She didn't know exactly which organ Ivan had chosen to abuse, but it was a dull ache that seemed to be rising in her.

Maclin stepped forward, aggressively. Brock's men instantly reacted by raising their weapons.

Quincy was to her left with his weapon trained on Brock. Maclin hadn't even heard Phee move, but somehow, in an instant, he was four feet to her right with his shotgun leveled at Brock's head. She hadn't drawn her weapon, but her hand was resting on it, still in its holster. Maclin pulled her phone out instead. "You want a Waco on your hands. I can easily make it happen. Trust me, we're not afraid to die."

Brock laughed. "Only a fool dies in vain. You would love to turn this into a Waco, wouldn't you? Sorry to disappoint you, but the time of our martyrdom will be at our choosing, not yours. And when that time comes, remember: One dies. Twenty rise."

As Brock lifted his finger, the men surrounding him lowered their weapons. Cameron, whose gun was pointed at Phee, was the only one not to comply.

"Cameron!" Brock admonished.

As the last weapon was finally lowered, Maclin took two more steps forward, intentionally bumping the table with her thighs with enough force that his ashtray overturned, spilling his cigarette butts and ashes.

Maclin put her hands on the table and leaned over Brock, their faces just inches from each other. "You're nothing more than an abnormality, you simple fuck. It's almost laughable that you love Hitler as much as you do, because you being an albino, he would have had you killed just as easily as my kind." She looked at the other men. "I guess neo-Nazis are more concerned with the impressiveness of a man's wallet than the purity of Aryan blood. And for the record, I never was good with hypotheticals—I prefer facts and reality much more. You need to suck on this unassailable fact: not only am I a Jew, but I'm *the* Jew who gets to flush you and your lackeys like the pieces of shit that you really are."

Brock smiled at her. "Pretty predictable, you overestimating your abilities and greatly underestimating ours."

"Am I? I know all I need to know about you and the rest of these inbred clowns. I could smell you the second I walked through the door. It's not hard—there's a stench that you've all carried with you your entire lives. All the fear and pitifulness. You have every right to be afraid because I'm the nightmare that you let through your gates. The Jew who's hell-bent on your annihilation. Yeah, I'm the one who's going to make it happen. I'm the one who's going to teach you and the rest of the lice you call brothers more about extermination than you ever wanted to know."

She raised her phone and snapped a photo of Brock and the men. "By the way, you shouldn't smoke in a church. It's bad for your health—and your soul."

As she turned to leave, Quincy and Phee walked backward, keeping a steady eye on Brock and his disciples.

The three partners got in the car without saying a word. Phee and Quincy looked at each other, neither ever having seen Maclin seething the way she was. Her anger made her forget about her pain long enough for the wave to subside. Quincy was the first to break the ice. "Well, at least Phee kept his word and didn't lose his temper."

As Maclin settled in behind the wheel, she couldn't help but smile, which then led to brief laughter from all three.

She nodded at Quincy. "Do me a favor and check the glove compartment to see if there are any evidence bags in there."

As he did as she asked and handed her a clear plastic evidence bag, she turned so that both men could see clearly the cigarette butt that she held up by the stem, careful not to touch the filter.

"Not bad. Not bad at all," Quincy commented.

"What's your thinking on a game plan since we don't have anything legally?" Phee asked.

"I'll email the pics to Langley to see what kind of facial recs we get back. See if we can't put an ID to them all. If we run Asshole's DNA, I know it won't stand up in court, but we'll at least know if some of the foreign blood found on Shaka's body comes back to him."

"Speaking of assholes, heads up," Phee nodded toward an approaching Ellis Brock, Jr., who was coming up on the driver's side.

Maclin lowered her window.

"Agent Maclin, detectives, I wanted to apologize to you. Just so you know, I don't agree with my father, but around here we're all subject to his will. No matter how things look on the surface, not all of us are what you think. My father is a dinosaur who simply refuses to accept that he's already extinct. Enjoy the rest of your day."

As the boy walked back toward the house and Maclin hooked a hard U and drove through the gates, Phee snarked, "Wow, how very white of him."

"Damn, can you imagine growing up with a monster of a

father like that? We gotta cut him some slack, Phee; he's only a child. Children are what we teach them," Maclin stated.

Quincy jumped in. "Yeah, Junior's fucked no matter how you cut it. Not sure how you ever bounce back from this kind of upbringing."

"Don't let his size and age fool you—he was just a little too convincing in his church performance for my taste. I'm just saying…"

"Phee, he's thirteen." Maclin cut him off. "Anybody can see he's nothing more than a trained seal, doing whatever circus tricks he can to please his father. You look into his eyes, you can see there's definitely something worth saving. Boy genius or not, at the end of the day, he's still just a kid."

"Yeah, well so was Hitler once," Phee fired back.

Maclin parked the car next to the van, but as she went to get out, Phee placed a hand on her shoulder.

"Janet, hold up for a quick sec. I've got something to tell you, and I don't want you to get mad."

"It wouldn't be the fact that you left an open burner in the church to illegally eavesdrop on our Aryan brothers, would it?"

Quincy and Phee were equally surprised.

Phee stammered, "How did you…?"

"At first I wasn't sure, but I thought I saw Burns slide the phone to you before we left. But quite honestly, the thing that gave you away was the chewing gum. I've seen you in some pretty intense situations, and you've never once felt a sudden urge to chew gum, let alone throw a wad of it in your mouth before a big interview. And somehow, between us entering and exiting the church, it just disappeared. Did you *perchance* use it to stick the phone under the pew?"

Phee looked at Quincy and then Maclin, shaking his head that she read him so well. "Yeah, that's exactly what I did."

"It was a smart move. Doesn't change how I feel about doing things by the book, but the two of you are right—we're much too far behind to try to catch them while playing by the rules. The only options I see available to us won't be stopping them anytime soon. If we're not..."

Maclin was interrupted by Burns tapping on the rear passenger side window. Phee opened the door and got out, as did Maclin and Quincy.

Burns started low and quiet to Phee until Phee stopped him abruptly. "It's cool. Everybody's up to speed."

Burns looked in Maclin's direction. "Good, 'cause you all need to hear what's going down. It's fuckin' bad. I mean, like, real fuckin' bad."

37

Yesterday, we celebrated our country's independence; tomorrow, we celebrate its rebirth. Let them think they won the moment. After tonight, what will it matter? When the festering bodies of Jews lay choking at our feet and the air of this city is made thick with the ashes of Muslims, the world will know the might of a Christian God."

The audio quality of the playback wasn't great, so Burns turned the volume up as much as he could. Despite the fact that everything sounded distant and somewhat muffled, Maclin and the rest of the team were able to hear Ellis Brock clearly enough. They were also able to identify a second voice as Cameron's.

"What do we do about Jesse and Wallis? They haven't checked in and we can't reach 'em, which means more than likely they've been compromised. What do we do if we find out the cops got to them?"

"We stick with the plan. Scapegoating Ezra Pearl and the nigger was always a bonus, not the primary objective. We've created enough evidence to tie the two of them to the gas and bombs. It might not happen exactly the way we planned, but trust me, nothing will stop the coming war," Brock responded.

"We could always snatch two more to replace them," Cameron offered.

"At this point, we don't take any extra risks. None. That also goes for whatever revenge you want on the cops for what they did to your brother. After tonight, you can kill them all for all I care— but not until after tonight. Until then, everybody lay low. Right now, we just focus on our two targets. The Fed took a photo of everyone here, which actually helps us. All of you will stay here tonight. I'll have Doris make her gumbo. Set up the cameras. We'll broadcast a live Bible study so that we all have a couple of thousand hard alibis. I need to run a couple of errands, stop by the bank, and then come back and prepare tonight's sermon."

Burns hit the stop button on the playback. "They all left the church after that. That's all we got."

The van was quiet. A thick, immiserated type of quiet. Trapped in stasis. The team's immobility bordered on helplessness. There was no air in the tight space. It had been wholly sucked out by the frightening details of Brock's plans.

Phee was the first to break the silence as he eloquently summed up the gravity of the news with a single "Fuck!"

Maclin, who was standing closest to Phee, could feel the angry heat coming from him. She thought she even saw steam. "We gotta get back to the city to identify the targets as soon as possible," she ordered.

"We've got two. How the hell do we go about locating them?" Quincy asked.

Maclin ran the plan. "Burns, you and Skia work the mosque target. Use the time on your drive back to start pulling up a list of any large-scale Muslim events being held tonight. Check every community calendar that you can—and while you're at it, have somebody at the station check patrol assignments throughout New York for special events. Also, see if there are any Muslim holidays being celebrated. You're looking for mosques with the biggest following. Brock and his people are going to be looking to inflict maximum casualties. Call us on the road with whatever you come up with."

"Are we doing the same with the synagogues?" Quincy asked.

"No, that won't be necessary—I already know which target they'll hit."

"Rabbi Pearl, as I tried to explain to you and your fellow rabbis on the phone, we have it from a very reliable source that tonight's museum opening has been possibly targeted in a terrorist plot. We're imploring you to postpone the opening until we can apprehend those who are responsible."

The conference room in the museum was actually cold. The air-conditioning was on full blast, leaving the space feeling a bit frigid.

Rabbi Pearl seemed to have aged twenty years in the two days since Maclin had last seen him. She assumed that the skin beneath his eyes sagged under the stressful weight of his son's abduction and his resulting injuries. Although the elder Pearl was noticeably fragile, it was clear that he still ruled the room. In addition to Losher and Yael, there were ten rabbis present.

All eyes were on Rabbi Pearl. No one spoke or moved. They all stood by, obediently waiting for their leader to speak. The distant stare in his eyes made Maclin wonder if he was fully present or if his mind was wandering in search of more peaceful avenues. Despite the magnitude of her news, there was no sense of urgency in him. His reaction was a nonreaction. As she opened her mouth to speak again, one of the nearby rabbis raised his hand to politely silence her. Rabbi Zon Pearl was not a man to be rushed under any circumstances. The room was quiet save for the cold air proudly blowing through the vents.

Maclin finally heard him mumble something that she couldn't quite make out.

"Kristallnacht."

Maclin looked at Quincy and Phee in confusion. Then she turned to face Losher and Yael. Losher subtly nodded his head at her as though quietly imploring her to be patient.

Rabbi Pearl finally faced her, his voice clear but lamenting. "The Night of Broken Glass. That's what they called it. November 9th, 1938. I was seven years old when the Nazis came and made the streets of Germany rain with the shards of broken windows from Jewish businesses and homes. Little did we know that it was only the beginning of greater horrors to come.

"Night turned into day and then night again as they looted the shops and vandalized all things Jewish. No one stopped them. By the time they were done, a few thousand shops had been destroyed. Two hundred and sixty-seven synagogues had been burned. Our cemeteries were desecrated. Over thirty thousand of our men were herded like sheep and sent to the first of the camps. It was the last time I saw my father. My mother and I, along with so many other mothers and children, washed the blood in the streets with the tears that knew no end. Eventually they came for all of us, and no one stopped them. The more we waited on others to save us, the more we suffered and perished. And no one stopped them until it was too late. Agent Maclin, do you know why this place was named the Shoah Museum?"

"Because *shoah* means *never again*."

"Exactly. When the world speaks its name, we want all to be reminded that never again will we run and hide. Never again will we cower in the face of terror from those who come to harm us or threaten the very things we worship and hold dear. You have good intentions, Agent Maclin—but fear no longer shrinks us. You may see this as only a building, but we see it as a reminder that the world will never be able to turn its back on us again. That it'll never forget or minimize the atrocities that our people have endured. So, the opening tonight will proceed as planned. We will not leave. We will not abandon the soul of who we are."

"But..."

"You and I, we serve two different masters. You are a woman of man's law. I am a man of God's law. I submit only to His will, not to yours. God's grace will protect us even in the throat of insurmountable adversity. Man knows himself best in the cold of night. Faced with the winter of his fate, he is then most revealed. With all that's happened over the past few days, that way of thinking might not seem logical to you; but therein lies the essence of faith. When I went to see my son in the hospital, he told me that even in the bleakest moments of his ordeal he still believed God would not forsake him. It was his faith that turned an enemy who had abandoned him into an ally willing to die for him. God will not forsake us. Now, if you'll excuse me, our guests will be arriving at seven."

As soon as he started to rise, two rabbis stood at his side to offer assistance if necessary. It wasn't. He exited the door with the ten rabbis and Yael following closely behind. Losher was the only one who remained.

Maclin pleaded with him. "You have to get your sister to convince him..."

"She would never go against the rebbe's wishes."

"Over two thousand people are expected to be here tonight. Does he really want their deaths on his hands?"

"I can't speak for the rebbe, but the one thing I do know is everyone in this community is unconditionally faithful to him. For the record, this museum doesn't just represent the rebbe's life's work; it's everyone around him as well. That's what it means to all of them. This is one of the biggest events in most of these people's lives. They're not going to just turn away because you tell them to, no matter what you say."

Phee interjected, "We could just have the fire department shut the place down."

Losher pleaded with Maclin. "Janet, you yourself said that it is a *possible* target. Unless you can prove it a hundred percent, trying to stop this opening could be a huge mistake. They don't just see this as the opening of a museum; it's a holy event. If you try to shut it down, you might just end up with a holy war on your hands."

Maclin was thinking. Her brows were so tightly pursed that they almost touched.

"Can you get the blueprints of the building from your sister? We need to see the whole layout to get a better overview."

"Yeah, of course."

"How well do you know the building?" Maclin asked.

"You kidding? For the last two years, my sister came here every day obsessing about every detail. I can't tell you how many times she's dragged me here going over every inch of this building, making sure nothing was overlooked."

"Good. You can show us where everything is."

"Sure," Losher responded as he turned and headed for the door.

Phee stopped him. "Losher, how big is this building?"

"Just over sixty thousand square feet."

Quincy asked, "What's up with the air-conditioning in here? It's freezing."

"It's intentional," Losher said. "The museum is designed as a partially interactive experience—a journey through four seasons in Auschwitz. They're starting with the winter exhibition. I'll go check on the blueprints."

"There's no way in hell we search that much square footage thoroughly in an hour," Quincy said.

Maclin nodded her head in agreement. "Just means we have to be smart about how we narrow this down."

"What if Losher is right and somehow we're wrong—which, for the record, I don't think we are. But as long as there is a possibility, we gotta think about the optics on how we handle this," Quincy offered.

Maclin started pacing, partly to think better and partly to quell the steady rise of her frustration.

"'When the festering bodies of Jews lay choking at our feet.' That's what Brock said, right?" Quincy asked.

"He's gotta be talking about the Zyklon B!" Maclin exclaimed. "What better way for them to make a statement than gassing tonight's opening?"

"Now, it makes perfect sense!" Quincy added. "Starting with the Abramovitz brothers, they've been trying to reenact scenes of genocide from the death camps."

"My money says that they release the gas through the air-conditioning," Maclin mused. "That would be a pretty effective way to distribute it throughout the building."

"Yeah, but I'm sure there are other ways to do it as well," Phee countered.

"When we were at Brock's ranch, there was an HVAC van in the driveway with a AFABT bumper sticker," Maclin said. "I'm just saying, the first thing we need to check out is the HVAC system on the blueprints."

"One way we can find out if your hunch is right," Quincy responded as he pulled out his cell. "Burns and Skia ran all the plates. I'll run the van through NVLS to see if we can track where it's been in the past month. If it's parked anywhere near here, we'll know."

Phee's phone buzzed with an incoming call. "What's up, Burns? We were just about to call you. Text Quincy the plates on the van from Brock's place. How are you and Skia making out?" He looked at Maclin and Quincy as he listened. He nodded his head a couple of times. "I think you're right; that one definitely makes the most sense. When you get there, talk to whoever you need to so that you can do a roundabout on the DL. Everything on the low unless you find something concrete. Keep us in the loop."

He hung up the phone and put it back in his pocket. "Burns and Skia think they may have discovered the Muslim target. There is a visiting imam from Syria who's been very critical of Israel. He's speaking tonight at eight at a convention hall up in the Bronx. They're expecting about eighteen hundred people. According to the event's website, some of the members from Umoja will be in attendance. Burns asked a buddy of his who's a bomb tech to meet them there to do a low-key walkthrough to see if they need to evacuate."

After Losher returned with the blueprints, they followed him up to the roof because it had the most obvious access to the air-conditioning unit. They seemed both relieved and disappointed that everything was intact and there was no compromise to the giant HVAC unit. Since starting at the top had proven fruitless, they moved their search to the basement. Losher led them through the boiler room, where they inspected three large water heaters as well as the condenser boilers, which sent chilled water throughout the building. Once again, they found nothing. Next in their search was the large utility room that served as both the guts and the brains of the building. Maclin stood back and took in the many lights and levers on the control panels. It was all state of the art. There was a security guard sitting in front of a bay of monitors surveilling every interior quadrant of the building.

"How long is the surveillance footage stored in the system?" Phee asked the guard.

"It's all digitized. Right now, it's programmed to store up to a month."

Quincy read off the screen of his phone. "NVLS puts the van parked on this block the day before yesterday."

"Pull up everything you have for Saturday," Phee instructed the guard, who immediately started pulling up surveillance footage.

Maclin nodded. "Makes sense for them to have planted something then because they knew no one would be working on the Sabbath."

Losher looked a bit confused. "If you don't mind me asking, what is NVLS?"

"National Vehicle Location Services. They're tied into hundreds of cameras throughout the five boroughs. Helps us to be able to track and ID pretty much any vehicle in the city," Quincy said.

The guard fast-forwarded through frame after frame of empty rooms, showing the team that the interior hadn't in any way been breached. There was a collective sigh of frustration.

Maclin looked in Phee's direction and saw him reading a text on his phone. From the look on his face, she knew what he was going to say before he said it. "Burns and Skia found the C-4 at the convention hall up in the Bronx. Bomb squad is on the way," he said.

"This has to be the second target. I know the threat is here somewhere," Maclin said with a little bit of exasperation.

"We'll find it," Phee said supportively.

"Pull up your exterior cameras," Quincy commanded the guard.

Several videos showing footage from outside the building played over the bank of screens. Quincy looked at the one monitor that showed nothing but blackness.

"What's up with the blank screen?"

The guard pressed a few more buttons, but nothing changed. He looked up the log and told them, "Looks like it was offline for an hour on Saturday. Must have been broken."

"Or intentionally disabled," Maclin chimed in.

"Where is this camera located?" Phee asked.

"On the north side of the building," the guard instinctively pointed.

The guard led them around the side of the building as they walked in the direction that the camera was pointed. Part of the two-story concrete wall was covered by eight fixed twelve- by twelve-foot-high metal louvers that were connected as a single unit. The metal covers were designed as metal slats to allow fresh air to be drawn in.

The guard turned around and faced them. "If you want my opinion, this would make perfect sense. Air intake is sucked in through these vents for circulation after being filtered through what's called the makeup air unit and then dispersed throughout the building."

Everyone, including Losher, stared at him oddly.

"Hey, I've worked enough security jobs on construction sites to have picked up a few things here and there."

There was a twenty-foot-long horizontal, ventilated planter box on the ground just five feet from the last louver closest to the corner of the building. As Maclin slowly lifted the lid of the planter, she revealed several keg-sized canisters, each attached to what looked to be timing devices.

"Evacuate the building right now. We need to get Hazmat out here along with the bomb squad."

38

Rabbi Pearl refused to leave. Maclin saw the fear in the eyes of some of the other rabbis, but the rebbe was unwavering. He stood before her, shoulders hunched forward, his back slightly curved from age and endurance. The tiny holy man reminded her of a frail Atlas shouldering the burden of a troubled world.

"We cannot leave and let them win."

"They only win if you stay and die."

"God will protect us."

"Be that as it may, you have no choice in this matter. We have to get you and everyone else out of the museum as soon as possible."

"The museum must open."

"And it will. Just not tonight."

Maclin's voice was stern, removing any false perception of what was negotiable and what was not.

"I will not leave!"

Maclin in no way masked her growing impatience. It was there in the heavy sigh just before her words. "With all due respect, you no longer have any..."

"There is a way for all of us to get what we need."

An unexpected voice diverted their attention. Although a bit tentative, it was loud enough to turn everyone in its direction. Yael was, as usual, taking a position on the periphery of the room, behind Maclin and the men. The rabbis looked at her with stern eyes, each look more chastising than the other. Despite the gravity of their crisis, the act of Yael speaking without invitation—and, more importantly, without the rebbe's invitation—was received as some unspoken violation. When one of the rabbis opened his mouth to quiet her, Rabbi Pearl silenced him instead.

"Let her speak."

Yael stepped forward as the men parted and let her into the semicircle they had formed behind Rabbi Pearl. "I believe if we all work together, we can address the safety concerns and still open the museum. Agent Maclin, based on how much time it took you to do a preliminary search, how long would you need for your people to conduct a more thorough investigation of the building to make sure there are no more threats?"

"Hard to say—three, maybe four hours. First, the bomb squad will have to do a sweep. If they use the dogs, it'll go a lot faster. But after that, Hazmat will have to remove the materials we've already found; then they'll have to do their own sweep to see if anything was missed."

"Okay, so it's almost 5:30 now. If there were two Hazmat teams working simultaneously, starting at opposite ends of the building and meeting in the middle, would that expedite things?"

"In theory. But that's not how it's normally done."

"But you being the FBI and handpicked by the mayor, you could make that happen. Am I right?"

"I suppose so."

"If it's confirmed that the canisters you found are the only threat, could the search be contained to three hours?"

"I couldn't guarantee that. But once again, in theory it could be done."

Yael turned to Rabbi Pearl. "Rebbe, I believe that faith, not theory, will carry this night. I don't think it a coincidence that a woman born of Jewish blood has been placed in charge of this investigation. She's already saved your son and discovered this threat here tonight. If God has in fact put her here, as light in this darkness, then our faith in Him now requires us to show some faith in Agent Maclin and her team.

"In the meantime, we can divert the caterers and our guests to the synagogue, where we can do a prayer service, followed by the testimonials from the survivors. By the time we do a reception there, we will have easily taken up two, two and a half hours— which only pushes the original time back an hour and a half or so. If we walk the block between the synagogue and the museum as a congregation and community, that would be a statement of unity as well as defiance in the face of our enemy's attempts to destroy us. Think of it, two thousand Jewish strong, taking the

night back from hate and fear. What better way to honor the victims of Kristallnacht, as well as those who perished in the camps?
Tonight's opening could be even better than we ever dreamed—
because the entire world would know of it."

Rabbi Pearl addressed Maclin. "Agent Maclin, you would do
everything in your power to make this night happen?"

Maclin looked at the rebbe and then at Yael, now standing
in front of the men who had regarded her as something less than
equal. It was she, not they, who swayed the unswayable rebbe. It
was the reasoning of women amid a roomful of men that turned
conflict into hope.

"Yes, I will. You have my word," Maclin responded.

Rabbi Pearl reached out and squeezed the back of Yael's hand
and nodded his consent. "We have work to do." He then walked
toward the door as his entourage followed. Just before Yael exited the
room, she mouthed a *thank-you* to Maclin. Maclin turned back to
Phee and Quincy. "Well, like the rebbe said, we've got work to do."

Maclin honored her word. The search took two hours and forty-
six minutes. She orchestrated everything seamlessly. The NYC
bomb unit had already been deployed to the convention center in
the Bronx, so she brought in two Fed bomb teams from Manhattan
and New Jersey. They each showed up with two bomb-sniffing
dogs. She wrangled three, not two, Hazmat crews that reported
all updates to either her, Quincy, or Phee. She pushed them but
reminded them to be as thorough as possible. After the coordinated

sweep of the building, it was confirmed by all that the original canisters were in fact the only threat.

Maclin called Yael directly. She wanted her to have the glory of telling Rabbi Pearl that the museum would be able to have its opening in the time frame that they had hoped for. She ordered three cruisers to block off the traffic in the one-block stretch between the synagogue and the museum. Twenty minutes after the last of the crime scene techs had left, Maclin, Phee, and Quincy stood just outside the museum and witnessed the approach of Jews two thousand strong marching down the street, lighting the night with the candles they held. It was a sight. They came arm in arm, a wall of solidarity. The night was lit by the glow of their march. As they got closer, Maclin could see the flicker of candlelight illuminating many tear-streaked cheeks of the faces in the crowd. Even though she stood off to the side, as the crowd filed past she felt herself marching along with them.

She may not have walked shoulder to shoulder with them, but she still felt a shared sense of ownership of the night, of the crowd's victory in the face of hate. Although her role in their triumph was anonymous to the masses, she floated with the knowledge that she was partly responsible for their forthcoming celebration.

As she watched Rabbi Pearl leading the mass of people through the front doors of the museum with Yael and her husband there by his side, she felt a swell of pride. Having been for the past several years of her life a self-proclaimed loner, she had all but forgotten the feeling of being part of a collective. Aside from Quincy and Phee, she had allowed herself to become a kithless island, singular and tribeless. The very thing that her obsessive independence had denied her was now her greatest reward. She accepted it, even welcomed it. Welcomed it all. The epiphany. The pardoning. The unspoken invitation. The awakening. The submission. Now that she had finally heard the ancestral knell as resounding as a shofar assembling her tribe, Maclin silently answered its beckoning. Her inclusion, even if only from an honorary perch, gave her a sense of connection that she wasn't very familiar with. She stood between Phee and Quincy. As the crowd continued passing them to enter the building, Maclin felt her cheeks cooled in the warm night by the tears streaming down her face.

Fifteen minutes after the last of the crowd had entered the building, Phee got the call from Skia and Burns informing her that the bomb threat in the Bronx had been neutralized. Maclin assigned six uniforms to patrol the perimeter of the museum just as a precaution, before leaving with Phee and Quincy to rendezvous with the other half of their team. Phee suggested that the five of them meet in New Jersey at the same diner parking lot where they'd met Shaka just a few days prior. Although they were closer coming from the Bronx, Burns and Bobby Skia were still the last to arrive. As Burns got out on the passenger side, he held up a white plastic shopping bag. "We had to make a stop to pick up a little libation. It's been a helluva day."

Bobby Skia walked around from the driver side. "Bomb squad found thirty-seven pounds of C-4. Brock and his people were definitely trying to make a hell of a statement."

"Same intent at the museum," Quincy chimed in. "There was enough gas in the canisters to take out everybody in there and then some."

Quincy and Phee leaned against the hood of Phee's Rover as Maclin stood close by. The vehicles were parked in the empty lot with the front ends facing each other with just ten feet between them.

Burns pulled out two Corona six-packs from the white shopping bag and turned to face Maclin. "Look, I know you're probably not cool with a drink since we're technically still on call. And even though this shit may get worse tomorrow, today we saved lives, most likely in the thousands. Most cops I know would think that's a good enough reason to throw back a cold one."

Maclin looked at him stone-faced. "Burns, would you shut the hell up and pass me a beer?"

Burns, a bit surprised that she actually showed a sense of humor, smiled and obliged her, then passed a bottle to everyone else. Phee poured a sip of beer on the ground. "To Shaka, our brother in blue who doesn't get to end this thing with us."

Everyone else followed suit and poured out a sip of beer before drinking. The mention of Shaka's name brought the mood down. Maclin's demeanor soured even more when her phone vibrated and she read an incoming text.

"My guy in the lab just confirmed that the DNA from Brock's

cigarette is a match for one of the foreign blood samples found on Shaka."

"Fuck me," Burns sputtered.

They were all left reeling, trying as best they could to channel the news in a meaningful direction. They all sipped their beer in silence until Bobby Skia finally spoke: "So, I hate to be the one to ask the obvious question here—but what are we gonna do?"

Phee finished off his beer. "Whatever it is, we need to do it quickly. I mean we now have confirmation that he was in on Shaka's killing, but we can't do anything with it. It's also a safe bet that they'll be looking to retaliate since we squashed their two hits. We sure as hell don't wanna just wait around and see what these assholes do next."

Maclin took another swig before speaking. "I couldn't agree with you more, but I don't know what we can do. We've gotten this far on illegal intel, but we're gonna need much more than that to really stop Brock and his clique."

"We just gotta get some kind of valid warrant to bust him on something—shit, anything—just to buy time," Burns said.

"What about a John Doe CI? We should be able to find a judge to sign at least a surveillance warrant based on intel we got from a reliable source," Skia posited.

Maclin opened a fresh beer, sipped, and then started her habitual pacing.

"Okay, so let's say we do go so far as to make up a CI. What happens when they need to be produced to corroborate?" she lobbed back.

"CIs drop out of sight all the time. We'll deal with that when the time comes. Right now, we just gotta disrupt them any way we can." Burns was adamant.

Quincy jumped in, the constant voice of reason. "Janet's right—we gotta put them down from something solid. Something that'll stick. He can afford the kind of lawyer who would have him out in twenty seconds."

"We just gotta put them down. I don't give a fuck if it's for jaywalking, as long as we get those animals off the streets," Burns stewed.

Maclin stopped pacing and stared at Burns, who in return stood more erect, defensively preparing himself for the oncoming lecture.

Maclin stepped closer to him. "Burns is absolutely right."

Everyone looked at her confused, especially Burns. Quincy jumped in. "What do you mean, he's right?"

Maclin looked as though she was scuffling with an idea that was still forming. "He's right about the jaywalking part."

"All right, I'm officially confused. We're gonna try and arrest Brock for jaywalking?" Phee asked.

"Of course not. But maybe we've been going at this the wrong way. What if we Capone him?" Maclin floated the question.

"What do you mean?" Bobby Skia asked.

Quincy smiled and nodded at Maclin, then turned to Skia. "Feds never got Capone for the really bad shit he did. They just followed the money and busted him on tax evasion."

Maclin addressed everyone. "Always follow the money. I'll assign a federal forensic accounting team out of Langley to go over every LLC, every transaction, loan, you name it. Makes no differ-ence how much money people like Brock have. Trust me—they're always looking to beat the system in one way or another. We just gotta catch him dirty."

"So we gotta wait till morning?"

"Yeah, that way I can assign the best team," Maclin answered.

"Why wait? Every minute Brock is free means that something bad is more likely to happen. One way or another, we gotta end him. We need a legal warrant on him as soon as possible. You've got your team right here. We head back to the precinct and jump on every computer we can. You can teach us what to look for. We'll pull an all-nighter if we have to." Phee was damn near plead-ing with her.

Maclin looked at the men and saw the same need in their eyes. Phee was right: she had all the team she needed.

As they headed back to their vehicles, Maclin saw the cell phones being pulled out. Phee, Quincy, Burns, and Skia all had loved ones who needed notifying. There were people who worried about them. People who cherished their return. She found herself dialing Losher. He may not have risen to the level of significant other, but he was certainly significant enough that she wanted to hear the light in his voice.

"How was the opening?"

"It was amazing. My sister cried from beginning to end. Actually, most people did."

"Does that include you?"

Losher laughed. "Even if I did, do you really think I would tell you?"

"Good point." Maclin smiled.

"You did some amazing things today, Janet."

"We still have a lot of work to do to end it all."

"I was wondering if I could see you tonight. Just—see you."

"I have no idea when we're finishing up. It'll probably be an all-nighter."

"Makes no difference how late—I'm off for the next two days. If you arrange for the front desk to leave a key for me, I'll be waiting whenever you get there. Or just meet you for breakfast, if that works better for you."

Maclin hesitated, more out of habit than anything. After a second or two she heard herself say, "I'll wake you when I get there."

39

Brock's financials just came in. I woke up my IRS contact who heads up the Criminal Investigation Division in Langley, and he's pretty thorough—so we should have everything, business and personal. Quincy, I need you and Phee to go over all of his bank accounts and transactions, along with investments. Dig into it like you're doing an asset forfeiture investigation."

Maclin held up her iPad. "By the way, I also got back the facial recs on Brock's cohorts. Most of them just have a few petty things here and there, but a couple of them have done real time. I'm forwarding their details now."

Maclin sat on the corner of an empty desk while Quincy and Phee settled in front of two available desktops in the detective's division of the One-Nine. It was just past midnight and the precinct was pretty quiet, with most of the detectives out in the field.

The two regulars who were still there were asked—quite persua-
sively—by Burns to temporarily relocate so that the team could
work in private.

Although Maclin wasn't feeling well, she put up a good front.
She was tired and halfway buzzed from the two beers she'd had, so she
was reluctant to take her medicine and risk getting sleepy. They had
too much work to do. Phee, Quincy, Burns, and Bobby Skia were
all dialed in to Maclin sitting in front of them doling out instructions.

"Burns, you and Skia look up all of his property holdings,
LLCs, and DBAs. I'll start combing through his tax returns for the
past ten years. First thing we need is a very clear picture of where
his money is and how he's using it. None of us are accountants—I
get it—but if we dig in the right way, there's a chance we come
up with something useful. The key is to look for anything that
pops, even if just a little. Something doesn't look or even feel right,
highlight it and let's discuss it. Trust me, there are enough federal
regulations for us to catch him in violation of one thing or another.
I like the odds of us coming up with something."

Even when her stomach started cramping, she still refused the
mercy offered from her pills. She couldn't risk it. If Ivan was going
to come for her, she would have to fight him without the aid of
her medicine. She would deal with the pain head-on—because
nothing was going to stop her.

It was slow going. A bit mind-numbing. The hours crept by
tediously, yielding much more frustration than progress. Maclin
was tired and knew that the rest of the team was as well, but none
of them were built to tap out. Her eyelids drooped at will with

fatigue. Just like everyone else in the room, she had been up since seven and had now been going nonstop for seventeen hours.

They all periodically took short walking breaks as a means of fighting the lethargy. The heat certainly didn't help. It was eighty-seven degrees outside, but the un-air-conditioned precinct felt like it was somewhere north of ninety. The team was beyond the heat. Beyond the sweat and discomfort. All that had been unbearable was now nothing more than an afterthought. They no longer complained or even made mention of it because their singular focus left very little room for anything other than following the trail of money in hopes of finding useful crumbs.

Aside from the four properties Brock owned in the States, the team also discovered real estate holdings in both Berlin and Moscow. There were a few false alarms. After a while, the numbers and words started blurring together. Burns and Bobby Skia thought they spotted some irregularities on some property loans, but Maclin pointed out that nothing on the loan applications was technically illegal.

It wasn't until 3:29 a.m. that Quincy found something that Maclin could use.

"He's got five bank accounts. Two in Manhattan, two in Vegas, and one up in Eagle's Hill. That's his primary account. He's been flagged with a suspicious activity report four times in the last two months."

"What was the SAR for specifically?" Maclin asked.

"Twenty-seven withdrawals of nine thousand dollars over the last two months. Even though he was trying to fly under the radar by keeping it less than ten Gs, he triggered a flag by visiting his safe deposit box four times in one week," Quincy answered.

"A quarter of a million dollars. You can definitely start yourself a war with that. He must have something pretty important in that safe deposit box," Phee suggested.

Maclin cracked a sly smile, happy for the break. "We'll find out soon enough. Multiple SARs will easily get us a warrant. I'll write it up and call it in now. We'll have it in a couple of hours. Good job, guys. I suggest we all shut it down until then, get a little rest, and serve the warrant as soon as the bank opens. Looks like we've got a long day ahead of us."

She got Burns to drop her off at her hotel. Since they only had three hours' downtime, Maclin didn't want Phee to drive in the opposite direction of the George Washington Bridge. As she rode up in the small hotel elevator, she took out her medicine and popped two pills. Her insides felt mangled. She was tired, weak, and dehydrated; the day and the heat had finally taken their toll. Ivan reminded her of his might, of the incontrovertible fact that no matter how distracted she may have convinced herself of being, she was never free of him. He reminded her of that wretched truth in the best way he knew how: with pain and nausea.

It had completely slipped her mind that Losher had said he would be there. Maclin had long forgotten the consolation of a man waiting for her return. She quietly undressed, not wanting to disturb his deep sleep.

After Maclin was completely naked, she sat on the floor next to the bed and watched him, listening to the low snore he emitted. She envied his peace. Despite how tired she was and how desperately she needed sleep, she knew her cancer had other plans. Since Ivan wanted to play, it made very little sense to her to get in bed knowing that she would only toss and turn as her illness worsened. She never knew how long it would take to recede. The current pain was dull, which she preferred over the sharp, stabbing alternative. Her insides felt like a mutiny of sorts. Her stomach ached in protest.

She kept her eyes on Losher, hoping that her focus would help ease her through the wave of sickness. Maclin stared at him in silence, knowing for a fact that—although for different reasons—he had been guilty of similar acts of voyeurism. It was now her turn to be the examiner. She'd woken many a morning after one of their trysts to feel his eyes taking in every inch of her. Catching him on more than one occasion attempting to count the field of freckles that canvassed her body. Or inexplicably captivated by the parts of her that she found least interesting. There were many times over the course of their lover-ship when she was convinced he looked at her not just to see her but rather to see *into* her. Even during casual conversation, he seemed to always be probing for something more—something hidden and intangible that registered much deeper than skin, lips, eyes, hair, breasts, or even bone. He left her at times feeling that he was looking for the palpability of her soul. Whether he found it or not, he never retreated.

When she was a child, Maclin's parents called each other the same nickname: *bashert*, a Yiddish word meaning "destiny" but more commonly "soulmate." Maclin had always thought of Willington as having been the love of her life, despite the fact that he left her feeling a need to hide the darker parts of herself from him. She now began to realize that it was in fact Losher who had been the only lover that had not just loved her for her light but accepted her darkness with no judgment. He was the only man who loved her unconditionally. She wondered if he was her true *bashert*.

She watched his eyes flutter, then open and stare at her in confusion.

"Why are you sitting on the floor? Come to bed."

"I've only got a couple of hours before I have to get back to work. I have something to tell you, but I need you to just listen. I know there's a longer conversation to be had, but I'm just asking you that it not be now."

Losher sat up in bed as Maclin remained seated on the floor.

"Are you okay with that?" she asked.

Losher did his best to manage his growing concern. He opened his mouth to speak but then just nodded at her.

Maclin breathed in deeper than usual. As uncomfortable as it was for her, she looked him in the eyes and blurted out, "I've been diagnosed with stage IV ovarian cancer that has metastasized."

She didn't give him the opportunity to say anything. She rolled her words together uninterrupted.

"I got three different opinions that all say the same thing. The last one came from the best there is, Dr. Winston Quinlan. That's why I originally came to New York five days ago. He said I was looking at two, three months tops. I'm sorry to tell you like this, and I'm sorry that I'm really not in any shape to talk about it the way I know you would want to. But the truth is, my brain is fried and my body aches. I'm just waiting for my medicine to kick in so I can hopefully get at least a little sleep, wake up at six, and then jump right back into the madness. I'm totally being selfish here and I get it, but I had no idea how to tell you. How to tell anyone. So please forgive me. I know it's a lot to just blurt out, but I just felt I at least owed you the truth."

When she was done speaking, she watched him get of bed and sit on the floor next to her. She was aware of the release immediately, the weight lifted from the unburdening of a horrible secret. She felt unrestricted. When he put his arms around her, she welcomed them as much as they welcomed her. As she buried her head into his chest, she felt the heavy thumping of an anxious heart. Despite his calm, she knew her news was shredding him. She had very little doubt that he held on to her tightly as much for his sake as hers.

For the first time since her diagnosis, Maclin cried. It was a long, hard, angry cry. She cursed Ivan and questioned God. When she was done, Losher's hold offered a safe landing for her. Per her request, he made no inquiries, he offered no well-intentioned but meaningless platitudes. Instead, he gave her what she needed most: strong arms, a loving heart, and the simple affirmation that she was not alone.

Maclin woke at his nudging. When she opened her eyes, he was staring at her. "You said you had to be up by six."

They were still naked on the floor in the same spot they had been in before she dozed off. The only difference was that somehow Losher had retrieved the pillows from the bed without disturbing her. The fact that sunrise was spilling through the window made her question how long she had actually been asleep. Although she was exhausted, she focused more on the fact that her body didn't ache. She didn't quite know how he had done it, but Losher had somehow negotiated Ivan's retreat. Somehow, he got the pain to release her enough to sleep, and even keep its distance when she awoke.

As she looked at him, she wondered how long he had watched over her. His arms were still firmly around her, as though he was trying to protect her from things that they both knew there was no protection from. It was evident that while she slept, he'd cried. His eyes told her what she already suspected. She saw the wounding in them, the slow crumbling that he tried to hide from her. The more she looked at him, the more she saw the toll of all the unanswered questions and the gnawing need to know more. They stared at each other without speaking until Maclin reached up and kissed him.

"I just want to say thank you."

"Even though I felt like there was something wrong, I never imagined it was anything like this."

"And all this time I thought I was doing a decent job at hiding it."

"You're good at hiding a lot of things, Janet, but that couldn't stop me from feeling that something was off. I just didn't want to risk pushing you away by asking questions I knew you wouldn't answer. Now that it's out, what do we do?"

"We?"

"Yeah, *we!*"

"I really do appreciate you wanting to help and all, but…"

"There are no buts. Look, I know that whatever it is that we've been doing for the last two years has been strictly on your terms. I'm not blaming you, because I was the one who went along with it. Took whatever parts of you that you chose to give, even when it was mostly just bits and pieces. We can pretend all we want that this has all just been about great sex, but I've always known that beneath that there was something even greater. I was just hoping that one day you'd be brave enough to accept the fact that you deserve more than you actually allow yourself to have.

"Whether you're cool with it or not, the terms are changing. If you're gonna fight this thing, you don't get to be a coward anymore. I don't know if there are any miracles left or if Quinlan is right and you only have two or three months. Either way, let's be clear: you don't get to do this alone, not when you have someone in this world who loves you as much as I do.

"I know you gotta go to work. When you get back, we talk. I mean *really* talk."

40

Burns and Skia were outside her hotel exactly at 6:30. Maclin got in and mumbled a "good morning" that was mumbled back by one of them, although she couldn't tell who specifically. Everyone looked tired, but none of them complained. The thought of having a lead that was credible, and most of all legal, was in and of itself the type of boost they needed. They swung by a townhouse on East 72nd Street to pick up the warrant from a federal judge whom Maclin knew personally, then headed uptown to meet up with Quincy and Phee.

The full team rendezvoused at a bodega up on Dykman Street. Quincy came out of the store with five cups of coffee and handed them out.

"Shouldn't be a lot of traffic going up in that direction. We'll be up in Eagle's Hill in about an hour and a half, just before the bank opens," Phee said. Maclin grabbed her coffee from him, walked over to his Rover, and got in the back.

The drive felt good. It was quicker than she had anticipated. For most of the trip, she fretted that the pain might make its way back to her. That Ivan would strike with a vengeance. She allayed her worry with thoughts of Losher. Their talk had certainly given her plenty to think about. The hardest part was accepting that he was an innocent who had now enlisted in her war. When the carnage started mounting—and there would certainly be plenty of it—there would be no disputing that the price of him loving her would sentence him to more than his fair share of misery.

He'd volunteered himself to the fire. He was now, as Phee would say, her *ride or die*. Her faithful soldier to the end. They were intertwined, not just with each other but also with Ivan. She could no longer think of Losher without thinking about her death. Although her fate was hopeless, she believed with all her heart that Losher would be fighting right there with her till the end. She at least owed it to the both of them to heed his words from earlier when he'd told her she was no longer allowed to be a coward.

Phee, followed closely by Burns and Skia, pulled into the driveway of the Eagle's Hill Municipal Bank ten minutes before it opened. The manager got there right at nine. He was a man who was not just short but oddly mushed. A squat man, with a thick mustache that looked too big for his squatty face. He hadn't gotten the fashion memo that polyester suits went out in the '70s. His name was Monroe Felton, a folksy type who didn't hide the fact that he didn't much care for city folk, especially those with badges and warrants. He only spoke when spoken to and, even then, he tried as best he could to keep his response to as few words as possible. The team followed him to the safe deposit room in the basement of the building. The room was only fifteen by fifteen feet, with around two hundred boxes. There was a single chair and a table in its center. As Mr. Felton crossed to the box belonging to Ellis Brock, he hesitated before inserting his master key. "Can't imagine what you folks might be looking for. Mr. Brock is a pillar of our community. He's one of the most generous neighbors any of us could ask for or..."

"Would you please just unlock the box, sir?" Maclin cut him off.

After he unlocked the eight- by eight-inch door that housed the box, Maclin stepped forward and retrieved it. "Thank you. We'll take it from here."

As Maclin placed the box on the table, the team gathered around as the manager stood off to the side. After donning a pair of latex gloves, she hesitated just a little before opening the lid. Although they had no specific idea what to expect, there was a collective sense of disappointment when their search yielded only some old family photos, a copy of Brock's will, and the deeds to half a dozen properties. There was absolutely nothing incriminating.

"Shit!!!" Phee hissed.

"Doesn't make sense. You don't come here as often as he has just to look at this crap," Quincy mused. "Maybe on his last trip he took out whatever was so important."

Maclin, pissed, turned to the manager. "Mr. Felton, is this the only safe deposit box registered under Ellis Brock's name?"

"Yes, it is. I told you that there was nothing for you to find. Mr. Brock is nothing but a decent man."

Maclin pressed harder. "Let me rephrase my question to you. Does he possibly have another box here even if it's not registered under his name?"

The second Phee saw him hesitate, he jumped in. "You might wanna think long and hard before you answer. If necessary, we can have a warrant here within the hour to search every box in here. I'm sure your customers would be pretty pissed about that. But trust me—that would be the least of your worries. If we find that you are lying or withholding information, we can and will hit you with felony obstruction of a federal murder case. You'll end up in prison so long that the suit you're wearing will have had time to come back in style and go back out again. You don't wanna fuck with us."

Felton looked at Phee, then Maclin, and stammered something unintelligible before moving over to one of the two largest safe deposit boxes in the room and unlocked it. Phee moved him to the side before taking out the box—which was almost twice the size of the first one—and placing it on the table.

When Maclin opened it, the team discovered a treasure chest of sorts. Quincy gloved up and helped her remove a ledger and a thick photo album that was on top of at least half a million dollars in a canvas satchel. As Quincy thumbed through the ledger, Maclin opened the album. She looked increasingly more troubled with the turn of each page.

Phee turned to Burns. "Burns, would you and Skia bring Mr. Felton here upstairs and have him show you all the video the bank has that corresponds to the dates Brock was in here? Start with his most recent visit."

As Burns motioned Mr. Felton to lead the way, Phee stopped them when they reached the doorway. "Keep an eye on him, and don't let him send any texts or make any phone calls."

"Sure thing," Burns responded.

Quincy leaned against the table as he thumbed through the ledger. "Gotta hand it to Brock—he's definitely thorough and old-school. No cyber handprint. This thing goes back to the late '80s. He's got a category for every member, their profession, donations, and even a list of silent supporters. They run the gamut. Everything from menial laborers and farmers to politicians, lawyers, doctors, even law enforcement. He's brought in three times as much as he reported for the church or his personal taxes. For every dollar that goes to the church, two dollars goes to his personal holdings. Looks like he's laundered millions. Not just from the government, but from his own people as well. Guess we really do Capone him. If nothing else, we got him on tax evasion."

Maclin, who was still engrossed in the photo album, placed it on the table so that Quincy and Phee could see what she was looking at.

"Oh we've got him on much more than tax evasion."

She felt a little lightheaded, so she sat in the chair as Quincy and Phee stood on either side of her looking over her shoulders. Although she had already perused the album, she started from the beginning for her partners' benefit.

The first photo was a rare shot of a beaming Hitler standing over a large pit filled with the bodies of dead Jewish concentration camp victims. The pics that followed were a detailed, pictorial account of varying denominations of white supremacists. Nazis, KKK, skinheads, and extremist alt-right groups. There were graphic photos of victims of the Holocaust, as well as lynchings and immolations of black men.

"It gets a lot worse," Maclin warned. She hesitated slightly before continuing to turn the pages. She had to steel herself for what she had already seen, already knew was coming: the second half of the book was image after image of the torture and killing of Jews and blacks. It was a firsthand account of victims just before death. The chronological documentation of not just dying but more specifically of being murdered. Body after body of what she assumed were from several cold cases.

Three pages of the album were dedicated to the slaughter of the Abramovitz brothers. Various stills of the rabbis' faces twisted in agony. Before and after images of what was easily assumed to be their final breaths. Eyes opened. Eyes closed. There was a photo of them lying in a pool of each other's blood. The final pic was exactly how Maclin, Phee, and Quincy discovered them on the dais at the synagogue: back to back with their bodies sewn together. Although it took some doing, the trio did a fairly decent job of stomaching their way through the horrifying images—that was, until they turned the page and found the swollen gaze of Shaka looking back at them. His face was bloodied, and one eye, purple from bruising, was closed shut. The next three photos of him were various shots of his lynching.

Maclin closed the album and refused to look directly at either Quincy or Phee. She was having a hard enough time holding it together and remaining professional; seeing the brokenness that she knew was in their eyes would have staggered her even more than she already was.

They were all still silently processing the horrible things they'd seen when Burns entered with his phone in his hand, oblivious to their pain. "Didn't get much from the videos. His last few visits were pretty much the same thing. The last time he was in here was right after we left yesterday. I just did a quick screen grab of it to show you."

Burns showed them a video recording of Brock sitting alone at the same table that they were now crowded around. Burns paused the video and enlarged the image to see the word PASSPORT on the item Brock removed from the box and placed in his shirt pocket. After Burns resumed playing the video, they saw Brock reach into a small shopping bag and pull out a bottle of wine and a glass. He popped the cork, made a long pour, and then casually sipped wine as he seemed to savor each page of his book of death.

"The sick fuck is gettin' off on this shit," Phee spit out.

"What's in the album?" Burns asked.

Quincy nodded at him to look for himself. "Start at the back. It's Shaka, and it's bad."

Everyone was quiet as Burns thumbed through just a couple of pages of the album. "Jesus Christ. Jesus H. Christ!" he exclaimed.

"It's like torture porn to him," Quincy added.

"He just buried himself. We need to go now and finish the job," Burns said.

Burns directed his question at Maclin. "So what's the play? Do we wait for a warrant to go bust his ass?"

Phee didn't wait for her answer. "The longer we wait, the more time we have for things to go sideways. Ten seconds after we walk out these doors, my money says the bank manager drops a dime to let Brock know we got to the second box. He'll know we have him and that we're coming for him."

Maclin thought for a second before responding. "We'll shut the manager down even if we have to take him with us on an obstruction claim. Good news is, we don't need to wait on a warrant."

"Why not?" Quincy asked.

"Because as soon as we left him yesterday, he came here and removed his passport. Not to mention one of his LLCs has holdings in Russia—which of course is a nonextradition country. He's a bona fide flight risk."

"Just so that we're clear: we show up to arrest him and don't expect him to come peacefully," Quincy stated.

"That's exactly what I'm hoping for," Maclin responded.

They didn't pass any cars as they drove down the main road to Brock's compound. When they were a half mile out, Phee, who was in the lead, pulled over to the side, followed by Burns. As they all got out, Skia opened the back door to let the bank manager out.

Quincy approached him. "End of the road for you."

"What are you doing?" Felton was confused.

"Letting you go back to work."

"But we're at least two miles from the bank."

"Well then, I suggest you pace yourself," Phee shot back.

After Felton glanced in the direction that they came from and the long, isolated stretch of road before him, he turned and pointed at Burns. "He took my phone earlier. I'd like it back."

"Sure thing." Quincy nodded to Burns, who then took out the phone and smashed it on the pavement as Felton looked on in shock.

"What the hell is wrong with you? Why did you just break my phone?" Felton was irate.

"I'm sorry. It slipped out of my hands," Burns said smugly.

Phee couldn't help but grin. "You should look at it this way, Mr. Felton: he may have just done you a huge favor. Protecting you from doing something stupid. If I were you, I'd start walking before we decide to take you in for not being straight with us earlier."

Felton looked back over his shoulder as he walked off. The team huddled around the front of Burns's car as Maclin laid out the game plan.

Maclin looked at an incoming text. "We'll have agents on the ground here in thirty minutes. And before any of you start telling me why we can't wait thirty minutes, don't bother—because I have no intention of us waiting. The longer we do, the greater the risk of this going the same way Waco did. We go in now, maybe we'll have the element of surprise on our side. Then again, there's a chance we don't make it out of there. Five of us against at least thirteen of them. But I'll take those odds with the four of you by my side any day."

"Careful, Agent Maclin—you're gonna have us thinking that some of this NYPD blood has rubbed off on you," Burns joked.

"Yeah, well, I hear they've got shots for that kind of stuff," she lobbed back.

As Maclin caught Quincy's and Phee's eyes, they just nodded at each other.

"All right then, let's get this party started." Burns motioned for them to follow him to the back of his Crown Vic. He unlocked his trunk but was able to open it only three inches. Maclin couldn't see exactly what he was doing after he reached his hands into the small space with a different key. Three seconds later, the trunk opened fully, and she saw the opened padlock that dangled from a half-inch-thick chain that was bolted to the bottom and top.

"Just an old trick we do. Somebody pops your trunk, but they still can't get in," Skia said to Maclin as she looked on curiously.

The trunk looked like a traveling armory. There were two flash-bang guns with accompanying concussion grenades and a sledgehammer with the name *Miss Doris Knockers* carved into the wooden hilt. Along with the twenty-something guns there were zip ties, police radios, and a team raid bag, which was a duffel stuffed with six level-three bulletproof vests.

Maclin, a bit surprised, looked at Burns, who simply replied,

"There's no such thing as too many guns and ammo. Don't ask— just trust me, you don't wanna know."

She nodded at him, grabbed a vest and a Ruger SR9 to go with the Glock she was already packing. She loaded extra clips for both guns as they all got suited and booted for the raid. Quincy's selection for an additional handgun was a Smith & Wesson Bodyguard 380, complete with a red laser. Phee's and Skia's weapons of choice were identical. Along with their Walther PPKs, they both grabbed double-aught shotguns, which they simply referred to as Crowd Pleasers. Maclin looked at Burns, who was loading several clips for his two Beretta M9s, and saw that he couldn't help but beam as he watched everyone preparing.

"Burns, when we get there, show us where you hopped the fence—we'll use that as our point of entry. We split up as soon as we put boots in the yard. We'll clear the house first. Quincy and I will go through the front. Phee, go around the back on the north side. Burns and Skia, take the east side. One click on the radio to let me know you're in position. The three of you will enter through the back door. When I give two clicks we all go in. Any questions? All right then. It's time we ended this thing."

After the last clip had been loaded and the last detail discussed, the team took just a second to breathe and ground themselves. They went through the smallest of rituals, which was meant not only to center themselves but also to help put them in sync with each other.

There were game faces, shoulder taps, and fist bumps, but no words. There were no "Good lucks," no "We got this" because, although it was unspoken, they knew all they had was a meager plan and a mile of hope. If they came up short on either end, they were fucked. They banished all fear. There was no room left for either anxiousness or doubt. As they prepared for the expected battle, their main focus was psyching themselves beyond their mortal limits. They were no longer just five cops on a mission but rather the gathering of five storms. They got in their vehicles and headed toward Brock's compound, loaded for bear.

41

Quincy and Maclin were the first two over the fence, weapons extended. As soon as Bobby Skia—who was last—hit the ground, the team split up and took off on a low run toward their designated spots. Maclin and Quincy snuck up onto the front porch and carefully posted up on both sides of the door, carefully avoiding the doorway—or "vertical coffin" as cops often called it, since it's the most vulnerable spot for gunfire. Their moves were precise. Economical, even.

There was one click on her radio, letting her know that the rest of the team was in position in the back. As Quincy picked the lock, Maclin peeked into a nearby window, looking for motion. When she saw none, she keyed her radio twice as she and Quincy slipped into the front door in a silent breach. They communicated with each other through a series of quick hand gestures. The team collapsed the room as Phee, Burns, and Skia worked their way to meet Maclin and Quincy in the middle.

The two-story house had a wide-open floor plan. The team cleared the kitchen, living room, office, dining room, den, and two guest bedrooms before moving upstairs. Burns and Bobby Skia stood sentry on the first floor as Maclin, along with Quincy and Phee, crept up the two flights of stairs. As they reached the top landing and the old wood floor creaked under their weight, they stood frozen for a few seconds and then continued their sweep.

There were five doors, four of which were closed. They each moved to separate doors and slowly turned the knobs. They were all as quiet as mice walking on cotton. Quincy and Phee disappeared into two bedrooms as Maclin cleared a small hobby room. The next door she tried was nothing more than a large linen closet.

As she reached the end of the hall, she heard a toilet flush and saw a shadow move underneath the bottom of the door. Quincy and Phee, having cleared their rooms, were just reentering the hallway when she directed their attention toward the bathroom.

Suddenly the door flew open and the trio found themselves, guns pointed, looking at the terrified face of Ellis Brock's young son.

"It's okay, you're fine. We're here for your father. Where is he?" Maclin asked in a low voice.

The boy stood before them, frozen, looking from one to the other.

"We're not going to hurt you. Do you understand me?" Maclin tried to ease his stress.

The boy nodded at her but kept his eyes on her lowered gun.

She pressed her gun to the side of her leg to further shield it from him. "I need you to tell me where your father is. Can you do that? Help us so that no one gets hurt, okay? Where is your father?"

When the boy finally spoke, his voice was soft, measuring barely above a whisper. "He's out back in the church."

"Is he alone?" Maclin pressed.

"No, they're all out there."

"Who do you mean by all?"

"Everyone from yesterday."

"Where's your mother?"

"She went to the market to get some more eggs."

Being so close to the boy, Maclin saw behind the ocean-blue eyes a sea of melancholy. She gently placed her hand on his shoulder. "Would you do me a favor and go to your bedroom and wait in the closet? When this is all over, I promise to come for you, okay?"

As the boy stood frozen in place, Maclin repeated, "I promise."

The boy looked at Phee and Quincy and then back at Maclin. "Okay."

He turned and walked slowly toward his bedroom, then turned back. "Are you going to kill my father?"

"That's not why we're here," she tried to assure him.

"But you should. You should *kill them all.*"

Ellis Brock, Jr., turned and walked toward his bedroom and closed the door behind him without looking back.

Maclin glanced up at Jesus and his disciples. She scanned the stained glass image of the Last Supper as she and the team jogged to the church. As they separated and took up different positions for the raid, she and Phee hurried toward the east entrance. As soon as she keyed her radio, Burns tossed a nine-banger flash-bang through one of the eight-foot-high windows. They only had five seconds. Five seconds to capitalize on the disorienting effects of the nine concussive blasts. The flash-bang was always a dependable breach technique because it compromised the designated targets by both impairing the photoreceptors in the eyes and disturbing the fluid in the ear, causing a loss of balance.

Maclin and the team moved quickly to take advantage of the group's temporary blindness and vertigo. Phee swung the Doris Knockers sledgehammer as hard as he could, busting open the side door as Quincy came through the front and Skia and Burns came in through the west entrance. Maclin did a quick count of the group and put them at thirteen, including Brock.

"FBI!!! Do not move. Ellis Brock, you are under arrest," Maclin shouted. Brock and his men were trying to orient themselves. Maclin and the team immediately advanced to the perimeter of the room, positioning themselves into the Devil's Triangle formation, which was not in fact an actual triangle but rather the five of them alternating their positions as they approached from three sides, so as not to create a crossfire situation. It was a strategic ballet that the team executed flawlessly. They had succeeded in catching Brock and his men off guard. The situation seemed to be contained.

And then it wasn't.

One of Brock's men, after getting his bearings, came up firing in Maclin's direction. Even though she cut him down quickly, the shooting led to chaos. All of Brock's men were packing. Since they were essentially cut off from the exits, they flipped the massive walnut table that they had been gathered around and butted it up against the large pipe organ, forming an effective L-shaped rampart. Gunsmoke wafted through the air as shots were exchanged. Maclin, Phee, and Quincy hid behind pews. Burns and Skia, holding down the rear, did a good job of keeping their targets pinned down.

However, Brock and his men held a tactical advantage by having the higher ground of the pulpit. As the clank of guns being reloaded echoed throughout the church, there was a lull in the gunshots. Phee army-crawled within twenty feet of Maclin, who was across the aisle of pews. He spoke to her in a raised whisper, "We gotta get them to break rank; otherwise, we'll be in a standoff longer than we want."

"I agree," Maclin said. "Any ideas?"

"Yeah, like you told me at the morgue, I just gotta do what I do best." Phee rose to a half stance and sprinted up the side aisle, which got him closer to the stage. A couple of gunshots were fired at him but missed. Once he was secured behind a thick column, Phee fired off a few shots of his own then shouted out, "Hey Cameron, how's it going? Remember I told you that I was gonna be the one to end you? I've come to keep that promise. I get to add you to my list along with your bitch-ass brother. Maybe when I'm done with you, I'll go track your father down for the trifecta."

Brock's voice could be heard loudly. "Cameron, get back here! Now!"

A few seconds later, Cameron darted from behind the table,

firing in Phee's direction. As two of Brock's other men tried to follow Cameron to lay down cover fire, the red dot from Quincy's laser landed on the chest of one them, dropping him as Maclin clipped the other. Burns and Skia shot the ends of the table to keep the other men pinned down. The wood splintered and chipped, but the eight-inch-thick tabletop was much too dense to be completely penetrated, even from Bobby Skia's shotgun blast from twenty feet away. He was, however, able to pump a face full of buckshot into one of the men who raised his head above the table. But Bobby Skia exposed himself just a second too long and took a hit in the neck as a result. As he fell backward, Burns rushed to his side, taking out his partner's shooter in the process.

Ranks were now broken on both sides. With Skia down, the defensive line was compromised. Brock and his men were no longer pinned down behind the table. As they fired several shots at Quincy, Burns, and Maclin, they attempted to escape through a side rear exit. Quincy cut off their path to the door as he took down their lead man.

They all dropped down and crawled to the front pews to use them as a barrier. Maclin knew that they wouldn't be able to keep the men from escaping for much longer. She looked to her side to see Phee and Cameron shielding themselves behind opposite posts, firing at each other. Suddenly, Phee sprinted back in the direction of the door he and Maclin had entered. Cameron gave chase, firing all the while. Phee ducked and dodged as he ran, randomly firing back over his shoulders. The man who Maclin had clipped was limping behind Cameron and firing at Phee as well.

Although Cameron was moving too quickly for Maclin to get a clear shot at him, the wounded man trailing him was an easier target. She fired three shots. Two hit home and put him down. When she saw Phee heading for an exit with Cameron closing in on him, she realized that her partner was leading his pursuer into a clear line of fire for her. She heard a volley of shots and turned to see Brock and his five remaining men just before they reached the door.

If she waited for the right second, there would be a brief window of opportunity to get a good shot at Brock—but she also knew that Phee needed her assist. She sacrificed the shot at Brock and turned back just in time to get a perfect angle on Cameron, who was closing in on Phee as he hid behind a column. Maclin's shot hit Cameron in the arm, spinning him just a little in her direction. He fired back, hitting a pew just a few inches from her head. As soon as he turned his face back in Phee's direction, it was met full force with the violent collision of the sledgehammer.

Maclin fired three more shots into him before he fell. Cameron was dead two different ways before he hit the ground. As Brock and the remaining five men shot their way to the exit, Quincy was able to wound Brock in his leg. One of his men helped him out while the others fired back at the team. As Maclin and Phee hurried over to assist Quincy, they saw Burns ten feet away, holding Skia and applying pressure to the nickel-sized hole in his neck, doing his best to stanch the heavy bleeding.

"Don't worry about us; I got him. Go get Brock," Burns yelled. As soon as Maclin, Phee, and Quincy approached the open door, bullets pelted the wood at the entryway. Just before she retreated, she was able to see Brock being led off by two of his men while the other three had taken up position, one behind a combine harvester and the other two behind a giant oak. Maclin and Quincy ended up on one side of the door as Phee leaned on the other side.

"Three shooters. They're trying to keep us pinned here to buy Brock some time," Maclin said.

Quincy looked at Phee and asked, "You or me?"

"You."

Quincy reloaded the Smith & Wesson 380 and bolted in the direction of the front door. Phee randomly fired outside the side entrance to keep the shooters engaged. Three of his bullets ripped chunks of bark from the giant oak that had, unbeknownst to him, played its part in Shaka's death.

When Maclin peeked through the doorway, Brock's men immediately returned fire, one bullet exploding splinters just an inch from her head. She nodded toward Phee at the near miss then listened for the radio, her chest heaving from the adrenaline burst of having just cheated death.

There was a second of quiet and an untruthful peace. The sound of Quincy keying the radio twice crackled in the still air. Maclin looked at Phee, then fired a few shots. They both saw one of the men go down, the center of his chest blooming red. The green grass beneath him was now soaked in blood. Phee and Maclin reloaded, then alternated firing—but the men were strategically positioned behind their cover.

Phee bolted through the door, firing all the while in an attempt to draw the two shooters out more. As soon as the men took the bait and exposed themselves, Quincy came around the corner of the church and blindsided them. Two clean shots. Two clean kills.

The trio took off immediately in pursuit of Brock and his two remaining guards. They split up when they came around the corner of a barn. Quincy went left, Phee went right, and Maclin headed straight to a cellar door egress. She cautiously descended the stairs, gun first. The tunnel was dank and reeked of damp fertilizer. As Maclin reached the bottom of the stairs, she could just make out in the darkness the silhouettes of Brock and his men ten yards ahead, racing toward a bunker door.

She keyed her radio as she ran. "I've got eyes on Brock in an underground tunnel. Follow the cellar doors."

As Maclin chased after her prey, she was momentarily blinded by the stinging sweat that burned her eyes. The back of her throat felt like the Sahara and her calf muscles started cramping. She didn't know if it was the heat or the exertion, but her running woke Ivan. He stirred with a roar. She thought he couldn't have come at a more inconvenient time. He reminded her once again that her body still belonged to him. There was a shooting pain that started in her groin area and quickly made its way up to her solar plexus. Ivan set her lungs on fire. Maclin slowed but never stopped. She refused to let anything prevent her from catching Brock, including her temperamental cancer or even the inconvenience of death.

Maclin fired down the narrow passageway at will, trying to prevent the trio from reaching the safety of the bunker door and the potentially dangerous possibilities that existed on the other side. The man pulling up the rear went down, and the final guard who was supporting Brock took a hit in his side. He limped forward, ushering Brock into the bunker. As Maclin started gaining on them, Brock pushed the man backward, attempting to close the door on him.

"Ellis, what are you…?" were the final words he uttered as Maclin unloaded her clip into him, blowing him forward just enough for his arm to fall in the door's path, preventing it from closing. While Brock was trying to kick the arm free, Maclin extended both her hands, running with everything she had left full force into the closing door, knocking him back in the process. The six-inch-thick steel door knocked the wind out of her.

She felt her right wrist snap as she crumpled to the ground with a broken hand. She was left dizzy from the pain but quickly sobered once she realized Brock wasn't on the ground in front of her. She forced herself up, her wounded wing dangling by her side. She pulled out her second gun with her left hand and walked deeper into the bunker, passing a dozen drums of the deadly gas compound Zyklon B. As she came around a corner, she was able to see how huge the bunker really was. The space was easily forty feet wide and sixty long, with a narrow tunnel at the end that led to a dark unknown. It was heavily stocked with blankets and cots, first aid kits, sleeping bags, food rations, stacks of bottled water, and military-grade weapons. It could have easily accommodated thirty people for at least a month. As she moved even deeper into the makeshift room, she heard the heavy steel door slam shut behind her. She pivoted and pointed her gun in its direction. Since she wasn't a southpaw, it didn't feel as natural as it did in her right hand.

The metal felt a little heavier and seemed to drift a centimeter or two from her aim.

There was a shadow sneaking just around the corner of barrels, getting closer to her. Maclin's trigger finger started slowly pressing against the metal stem. Just as a body came into view and she was about to squeeze, she recognized Ellis Brock's son. Although she kept her gun pointed on him, she relaxed her grip ever so slightly. When she heard movement behind her and turned her head, the split-second distraction allowed the boy the advantage of raising the gun that he had resting by his side. When she glanced back at him, his eyes were cold and she saw the barrel of a nine-millimeter staring back at her. The boy fired twice, hitting Maclin both times. The first bullet tore through her shoulder while the second hit her center mass. Even though the full impact of the body shot was lessened by the chest plate of her Kevlar, her body still felt like she'd been hit with Phee's sledgehammer. She had never felt such excruciation. Not even Ivan's worst blow could compare. She dropped her gun as she fell backward. First came the pain; then she was swallowed whole into blackness.

She wasn't sure how long she'd been out, but when she came to, she saw Ellis Brock and his son looking down on her. Her head was uncomfortably propped against the bunker's stone wall, and the upper part of her arm was covered with her blood. The senior Brock was sitting on a crate while tying gauze around his leg to stop it from bleeding. There was an AR-15 assault rifle by his side.

The boy knelt down close to Maclin's face, studying her as if she were an insect in a jar. He listened as his father spoke to her.

"It's a good thing for all of us that you were wearing a vest. We wouldn't want you dying too quickly. So, did you really think that you were capable of killing me? That's the problem with deluding yourself that you're the chosen ones: that inevitable moment when life reveals that you and the rest of your people are nothing more than self-entitled parasites. You were born from weakness, and that's how you deserve to die. Isn't that right, son?"

Ellis Brock, Jr., jumped in on cue, finishing his father's thoughts. "Annihilation is the fate of the wicked and the weak. Hitler understood that. Exterminating you is for the better of the whole. You're a malignancy, just like the niggers and border rats. We were born from power. That's how we made this country great once and how we will make it even better than it ever was. Your Torah doesn't make exceptions for killing, isn't that right? Fortunately, the Bible is a little more flexible. You could never defeat us because we have God on our side, and we're willing to do whatever it takes."

Maclin no longer had questions regarding whether the boy was his father's puppet or if he was, in fact, a full-fledged hatemonger. As she looked in his eyes, she saw him for who and what he really was. She saw the vicious ownership. He was hate personified.

She saw the old, warped soul deep beneath the youth in his eyes. It had been there all along—she had just been too optimistic to see it.

Ellis Brock, Sr. spoke to his son: "A man's first kill is the most important one because that's the one that defines him. Here, take my gun and put her down the right way. Aim for the stomach; let her bleed out slow and hard."

When the boy tucked his handgun in his waistband and moved to retrieve his father's AR-15, Maclin's limp arm instinctively dropped to the side of her hip, brushing across her radio only to land on an empty holster. When he crossed back to her and toyed with her by pointing the nozzle of the weapon at her, she stared back at him with neither rebellion nor fear. She was still. Everything about her was minimal: her movement, her breathing, even her thoughts. There was simply nothing left save her resignation. The only good thing about Ivan was that he had already prepared her for her end. He filled her head with constant thoughts of death. Whether it was the cancer or even the probability of her not surviving the raid, she knew death was coming for her. She just never imagined it would be at the hands of the sad-looking boy with ocean-blue eyes.

After he finished wrapping his injury Ellis Brock, Sr. stood gingerly on his wounded leg. "We gotta take the tunnel—that door won't hold them out forever. When we make it out, there are plenty of people who will hide us. Go ahead; put the muzzle underneath her vest and just shoot," Ellis Brock commanded.

The boy poked her in her broken wrist with the tip of his rifle.

"I'm not sure if it's any consolation to you, but at least you'll be credited with killing my father. I'm sure that will make you some kind of a hero."

Ellis Brock limped over to his son. "What the hell are you talking about? I told you to just aim and…"

His sentence was interrupted as his son suddenly turned and shot him. The sound made Maclin jump.

Brock didn't fall right away. He teetered for a few seconds as though he was much too confused to die. He pawed at his wound helplessly, trying to stop the bleeding. When he finally went down, he landed on his back. Maclin could hear his lungs collapsing when the sound of his breathing became a high-pitched hiss similar to a punctured tire. Brock, Jr., leaned the rifle against a crate as he moved closer to his father and knelt beside him.

Maclin saw Ellis Brock struggling to speak. The best he could do was squeeze out the word *why*.

The younger Brock answered him very matter-of-factly: "If we are really going to win this war, there isn't any room for people like you. Not when you put your own ego and greed before the cause. What kind of man steals from his own people? You're a weak leader. I'll be better."

He removed the handgun from his waistband, pointed it at his father's heart, and pulled the trigger.

The bunker was silent. Ellis Brock, Jr., stood over his father for a minute or two. Maclin assumed it was the closest thing to mourning that he had to offer. Even though she tried for movement, her body still didn't work. It hurt too much for any meaningful function. Her sternum was severely bruised, and there was most certainly a broken rib or two. When the boy came over and sat on the ground in front of her, Maclin thought he looked instantly older. There was a hollowness to him. More burden in his eyes than when she'd first met him. He'd played her and played her well. What she had mistaken for youth was cunning. What she had mistaken for innocence was in fact evil. He now looked every bit the part of the boy who would be king.

Phee was right: Hitler too was once a child.

When he spoke, even the timbre of his voice was slightly different.

"Now you know what I meant when I said my father was a dinosaur who didn't know he was extinct. I've been waiting for the right moment for a while now. Killing him was a lot easier than I thought because, the truth is, I love the cause much more than I ever loved him. His old-school ways of doing things are counterproductive. I told him that trying to create this whole race war thing was a mistake. He was too simpleminded to see that ultimately all it would do was demonize us and sanctify our enemies. You know how we take back this country? Not under the cover of darkness but by hiding in plain sight. With education, high positions in finance and law enforcement. Not by lynching niggers and gassing Jews for entertainment but by controlling the government and judicial system. When we control the laws and the money, just like Hitler, we'll certainly control the people. We'll no longer have to worry about the Jewish problem or the black problem or the immigrants. I'm thirteen years old. By the time I'm twenty-five or even thirty, this country will be ours again."

"Sounds like you've thought of everything," Maclin said.

"That's because I have."

Maclin smiled, "What about NYSPURN?"

Brock, Jr., looked a bit bemused. "What the hell is that?"

"It's the communications and data system for law enforcement throughout the state of New York."

As he looked at her even more confused, she made a small hand gesture toward the radio on her hip.

"Our radios. Certain channels allow me to communicate with my partners on-site, but if I switch to the base channel, then not only are we heard by over thirty thousand cops statewide but it goes through Central Dispatch and is automatically recorded."

"You're making that up."

"Am I?"

The boy stared at her, searching her eyes for even the slightest hint of a bluff.

"Yes, you are," he concluded.

Maclin remained calm. "Dispatch, would you please play back a part of our conversation?"

Nothing came back but silence as the two of them continued staring at each other. The boy raised his 9 and pointed it at Maclin's forehead. "Nice try."

As his index finger found the trigger, Maclin's radio squawked. Brock, Jr., heard a staticky playback of his own voice: "...*killing him was a lot easier than I thought because, the truth is, I love the cause much more than I ever loved him. His old-school ways of doing things are counterproductive.*"

"Thank you, Dispatch," Maclin interrupted.

He kept the gun pointed at her but was inoperative by the revelation. Gone were the confidence and the hubris of his youth. She could see his mind racing as though he was searching for a possible spin on his admission. Maclin saw his fear turn to anger at the realization that he had been outsmarted by her. She didn't break her stare. "You look like you're trying to figure out whether there is possibly an angle for you to try and play. I gotta be straight with you—there is *no* angle to play. So now your next move is whether or not you add killing a federal agent to your list. It may or may not be a disappointment to you, but I'm not afraid to die, especially not for this. Isn't that the point, that we're willing to die for what we believe in? I still end up better than you."

"What are you talking about?"

"Because you only get to kill me once. Your death, on the other hand, will feel like an endless loop. You've been recorded confessing to a premeditated murder. You're clearly intelligent beyond your years and therefore able to fully comprehend the consequences of your actions. And because of that, you will definitely be tried and convicted as an adult and put away like one as well. New York still has the death penalty. You'll be the youngest to ever receive it.

"But I think that would be the least of your problems, because you'll actually never make it to the ball. You'll spend the rest of your days with hardened criminals. And don't think for a second that the white supremacist will protect you inside—because they'll think your father was a hero for what he attempted, and you a traitor for killing him. All the black and Latino men in there will know who and what you are, and they'll remind you of that every chance they get. You wanted to be at the top of the food chain? You will be, trust me. A pretty white boy with golden hair and blue eyes? You won't be able to keep them away. The men that you've always feared and thought of as animals—and even new ones that look just like you—will show you firsthand just how base they're capable of being."

Maclin saw the first signs of defeat in his face. He blinked rapidly, as though he was trying to keep horrible images and thoughts at bay. There was a slight quiver to his bottom lip. When she saw fear in the young boy's eyes, she pressed on even more.

"They get to take everything that you ever thought you were. Your body first and foremost, but also your mind and whatever you claim as a soul. Every time they come for you they'll take parts of you, things you never get back. You might not believe it now, but you'll think of this conversation every time you're violated.

"*That's* how I win. It's also how you die, a little bit each day. Until there's nothing left of you. So one night when you know they're coming for you, coming for their sport, and you just can't take any more of what the animals will do to you, that's when they find you hanging in your cell—dead before you've even made it to the age of fourteen. So whatever you want to do to me, I'm ultimately fine with because I get to die with the satisfaction that unlike you and your father, I go out on my terms—which is a fate far greater than yours. Because I know what's waiting for you on the other side of these walls."

The boy's face was wet. Tear after tear ran down his cheeks as his body shook in small convulsions. The handgun that he pointed in her face trembled incessantly. If he was expecting fear from her she gave him calm instead. She stared back at him, seemingly undaunted by the threat of death. He lowered his gun and placed the muzzle of it between the bottom of her vest and the top of her navel.

It was then that he shot her. Once in the gut.

Through his tears he warned her, "You get to die slow. Not on your terms. Mine. You don't win. None of you will ever win because we'll keep coming. One dies. Twenty rise."

He put the gun in his mouth and pulled the trigger.

Maclin couldn't feel anything. At best, she could only suck in half breaths. She could see her fingers, hands, legs, and feet. She could see her bloody abdomen and the red pool beneath her, but she couldn't feel anything. Not even the pain of her injuries. She would have welcomed it, because it would have been something. The aching and agony would have at least been evidence of her body still in negotiations with life. She would have even welcomed Ivan because no matter how cruel and overwhelming he was at times, he always reminded her that she was still alive. Instead, all she was left with was the numbness from head to toe.

The only thing worse than pain was the nothingness. When a silent shadow fell across her face and blocked her drooping eyes from the light, she knew she wasn't alone. She knew that death was there beside her.

42

There was no parting of clouds or luminous light shining the path to Heaven. There were no cauldrons of fire or stench and torments of hell. There was only the in-between. The vast acreage of a human weigh station. It was higher than earth and lower than sky. An infinite valley of unanswered questions and a bottomless ocean teeming with regrets. There were memories taller than redwoods, all yearning for recognition and to be laid claim to. Precious moments, now illuminated even more through the prism of hindsight.

Everything was presented in snippets, 3D images of tiny extractions of an entire life. They were all the highlights: mother, father, brothers, childhood, adolescence, and adulthood. Schools followed by the Academy followed by the meritorious ascension of an honorable career. The men who had impacted her life the most: Willington, Losher, Quincy, and Phee. Two were lovers who loved her, and two were partners who adopted her into their tribe. There was of course Ivan and the sentence of her cancer. There was the heartbreak of miscarrying a child and the healing joy of the uncanny bond she instantly felt with Phee's daughter Dolicia. Her life, if weighed on a balance, tilted much more in favor of the triumphs than tragedies. Her love measured far more heavily than her hate. Her optimism registered more substantially than her despair. By all meaningful standards, her life mattered.

When she opened her eyes, Phee and Quincy were there by her side. She was able to make out—from the cast on her hand along with the tubes and wires connected to her and a host of machines—that she was in a hospital. The partners stood on both sides of her bed. They were unshaven and there was blood, more than likely hers, on their clothes. She was groggy. It took a minute for her to be able to speak, and even then it was a weak whisper: "Did we...?"

"Yeah, we got 'em all," Phee interrupted.

"Bobby Skia?"

Quincy hesitated. "He didn't make it."

As Maclin thought about Skia, tears immediately ran down the sides of her face.

He continued, "Burns has been with the family the last two days."

When Maclin looked at him oddly, Quincy clarified. "You've

been in and out for two days. Mostly out. It was real touch-and-go both during and after the surgery, but the doctors say you'll recover from your injuries."

Phee joined in. "We airlifted you back to Manhattan. Quincy and I stayed because we both wanted to be here when you pulled through. Losher is making sure you get the best that everybody here has to offer. You're getting the full VIP treatment. The head of the FBI, the mayor, chief of police, everyone's been here to check on you."

Maclin saw Quincy and Phee share a look and immediately felt that there was something they weren't telling her. She first saw it in the stealthy glances they exchanged and then heard the awkwardness in Phee's voice.

"Listen, Janet, we uhh…well, when we brought you in we overheard Losher tell the surgeon about the cancer. He assumed we already knew. I'm so sorry. Quincy and I thought whatever was wrong might be more serious than you implied but had no idea how bad it really was. The day that you came to my house for lunch, before all of the madness started, was that what you were coming to tell us?"

Maclin nodded her head.

Quincy held her hand as he spoke. "I know there are people here much smarter than me when it comes to this kind of stuff, but I'll tell any one of the experts that they don't know you, Janet. Not like we do. I doubt that they've ever met a warrior like you. It should go without saying, but any fight that you show up to, Phee and I got your back."

Phee grabbed her other hand. "You fight. We fight. Like I told you once before, you don't get to break up the band that easily."

Maclin smiled as she looked at Quincy and Phee. She saw more clearly the blood on their rumpled clothes. Their eyes were heavy with fatigue. She saw the toll that the case had taken, the mourning of fallen comrades as well the singe of hate that no matter how hard they tried to shake would forever shadow them. She saw the rubble left in their lives. They still wore her blood on their clothes because they hadn't left her side for two days. She was moved beyond measure that they had put their own lives and loved ones on hold until they were certain that she had come back to them.

Phee started laughing. "By the way, I've got a good one for you. Spider told me that Ezra and his father invited him to Shabbat when he's up to it."

"You're kidding," she muttered. Maclin looked at him incredulously. "So what did Spider say?"

"He'd go only if Ezra went up to Harlem first. Who knows— maybe a kosher-soul food restaurant is in their future."

Each time Maclin attempted to laugh, she ended up wincing from her stomach wound.

Phee's phone vibrated. "It's Brenda. I need to check in with her and the little one. I'll just be a little bit. I'll tell one of the nurses to let Losher know you're awake. By the way, somehow we lost the half mill that we confiscated from Brock's safety deposit box. The good news, though, is that Shaka's wife and daughter will be taken care of."

"So much for plausible deniability." Maclin smiled. "Somebody once told me that everything that is right isn't always legal and everything that's legal isn't always right."

"I'm glad you're back, Janet." Phee headed out the door.

As he left, Quincy patted the back of Maclin's hand. "Losher has been running up here in between patients every half hour to check on you. He's a good man."

"I know he is."

"And anybody can see that he's heart over head in love with you. He's the kind of man you want to have in your corner, Janet. He's like Phee and me: he'll always have your back. Just a heads-up, the two of them have already talked it through, and as soon as they let you out of here you're going to stay in Phee's guesthouse so we can all keep an eye on you. Phee told Losher he could come out and stay with you as much as the two of you want. Do yourself a favor: don't try to protest, 'cause it's nonnegotiable."

"I thought everything in life was negotiable."

Quincy smiled. "Not when it comes to family."

He pulled up a nearby chair and sat down. His weariness was as obvious as it was instantaneous. The more Maclin stared at him, the more he seemed to melt into the chair.

"You know you look like shit, right?" she joked.

"Well considering that's exactly how I feel, I guess that makes sense."

Maclin looked at him—her partner, her brother, her co-protector.

"I'm sorry that you and Phee didn't hear it from me. I owed the two of you that much. I just couldn't bring myself to…"

"Janet, stop. You didn't owe us."

"It's the only time I've ever not told the two of you the truth, and I hated every second of how it felt."

"Trust me, we both get it. This is not about us right now; it's about you. What you're going through and what you need to make it through. It's not always easy sharing bad things with the people you care for most."

"Well I just never want to feel like I'm not being a hundred percent straight with you or Phee. The three of us have been through too much together for anything less."

Quincy didn't respond. He just sat in his chair and looked at the wall. He was quiet and even looked a bit distracted. She could tell from his silence that for some reason she had lost him. Maclin didn't know why the conversation had wilted. The room suddenly felt segregated: there was his side and her side. Even though they were less than three feet apart, there was the narrowest of valleys that divided them. Quincy was often a tough read. Unlike Phee, who was incapable of biting his tongue, Quincy was more likely to suppress how he felt.

Maclin let it go. Whatever it was, she knew he'd come back when he was ready.

Losher entered the room a few seconds ahead of Phee. He was winded just enough to let her know he had come running when he got the news she was awake. Whether he had been in the middle of rounds, in a consultation, or otherwise engaged with patients or colleagues, his presence reminded her that she was his priority. She hadn't seen him in his scrubs and lab coat since first meeting him after she was admitted into his ER two years prior. Her first thought of him then was that he certainly looked the role of the indomitable doctor. But now, as he came through the door, she saw something else in his eyes. It was the bundle of fear, relief, and hope.

When Quincy had mentioned earlier that her surgery was touch-and-go for a minute, it was a bit of an understatement. Losher was the one who told her that she had died. That for twenty-three seconds her heart had stopped and she had flatlined.

Her mind was a field of questions. If it was hate that had killed her, then was it within the realm of possibility that it was love that brought her back? She hadn't necessarily cheated death. It was merely a postponement. Even that in and of itself was a victory. It was because she chose to embrace it that way. The three men in the room—one a lover and two her brothers—were both her family and her army because they chose to be. Unlike the parameters of the inherited bonds that they were born into, the three men had chosen her and she in return chose them. As she looked at the nucleus of her tribe, she remembered her mother telling her as a child that ultimately life came down to choices. Maybe not every-thing, but certainly the things that mattered. Things like love, God, and hate. Not God of the skies, although that too was a choice, but more specifically God of the heart.

She knew that Ivan had more pain in store for her. That there would be miserable days ahead and the only fortitude that she would have to fight him was finding the light, even in the shadows of doubt and adversity. She'd thought about how life had often dealt her what she saw as a losing hand, and yet she had still survived. Flourished, even. Surrounded by people who believed in her so much that even in the face of death they refused to give up on her.

She thought about the times she doubted God—not His existence but His compassion. When her mother died and again when her fiancé was murdered were the most difficult times. Those were the times that she too died, even if only in pieces. She blamed Him for being mute when she needed His voice most. At the times she needed Him nearest, He seemed to be the farthest away. She had no answers for the questions of why she hadn't heard Him in years but could hear Him so clearly now. She heard Him when He told her that there were still sunrises left to warm her. Gardens with daylilies to behold. Conversations with Him to be had. There were still debates and laughs and stories to be shared with Quincy and Phee. Time left to marvel at the preternatural connection that she had with an angel named Dolicia whose eyes lit up rooms and hearts with very little effort.

He told her that despite the blows that life and Ivan had dealt, there was still enough magic left in her to brighten the eyes of an angel. He told her of the joy to be found in the unconditional surrendering of her heart to a man who truly loved her. Maybe He had spoken to her long ago, but because she was so smothered in bitterness and self-pity, she was either unable to or out of anger chose not to hear Him. The things He told her now were the weapons in her arsenal she had on the days that Ivan threatened to undo her. She completely trusted that she had what was most needed. If the things she learned as a child were true—that life was ultimately about choices—then Maclin was well armed with the mother of them all: faith.

EPILOGUE

Maclin woke before dawn. She took her meds and then said a
morning prayer. It was a new ritual she'd started in the week
since she'd been discharged from the hospital.

Losher was sleeping soundly beside her. She moved quietly,
trying not to disturb him since he hadn't gotten to bed until after
1:30 a.m. following being on call for forty-eight hours straight.
She wanted him to have the peace of a lazy Saturday. He had been
staying with her in Phee's guesthouse as much as he could. She
missed him on the nights that he had to stay at the hospital. Like
her prayers, he had become a welcome ritual.

She eased herself to the side of the bed, her stomach still tender
from her wound, her hand still in a cast. She reached for her phone
on the nightstand. Even though there were several emails, she
scrolled past them to find the one she was looking for. It was from

Rabbi Pearl. Each day he sent her a different passage from either the Torah or the Talmud as well as secular words of wisdom and inspiration

> *Do not be daunted*
> *By the enormity of the world's grief.*
> *Do justly, now.*
> *Love mercy, now.*
> *Walk humbly, now.*
> *You are not obligated to complete the work,*
> *But neither are you free to abandon it.*

She slipped on a pair of shorts and Losher's favorite "Just Do It" T-shirt and slowly tipped out of the room to go catch the sunrise. She walked gingerly, slightly bent at the waist. Although it took more effort to navigate around her physical limitations, part of her reward was that as soon as she made it outside, she was greeted by the scent of night rain that still lingered in the morning air. She could also smell the citrus from the potted fruit trees. It was the dawning of a beautiful day. The heat wave had broken, and the East Coast once again felt normal. When she made it to about thirty feet from the garden, she saw the lone silhouette of Quincy sitting in the gazebo.

As she got closer she spoke out. "You're the only person I know who requires less sleep and sanity than me."

Quincy rose and crossed to escort her the last few steps of her journey. "I don't know if that's a compliment or a dig."

She smiled at him in the dim light. "That was the desired effect."

"I was just beginning to wonder whether you were going to make it this morning."

"Wouldn't miss it for the world."

"How are you feeling?" He sat her down.

"Not bad, all things considered. Losher got me into a new trial program over at Sloan Kettering that's gotten pretty decent results with some of their stage IV patients. I start on Monday. Who knows?"

"Never underestimate how far a little hope can carry you."

"Even though I told Director Tuttle everything that's going on with me, for some reason he and the president still don't want to pull the plug on naming me general council."

"Maybe it's because none of us are willing to give up on you, Janet."

There were stretches of conversation followed by swaths of silence. Maclin felt at times that Quincy wanted to say more than he allowed himself. They stayed in the garden longer than they ever had before. The morning air was comfortably cool; a soft breeze swirled around them. It was the same gentle gust that carried the sounds from the kitchen that had escaped through open windows and floated in their direction. They heard the clatter of pots and pans and the familiar pitch of a young girl's laughter.

Maclin smiled. "Sounds like a certain little angel is up."

"Brenda told Elena that every morning as soon as Dolicia wakes up, she asks for you. I think the two of you were related to each other somehow in another life," Quincy joked.

Although she smiled, she took what he said more seriously than he intended.

What if it were possible? What if her previous notions of spirituality were all wrong? Maybe, contrary to what she had believed all her life, she and everyone else weren't just humans having spiritual experiences—but rather spirits having human experiences. Maybe life was a mysterious continuum, one that bent and made allowances for past encounters and the intersecting of souls. She no longer stood immovable on her lifelong absolutes.

"For what's it's worth, I think you and Elena should stop just talking about having kids and start actually having them," Maclin blurted out.

"Wow. Where did that come from?"

"I was thinking about Dolicia and how when she walks into a room she lights it up. I know what being on the job can do to us. Dealing with all the ugliness and horrible things that we encounter. We get to see the worst of what people have to offer."

"Yeah, but…"

"Let me finish. Quincy, I know you're scared to bring a child into this kind of world. I totally get it. But what if, ultimately, that's our best chance of really shifting the balances? At the end of the day, isn't that what we're trying to do? One thing we know for certain is that the darkness will always come. Rabbi Pearl sent me something the other day that said, 'There is no source of darkness, only the absence of light.' Quincy, we need more light in this world."

Quincy was quiet. She saw him processing. His expression was blank. Just as she thought she had lost him, he lowered his head and spoke.

"Maybe that's what I've lost faith in. I don't always know

whether I can tell the difference between the darkness and the light. I used to, but I'm not so sure anymore."

From the way he refused to look at her, she could feel that he was getting more and more uncomfortable. Maclin just sat there quietly, careful not to press him in any way. His energy changed, and he started getting fidgety. He stood and walked to the edge of the gazebo to try to hide it from her.

"I need to tell you something in confidence," he said. "I haven't even been able yet to talk about it with Phee, and it's killing me. Like you said in the hospital, we've been through too much together to not be straight with each other."

She had never seen Quincy like this. So conflicted. So unsure of himself.

After a few seconds of silence, he finally spoke.

"The other morning when you came out here and I told you I was working on something?"

She nodded.

"A buddy of mine who I went through the Academy with is now running a homicide department out in Chicago. They caught a pretty bad case about a week ago. Then another one a couple of days later. He reached out to me because it looks like a copycat of the first case you and I worked together."

"The Deggler case?"

"Yeah. I went over every detail a few times. I compared the MO—and trust me, it's identical."

"How could it be identical? We never publicly released the details of how the victims were killed."

"I know."

"So how's that possible?"

"What if Deggler had an accomplice, a confidant who knew exactly how he was committing the murders? What if that accomplice decided to continue what Deggler started? I need you to trust me on what I'm about to tell you, Janet. I'm pretty certain I know who it is. Actually, I'm positive."

"Who do you think it is?"

"My brother Liam."

Acknowledgments

Thanks to God first. Always.

No matter how long or difficult the journey, the seemingly impossible was made possible with the tireless aid and dedication of three women who proved to be game changers.

Rockelle Henderson, my agent, master strategist, and consummate cheerleader. You've made my dreams your dreams, and you have made it your mission to find new ways to bring them to fruition.

Lavaille Lavette—the baddest of bad asses. I'm always amazed at how many different hats you wear and how you consistently make magic happen.

Yona Deshommes—you came on board our team with the force of a tornado that impressively keeps moving us forward.

I also want to thank my assistant Penni Wasserman for having my back and keeping the team moving with effortless precision, because it really does take a village to raise a book.

I truly appreciate all of you ladies and the profound impact you have made on me.

I would also like to thank:

412 ERIQ LA SALLE

Brian Luce—throughout my career I've worked with many talented technical advisors on TV and movie projects, but you have always been the crème de la creme. Your integrity as a cop and your knowledge of procedure in law enforcement has elevated me as well as every artist that you've worked with. Your generosity in allowing me to pick your brain and authenticate my characters and story is simply priceless. Can't thank you enough. You do the badge, the public, and your father proud. Love you, Brotha.

David Appel—From the day that Luce told me that he wanted to introduce me to "one of the highest ranking Jewish cops in Chicago," you've treated this book as though it were a part of you. On countless occasions you've educated and guided me through specifics of Jewish culture and religion. The book is more grounded and credible simply because of you always having my back. Thanks for serving as honorary Godfather to this story.

Thanks to the readers of this series. Your support and inspiration truly means the world to those of us that have stories to tell.

About the Author

© Lori Allen

Actor-director Eriq La Salle is best known to worldwide television audiences for his award-winning portrayal of the commanding Dr. Peter Benton on the critically acclaimed and history-making medical drama *ER*. Educated at Juilliard and NYU's Tisch School of the Arts, he has credits that range from Broadway to film roles opposite Eddie Murphy in *Coming to America* and Robin Williams in *One Hour Photo*. La Salle has maintained a prolific acting career while at the same time working steadily as a director, taking the helm for HBO and Showtime in addition to series such as *Law & Order*, *CSI: NY*, and *Under the Dome*, to name a few. He lives in Los Angeles, California.

Twitter: **EriqLaSalle23**
Facebook: **EriqLaSalle**
Website: **IAmEriqLaSalle.com**